Fictions of India

This book is dedicated to my Mum and Dad,
for all they have given me.

Fictions of India

Narrative and Power

Peter Morey

Edinburgh University Press

ATLANTIC®
PUBLISHERS & DISTRIBUTORS

ATLANTIC®

PUBLISHERS & DISTRIBUTORS

7/22, Ansari Road, Darya Ganj
New Delhi – 110 002
Tel: 2327 3880, 2327 5880, 2328 0451
Fax: 91-11-2328 5873
E-mail: info@atlanticbooks.com
Website: www.atlanticbooks.com

Published in India by
Atlantic Publishers and Distributors, New Delhi
in association with
Edinburgh University Press Ltd
22 George Square, Edinburgh, U.K.

First published 2000 by Edinburgh University Press Ltd
First Indian Reprint 2005

ISBN 81-269-0555-7

Typeset in Monotype Apollo by
Koinonia, Bury, and
printed in India by
Pushp Print Services, Delhi

Contents

Acknowledgements

I wish to acknowledge the assistance received from a number of quarters in the writing of this book. Help, both intellectual and practical, has been forthcoming from so many sources that it would be impossible to name them all. Those individuals and institutions mentioned below have been particularly generous with their time and professionalism, so much so that I consider them to be significant contributors to whatever merits the book possesses, while also being entirely innocent of its undoubted faults and inevitable oversights.

Thanks go to erstwhile colleagues at the Universities of Sussex and Leeds, and University College, Worcester. In particularly I wish to thank Professor Shirley Chew and Dr Elleke Boehmer, whose example taught me the value of attention to texts in context, rather than vice versa, Professor Roger Ebbatson at Worcester, who not only offered quiet encouragement, but also intervened to help me balance research with academic commitments and tied up the loose ends I left behind when moving on to a new post, and, especially, Dr Geoffrey Hemstedt at the University of Sussex. Geoff is a powerful, fluid thinker and inspirational teacher with apparently infinite resources of patience and a formidable attention to detail. My life, and not merely the academic side of it, is richer for having known him.

I also wish to acknowledge the generous assistance forthcoming from the libraries at the Universities of Sussex and Leeds, Senate House Library and the School of Oriental and African Studies Library, University of London. Thanks also go to the staff at the British Library for their promptness and efficiency, and at the University of East London Library. In the latter instance, Roy Hobson and Stella Lebrun deserve plaudits for calming the sometimes troubled waters of research during the final stages of this work, not least by procuring material from the four corners of the earth – well, India and Canada anyway – via the interlibrary loan system.

A debt of gratitude is owed to Professor Roger Bromley and Dr Patrick Williams of Nottingham Trent University. Both have offered support, suggestions and constructive criticism when necessary. In terms of preparation of the manuscript, I wish particularly to thank Kate Peel who gave her time freely and cheerfully and Olive Farnham who has been involved from beginning to end and without whom the ideas contained here would probably have remained an illegible jumble.

Thanks are also due to Jackie Jones and the team at Edinburgh University Press for seeing the project through to completion. I also wish to thank Amina Yaqin, whose many qualities are legion and to whom I owe more than I can ever repay.

All the above have, in their different ways, played a part in bringing this work to fruition. I hope this book is some kind of reward for their faith and efforts.

Abbreviations

The following abbreviations are used in Chapter 1 when discussing volumes of short stories by Kipling:

L.H.	*Life's Handicap*
P.T.H.	*Plain Tales from the Hills*
W.W.W.	*Wee Willie Winkie*
D.W.	*The Day's Work*
M.I.	*Many Inventions*

Introduction: Post-Colonial Criticism: A Transformative Labour

> ... if we study the impulses giving rise to ... [the European novel], we shall see the far from accidental convergence between the patterns of narrative authority on the one hand, and, on the other, a complex ideological configuration underlying the tendency to imperialism. (Edward W. Said, *Culture and Imperialism*)

> Criticism is not an 'instrument' or 'passage' to the truth of a text, but a transformative labour which makes its object appear other than it is. (Terry Eagleton, *Against the Grain: Essays 1975–1985*)

In Rudyard Kipling's short story 'The Head of the District', Khoda Dad Khan, the leader of a population of warlike tribesmen laments the impending death of the much-loved English Deputy Commissioner Orde Sahib, by addressing him in the following terms: 'thou art our father and our mother ... What shall we do, now there is no one to speak for us?' (L.H., p. 121). Somewhat uncharacteristically, Kipling's text here lays bare the power of representation in the colonial situation, albeit in a tale which ultimately resolves itself into a story about the unsuitability of Bengali Hindus attempting to rule over, represent and speak for North West Frontier Muslims. Orde can speak on behalf of these tribesmen in the corridors of power and, perhaps more importantly, he can represent them, their legends and history, to themselves; Orde has thoroughly digested local folklore and is able to enthral young and old with the power of his storytelling. An issue clearly foregrounded in this text is that of narrative and power. As a good imperial servant Orde Sahib stands at the midpoint of the processes of colonial representation: while representing India to policy makers in Government House he is also suffused with that more deeply ingrained 'knowledge of the native' which built imperial power in the first instance and which emerges, robed in the garments of common sense and first-hand experience, to construct a knowable community of India. Having space to narrate means having power. The story of English language fiction on India is also the story of a struggle around representational politics: British writers seek to represent the Indian; colonized Indian writers strive for a space in fiction to represent themselves; and post-colonial Indian authors offer to articulate identities for Indianness which avoid ethnically specific state-sponsored versions.

This book is an investigation into the relation of narrative technique to hegemonic ideologies in the work of a number of fiction writers on India in the English language. It applies strands of colonial and post-colonial debate, ideas from narrative and reception theory and a sense of historical context to selected works by Rudyard Kipling, E. M. Forster, John Masters, J. G. Farrell, Paul Scott, Khushwant Singh and Rohinton Mistry. The study begins from the premise that there is a demonstrable relationship between narrative power, exerted over a text, and what Edward Said calls 'the gross political fact'. Of course, such a relationship extends beyond the school of British writing on India – it is particularly important for post-colonial Indian writers seeking to contest both colonialism and later, but not unrelated modes of civil oppression – but its study is particularly appropriate in the field of imperial fiction, hence the perhaps disproportionate weighting given to British writers here. This association is never simple – indeed in Kipling, for example, it will be seen to be highly complex – but, in one way or another the hierarchies, inclusions and exclusions of the 'small world' of the text can be linked to larger power relations under imperialism and beyond.

From this certain questions arise for which this study will undertake to provide tentative answers as it proceeds. First, there are issues concerning the mediation of positions of domination and subjection and the currents of power resulting from them. Are these viewed as unidirectional and uncomplicated, or fluid and in constant motion? We must examine the fictional strategies used to gain power over, depict and 'speak for' India and, by extension, which narrative forms are chosen and what motifs and images circulate. Indeed, do the writers recognize that what they offer is a 're-presentation' of India and not the essence of the object itself, and are they conscious of themselves as belonging to a tradition of writing which purveys such 'representations'?[1] The answer to this question is particularly important for colonial novelists since Britain's knowledge of India was dependent on steadily accumulated texts of many kinds – geographical, anthropological, legislative, commercial, military and strategic and fictional. When these texts converge a corpus of knowledge is created and a sanctioned discourse about India is born which works to perpetuate the outlook and role of the colonizer. It is proposed to examine the ways in which the texts under scrutiny use this ready-made discourse. How aware of tenacious ideological constructions do the texts appear to be? Perhaps a certain irony is necessary in the project of a British writer attempting to represent India after 1947. Do the writers enlist or resist ironic perspectives? Concomitant with questions of power is the British will-to-know that facilitated colonial governance. How does this will-to-know appear in the texts? How is the matter of racial and cultural difference addressed, and how do the narratives use and develop conventional orientalist ideas of Indian alterity or 'otherness'? What typologies occur and recur? For instance, how does the English writer handle those cliches of orientalist discourse, eastern illogicality, malevolence, mystery, bestiality, brutality, fecundity and sexuality? How are such typologies given currency? What narrative ends do they serve? Likewise, for post-colonial Indian writers questions arise such as: what is the nature of the discursive forces which have sought to delimit and enforce notions of India and what it is to be Indian? what are the polyphonic potentialities of narrative fiction which enable it to resist such perspectives? and how can one metaphorize the plurality of India and so avoid the kind of replication of monocular colonial ways of seeing which have from time to time returned to haunt post-colonial self-definition in national politics?

Although not following a single preordained theoretical model, the concern with narrative and power might enable one to situate this study in a space created by the approaches of narrative theorists such as Bakhtin and Genette on the one hand, and Marxist critics such as Jameson and Eagleton on the other. My approach is based on the assumption that narrative technique consists of a number of available forms and registers functioning largely in, and as part of, existing discourses. However, by the complexity of their deployment they are also able to test discursive boundaries and highlight inconsistencies bespeaking anxieties and therefore the inability to exert complete representational control. The tradition of British narratives of India belongs as part of the wider discourse of empire. Thus 'imperial narrative' and 'colonial discourse' are treated as closely connected since the former can be said to exist within the latter. The terms are slowly prised apart as my analysis gets under way and as they divulge incongruities and gaps in the discourse. In short, the first three chapters begin from a presumed unproblematic understanding of the writer's relation to the discourse as shown in his texts, but interpretation soon spirals away to draw out the ever-present ambiguities and ambivalences.

Adorno suggests that for any writer social contradictions are made manifest in a work of art as problems of form. Hence, this study concentrates on the formal aspects of the texts, particularly at points where such problems appear related to ideological or historical anxieties. Traced closely, in their manifestations as hesitations, gaps and absences, formal problems can be made to yield up a suppressed or forgotten historical moment, much in the way Jameson recommends a 'symptomatic reading' to 'restore to the surface of the text the repressed and buried reality of this fundamental history'.[2] This is the kind of reading used in the chapters on British writers. In the case of Rudyard Kipling, analysis of the relation of power and knowledge reveals the writer's technical awareness of the link between textual apprehension and imperial stereotypes. However, a closer examination of his own deployment of an unreliable narrator, and his use of political allegory and the repression he must enact on his text in order to gain control of these allegorical meanings, discloses a fundamental strain under which the solid-seeming wall of his imperial narrative buckles. E. M. Forster writes at a time when the imperial voice was being loudly answered by a previously ignored Indian discourse. *A Passage to India*, while foregrounding the dialogics of the imperial relationship, also provides evidence of Forster's ambivalent attitude towards the other, non-Eurocentric culture, as do his essays on India. These ambivalences are traced to their source in Forster's liberal humanist individualism which is at odds with the kind of radical collectivist action inspired by Indian nationalism which, in its mobilization of previously silenced, marginalized subaltern groups, refuses to answer the colonizer antiphonally. Coming after independence, John Masters uses Kiplingesque tropes, situations and power relations to mythologize the colonial encounter and thus preserve the white man's legacy. However, his post-independence position requires that he acknowledge that the colonized has a voice and will use it in the retrospective world his novels evoke. He attempts a form of cultural relativism in his most ambitious novel, *Bhowani Junction*, with its first-person multi-narrator technique and claims to narrative neutrality. Yet even here the voice of the Indian and the Eurasian is always filtered and carefully controlled by a meta-narrator who acts to recolonize it.

In contrast to Masters, J. G. Farrell recognizes the basis of imperial modes of self-perception and aggrandizement in cultural forms. In his Booker Prize-winning novel *The Siege of Krishnapur*, Farrell simultaneously invokes and subverts the cultural modes most closely associated with imperial myth-making, such as the adventure story, the Victorian collection, heroic painting and photography

– and their contemporary equivalent, the motion picture – to puncture the pretensions which buoy up the British self-image even today and which have allowed an ongoing romanticization of the colonial connection with India. Paul Scott's *Raj Quartet* enacts the fragmentation of traditional historiography and imperial certainties. It incorporates a circular, reverberatory technique and experimental syntax, instead of the dogmatically linear narrative which had previously characterized the genre. A fragmentary collage technique – corresponding to the stages of the historian-narrator's search for the truth and consequences of the Bibighar Gardens incident – relativizes different versions of a single event to expose as contingent the apparently timeless, authoritative British narrative, while paradigmatic or 'epic' character types are explored and undermined. Contradictions in the discourse give space for another voice, of the kind attended to in the work of Homi Bhabha. The hybrid Hari Kumar becomes, in this reading, less a valorized part of the grammar of liberalism than an act of narrative infiltration which unravels homogeneously imagined racial and national identities in a way that anticipates much writing by authors from the former colony itself. Those writers are represented here by Khushwant Singh and Rohinton Mistry. Much critical work has addressed Salman Rushdie's playful deconstruction of exclusionary cultural and national identities. This study argues for such tactics as forming an ongoing feature of much post-colonial Indian writing in English. Specifically, Khushwant Singh's *Train to Pakistan* and Rohinton Mistry's *A Fine Balance* are here analysed in the light of Fredric Jameson's contention in the well-known essay 'Third World Literature in the Era of Multinational Capitalism', that the story of the individual in 'third-world' literature always has a 'conscious and overt' allegorical relationship to that of the public or national culture. This study argues that rather than appearing as the 'story of India' endlessly rewritten, the work of post-colonial Indian authors inscribes an understanding that there is, in fact, no 'story of India' as colonial fiction and historiography once claimed, only *stories*, and it is in the recurring tropes of space and the body that this may be seen most clearly. In the texts under scrutiny these images constitute part of an attempt to think through partition and subsequent Indian history – including Indira Gandhi's infamous 1975 State of Emergency – and reclaim colonized space and its bodies from both external and internal forces of oppression and discursive power. In these texts, I would argue, one can see a movement of topographical and tropological decolonization for Indo-Anglian fiction, one which acknowledges that national allegory is not merely multifarious and split – as indicated by the diverse ethnic and religious composition of post-colonial India – but that it may be woven into the fabric of a collective national memory.

In studying colonial fiction, Jeremy Tambling's observations about the relation of ideology and literary form could serve as a guiding principle, particularly for the chapters on Kipling and Masters; 'A text may well show up the silences and the gaps in the ideology, for instance, by the way its own explanatory force stops short, owing to its involuntary commitment to an ideological standpoint'.[3] However, these chapters do not offer merely a reading for ideology in the Machereyan sense, as ideology nearly always appears at surface level in fiction dealing with empire; writers either support or are opposed to the idea of empire and use their writing to justify these views. Rather, British fictions of India impose their own generic conventions in terms of structure, metaphor and symbol, character interaction and so on. The first five chapters of this study are designed to explore the degree to which respective writers internalize and reproduce these conventions, or show awareness of, problematize or subvert them. They can best be viewed as a series of experiments with certain takes on paradigmatic texts which offer to expose narrative's relationship to power in new ways. Accordingly, the aim is not to demonstrate a hard and fast link between certain narrative choices and ideology that will be fixed forever after, but to suggest some ways in which these choices serve or call into question established discursive power relations in the particularly fraught arena of the British-Indian connection, and, in Chapter 6, in post-colonial India, where abuses by those in power have continued, sometimes in shapes that strangely recall the autocratic drives of colonial oppression.

From this it should be noted that this book does not seek to present a cultural or social history of English literature on India. At most it will offer a series of snapshots showing the way history seems to impinge on the possibilities for narrative strategy. This is partly because several recent texts have given useful and contextually detailed readings of colonial discourse in India.[4] However, it is also because the argument contained herein is intended to be cumulative in effect, for which it is necessary to keep a reasonably sharp focus on the texts themselves and how their meaning is created in narrative terms. Having said this, it is of course the case that there is no such thing as neutral description, as any study informed by Said's work must immediately concede. Even Aijaz Ahmad, who has been highly critical of aspects of Said's work, reminds us:

> When it comes to a knowledge of the world, there is no such thing as a category of the 'essentially descriptive'; that 'description' is never ideologically or cognitively neutral; that to 'describe' is to specify a locus of meaning, to construct an object of knowledge, and to produce a knowledge, that will be bound by that act of description. 'Description' has been central, for example, in the colonizing discourses.[5]

Such a stricture clearly applies to this study also, and readers will undoubtedly draw their own conclusions about its relationship to dominant critical ideologies. I am not saying that some readings are more ideological than others, but that there are other factors to consider: specifically, the role of rhetorical tropes and conventions which reveal ideology but also probe its inconsistencies. The point is precisely not to see form and ideology working together, but to explore places where they pull in opposite directions. Consequently, I am not here claiming to be deploying anything as frankly unpost-colonial as a superior methodology to those which have gone before, merely the interpretative possibilities of a number of interlinked approaches in the study as a whole, focusing on their relation to narrative technique. History is, of course, an important part of all this, but my particular interest is in the kinds of connection we can trace between the anxieties and preoccupations of the colonizers – for example, about securing the apparent consent of the colonized and so seeing themselves as all-powerful and loved – and their expression in fiction.

Benita Parry has described the tradition of liberal criticism that for years dominated study of imperial fiction:

> Affiliated to the hegemonic explanatory order and written within the same ideological code as the discourse of colonialism, this putative oppositional discourse rebuked colonialism as the unacceptable face of Western civilization, while endorsing the affirmations and prohibitions authorized by the culture pursuing and implementing colonial power.[6]

She sees the signal achievement of the colonial discourse analysis which has been prominent since Said's *Orientalism* (1978) as 'moving the discussion of the colonialist text as an authentic portrayal of reality, to a system of ideological representation which such writing produced'.[7] This is an assessment with which I completely concur. In part this study is predicated on the fact that, for a British writer, merely producing a novel or a work of criticism sympathetic to

Indians is not sufficient to liberate them from the tradition of misrepresentation which is inherent in forms of depiction which have gone before, accompanied and contributed to imperial policy and power. However, it is just as important to be vigilant against the most programmatic excesses of what one might describe as the more vulgar strain of 'oppositional' colonial discourse analysis too. One should recall Said's warning that:

> Today's critic cannot and should not give a novel legislative or direct political authority: we must continue to remember that novels participate in, are part of, and contribute to an extremely slow, infinitesimal politics that clarifies, reinforces, perhaps even occasionally advances perceptions and attitudes about England and the world.[8]

Understanding how writers may be interpellated helps to explain the way narrative too can entice readers into a certain value system. Exposing this process in imperial fiction has been both necessary and valuable. Yet such approaches seem, in some cases, to have hardened into an orthodoxy by which texts are constantly and somewhat tediously read in a schematic manner to 'reveal' their ideology, thereby absolving the critic from any need to engage with the way texts, in their own narrative dynamics, problematize and sometimes even subvert the operation of anything as general as discursive power. Indeed, it could be argued that such vulgar readings for ideology replicate a colonial determinism by 'revealing' that Kipling, Forster or Scott cannot help but write in a way complicit with colonialism ... QED. Dissatisfaction with both liberal criticism and a certain strain of colonial discourse analysis begs the creation of a different agenda. Thus, what follows is a sequence of eclectic and shifting, but text-centred, readings which emphasize the discrepancy between the presumed ideology of the writer – or their narrator persona – and the post-colonial reader informed by the end of empire and aware that the anti-colonial utterances of that empire's former subjects were always instrumental in contesting, and ultimately decisive in the demise of, British rule in India. It seeks to trace the extra resonances that, for example, Kipling's Indian fiction – written at the height of empire for a readership just then awakening to the enormity of its acquisitions and responsibilities – takes on in the cosmopolitan, post-imperial world.

Thus, the perspective offered here is not inherently more 'enlightened' – always an ambivalent word – and further along the road to salvation than previous, say liberal, perspectives. It is just that for a reader living at the beginning of a new millennium, when the process of release from direct political control has largely been effected, our ways of reading cannot be expected to remain uninformed or undisturbed by the end of empire and the articulation of previously silenced or marginalized subject positions. A post-colonial perspective is ultimately located in the text's readership, since its point of recognition is there and its meaning is created in 'a process of recreative dialectics' with the reader.[9] A post-colonial reading is made possible not least by history itself, by the convergence or discordance between the moments of writing and reading. In this way, rather than reproducing empathetic liberal readings or frosty ideological excavations, post-colonial criticism may break free from the unspoken yet persistent gravitational pull of authorial intention and truly become a transformative labour. Narrative and reception theories appear to offer one valid means of elaborating post-colonial systems of reading applicable to British texts seeking to write, or rewrite, the imperial encounter. Wolfgang Iser concludes that:

> Meanings and truths are by nature influenced by their historical position and cannot in principle be set apart from history. From this arises the suspicion that literary texts are resistant to the course of time, not because they represent eternal values that are supposedly independent of time, but because their structure continually allows the reader to place himself within the world of fiction.[10]

One might continue this idea by pointing out that the reader's position within the world of fiction inevitably changes with the passage of time and the modifications in the dominant ideology it throws up, as well as with the various national, cultural and racial dimensions of that ever-changing readership. Thus it is proposed to emphasize plurality in this study to uncover what I have called the interpretative possibilities of each text, and the way these possibilities may have changed over time. Ideology enters the equation because it dictates the salient forms of the genre of British fiction of India and, therefore, any anomalies or innovations immediately lend themselves to scrutiny. Such an approach stems from a conviction that indeterminacy is much more prevalent in these fictions than has been appreciated. In other words, the incompletions and inconsistencies of the texts do not simply display the writer struggling with the fetters of his or her moment, but also enable the reader to interact with the text to produce a meaning which subtly reflects his or her own age and its concerns. It might be objected that this is to encourage anachronistic and, therefore, unjust interpretations, but to make such an accusation would be to forget that the works themselves participate in a discourse which relies upon the consent of its addressees: hence my argument that post-colonial criticism should be a transformative labour. This book is not interested in authorial intention. The best way of reading colonial fiction of India now might be to approach it, and the grandiose claims it often enshrined and codified, at an oblique angle to the reading it invites.

That is, reading, like writing, responds to history as well as helping to shape it. The influence of historical process can be felt not only in the text but also in its possible readings, despite the best efforts of imperial myth-making with its investment in immutable India. Hence, when dealing with British writing, it is important to delineate different phases of the Raj, mark the historical moments of the texts and assess the significant differences between pre-independence and post-independence writing. After 1947, issues of self-criticism and nostalgia come to the fore. Memory is particularly important in the projects of returned Anglo-Indians and others more dispassionately observing the Raj in its death throes. They share a concern for the idea of empire and its psychological co-ordinates as integral to the identity of its servants. The passing of the 'imperial mission', therefore, brings a sense of loss, sometimes seemingly for the author as well as his characters. (Clearly, this is different for Indian authors operating at this time – such as Raja Rao and Mulk Raj Anand – for whom the project of fiction had been to contribute to the imagining of a unified nation free from the British, and for whom this necessity gives way, after partition, to the dissection of the post-colonial body politic, often through the story of representative groups or individuals. Not for them the rather parochial and blinkered benign construction of Britain in India which has subsequently fed into a post-imperial conservative revisionism.) Although there is a generally shared view of the extent, if not the nature, of Britain's responsibilities toward India, Kipling and the later writers incorporate their fundamentally problematic relation to established orthodoxies in the texts they produce. After independence the writers themselves have to re-read the Raj, so to speak.[11] John Masters, for example, promotes the continued viability of the imperial service ethic in stories which reanimate generic commonplaces while nevertheless acknowledging the historical terminus formed by independence. In writing of Masters it has been necessary to stress the difference between what I take to be a post-colonial perspective and the kind of *post-independence* perspective visible in his adventure novels. A post-independence perspective can be defined simply as a consciousness of coming after the moment of Indian independence. A post-colonial perspective, in my usage, assumes a degree of freedom from a colonial mindset: an assumption not applicable to Masters if one examines the staple elements of his technique and the kind of implied reader he appears to court. His reversion to Kiplingesque fantasy in a post-colonial world contributes to a highly embroidered set of narratives of self when away from the metropolitan centre. They are heroizing and ultimately reactionary repositories of conventions for writing about India. The clearest instance occurs in the repeated use of the figure of the walnut-stained Englishman passing among the Indians as one of their own. Yet this narrative trick was travestied and reduced to a joke by Forster thirty years before Masters begins his novel cycle, in the figure of the deluded imperial policeman, McBryde, who tries this sort of thing at the time of Dr Aziz's trial in *A Passage to India*. Cultural cross-dressing for power and knowledge is not intrinsically a joke – consider the continued potency of the T. E. Lawrence legend – but it is exposed as a redundant form, a hollow fantasy about control, when applied to an India which political developments between the eras of Forster and Masters have revealed to be irretrievably out of control. Masters hopes to be borne aloft by certain traditions of writing about India he claims are innocent and valid, yet he falls upon the thorns of ideology and bleeds. Forster's writing, by contrast, shows an awareness of the potential malice of certain hackneyed conventions and brackets them as part of a problematization of the matter of speaking for India. Awareness of the genre's codes is even written into Kipling's work comparatively early in its development. By the time of J. G. Farrell and Paul Scott the wholesale dismantling of generic conventions has become central to a reckoning of the imperial legacy in fiction, and can be seen as the linchpin of both the *Siege of Krishnapur* and the *Raj Quartet*.

Until recently, vigorous exclusionary readings often asserted 'the colonial' and 'the post-colonial' to be antithetical and mutually exclusive discursive entities: the former being associated with the colonizer and the latter with those once colonized. However, in the last few years the work of critics such as Homi Bhabha has led to a recognition of the connection between colonizer and colonized, in terms of identity formation, as a reciprocal if unequal site of exchange. Likewise, the somewhat reductive assertion that there is an essential, intractable opposition between British and Indian writing in English on the level of narrative has been challenged by criticism which instead highlights the mutually influential elements of their relationship; I refer in particular to Sara Suleri's *The Rhetoric of English India* and Elleke Boehmer's *Colonial and Postcolonial Literature*. Indeed, my understanding of the relation between colonial and post-colonial writing on India – and thus the arguments that follow – are to some extent in accordance with Boehmer when she says of post-colonial literature:

> Rather than simply being the writing which 'came after' empire, postcolonial literature is that which critically scrutinizes the colonial relationship. *It is writing that sets out in one way or another to resist colonialist perspectives.* As well as a change in power, decolonization demanded symbolic overhaul, a reshaping of dominant meanings.[12] [emphasis added]

Although Boehmer largely concentrates on writing from the former colonies in her book, what is being argued for in this study is, among other things, a redefinition of the critical category 'post-colonial'. Both colonizer and colonized share a history that subverts easy binarisms, both are in part constructed by imperial ideologies, therefore, both are, in their different ways, post-colonial subjects. In taking this line it is certainly important to differentiate between the possible connotations of 'subject' here; the general condition of having one's subjectivity created by the colonial encounter is vastly different from the very acute experience of being in subjection to it. Similarly, the notion of a shared history for colonizer and colonized runs the risk not only of ignoring the matrix of domination, but also of blurring issues of cultural specificity. However, readings which acknowledge some degree of mutuality perform the service of contesting the polarities of irreconcilable difference upon which colonialism constructed its edifice of power and knowledge. This is certainly an important revision since the 'post-colonial' can be said to be as much a set of aesthetic and political issues and choices as a geographically or racially determined set of subject positions.[13]

These redefinitions embolden me to advance an interpretation of the novels of J. G. Farrell and Paul Scott as examples of *post-colonial* fiction, since both partake of oppositional and interrogative narrative practices which recognize and work to dismantle the staple elements of imperial narrative. They are, of course, post-colonial in a different sense from writers such as Khushwant Singh and Rohinton Mistry. Nevertheless, they highlight the complicitous hegemonic drives of certain conventions of representation and seek to explore and challenge them.[14] In these terms, Scott provides a prime example of a demonstrably post-colonial writer, since his terms of reference are both the run-up to 1947 and the historical overview which explicitly situates itself in the 1960s and 1970s, at the defining moment for that most tangible and fraught legacy of empire, immigration and race relations in Britain itself. (The inadequacy of the term 'post-imperial', often applied to these writers – which fails to distinguish between radical and conservative aesthetic moves – perhaps calls for the creation of an alternative term such as, for example, 'post-orientalist', more applicable to writers like Farrell and Scott who show an awareness of the way in which orientalist structures of thought underpinning empire are textually determined and transmitted, and who intervene in this transmission in a radically destabilizing way.)[15]

In addition, it will be noted that a shadowy figure haunts this work, whom I have chosen to call the post-colonial reader. This reader is deliberately ill-defined, or at least defined in the broadest sense of a reader who comes after decolonization and has the critical and experiential faculties to contest colonial ways of reading invited by certain narrative forms, such as the mode favoured by Kipling and Masters which might be described as imperial romance.[16] Its air of generality stems from the fact that the study argues that fruitful examination of colonial and post-colonial cultural productions should not only resist prescription, but encourage plurality of interpretation. In short, the post-colonial reader here envisaged, is one who is able to recognize and resist enticement into acquiescence in the value systems offered to the implied reader of a text such as Kipling's 'The Mark of the Beast', or Masters' *Bhowani Junction*. The implied reader's role as inscribed within such imperial romance narratives, is contrasted with the existence of a reading subject – the 'real reader' in Iser's terms – with an alternative set of political priorities and what I describe in Chapter 1 as an 'oppositional literary competence'. Of course, not every modern reader will wish to resist the seductive wiles of imperial romance. Nor is it necessarily the case that reading location or cultural identity will finally determine one's responses to such texts. Clearly there are, and should always be, as many readings as there are readers. My point here is that, while I acknowledge the existence of gendered and racialized reading positions and of the particular contexts of reception, it would be presumptuous of me to articulate a response for them. Therefore, the post-colonial reader in this study remains an idealized construct, a super-reader used to expose the central relationships of narrative and ideology, and endowed with the spectral ability to identify and contest power drives in narrative whenever they occur. (S/he is of course *my* implied reader.) Any assumptions made in these pages about the experience of post-colonial readers coming to these texts is based on the shared nature of their historical moment rather than in the specificities of a multitude of subjectivities and different legacies of imperialism in 'the real world' – South Asian, African, diasporic and so on. The heterogeneity of such experiences is, quite literally, more than I can say. Nor does this study engage with the currently contentious issue of how best to recover the voice of the native in the colonial text. I am content merely to point towards its unsettling presence in the interstices of a text such as *A Passage to India*.

In the last chapter, dealing with the Indian writers, it has been necessary to incorporate a slight shift in methodology and a broadening of focus in the treatment of history. This is because these two post-1947 texts, recounting events taking place during partition or many years later, are plotted around specific historical incidents: in *Train to Pakistan* the social disruption and carnage of partition, and in *A Fine Balance* the brutal oppression and injustices inflicted by Indira Gandhi's regime during the Emergency. As these are actual events – whereas history is read into the colonial texts symptomatically – a greater sense of context has been deemed necessary. Likewise, a brief overview of at least part of the evolution of Indian writing in English is needed to situate Khushwant Singh and Rohinton Mistry – not least because all self-aware Indian literature in English has at the outset had to negotiate issues of narrative and power. Critical interest in this topic has often centred on what has been known as the 'language question', to do with the validity of English as a vehicle of expression for Indian literature. This is understandable since the malleability of English for the purposes of creating (or recreating) the rhythms and idioms of class and regional utterance is an inherently political issue which has exercised a number of writers, from Bankim Chandra Chatterjee and Raja Rao to G. V. Desani and Salman Rushdie.[17] In the chapter here, my interest is in those strategies and devices which may be seen as both reclaiming the space and peoples of India from traditions of representation outlined in earlier chapters, and contesting those ongoing abuses of power, both physical and discursive, which have characterized the creation of the nation of India in 1947, and subsequent attempts to regulate and curtail the proliferation of elements within it which deviate from official ethnic and social prescriptions.

In *Train to Pakistan*, Khushwant Singh shows the break-up of a traditional, co-operative, intercommunal way of life in the emblematic village of Mano Majra. His story depicts the march of an ethnic nationalism which operates through the marked bodies of its subjects, and which roots out and eliminates elements not carrying the requisite physical signs. Yet against this increasingly frenzied and violent national sifting, the novel posits intercommunal relationships – such as that between the Sikh *budmash* Juggut Singh and the Muslim weaver's daughter, Nooran – and makes them stand as a symbolic bridge beyond blind nationalism, like the bridge which carries the Muslim refugees fleeing on the train to Pakistan. *A Fine Balance* uses the central image of a quilt to symbolize the complex texture of post-colonial India as experienced by the novel's main protagonists, a Parsi student and his 'aunt', and two Hindu tailors. The metaphor also serves for the multiple interconnections of caste, region and class the text traces as it creates a canvas incorporating the polyglot, multivalent reality of India – including rich landowners and beggars, hair collectors and entrepreneurs – which defies the monomaniacal, authoritarian impulses of Indira and Sanjay Gandhi as expressed in the Emergency legislation. The choice to focus on space and the body in this chapter suggested itself because both have traditionally formed fields of contestation for discursive power in personal and national politics. For example, as previous chapters demonstrate, British fictions of India reveal an obsession with the challenges to control posed by the Indian body: J. G. Farrell exposes how anthropology, ethnography and photography sought to contain it through description; Kipling's supernatural tales link its transformative power to a dissolution of those differences on which imperialism is based; for Forster it is an eroticized icon beyond narration and therefore discursive power; and its potential both as sacrificial object and as generic counter are explored by Paul Scott. Bodies undergo transmutation, fetishization and gruesome corruption in the writing of Khushwant Singh and Rohinton Mistry, all played out in spaces – villages, fields and rivers, cities, mountains and slums – which mark the limits of national society's ability to live at peace with itself. Moreover, by examining the work of a Sikh writer and a Parsi, both of whom offer visions of India and Indianness which are fundamentally at odds with both colonial and subsequent Hindu nationalist orthodoxies, we may perhaps glean a new perspective on what it has meant to be part of the Indian polity at crucial times in the years since the end of empire, and gain another insight into the possible relationship of narrative and power.

As the phenomenal success of Indian writing in English among readers and prize-panel judges in recent years testifies, the distinctive qualities of South Asian fiction – blending written and oral traditions, teleological and cyclical understandings of history and narrative and a reinvigoration of both language and genre – should instantly belie any inadvertent sense, caused by the structure of this book, that Indian novelists merely labour in the long shadow of British writers, incapable of producing anything which does not have its source, in one way or another, in something someone else has written. On the contrary, were it fruitful to reanimate superannuated critical commonplaces about a 'main road' of the novel in English, it might be possible to claim that the post-colonial novel – some of the most striking examples of which have been furnished by Indian writing – has in some sense now come *to be* that main road, rather than some shady and slightly exotic side-street. Less hyperbolic, but more accurate, might be the idea that the colonial experience and its endless reverberations in the comings and goings of its former subjects both in the metropolitan centres of the West and in India itself, receives one of its most vibrant commemorations in Indian fiction in English.

Much of this writing has been by women. Their absence here, or rather their presence merely as brief references in the spirit of 'further reading', underlines what I have already indicated: that this study does not aim to offer any kind of comprehensive account of writing in English about India. South Asian women, from Nayantara Sahgal, Anita Desai and Bapsi Sidhwa to Mahasveta Devi and Arundhati Roy, have produced texts foregrounding issues of narrative and power, sometimes in the form of that personal power politics affecting gender relations; indeed, Nayantara Sahgal's *Rich Like Us* (1983) offers an interesting counterpoint to the Mistry novel studied here. Overall, the examples chosen for close analysis were selected because they seemed to illustrate certain indicative features of narrative's relation to power, as well as offering the chance to explore a certain critical trajectory reflecting the course of wider interests in the discipline: analysis of the relation of narrative and power diagnosed by Said; the reliance of the mechanics of imperial self-confidence on a sense of dialogue; and the collapse of the concept of 'pure' colonial identity at a moment of crisis as it yields to hybrid voices and alternative ways of reading. Gender issues, like those of sexual politics more generally, clearly coincide with narrative and power. However, to do justice to them one would need to explore theories of gender difference, the construction of masculine and feminine paradigms, the normalization of sexual desire and so on, taking the study toward yet another region, one ably charted in recent works by Joseph Bristow, Christopher Lane, Jenny Sharpe and Lola Chatterjee.[18]

What emerges from this study is a picture of fiction on India that at some level always incorporates an awareness of the Janus-faced nature of narrative authority. In the work of imperial romance writers such as Kipling and Masters the neutrality of rhetorical devices is parenthesized even as it is asserted. These writers seem aware of the shaping incursion of ideology but, like a dog chasing its tail, circle incessantly in an attempt to swallow its traces. Forster's narrative, to some degree more candid about the need to acknowledge the proximity of typologies in character and voice to the power drives of empire, must still trip and stumble over the dialogic process before identifying silence as the only narrative space in which powerlessness can express itself. It is ironic that Farrell and Scott have sometimes been criticized for a Eurocentric focus since the lesson they seem to have learnt, and which they inscribe in their texts, is that when one chips away at the edifice of colonial self-perception one will eventually expose the crumbling masonry of walls which encircle the entire set of knowable communities and possible relations under colonialism: the fragments shored against the ruins of empire. For Indian writers such as Khushwant Singh and Rohinton Mistry, the issue of discursive power is still of vital importance in a post-colonial world where the definition of 'India' and 'Indian' is often constructed monologically and where the polyphonic potentialities of fiction offer a space for voices speaking from outside socially sanctioned narratives of nation. Likewise, for the critic, defining a particular set of narratives of India as in some way paradigmatic carries with it the danger of simplification and canon-formation. Nevertheless, the emphasis placed in this book on a multiplicity of interpretative possibilities may contribute to the current reconnoitring of a space beyond the frontiers of liberal criticism and the kind of discourse analysis which, taking Kipling at his word, sees colonial and post-colonial narrative as a site where 'East is East and West is West ...'. As Sara Suleri remarks:

> The postcolonial condition is neither territorially bound nor more the property of one people than of the other: instead its inevitably retroactive narrative allows for the inclusion both of its colonial past and of the function of criticism at the present time as necessary corollaries to the telling of its stories.[19]

To conclude in a similarly Arnoldian vein, the hypothesis advanced here is that, taken together British and Indian fictions of India, along with the possibilities for re-reading them, may be seen as the fruit of a forced and sometimes brutal but always rich and dynamic interchange, rather than as the cultural debris left when ignorant armies clash by night.

Notes

1. Edward W. Said, *Orientalism: Western Conceptions of the Orient*, pp. 272–300.
2. Fredric Jameson, *The Political Unconscious: Narrative as a Socially Symbolic Act*, p. 20.
3. Jeremy Tambling, *Narrative and Ideology*, p. 90.
4. See for example, Teresa Hubel, *Whose India? The Independence Struggle in British and Indian Fiction and History*, and Gail Ching-Liang Low, *White Skins/Black Masks: Representation and Colonialism*.
5. Aijaz Ahmad, *In Theory: Classes, Nations, Literatures*, p. 99.
6. Benita Parry, 'Problems in Current Theories of Colonial Discourse', p. 33.
7. Ibid., p. 32.
8. Edward W. Said, *Culture and Imperialism*, p. 88.
9. Wolgang Iser, *The Act of Reading: A Theory of Aesthetic Response*, p. x.
10. Wolfgang Iser, 'Indeterminacy and the Reader's Response in Prose Fiction', in J. Hillis Miller (ed.), *Aspects of Narrative: Selected Papers from the English Institute*, p. 43.
11. Re-reading the Raj has also occasioned some gleefully taken opportunities for parody and pastiche among Indian novelists, as well as less acrobatic reconsiderations of the British-Indian connection. Regrettably, these fall outside the scope of the present study, but would offer excellent case studies for a similar treatment. For sheer enjoyment the reader is referred to such texts as: Shashi Tharoor, *The Great Indian Novel*; I. Allan Sealey, *The Trotter Nama*; Gita Mehta, *Raj*; Vikram Chandra, *Red Earth and Pouring Rain*; and Mukul Kesavan, *Looking Through Glass*. The pinnacle of such narrative achievements, and in a way their progenitor, remains Salman Rushdie's, *Midnight's Children*.
12. Elleke Boehmer, *Colonial and Postcolonial Literature*, p. 3.
13. The question of who claims 'post-coloniality' is a current concern of much criticism in this area. For a representative spread of issues and positions around the term 'post-colonialism' see: Patrick Williams and Laura Chrisman, 'An Introduction', Vijay Mishra and Bob Hodge, 'What is Post-colonialism?', Anne McClintock, 'The Angel of Progress: Pitfalls of the Term "Postcolonialism"', all in Patrick Williams and Laura Chrisman (eds), *Colonial Discourse and Post-colonial Theory: A Reader*. See also, Edward W. Said, 'Intellectuals in the Post-Colonial

World', pp. 44–6; Ella Shohat, 'Notes on the "Post-Colonial"', p. 103; Arif Dirlik, 'The Postcolonial Aura: Third World Criticism in the Age of Global Capitalism', pp. 328–56; and Kwame Anthony Appiah, 'Is the Post- in Postmodernism the Post- in Postcolonial?', p. 353.

14. In the Introduction to *Past the Last Post: Theorizing Post-Colonialism and Post-Modernism*, Helen Tiffin cites post-colonialism as being characterized by having two 'archives':

> The first archive here constructs it as writing ... grounded in those societies whose subjectivity has been constituted in part by the subordinating power of European colonialism – that is, as writing from countries or regions which were formerly colonies of Europe. The second archive of post-colonialism is intimately related to the first, though not coextensive with it. Here the post-colonial is conceived as a set of discursive practices, prominent among which is *resistance* to colonialism, colonialist ideologies, and their contemporary forms and subjectificatory legacies. (Ian Adam and Helen Tiffin (eds), *Past the Last Post: Theorizing Post-Colonialism, and Post-Modernism*, p. vii)

Clearly Scott and Farrell belong in the second archive, according to my usage. Peter Childs and Patrick Williams also offer an acknowledgement of the interrogative nature of Farrell's writing when, at the start of their text, *An Introduction to Post-Colonial Theory*, they describe Farrell as 'a post-colonial chronicler of the British Empire's moments of crisis', Peter Childs and Patrick Williams, *An Introduction to Post-Colonial Theory*, p. 1. I do not take their use of the term to be merely chronological here.

15. In *Whose India?* Teresa Hubel follows Gyan Prakash's lead in defining the kind of historiographical texts which 'deconstruct the colonial discourses of nationalism and imperialism and expose what has been placed under erasure by these discourses' in conventional histories of India, as 'post-Orientalist'. In the same way, Farrell's and Scott's texts are self-conscious in deploying and ironizing the conventional elements of what is sometimes known as Raj Fiction, recognizing them as contributing to that myth of imperialism-as-natural which Roland Barthes elsewhere describes as 'imperiality'.

16. I understand the term 'imperial romance' in the sense in which it is often used by late nineteenth-century critics to differentiate between domestic fiction – frequently identified with realism and traduced as the sickly and effeminate 'novel of manners' – and an outward-looking (read imperial) tradition, drawing on other romance genres such as the Gothic, and deploying stock characters and situations. Hence the term remains applicable to the writing of John Masters, seventy years after Kipling. The distinction has recently proved fruitful for contemporary critics of imperial adventure fiction such as Patrick Brantlinger and Gail Low. See Patrick Brantlinger, *Rule of Darkness: British Literature*

and Imperialism, 1830–1914; and Gail Ching-Liang Low, *White Skins/ Black Masks*.

17. See Meenakshi Mukherjee, *The Twice Born Fiction: Themes and Techniques of the Indian Novel in English*, especially Chapter 7, 'The Problem of Style'.
18. See Joseph Bristow, *Empire Boys: Adventures in a Man's World*; Christopher Lane, *The Ruling Passion: British Colonial Allegory and the Paradox of Homosexual Desire*; Jenny Sharpe, *Allegories of Empire: The Figure of Woman in the Colonial Text*; and Lola Chatterjee (ed.), *Woman, Image, Text*.
19. Sara Suleri, *The Rhetoric of English India*, pp. 21–2.

I Gothic and Supernatural – Allegories at Work and at Play in Kipling's Indian Fiction

It becomes clear ... that the social and literary functions of the supernatural are one and the same: it is a question of breaking the law. Whether it occurs within social life or within a narrative, the intervention of the supernatural element always constitutes a rupture in the system of established rules, and this is its justification. (Tzvetan Todorov, 'The Fantastic in Fiction')

All literary works are determined by their relation to an ideology ... the excellence of the novelist lies not in his ideology but in the fact that he confronts an ideological utterance with a fictional utterance. (Pierre Macherey, *A Theory of Literary Production*)

Rudyard Kipling arrives on the literary scene of Anglo-India just as the arteries of imperial governance are beginning to harden. The pragmatic and utilitarian impulses of the first half of the nineteenth century, with their reforming zeal, which yet retained a place for friendly interaction with existing Indian society, have given way to a dour scepticism about the value of Indian character and culture and an increasingly overt reliance on repression. The roots of this change lie in the psychological impact of the Mutiny of 1857 which continues to haunt Anglo-India and its cultural productions up to, and beyond, independence.

As a result, Kipling's Indian fiction is marked by profound concerns over imperial security. His stories are littered with descriptions of the best way of exerting power over the native and what happens when the promptings of the *cognoscenti* in India are ignored by the metropolitan powers-that-be. Yet the strategic employment of both carrot and stick in politics bespeaks an unease over the continuance of British power which contradicts the oft-stated luxurious confidence encouraged by an all-seeing imperial eye. Kipling's early fiction actively reveals such misplaced complacency in a narrative technique, which, while obeying the imperatives of power-knowledge, distances the putative narrator from both reader and an author who appears often to be laughing behind his hand. While Kipling's technique in these first tales is not as complex as it becomes later it is certainly more complex and problematic than it has been given credit for and, I would suggest, reveals much about the tenuous nature of the moral and political power of the Raj through the narrative 'will-to-power' used to exert control over the colonized Other, and about thinly veiled anxieties regarding both politics and questions of literary representation. In spite of themselves and their apparently complete formal qualities, Kipling's narratives are often infiltrated, subverted and disrupted, both by uncertainties which imperialism would prefer to ignore, and by the Other which imperialist discourse seeks to keep at the edge, on the fringes and in a carefully defined and subjugated space.

As a result it is proposed to engage with Kipling's early fiction in this chapter, and to show how his highly ambitious narrative practices relate to power. That narrative ambition appears in his very first volume of 'turnovers' culled from the Lahore Civil and Military Gazette and compiled as *Plain Tales from the Hills*, in the form of an undermined and unreliable narrator-figure whose foregrounded shortcomings call into question many of the views he apparently represents.[1] For example, in 'Miss Youghal's Sais', the narrator is initially linked to censorious Anglo-Indian opinion of Strickland's habit of 'going Fantee among natives', through his description of the policeman who 'dabbled in unsavoury places which no respectable man would think of exploring – all among the native riff-raff' (P.T.H., p. 51). This may well be irony – the success of Strickland's courtship of Miss Youghal validates his unorthodox methods – but such an explanation will not suffice in the highly problematic tale of transgressive interracial love, 'Beyond the Pale', where the segregating narrator occupies an epistemologically dubious position and the 'lesson' ('lessons' on the morality and social codes of Anglo-India characterize *Plain Tales*) remains triumphantly equivocal. The status of the narrator's knowledge is called into question in 'Beyond the Pale'. Despite his socially sanctioned statement in the opening paragraph: 'A man should, whatever happens, keep to his own caste, race and breed. Let the White go to the White and the Black to the Black' (P.T.H., p. 162), it appears that the narrator too has a transgressive knowledge of the Other which calls into question his position as a champion of Anglo-India's binarist values. Having noted Trejago's excess of acceptable knowledge – the inference being that knowledge gives power up to a point, after which there is a real danger of the kind of emotional and intellectual assimilation which serves to undermine carefully constructed racial hierarchies – the narrator comments on Bisesa's chosen method of communication with her errant lover: 'No Englishman should be able to translate object-letters', as Trejago can. Yet the narrator proceeds to reveal, sign for sign, the meaning of Bisesa's fragmentary epistle. This kind of narrative vision, or 'double vision', implicitly undermines the separatist sentiments of the opening paragraph and contributes to a deferral of meaning, a neutralization of the narrator's initial didacticism, and the equivocation noted above. It is an early example of Kipling's experimentation with the problematic narrator figure, which becomes such a feature of both the Anglo-Indian and later fiction. In putting such ironizing distance between himself and the textual spokesperson, Kipling confounds the easy assimilation of the 'real author' and the 'implied author' who 'lives' only in the text.[2] *Plain Tales from the Hills* and the other Anglo-Indian volumes are extended experiments with different narrative voices and positions. Kipling does not seek a constant authoritative and authorial standpoint. The result has been that certain critics have been frustrated in their attempts to equate Kipling's views with those of his narrator-personae in a direct way: being unable to obtain a consistent set of political and racial opinions thereby.

In the same way, critics have been irritated by the habit of punctuating these early narratives with fragments of other tales which the knowing narrator then withholds. Likewise, the phrase, 'but that is another story', forms something of a refrain in Kipling's first volume.[3] Certainly, the persistence and obtrusiveness of this device indicates the rough edges of a still-developing technique. Yet, I would argue that it serves a similar purpose to the double-vision strategy described above, and that hostile critics have failed to perceive that such intrusions and interruptions, which may indeed serve to alienate the reader from the narrator through their annoying insistence, are designed to do just that; after all in so many of the Anglo-Indian tales the narrator is undermined and his views shown to be palpably flawed. These persistent intrusions reveal the narrator as a censorious and opinionated storyteller revelling in his role as keeper and dispenser of knowledge. Kipling's own 'alienation effect' serves as a measure of the distance he puts between himself and his narrator-persona. The extent of his development as a writer can be appreciated by the degree to which such devices become internalized in the structure of later texts such as 'Mrs Bathurst' and 'Dayspring Mishandled', where several narratives contend for pre-eminence within the body of the meta-narrative. (Such internalizing may be seen in embryonic form in 'A Conference of the Powers',

'The Phantom Rickshaw' and, most effectively, in 'On the City Wall' where the panoramic vision and supposed knowledge of the narrator-protagonist, in whom we are initially encouraged to place our confidence, is entirely undercut when he is duped into assisting in the gaol-break of a former resistance leader, organized by Hindus, Muslims and Sikhs working in concert.)

The status of Anglo-Indian knowledge of the colonized Other, touched upon in 'Beyond the Pale', forms a central concern of stories in this and other volumes, and comes to be linked to its co-efficient, power. Thus, in 'The Bisara of Pooree' (P.T.H.), the orientalist axiom: 'All kinds of magic are out of date and done away with, except in India where nothing changes in spite of the shiny top-scum of civilization' (P.T.H., p. 225) – juxtaposing the imagined eternality and stasis of the East with the rational, civilized West – leads into a tale in which the mesmeric effect of a talisman is combated by another figure with transgressive knowledge. The significantly named Man who Knew is 'different from most Englishmen', and it is his imaginative difference which enables him to credit the powers of the Bisara and take the appropriate steps to neutralize them. The Man who Knew 'knows' Indian lore intellectually and also imaginatively. He occupies a middle ground and, as such, is empowered to a greater degree than the conventional orientalists, Mr Gubernatis (Professor of Sanskrit) and Max Müller (Professor of Philology) who stand outside the Orient and translate it for the Occident. We are told that, 'In ordinary ears, English ears, the tale [of the Bisara's powers] was only an interesting bit of folklore' (P.T.H., p. 227). Yet, like the Man who Knew, the narrator perceives the story as more than mere folklore. Although he issues certain disclaimers from time to time, he is able not only to reveal what the Bisara signifies in Indian culture, but also to demonstrate its properties in action as he tells the tale. Eastern folklore is framed and validated within a Western narrative, and although the text does not itself enact a struggle between Indian 'magic' and Western rationalism – in the way that some of the supernatural stories in *Life's Handicap* and *Wee Willie Winkie* do – the inconclusive ending prefigures the anti-teleological thrust of stories like 'The Mark of the Beast', and suggest Kipling's problematic desire to stand imaginatively between two cultures while remaining politically allied to just one.[4]

A commonplace of a certain strand of recent imperial study is that the late nineteenth century saw an increased use of improved surveillance techniques and a relatively smooth incorporation of Indians within British hegemony. However, I would argue that the British empire in India displays a fraught connection to more sophisticated modes of governance.[5] The ambiguous position of the British in India – on the cusp between surveillance based operations of power and a power enacted on the body of the colonized – was witnessed by numerous late nineteenth-century figures. For example, Fitzjames Stephen described the funeral of the assassinated Viceroy Lord Mayo in 1872, which was surrounded by all the pomp and ceremony an outraged imperial power could muster and was accompanied by a hatred and fear, bordering on paranoia, on the part of the now explicitly vulnerable British toward any native not displaying the required degree of reverence and solemnity. Stephen commented, in respect of the troops, cannon and gun carriages in the funeral procession: 'everything rests upon military force. The guns and the troops are not only the outward and visible marks of power, but they are the power itself to a great extent'.[6] Similarly, Theodore Morison noted the effect that great spectacles of princely power had on the native and advocated an increased use of such spectacle by the Raj.[7] It was argued that Indians preferred a forceful and visible form of government. It was what they understood and deferred to as their history had been one of despotic rule rather than participation in a functioning parliamentary-type system. Partiality and strength, it was claimed, excited greater respect and understanding in the native than impartiality and democratic reform.

The corollary of this essentially feudal piece of political science was that authoritarians within the Raj were able to advocate a repressive approach not only in cases of dissent, but also in everyday relations with the colonized and the enforcement of British jurisdiction. Hutchins has described the transformation in outlook by which the reformist, liberal policy adopted towards India in the early years of British rule was superseded, in a process that escalated after the Mutiny, by increasing autocracy and conservatism among those for whom the progressive democratization of England was a process to be bitterly regretted, and resisted in India at all costs. The result was that:

> In the later years of the century, Englishmen did not shrink from asserting that British rule was primarily based on force, because such a basis for rule had transformed itself from a charge which men were eager to refute, into an actual sanction of the moral superiority of that rule.[8]

Given this volatile historical situation, the theory of an empire based on an efficient system of surveillance requires closer scrutiny.

Kipling's Gothic and supernatural stories provide an opportunity for just such scrutiny.

Thus far my study has concentrated upon the way in which knowledge operates to produce political power, and how Kipling's narratives reflect and complicate this process. Such a thesis is based on that theoretical description of knowledge provided by Foucault, and more particularly Said in *Orientalism*: knowledge of a people or group of peoples, their customs, beliefs and patterns of behaviour, which makes it possible to exercise power over them, to govern them. However, when one comes to study those stories concerning Gothic and the supernatural in India which Kipling scatters among the more realistic tales of Anglo-Indian life, it is important to comprehend the subtle change which takes place in the nature and function of knowledge. Where a supernatural economy of power is shown to operate, knowledge, for the Anglo-Indian protagonist, ceases to be a mark of power. It becomes instead a general understanding or enlightenment as to the altered realities of his position as a victim of supernatural or unknowable phenomena. It becomes a source of instability and lack of power. In this sense the knowledge that something is supernatural acts as a subversion of power through knowledge, an ironic commentary upon it. Moreover, in certain tales one might claim that this supernatural absence-of-power constitutes part of an allegory depicting the unseating of the white man from his position of sovereign authority in India. That rationalism which has been the guiding light of Western intellectual development is suspended in a supernatural economy as the phenomena witnessed are not subject to empirically established laws of nature. To know that something which apparently exists is beyond the realm of human knowledge is, at the same time, a form of knowledge and a recognition of the inadequacies of that 'sovereign knowledge' by which England rules India: one simply knows that one does not know.

In this chapter it is proposed to examine certain stories in which a supernatural or Gothic economy operates, and to scrutinize the author-narrator's attempts to restrain the development of that economy to a point where it is no longer reclaimable through realistic teleological conventions. As we shall see Kipling achieves this more successfully in some texts than in others. The stories to be focused upon are 'The Return of Imray' (L.H.). 'The Strange Ride of Morrowbie Jukes' (W.W.W.), 'The Phantom Rickshaw' (W.W.W.) and 'The Mark of the Beast' (L.H.).[9]

The Orient as a land of mystery and strangeness is a long-established, if reductive, orientalist tenet. Kipling's supernatural and Gothic stories take this somewhat cliched idea as their base and use it to explore issues of imperial control and, I would claim, enact the struggle of colonizer versus an Ultimate Other in the formal qualities – the hesitations, lacunae, selections and omissions of the texts themselves. In reading along with this well-worn trope, the argument of this chapter proposes a recognition of how the very tradition of India as uncanny picks out blind spots *within* rationalist colonial discourse. The point is not that India is spooky – or that Indians deliberately act strangely as a strategy of resistance – but that in positing extreme alterity of this kind, colonial discourse itself identifies a space beyond its tenets and operation. The analysis of Kipling's stories is then about the comparative success or otherwise of Kipling's attempts to police the potential interpretative possibilities that ensue. However, at the outset, two key questions present themselves. What is the importance of the distinction between the Gothic tradition and what may be termed the raw supernatural? And what are the qualities which allow the supernatural to be read as a radical commentary on political relationships? The answer to the first question exists in the malleability of the Gothic genre. There is no obligation on Gothic texts to explain their resolution through the supernatural. For example, in works such as *The Mysteries of Udolpho* and *The Italian*, Mrs Radcliffe provides rational explanations for events that have appeared preternatural. The implications of such coy resolutions for a reading of the Gothic as subversive through its irrationality are immediately clear. Any event can be reclaimed for rationalism through an authorial will-to-power of the kind to which Kipling resorts again and again in the Indian tales of horror. This tendency of Gothic can be used to impose a consoling, one might say conservative, ending on what had appeared a wilful and radical text.[10] Thus, if it is the author-narrator's intention to use situations of horror as allegories depicting inversions of political power – as does Kipling in 'The Return of Imray' and 'The Strange Ride of Morrowbie Jukes', for example – it is then simple to restore the previously existing balance, or imbalance, of power. He merely has to explain in some way that the phenomenon described is an exception to established rules and display the eventual victory of those rules. The supernatural is not so easily assimilable, for if the author-narrator leaves a supernatural explanation in place he has effectively burned his bridges: whatever conclusions may be drawn, the fact of the unexplainable exists like a hole in his narrative.

The pliable nature of the Gothic convention makes it a convenient vehicle for the kind of disturbing yet ultimately conservative political allegory Kipling favours. Yet these qualities, at the same time, draw attention to the more irrevocable tendencies of the supernatural, and provide an answer to our second question. One can claim that the supernatural tales display a potential for independence from reactionary determinism, an antithetical allegorical potential, since an oppositional reading may see in them a coding of the breakdown of that rationalism on which imperial power is based. Potential allegories are those tales where the outlandish events narrated refuse to yield to the consoling schemes of teleological certainty. They remain recalcitrant, elusive tales in which ordinary Aristotelian narrative – the trumpet of imperial discourse – is choked off, and where resolution remains unattainable. The supernatural is always 'beyond', always inscrutably Other. As 'super-nature' the events described in these narratives are above and beyond the realm of the natural; that which is framed within nature and its laws as they have come to be understood through Western empirical observation. Francis Hutchins has described the late nineteenth-century attempt by British imperial discourse to represent English rule over India as natural or 'orientalized rule' – Kipling's contribution to the strategy being tales of 'imperial families' like the Chinns of 'The Tomb of his Ancestors' (D.W.) who are portrayed as being as much a part of India as the Indians themselves.[11] Yet if British rule is 'natural', anything, like the supernatural, which contravenes or transcends nature consequently calls into question the power and permanence of that rule. In this way the supernatural stands as a surrogate Other, a form of allegorical subversion, and must be combated in the stories by 'knowledgeable' figures like Strickland. Whether it is made manifest in the form of a *doppelgänger*, through ghosts or by bestial regression, the attack by the Other on the role of Western rationalism performed in the supernatural possesses a power of contribution to the decolonization process since its phenomena refuse the parameters defined for them both by imperialist rationalism and the attempted containment operation enacted by the author as he constructs the narrative.

Those narratives which employ what I have termed the Gothic and that may therefore be read as straight allegories include 'The Return of Imray' and 'The Strange Ride of Morrowbie Jukes'. They depict temporary inversions of racial and imperial power relations: in the first case between master and servant, and in the second between the colonizing and colonized races. In stories where the supernatural remains undiluted, and which display allegorical potential – such as 'The Phantom Rickshaw' and 'The Mark of the Beast' – power is problematized and the text itself, the mechanics of the telling, forms a site of struggle which is only resolved through premeditated authorial action, and which reveals the inadequacies and contradictions of privileged narrative positions. What one must bear in mind is that the straight allegories are consciously such and Kipling as author and ultimate authority is empowered to impose the desired (conservative) ending; Imray's treacherous servant pays the price for his actions and Morrowbie Jukes is rescued. Furthermore, the incidents themselves are isolated, framed and hemmed in by the continued operation of an imperial order projected by the narrator beyond the boundaries of the text; the bad servant is only one among a number of faithful servants, like Dunnoo the dog-boy who rescues Jukes, while Jukes' pit is an arena of suspension not obliteration, an anomaly, and the reader is always aware of imperial jurisdiction carrying on normally somewhere outside. However, those texts displaying allegorical potential are not reducible to the level of imperialist morality plays. They exhibit a disconcerting 'life' of their own in that no imposed resolution is adequate to erase contradiction. The author-narrator avoids judging between the contending narratives in 'The Phantom Rickshaw' and in so doing calls attention to the preferential treatment of imperialist, as opposed to dissident, narratives in the Anglo-Indian fiction as a whole. Similarly, while 'The Mark of the Beast' may depict the salvation of Fleete from the wrath of the 'Gods and Devils of Asia', that source of subversive power which set in motion the train of retributive events is still at large in the empire, and the methods used to effect Fleete's rescue are morally ambiguous to say the least.

Of course, potential allegories like 'The Mark of the Beast' require a conscious act on the part of the reader to realize their potential and bring them into existence as allegories; just as the conservatism and reassuring denouements of the first kind are the product of conscious suppressions and omissions on Kipling's part. Effectively, one must adapt Jonathan Culler's idea and exercise an ironic or oppositional literary competence. One must take one's place as the implied or implicit reader sought by the text, but at the same time reject the role of complicit reader the author encourages: compliant in producing a meaning for the text through evasion and political manipulation. Indeed, one must, with Macherey, read the text 'against the grain of its intended meaning',[12] not so much to reveal ideology, since its presence is unavoidable in Kipling's work, as to reveal ideological-literary anxiety.

Martin Green has described the imperial adventure tale genre, to which much of Kipling's work belongs, as 'the energizing myth of English imperialism'. He supports Lévi-Strauss' view of the political nature of myth in modern societies; 'myths, while sometimes constituting models for their societies – to perpetuate beliefs or practices – sometimes instead expose the mainsprings of their societies, in all their contradictions'.[13] We have seen how inconsistencies in Kipling's work expose the mainsprings of imperial discourse in the realistic Anglo-Indian tales. It is possible to claim that the supernatural texts effect a more drastic exposure of self-contradictions within the discourse both in the non-linguistic methods of communication they choose, and by the challenge they pose to those easy binarisms which are the basis of racial-imperial hierarchies.

Colonial criticism following Said has often concerned itself with those simplistic dualities which form the garb of imperialism. Central among these is the master–slave relationship, as set forth by Hegel. In the majority of Anglo-Indian stories, position in this dialectic is defined by race. Crudely speaking the colonizer is master and the colonized is the slave. The supernatural introduces a dangerous ambiguity into this situation. One might say that it is a weapon of that ambivalence or hybridity recognized by Homi Bhabha – a critic of the phenomenological projection of 'Otherness' – which marks: 'the disturbance of ... [English imperialism's] authoritative representations by ... uncanny forces ... the paranoid threat from the hybrid is finally uncontainable because it breaks down the symmetry and duality of self/Other, inside/outside'.[14]

Many of Kipling's narratives take place amid the ruins of the master–slave dialectic. The difficulties of fulfilling the roles ostensibly decreed by that 'heaven-born/follower' dichotomy, explicitly stated by Kipling in some texts, reveal the colonial position as one fraught with dangers and characterized by struggle illustrated in the peculiar fluidity of power relations in supernatural texts. Extrapolating from this one can say that the 'hostile India' motif, which recurs with monotonous predictability in Anglo-Indian literature in general, is as much a projection on to the environment of anxieties over the instability of power relations as a description of practical discomfort. (Kipling combines the two in 'At the End of the Passage' (L.H.), a tale of mental breakdown liberally sprinkled with Gothic effects.) The supernatural itself forms a critique of those binarisms – subject/object, us/them, colonizer/colonized, English/Indian – through which imperial discourse seeks to perpetuate hegemony. In the horror stories, for example, those usually 'acting', the English, and those 'acted upon', the Indians, often change places. Once inversion is effected the rest of the tale is concerned with the attempt at redress and the reactivation of colonial power. The success of this endeavour is dependent on whether Kipling has reined in the text through Gothic or 'given it its head' through the supernatural.

The radicalism of the supernatural is paradoxically revealed by the conservatism of a Gothic text explicitly concerned with a practical demonstration and reinvocation of the master–slave dyad after its temporary violation. 'The Return of Imray' literally centres on a master–servant relationship and is designed to operate as an allegory of the loss of imperial power and the steps necessary to reassert it. The sudden disappearance of the civil servant Imray is a mystery. After a few months Strickland of the police – that transgressive figure whose hobby is gaining knowledge of India – rents Imray's bungalow. When the narrator quarters himself upon his friend, he is witness to unaccountable and disconcerting events. Strickland's dog, Tietjens, refuses to sleep in the house with his master at night and bays at the moon; a strange visitor apparently calls to see the narrator but disappears before they meet; and the narrator has the impression that someone is calling him during a stormy night. The implication in all this is that Tietjens, as a dog, has access to an extrasensory world not shared by the humans and has witnessed the manifestation of Imray's ghost. Despite the somewhat heavy-handed Gothic touches of the voice in the storm and the spectral visitor who may have been a trick of the light, at this point the tale still stands neatly poised between Gothic (conservative) and supernatural (radical) potentialities. However, the nature of the allegory, like the fate of the murderer, is sealed when Strickland, in pursuit of some snakes, discovers the body of Imray on the beam between the ceiling cloth and the roof. The rest of the narrative is concerned with the detection and punishment of the murderer and the reinvocation of the white man's power over the insubordinate native. Strickland's rationalism and relentless logic in pursuit of the murderer is invoked to underpin imperialist generalizations about the moral inferiority of Indians, as when Strickland remarks:

> 'If I call in all the servants they will stand fast in a crowd and lie like Aryans. What do you suggest?'
>
> 'Call 'em in one by one,' I said.
>
> 'They'll run away and give the news to all their fellows,' said Strickland. 'We must segregate 'em'. ('The Return of Imray', L.H. pp. 271–2)

Thus one sees recommended a policy of divide and rule to gain knowledge, and reinstate power, like that by which England seeks to control the wider empire in India.

Eventually, Imray's own servant, Bahadur Khan, admits to murdering his master because he believed that Imray had cast an evil eye upon his son, causing his death. Here is the centre of the allegory's horror: the body-servant's treachery recalls the vulnerable position of the sahib, and the very personal horror of the Mutiny, a recent and vivid memory for Kipling's Anglo-Indian contemporaries. Geoffrey Moorhouse has written:

> Much of the horror for the British sprang from the fact that natives they had individually known for several years, and trusted absolutely in their patronizing way, suddenly one morning cut to pieces parents whose children they had been cradling gently only a few hours before.[15]

(Indeed, one might say that mutinous scenarios form a persistent echo in Kipling's fiction. Apart from the allegories, 'The Head of the District' (L.H.), 'His Chance in Life' (P.T.H.), and 'The Tomb of his Ancestors' (D.W.), several other tales feature situations arising from rebellion.) The worst Anglo-Indian nightmare, the treacherous servant, is a metaphor for India in revolt.

Nevertheless, over against this horror is revealed Strickland's capacity for solving the mystery, while Bahadur Khan's confession is a handing over of knowledge to the sahib and an acquiescence in the process of power. Furthermore, Bahadur Khan's quasi-British sense of honour is shown to be intact by his preference to make redress through suicide rather than go to the gallows. His vindication of Anglo-Indian codes of honour and fidelity, in the teeth of his own treachery confirms the social *status quo*, and is part of the process of reinstituting the original set of power relations. At the end Strickland, somewhat smugly, diagnoses Imray's fatal mistake in touching Bahadur Khan's son: 'Simply and solely through not knowing the nature of the Oriental, and the coincidence of a little seasonal fever' (L.H., p. 276). Rationalism's reply is shown to be more than a match for a controlled eruption of what might have been the supernatural. Indeed, the ostensibly supernatural events of the story merely serve to help the English detective by convincing him that there is a mystery for him to solve. The supernatural is, therefore, merely a function of Kipling's text: helping to confirm the superiority of the colonizer. At no time does the English 'ghost' threaten to disturb the living Englishman's power, and once it has performed its role it disappears from the text never to return. Indeed, all those 'ghosts' raised in 'The Return of Imray' are successfully laid to rest.

So too Kipling acts to thwart the potentially disquieting consequences of a richer and more fully developed Gothic allegory, 'The Strange Ride of Morrowbie Jukes'. The full horror of the pit into which Jukes tumbles after his semi-delirious ride is established by the practical rather than imaginative character of Jukes' narrative. The detailed description of its geographical features and careful measurements reflect the civil engineer's cartographical first instincts; he deals with the mapping, planning and settling of land, a key part of the colonization process.[16] However, that the deference and hierarchies subtending from normal colonial power relations are here, somehow, in a state of suspension, is suggested when Jukes' search of the river front which bounds one side of the pit, for a means of escape is, 'the signal for a bombardment from some insane native in a boat' (W.W.W., p. 173): prefiguring Conrad's man-of-war shelling the bush in *Heart of Darkness*. However, here it is an example of anti-colonial, rather than colonial, aggression: roles are reversed with the colonizer at the mercy of the native, anticipating the allegory's nature.

That imperial race roles are disrupted here is made explicit when Jukes is confronted by the troglodytic inhabitants and reflects:

> I have been accustomed to a certain amount of civility from my inferiors, and on approaching the crowd naturally expected that there would be some recognition of my presence. As a matter of fact there was, but it was by no means what I had looked for.
>
> The ragged crowd actually laughed at me ... some of them literally throwing themselves down on the ground in convulsions of unholy mirth. ('The Strange Ride of Morrowbie Jukes', W.W.W., p. 174)

Similarly, Gunga Dass, an ex-government servant of Jukes' acquaintance and now a resident of the pit, tells his former superior that he has stumbled upon a town where the dead 'who do not die' – those given up for dead because of catalepsy or trance – are allowed to dwell by some unspecified authority. He utters a 'long low chuckle of derision – the laughter, be it understood, of a superior or at least of an equal' (W.W.W., p. 178). It is made clear to Jukes that there is no means of escape. The white man's sovereignty counts for nothing here and, despite Jukes' protestations and threats, no 'retributive justice', no imperial revenge, is possible in this unknown land. Jukes records that, 'Gunga Dass was at some pains to throw half a cupful of fetid water over my head, an attention for which I could have fallen on my knees and thanked him, but he was laughing all the while in the same mirthless, wheezy key' (W.W.W., p. 179). Native laughter in this tale is a kind of grim carnivalesque laughter that strips away the pomposity and pretension of the ruler.

Yet the real terror of the allegory is only brought into full relief when Jukes himself begins to recognize and acquiesce in the revised realities of his powerless state. He comments, 'being only a man [not a "heaven-born" now] ... I felt hungry and said as much to Gunga Dass, whom I had begun to regard as my natural protector' (W.W.W., p. 179), after which Gunga Dass verbalizes the inverted master–slave disequilibrium now existing: he 'propounded the terms on which he would consent to "do" for me'. Jukes is forced to admit, 'Here was a sahib, a representative of the dominant race, helpless as a child and completely at the mercy of his native neighbours' (W.W.W., p. 182). The political allegory is made explicit and Gunga Dass cites 'greatest good of greatest number' as the governing maxim, then gleefully proclaims, 'We are now Republic'. Empire is suspended and what is set in its place is a kind of perverse utilitarianism: a mockery of Western political systems. Republic constitutes a rejection of monarchy, of the Queen-Empress, and of the white sahib who is her representative. Here is a kind of revolution in which the 'Duke' is at the mercy of the proletariat. Hierarchies have collapsed and Gunga Dass and his fellows could rightly profess, 'to-Morrow we'll all be Jukes'.

However, at the height of its imaginative power, Kipling shies away from the revolutionary propensities of his narrative and 'The Strange Ride of Morrowbie Jukes' undergoes a kind of narrative breakdown. Morrowbie Jukes strikes Gunga Dass for refusing to tell him about the other sahib who had apparently fallen into the pit, whereupon, 'He stepped down from the platform at once and cringing and fawning and weeping and attempting to embrace my feet led me round to the burrow which he had indicated' (W.W.W., p. 191). The incident suggests that native fear of and deference to the white man is inherent despite the contingencies of their present position. In order for Kipling to resolve the allegory satisfactorily and reactivate colonial power it must appear that the 'natural order' has simply been temporarily upset. In the same way Jukes decides not to ask Gunga Dass the whereabouts of the dead sahib's gun, 'knowing he would lie'; although this is a defamiliarizing narrative, orientalist adages about native deceit are still in place, indeed their treachery is part of the horror. Likewise, when the sahib's escape route is discovered, Gunga Dass' eagerness to accompany Jukes back to 'terra firma' implies the native's realization of the overriding benefits of imperial rule instead of the pit's communal anarchy.

Armed with the sahib's notebook the Englishman literally reclaims the land step by step: mapping the uncharted territory in a process of recolonization. While it is suggested that the cartographer and the communicator – Dass is a former telegraph-master who deciphers the sahib's notes – need each other to effect escape, it requires an Englishman among all these natives to achieve it. Additionally, the white man must always be on guard for the black's treachery; as is demonstrated when Gunga Dass assaults Jukes leaving him senseless on the ground yards from freedom. Yet even this predicament can be salvaged by Kipling the eternal optimist; Jukes is rescued by the faithful servant figure of Dunnoo the dog-boy, who certainly is this man's best friend.

Kipling's idealized India comes to the rescue – the one that is happy with British rule – and his conservative will-to-power resurfaces in the slick and unlikely resolution needed to reactivate colonial power. The tale begins as an allegory of white loss of status and privilege: the 'nightmare scenario' in which a dissolution of imperial power relations takes place. It ends as a tale of British pluck, white moral superiority and the fidelity of those natives who know what is good for them. The text raises the question of how one survives, as a sahib, in a land where hegemonic signs are turned upside down, and then shrinks from an honest answer. To appreciate the disturbing radical possibilities of the events narrated one need only imagine the difference which would be made to the tale as allegory if Jukes had failed to escape from his pit and, say, his diary had been posthumously discovered containing this narrative; in other words, if British power were left in a state of suspension and not reactivated. (The horror of 'The Man who would be King', for example, exists in just such an inability to reactivate imperial power.) But this narrative is never told. Indeed, Kipling prevents any chance of such a narrative ever being told at the outset when the narrator introduces Jukes' own account, discussing the teller in the present tense, informing the reader that, 'He never varies the tale in the telling, and grows very hot and indignant when he thinks of the disrespectful treatment he received' (W.W.W., p. 169) and – surely a significant comment given Kipling's own adulterating project – that Jukes has 'touched it up in places and introduced Moral Reflections'. The narrator's introduction ensures we know that Jukes has escaped his ordeal. It consigns the tale to the level of an unpleasant dream. The narrative is thus effectively neutered, defused of any revolutionary inclinations, and this highly conservative tactic – policing the defamiliarizing inner-narrative – allows the imperial reader to enjoy the fright and sleep easily in his bed afterwards.

Supernatural tales, potential allegories, frustrate such narrative castration. In so doing they expose certain truths about the methods by which Kipling can manipulate those more plastic texts we have examined. 'The Phantom Rickshaw' provides an interesting example in its use of a self-destructive narrative as well as being a potential allegory of discursive forms in imperialism. Jack Pansay is apparently being hounded out of life by the ghost of Mrs Keith-Wessington, a former lover his heartless desertion has killed. Her sporadic materializations cause the termination of Pansay's subsequent engagement to Kitty Mannering and some kind of breakdown. However, the reader is never sure whether the ghost is real or a projection of Pansay's guilt. In his defiantly supernatural interpretation of events, the teller Pansay reveals himself as a self-consciously sophisticated refuser of language, rejecting and stifling any fragments of those other narratives which threaten to break through to contradict and censure him and his conduct while he tells his highly subjective and self-justificatory tale. Those voices which might record his selfish and unreasonable behaviour are pushed to the fringes of the text and quickly silenced. In the technique of inserted narratives and a found manuscript, 'The Phantom Rickshaw' has structural affinities with certain other nineteenth-century texts dealing with border-line states.[17] Yet Kipling's text is singular in Pansay's method of suppression, which provides a clue as to his author's mode of manipulation in the tales of horror, and how he apprehends and speaks for (one might say, 'colonizes') other narratives under imperialism.

The instigating narrator and Pansay's doctor, Heatherlegh, each has his own theory as to the cause of Pansay's condition. Heatherlegh has 'the right to speak authoritatively' and laughs at the narrator's imaginative, pseudo-Swedenborgian diagnosis that 'there was a crack in Pansay's head and a little bit of the Dark World came through and pressed him to death' (W.W.W., p. 125) – preferring his own empirical, medical explanation. Indeed, the reader's uncertainty is maintained throughout: even Pansay appears to waver under the initially beneficial auspices of the doctor, 'till I begin to suspect that I am an ungrateful, evil tempered invalid' (W.W.W., p. 126). These hesitations are written into the text, and the indeterminacy they produce at times recalls Henry James' *The Turn of the Screw*. Pansay, like the originating narrative voice, promises the reader, 'you shall judge for yourself' (W.W.W., p. 127), suggesting the text as a mystery the reader will be empowered to solve. Yet he immediately imposes a limit on the information we are to be allowed. Pansay refuses to say 'what manner of woman'

Mrs Wessington was, but tells us to be 'content with the knowledge' that they were once in love. Furthermore, he cajoles the reader in the guise of an appeal to a common sense code of reasonable conduct which he depicts Mrs Wessington as violating through her persistence: 'You will agree with me ... that such conduct would have driven anyone to despair. It was uncalled for; childish; unwomanly' (W.W.W., p. 129). The issue of Pansay's 'uncalled for', 'childish' and 'unmanly' conduct in his inconsistency and cruelty is deviously reversed and projected on to the other partner. Similar points, such as the alacrity with which he transfers his affections to Kitty and his unpleasant disgust on seeing the phantom rickshaw containing Mrs Wessington a few months after her death, are equally lightly tossed out, and are more apt to alienate the reader than enlist his or her sympathy. Yet this technique does draw attention to the ethics of the entire project of fiction-making and narrative structures. It broaches the question of how far we can trust Pansay in a text dealing with such an emotive subject and which has been designed, as Pansay himself eventually admits, to be read by Kitty, 'as some sort of justification for my conduct' (W.W.W., p. 152).

Pansay's account appears at odds with the events he describes. Moreover, those narratives which threaten to expose this discrepancy are immediately smothered. Pansay warns us to: 'Remember that – whatever my doctor may say to the contrary – I was then in perfect health, enjoying a well-balanced mind and an absolutely tranquil spirit' (W.W.W., pp. 131–2), which straightaway leads one to ask what the doctor would say to the contrary? Pansay anticipates a narrative that never fully materializes. In so doing he highlights those strongly conflicting narratives that could be told, belonging to the initial narrator, Dr Heatherlegh, Kitty and even Mrs Wessington herself. Pansay's behaviour toward Mrs Wessington is stingingly censured by both Heatherlegh and Kitty in the fragments of their versions Pansay allows us to read. Nevertheless, his tone remains self-righteous and unyielding to shame despite the other narratives with contending moral positions which persistently puncture his own story, rather in the way weeds break through the best laid road surface. It is because of such intrusions that we are never sure how far to take Pansay's word. Even Mrs Wessington's narrative is throttled after Pansay's conversation with the spectre. On the pretext of not wanting to stretch credulity further, Pansay silences the voice which would undoubtedly damn him. What Mrs Wessington says is unutterable as it would undermine the justificatory thrust of Pansay's narrative.

The twin possibilities of delusion and the supernatural are maintained because what we do hear of Heatherlegh does not incline us to put our faith in him anymore than in Pansay. To begin with, his theory of the spectre as a 'Stomach-cum-Brain-cum-Eye Illusion' brought on by overwork is weakened by Pansay's continued terminal decline. His zeal in attributing a rational explanation reveals him as paralyzed by the prosaic and unable to identify imaginatively with Pansay's plight. Heatherlegh, like Lockwood in *Wuthering Heights*, is a narrator who seeks to contain the unknowable but who does not understand it. He reaches instantly for the fact and reason with which his medical training has furnished him. As one of Kipling's physicians his task is both to treat Pansay and to cure the narrative of its irrational and dissolute impulses by subjecting it to the light of reason and imposing order upon it. Sandra Kemp points out:

> In a number of stories Kipling presents the agency of inspiration in terms of the powers and techniques of the doctor and of the detective: acting as writers of special competence these practitioners unravel stories from images of the dark and diseased territories of the mind.[18]

Heatherlegh, like Strickland, attempts to create from the chaos what one might call a pukka narrative, transcribing the irrational, supernatural Other which is synonymous with India, in a logical, sequential narrative form acceptable to a Western audience. (It is no coincidence that Heatherlegh is a consummate anecdotalist who tells Pansay, upon his confession, 'you've spoilt one of the best tales I've ever laid tongue to' (W.W.W., p. 141).) Nor is it fanciful to suggest that Kipling himself attempts such a project in the tales of horror where disquieting supernatural effects threaten the empire of rationalism.[19]

One might claim that the allegorical potential of 'The Phantom Rickshaw' is complex since the struggle it invokes is not a basic England/India confrontation, it has more to do with the manner of the telling and the creation of meaning. The treatment and suppression of dissenting narratives has consequences for Kipling's work as imperial storyteller. The unstable structure of 'The Phantom Rickshaw' appears to suggest that all narratives are merely shimmering, evanescent forms which provide only a partial view. It reminds us that we only ever have fragments or see one side of any story, and the same is patently true of the highly biased imperial story Kipling's tales provide.[20] Of course, as an aware craftsman Kipling is conscious of this problem. His answer is to conscript, or colonize, those other discourses which existed in the late nineteenth-century imperial world and travesty them. For example, liberal imperialism is portrayed and parodied in tales such as 'Without Benefit of Clergy', 'The Head of the District' and 'At the End of the Passage' (L.H.), where it is displayed as misguided and potentially dangerous. Anti-imperial discourse is attacked venomously in 'The Enlightenment of Pagett M.P.' and is elsewhere conceived as the province of jealous foreigners with designs on India, like those in *Kim*. Kipling attempts to colonize native discourse too by adopting the 'voice' of Indians in stories such as 'One View of the Question' (M.I.) and in the 'In Black and White' section of *Soldiers Three*. Kipling's considerable success in this last act of narrative colonization can be appreciated when one remembers the praise his depictions of native life and tongues have long elicited. However, detailed examination of almost every incidence of 'Kipling-the-Indian', will divulge a conservative 'message', put into the mouths of natives to make it appear objective. In fact this premise owes less to Kipling's authenticity than to the solidity of orientalist discourse. Kipling is 'speaking for' the Indian *in exactly the way* orientalism speaks for the native. 'The Phantom Rickshaw' performs a service in exposing the arbitrariness of narrative viewpoints. It is a text which calls attention as much to its frame – its Sjuzet as the Russian Formalists would say – as to the events related therein. Its structure is a model of power relations in narrative form, describing how voices are ordered and what they reveal about imperial discourse. It also exposes that inadequacy of language in view of which Kipling is unable to cosset the supernatural in a reassuring realist-Gothic structure.[21] When this happens, as it does in 'The Mark of the Beast' – and when a whole ideology is challenged by what it is unable to incorporate – a desperate situation demands desperate measures.

In *The Simple Adventures of a Memsahib*, Sara Jeanette Duncan comments, 'in India we know only the necessities of speech, we do not really talk'.[22] This is a revealing comment on the nature of communication, the redundancy of words, in a society in which so much is recognized by outward signs and received notions of 'good form'. However, one can apply the statement, with equal validity, to Kipling's supernatural narratives to register the discrepancy one perceives between the attempt to create a pukka narrative – by ordering and reclaiming events from the twilight of irrationality and confusion: forcing them to obey 'the necessities of speech' – and what this Ultimate Other would say if it was allowed to 'really talk'. In 'The Mark of the Beast' the attempt to discipline the delinquent narrative consists of a twofold manipulation of language: a conspiracy to misuse speech among the characters, and the manipulation of information by the narrator in an attempt to render events. His task is to narrate a happening for which the signifiers of his own culture are inadequate; that is, one involving the spiritual beliefs of another culture and containing elements of what the West tamely calls the supernatural. As we have seen, one option is to use Gothicism and there are certainly a number of Gothic descriptions in 'The Mark of the Beast'. However, when it comes to the retribution the West enacts, this cannot be represented or contained within a normalizing literary genre, as the violence involved is inimical to the author-narrator's view of the British–Indian relationship. Thus the narrator censors these events through lapses into silence, of both the text and, from time to time, its characters; they dare not say certain things, resort to cliches and try to deny the truth of what has happened. Indeed the tale is only completed at all through that multi-purpose will-to-power, this time on the part of the putative narrator and witness to the events. In order for Western cognitive systems to survive they must triumph over the dissolution of reason, implicit in the power of 'the Gods and Devils of Asia'; they must efface and outface it. To tell the story, even if, as the last paragraph suggests, it will not be believed, is to reintegrate irrational events into the rational, linear narrative valued by the West and to reclaim them as a fund of knowledge through which the West can frame, represent and govern the East.

An East/West power struggle is directly posited in the opening paragraph:

> East of Suez, some hold, the direct control of Providence ceases; Man being there handed over to the power of the Gods and Devils of Asia, and the Church of England Providence only exercising an occasional and modified supervision in the case of Englishmen. ('The Mark of the Beast', L.H., p. 240)

In this context Church of England Providence is as much a cultural symbol, a euphemism for Western power, as a literal, theological entity. A number of late nineteenth-century imperialists were quick to attribute British imperial power to the dispensation of an omniscient Providence.[23] In the mouths of paternalists, Providence comes to represent that 'moral right' by which the British rule India, projected in third-person terms to signify its objectivity, its naturalness.

However, here the words 'modified supervision' call attention to the reduction in that power which 'oversees'. For all his knowledge of the native, the detective Strickland is confronted in this tale with phenomena beyond the boundaries of his experience. As a result he is only slightly less vulnerable than the newcomer Fleete of whom we learn: 'His knowledge of natives was of course limited and he complained of the difficulties of the language' (L.H., p. 241). His lack of knowledge leaves him unprotected while language difficulties mean that he cannot read native signifiers, written, spoken or implicit. His drunken attack on the statue of Hanuman, the Monkey God, which provokes the wrath of the priests, is a result of his ignorance. Fleete's 'Mark of the B-beasht' parodies significations of divinity – the mark on Hanuman's forehead caused by his cigar-butt is a mockery of the Hindu caste mark – and turns it into a sign of the diabolic.

Hanuman has been 'defaced' and it is suitably ironic that vengeance should be initiated by the Silver Man, literally a faceless leper and thereby beyond Western description. By marking Fleete's chest, the Silver Man is able to cast some sort of spell on the Englishman which progressively reduces him to the level of a beast. He bolts his food like an ostrich, grovels about in the garden, Strickland's horses rear away from him in terror, and his own language becomes a bestial howl. In de-civilizing Fleete, this manifestation of native power burlesques British imperialism's much-vaunted 'civilizing mission'. Fleete's dehumanization constitutes a fall down that social Darwinian scale which characterizes nineteenth-century anthropological thought.[24] Such reversal defines him as now Other, something less than normal. It contains implicit value judgements about human worth based on race and culture. With this in mind, it is interesting to contrast Fleete's 'fall' from grace and his assimilation to beasts (and natives) with the role of the natives' own marginalized figure, the Silver Man. The leper is not an outcast on the basis of a normalizing judgement, as Fleete has now become, rather, he is brought to the centre of his religion's sign-system, the temple, and given an added power – that of retribution and disruption – which forms a challenge to British hegemony. It is the Western 'reading', that of the narrator and Strickland, that labels him sub-human.[25]

Such complication exemplifies this text's dialectical methods. A struggle, based on the double play of power – East over transgressive West and West over transgressive East – epitomises 'The Mark of the Beast' and is, at times, written into its structure. (For this story to be written at all the West must triumph but, as will be seen, the victory is somewhat pyrrhic.) Fleete's body becomes at once the sovereign's body (attacked) and the marked body of the transgressing criminal. The Mark of the Beast is, for both cultures, the sign of an alien power and an act of war. For the native it is an attack on the dignity and divinity of the god Hanuman that is punishable by retribution on the criminal's body. For the English it is an attack on the body of a white sahib, who stands in lieu of the Viceroy who stands in lieu of the Queen: an indirect assault on the sovereign.

The Silver Man's offensive presents a problem to Strickland, who makes it his business to know the native. Because it operates in a realm beyond the Englishman's understanding, the supernatural, Strickland's reaction betrays at once his bewilderment and consequent supplication to a higher authority, his urge for knowledge to acquire influence over the phenomenon, and that reflexive recourse to violence in the face of the unknown which is a common colonial reaction. He says of the Silver Man, 'I think I should peculiarly like to *lay my hands on him*' (emphasis added) (L.H., p. 249), recalling the Christian method of identification with another before God and, in this context, Christ's healing of lepers. (Likewise, the invocation of Christ represents a petition to the ultimate authority in Christian hagiology. With his preferred rationalism removed as an option Strickland appeals to a higher authority, yet one still within his own culture.) Yet the phrase also suggests the notion of procurement: in this case for examination to yield up knowledge. In yet another sense it records the frustration of powerlessness and a desire to inflict physical violence: 'just wait till I lay my hands on him!', the exercise of quite another kind of power and what will ultimately be required here. Thus the problem, and its possible solutions are presented. The text then proceeds to enact a struggle of its own in language. Those ideas and images which gainsay norms and threaten the illusion of benevolence that forms the foundations of imperial discourse, must be reclaimed in some way, made presentable, and the unpalatable necessities of the reactivation of power must be hidden behind a cloak of 'stiff-upper-lip' reticence. This can only be achieved by a determined and multifaceted manipulation of language. In a sense, the text is tortured, like the Silver Man, but not to confess anything, rather to enforce a conspiracy of silence about that which its narrator would not have heard.

Such a conspiracy originates in the English characters through fear. Although he is aware of what is taking place, Strickland at first refuses to communicate his knowledge – that kind of knowledge which bespeaks an absence of power – to the narrator: 'I can't tell you what I think now … because you would call me a madman' (L.H., p. 248). Strickland cannot say what he knows because to frame the phenomenon in words, to name it, would be to admit it, and its power, as fact. Equally, Western culture's signifiers are inadequate to this wholly Other signified they must attempt to pin down. For Strickland to claim as fact a phenomenon beyond the bounds of possibility is to leave the safety of imperial discourse – where everything is known, measured and classified – and journey into the, as yet, uncharted territory of irrationality, risking classification as 'mad'. In the same way the narrator falters in his diagnosis, 'I tried to say "Hydrophobia" but the words would not come, because I knew I was lying' (L.H., p. 251).

In the face of this sudden paralysis of Western language the narrator must discover new ways of uttering the unutterable. As T. E. Apter says of fantasy literature in general:

> figurative language becomes the only means of making literal assertions, for ordinary meanings fragment, expand, splinter, either because some new, unknown order prevails, or because the former order functions haphazardly or piecemeal. Thus the fantasist must piece together a new language.[26]

The narrator begins this process by reducing the horrors of Fleete's degeneration to a list or table of symptoms, narrated in a shocked staccato, in an endeavour to retain control over events: 'Strickland dashed into Fleete's room.[/]I followed,[/]and we saw Fleete getting out of the window.[/]He made beast noises in the back of his throat.[/]He could not answer us when we shouted at him.[/]He spat' (obliques added for emphasis) (L.H., p. 252). Yet, as the horror grows, both characters and narrator become more desperate in the search for linguistic control. Thus when the protagonists summon Dumoise the doctor to examine Fleete they tell him the patient has suffered dog-bites and, although Dumoise knows this is untrue, he agrees to certify that Fleete's anticipated death was caused by Hydrophobia. Through the tacit agreement to form a conspiracy by a re-naming of the 'disease', the ratification of the diagnosis in publicly digestible form and the agreement to maintain the conspiracy through an active (mis)use of language in the lie, the doctor and detective, Kipling's 'authorities' and authors of pukka narratives, merely admit their lack of knowledge and absence of power.

Here, as Dr Jekyll might have noted, is 'one of those affairs that cannot be mended by talking', and Strickland appears to admit as much when he recommends a course of action, rather than words:

'we must trust in Providence and go out softly with polo-sticks into the shrubbery at the front of the house' (L.H., p. 254) where the Silver Man now hides. As we know, Providence is currently in a state of flux so the plan may or may not work. However, the battle must be enacted on a physical, as well as metaphysical and narrative, level 'with all the tortures that might be needful'. Similarly, the narrator begins to admit the inability of English to codify and represent events when he concedes, 'the scene was beyond description'. Yet here the admission is charged with a political motive because, of course, what comes to be literally beyond description, and any inscription in the text at all, are the tortures the English inflict on the leper to force him to lift the spell. After describing trussing the leper, the narrator's self-imposed task of censorship begins: 'Several things happened ... but they cannot be put down here' (L.H., p. 255). Moreover, the narrator endeavours to justify the violence the sahibs use in an image which betrays the operation of physical repression beneath the veneer of benevolent supervision: 'I understood then how men and women and little children can endure to see a witch burnt' (L.H., p. 255). Witch burning is one example of that principle of the spectacle of power over the transgressing body designed to inflict punishment and restore eclipsed power. However, the act of restoring a power that has been eclipsed involves an implied acknowledgement of the temporary triumph of the transgressive power. Medieval torture traditionally reflects a dissymmetry between violating subject and all-powerful sovereign,[27] but in 'The Mark of the Beast', torture also involves its own supplication to its victim to return the body of his victim to 'normal'. It is a power that descends on the body of the criminal, but also requires him to bestow or hand down forgiveness to the original sinner.

Yet just as he is about to damage irreparably his ethic of benevolent rule, the narrator remembers himself and breaks off:

> though the Silver Man had no face, you could see horrible feelings passing through the slab that took its place, exactly as waves of heat play across a red-hot iron – gun barrel for instance ... This part is not to be printed.
>
> . . . .
>
> (L.H., p. 256)

This lapse into silence constitutes the ultimate use of the author-narrator's censorship. The principle of spectacle is to be denied the civilian reader. The operation must be hidden because this attempt to reintroduce an unquestionable power that can once again rely on supervision and surveillance involves use of that ur-power, physical coercion, which allowed colonization in the first instance. The narrator shrinks from depicting the brutal reactivation of sovereignty as it is anathema to the ideal of the British–Indian relationship. Yet, at the same time, in the teasing allusion to the instrument of torture, the heated gun barrel, the writer encodes a kind of knowingness into the text. The suggestion is that a true knowledge of the exigencies required by empire is the preserve of a Masonic few, the insiders, the imperial ruling caste. Thus a second implied reader is invoked, one who understands and approves of the force necessary to maintain control. This reader is a sympathetic contemporary of the author-narrator who can participate in the flirtation around violence in the way a post-colonial reader, deconstructing the text, can recognize but not condone.

Almost shamefacedly the Englishmen release the leper. The West has re-established its sovereignty over the East, although less by rational means than by violence, and even then the source of potential power must be returned to its natural environment. The trauma involved in a revelation of the arbitrary yet dependent nature of British power is revealed by Strickland's hysteria and the narrator's comment that, 'we had disgraced ourselves as Englishmen forever' (L.H., p. 258). Boundaries have been crossed, essential hierarchies violated. Fleete has been rescued, but at a price. In his desperation to reintegrate his characters under 'Church of England Providence', Kipling has his narrator paint a peculiar and otherwise irrelevant picture of Strickland, 'some years later', as 'a church-going member of society', to emphasize his cultural security and the tight control of his transgressive energies. And, indeed, the narrator disclaims his own narrative when he concludes: 'no one will believe a rather unpleasant story and ... it is well known to every right-minded man that the gods of the heathen are stone and brass, and any attempt to deal with them otherwise is justly condemned' (L.H., p. 259). Clearly this is heavily ironic: the narrator may have felt this before, but his experiences have disabused him. Yet it is consistent with that narrative will-to-power by which he has expunged unacceptable aspects and through which he has been able to draw the text to a comfortable and reassuring close.

Yet the ending to this truly supernatural tale can never be as neat and all-embracing as in the Gothic allegories. Western 'right-minded' knowledge has investigated, digested and tabulated 'the gods of the heathen'. The supernatural confounds this process since the phenomena it offers are beyond words: thereby interrupting the power-knowledge taxonomical current. To believe this story is to surrender power through knowledge. Belief is 'justly condemned' on rational grounds because 'stone' and 'brass' things do not behave in this way – and because affording belief means also affording a subversive power to the 'gods of the heathen'. It is precisely this territory of cognitive and political anxiety that 'The Mark of the Beast' plays upon. The uneasy peace of the ending is unable to disguise the fact that the narrative framework cannot contain the horror of events, just as imperial discourse cannot support what has happened to Fleete and, more to the point, what must be done to reclaim him. The attempt to normalize events through language, to reclaim them in speech, is doomed, owing to the metamorphic nature of the attack. In *The Gaping Pig*, Irving Massey describes metamorphosis as a rejection of language and conventional links between signifier and signified. He claims:

> metamorphosis is antilinguistic as a desperate measure; as a means of breaking in when there is no way of breaking out of the circle of language. It takes refuge in the physical, not because that is where it chooses to go, but because that is the only place where language cannot follow it.[28]

Just such an anti-linguistic 'language' is at work in 'The Mark of the Beast' and operates on Fleete's body, bypassing and subverting the colonizer's language, as well as functioning beyond the jurisdiction of 'the known'. Like Mr Hyde's irrational violence, this other power communicates by 'the mark' not 'the sign'.

Indeed, the strong central images of the mark and the faceless Silver Man work to counteract the reclaiming narrative drive of the English narrator. In so doing they work in the way suggested by Clare Hanson:

> the image (even the image in words) negates language with all its differences and deferrals ... Language, or narrative, cannot attain such fullness of expression ... it is by its very nature un-full, partial, analytic, concerned with endlessly ... multiplying logical and causal relations.[29]

Hanson's analysis identifies a tension between image and narrative as the operative force in Kipling's stories. In his description of the literary function of the supernatural, Tzvetan Todorov traces a coincidence of those authors favouring the supernatural, with its strong central images, and those who stress the development of action, who tell stories. For Todorov the basic narrative inscribes two types of episode: 'those which describe a state of balance or imbalance and those which describe the transition from one to the other. The first type contrasts with the second as the static contrasts with the dynamic, as stability with change'.[30] The dynamic quality of Kipling's supernatural stories introduces a change his imperialism cannot contain. The imbalance that characterizes the imperial narrative is inverted or redressed under the auspices of the supernatural. 'The relationship of the supernatural to storytelling thus becomes clear: every text involving the fantastic is a narrative, since the supernatural event or image alters the previous equilibrium, and this is the very definition of narrative.'[31] The supernatural is thus a sequence of images – of events within the text – which provide their own momentum or narrative through a kind of 'knock-on effect'. It is in this that the radicalism of the supernatural image lies.

Moreover, these large central images contribute to a critique of the ideology the tales apparently convey. For example, the image of the powerful yet dehumanized Silver Man questions the Englishmen's sovereignty over nature and the Other implicit in the very definition of empire as supreme and extensive dominion or absolute control. The uncertain resolution of several tales illustrates the position of Kipling's texts between historicist certitude and nightmare image; a position which owes as much to Macherey's 'unconscious' of the text, 'the play of history beyond its edges', as to Orientalist cliches about the terrifying Indian climate and topography, or to Kipling's own subconscious. The symbolic force of an image like the Silver Man is considerable in range and implication. In a sense the Silver Man connotes history, and those otherwise excluded historical processes – Russian ambitions and embryonic nationalism for example – that trouble the text's unconscious. In this way, almost by accident, Kipling confronts an ideological utterance with a fictional utterance: ideological anxiety appears through the fissures which constitute formal aspects of a fictional text designed to demonstrate British ingenuity and support 'vulgar' imperial ideology.

The intrusiveness of ideology is always accompanied in Kipling by uncertainty. Such uncertainty frustrates the writing, by characters, narrator and author, of pukka narratives, like that which the good-storytelling doctor aims at in 'The Phantom Rickshaw'. A virtuous Aristotelian narrative of beginning, middle and end, is something the stories strive for but never achieve. Yet Kipling doggedly persists with tales for which ideological platitudes are inadequate and that will rapidly run out of his control. This determination raises the issue of whether the supernatural texts begin as pukka narratives and degenerate, or whether the nominal narrator is, in fact, always struggling to impose order on an obstinate text. In fact, one might say, the text itself performs this struggle. To take 'The Mark of the Beast' as an example, it can be claimed that the reader is presented with a 'cool' text recalling what was, in view of the heated gun-barrels used for torture, literally a 'hot' moment. The narrative is being set down with the benefit of hindsight long after its events have been completed and the narrator should be able to organise and manage its contents. However, the orthodox operation of memory is interrupted by ideological anxieties which express themselves in the gaps and absences of the work, and suddenly we realize that two contradictory texts are being written. In one, Kipling's 'good' text, India is made complete by the presence of the British. Yet against this confident text there exists a subtext which, despite the author's best endeavours, does not 'understand'; the undermined narrator identified earlier is merely the tip of an anti-epistemological iceberg. The text's double project is to 'speak India', and to acknowledge and contain the contradictions, deviations and disobedience which appear when this act of imaginative colonization is undertaken. The strained peace which Kipling imposes when his problems prove insoluble forms an infinite resource of deferral: he avoids directly facing his anxieties but, at the same time, his texts are unable to escape from them.

In avoiding the conclusion towards which his narratives tend, Kipling transfers the burden of resolution and interpretation to the reader in a way that anticipates modernist poetics.[32] It is in this transfer that one may identify the distinguishing feature of potential, rather than realized, allegories. Potential allegories are 'do-it-yourself' allegories: the reader must make some sense out of them as Kipling cannot. They form areas where anxiety can no longer hide behind the regular structures of control. Kipling abdicates his authority as author. Potential allegories have a special, ongoing life as what they say, or more often what they do not say, changes in implication with succeeding generations of readers. While this may be true of all texts to a certain extent, the point is that the reader's willingness to empathize with the offered narrative position alters irretrievably with independence. After 1947 the British imperial world-view begins to crumble and that very different creature the post-colonial reader emerges from the rubble with a different set of political priorities. He or she brings to bear special historical knowledge which would have been unavailable to a contemporary of Kipling. The hindsight offered by a late twentieth-century perspective encompasses nothing less than the end of the empire Kipling presents. The post-colonial reader supplies that completion the author declines to furnish, in the light of decolonization. In short, the reader recognizes in certain strategies of evasion – those textual hesitations and omissions – seeds of doubt about the imperial project, its future and how to 'write' it. A text such as 'The Mark of the Beast' inscribes silence, like understatement, as an integral part of imperial discourse. It demonstrates that certain things stand outside the discourse and must not be said.[33] Kipling continually attempts to portray reticence, like endurance and self-sacrifice, as a valuable empire-building quality. He turns it into a symptom and testament of power: the more one is in control, and the more natural that control seems, the less one has to speak beyond issuing orders; censure of querulous or dissenting voices is an established feature of Anglo-India that Kipling's own fiction illustrates. This all too easily culminates in an attitude encapsulated in the dictum, 'never explain, never apologize'. It is a rejection of moral and political accountability and insures one against ever having to examine oneself or one's motives. In this way it eliminates from the discourse all that is disturbing and contradictory. Reticence characterizes the imperial narrative but the modern reader can deconstruct it and reveal it for the subterfuge it really is. From a crisis of grammar emerges a crisis of reading which the reader is able to resolve. As he or she does so the text changes from a vehicle for conservatism into an untameable source of power for the other. Kipling's supernatural tales no longer tell the story he originally wrote.

Notes

1. A cogent argument for the use of an unreliable narrator in Kipling is made by Moore-Gilbert in 'Rudyard Kipling: Writing and Control', in B. J. Moore-Gilbert (ed.), *Literature and Imperialism*.
2. David Lodge uses Seymour Chatman's idea of the role of the 'implied', rather than 'real', author of a text, in 'Mrs Bathurst: Indeterminacy in Modern Narrative', in P. Mallett (ed.), *Kipling Considered*, pp. 71–84.
3. Moore-Gilbert, *Literature and Imperialism*, pp. 96–7.
4. This aspiration receives its most celebrated articulation in *Kim*. Edward Said, in *Culture and Imperialism* and Patrick Williams in a polemical essay in *Kipling Considered*, have both recently engaged exhaustively with the place of *Kim* in the programme of narrative-knowledge-power, and it is not proposed to cover the ground again here. See Said, *Culture and Imperialism* (also his introduction to *Kim*, 1987), and Patrick Williams, 'Kim and Orientalism', in P. Mallett (ed.), *Kipling Considered*.
5. Fanon reminds us that colonialism itself is 'violence in its natural

state', in Frantz Fanon, *The Wretched of the Earth* (1967), p. 48.

6. Francis G. Hutchins, *The Illusion of Permanence: British Imperialism in India*, p. 115.
7. Ibid., pp. 160–2.
8. Ibid., p. 125.
9. For a different reading of the political undertones of 'The Strange Ride of Morrowbie Jukes', 'The Return of Imray' and 'The Mark of the Beast', see 'Rudyard Kipling: Writing and Control', in Moore-Gilbert (ed.), *Literature and Imperialism*. See also Gail Ching-Liang Low, *White Skins/Black Masks: Representation and Colonialism*, pp. 113–30. Gail Low's reading offers psychoanalytically inflected interpretations of the central incidents of these stories in terms of the precarious status of British identity and power.
10. Rosemary Jackson writes:

    > Gothic is a complex form situated on the edges of bourgeois culture, functioning in a dialogical relation to that culture. But it also conducts a dialogue within itself, as it acts out and defeats subversive desires. Hence the difficulty of reading Gothic as politically subversive. (*Fantasy: The Literature of Subversion*, p. 96)

    For a fuller exposition of the political uses of the Gothic in imperial adventure fiction see the chapter entitled, 'Imperial Gothic: Atavism and the Occult in the British Adventure Novel, 1880–1914', in Patrick Brantlinger, *Rule of Darkness: British Literature and Imperialism, 1830–1914*, pp. 227–53.
11. > The British characteristically believed they had mastered the subtleties of Indian society and learned how to run them to British advantage. It was also believed that British rule was itself Oriental, as ideally suited to Indian conditions as Hinduism itself. Fascinated by what was traditional in Indian society many Englishmen had become incapable of dealing with the fact of change. Fascinated by Indian tradition, they hoped to make British rule a part of that tradition. (Hutchins, *The Illusion of Permanence*, p. 184)

    Another aspect of this strategy surrounds the manipulation of Indian religious sentiment:

    > Theodore Morison pointed out that all Indian religions taught obedience as a religious duty; why should Indians not be encouraged to believe that obedience to the British was similarly a religious duty? Queen Victoria, so Morison noted, was already viewed in some quarters as something of a divinity. (Ibid., p. 169)

    There is a certain degree of irony and condescension in Britain's ideas of invoking a supernatural or theological basis for imperial government. In a different sense it represents a regression to pre-classical models of power since the concepts of Divine Right of Kings had been extinct in Western Europe since the French Revolution, while in British politics sovereignty and divinity had been separate since the death of Charles I and the creation of a secular political science by Hobbes and Locke in the seventeenth century.

12. Pierre Macherey, *A Theory of Literary Production*, p. 230.
13. Martin Green, *Dreams of Adventure, Deeds of Empire*, p. 55.
14. Homi Bhabha, 'Signs Taken for Wonders', pp. 155 and 158.
15. Geoffrey Moorhouse, *India Britannica*, p. 109.
16. They also induce belief in his tale; see Moore-Gilbert, *Literature and Imperialism*, p. 108.
17. These include James Hogg's *Confessions of a Justified Sinner*, Arthur Machen's *The Great God Pan*, and R. L. Stevenson's *The Strange Case of Dr. Jekyll and Mr. Hyde*, to name but three.
18. Sandra Kemp, *Kipling's Hidden Narratives*, p. 8.
19. Clare Hanson has written, 'His are archetypical "short stories" in English: he came on the scene when the well-plotted tale was at the peak of its popularity and was being industriously produced', 'Limits and Renewals: the Meaning of Form in the Stories of Rudyard Kipling', in P. Mallett (ed.), *Kipling Considered*, p. 85.
20. This issue is taken up by Paul Scott in the cyclical structure of his *Raj Quartet* which offers different viewpoints for the same set of events.
21. I am indebted to Kipling's most sensitive critic, J. M. S. Tompkins, for the phrase an 'inadequacy of language', although she uses it in an entirely different way in *The Art of Rudyard Kipling*, p. 199.
22. Sara Jeanette Duncan (1909), *The Simple Adventures of a Memsahib*, p. 309, quoted in B. Moore-Gilbert, *Kipling and 'Orientalism'*, p. 61.
23. These include the Earl of Meath, quoted in John M. MacKenzie, *Propaganda and Empire: The Manipulation of Public Opinion 1880–1960*, p. 232; and the Viceroy, Lord Dufferin, in Parry, *Delusions and Discoveries: Studies on India in the British Imagination 1880–1930*, p. 20. Rosemary Jackson comments that fantasies locate good and evil 'outside the merely human ... It is a displacement of human responsibility on to the level of destiny: human action is seen as operating under the controlling influence of Providence, whether for good or evil', Jackson, *Fantasy*, p. 53.
24. Jackson writes, 'Recidivism and regression to bestial levels are common post-Darwinian fantasies', ibid., p. 116. One can see another example of this popular sub-genre, which also features the fragmentation of language, in Wells' *The Island of Doctor Moreau*, and also in Forster's early tale 'The Story of a Panic', in *Collected Short Stories*, which also adopts the device of a priggish, undercut narrator.
25. Curiously enough, leprosy comes to be synonymous with the oppositional power of the other in Anglo-Indian literature; take, for example, Masters' Silver Guru who is a key figure in mutinous activity, in *Nightrunners of Bengal*.
26. T. E. Apter, *Fantasy Literature: An Approach to Reality*, quoted in Sandra Kemp, *Kipling's Hidden Narratives*, p. 31.

27. Michel Foucault, *Discipline and Punish: The Birth of the Prison*, pp. 48–9.
28. Irving Massey, *The Gaping Pig: Literature and Metamorphosis*, p. 187.
29. Clare Hanson in *Kipling Considered*, p. 96.
30. Tzvetan Todorov, 'The Fantastic in Fiction', p. 89.
31. Ibid., p. 90.
32. David Lodge exposes the 'polysemous', anti-teleological nature of Kipling's work and suggests an affinity with 'the acknowledged modern masters', in 'Mrs Bathurst: Indeterminacy in Modern Narrative'. It is to be hoped that these chapters have established the innovative nature of Kipling's narrative technique and will help to refute the misdirected generalizations which have blighted Kipling studies, exemplified by Ford Maddox Ford in 'The Critical Attitude', quoted in P. Faulkner (ed.), *A Modernist Reader: Modernism in England 1910–1930*, who says that James and Conrad are 'wholly concerned with their Art' while Kipling is not an artist at all 'in the strict sense', being more insular and ameteur than his cosmopolitan contemporaries, pp. 35–6.
33. In the same way, Macherey, 'Like a planet revolving around an absent sun, an ideology is made of what it does not mention; it exists because there are things which must not be spoken of', *Theory of Literary Production*, p. 132. Perhaps the most famous of many examples of this ethic in Kipling occurs in 'The Flag of their Country' chapter of *Stalky & Co*, in the hereditary and unspoken patriotism of the schoolboys, and the offence given by the 'Jelly-bellied Flag-flapper', Mr Raymond Martin, M.P.

II E. M. Forster and the Dialogic Imagination

> Language is always a matter of force, to speak is to exercise a will for power, in the realm of speech there is no innocence, no safety. (Roland Barthes, *Image, Music, Text*)

> No colonialism could be complete unless it 'universalized' and enriched its ethnic stereotypes by appropriating the language of defiance of its victims. That was why the cry of the victims was ultimately the cry to be heard in another language – unknown to the colonizer and to the anti-colonial movements that he had bred and then domesticated. (Ashis Nandy, *The Intimate Enemy*)

Kipling's fiction can be said to reflect and yet expose the illusory confidence of an age in which symbols of imperial authority were still believed effective as tools for British governance. E. M. Forster, in contrast, writes at a time of crisis for a power based on mutual visibility, spectacle and the grandiose gesture. Curzon's 1903 Durbar is a distant memory and Victoria, imperial matriarch, long dead. In their wake have come the First Government of India Act and the Amritsar Massacre (1919), the Khilafat Movement (1921–22), and the rise of Gandhi. By the 1920s there is an almost tangible anxiety about the continued efficacy of such symbols. The third book of James Morris' *Pax Britannica* trilogy, *Farewell the Trumpets,* is saturated with a sense of the hollowness of imperial symbolism as the twentieth century progressed. Morris comments on the empire of 1924:

> Its symbols had gone threadbare. The opulence of the Victorian heyday had been suited to an age of hope and progress, presided over by an almost mythical mother-figure. Since then the British had lost their grand optimism ... The time for posturing was over.[1]

Indeed, one might say that whereas historical flux appears in Kipling through gaps and the 'unsaid' of his texts, it provides an external dynamic for the confrontation depicted in *A Passage to India* in the insubordination referred to at numerous points; during the turmoil surrounding Aziz's trial a British car is stoned, Mohammedan ladies swear to take no food, and the sweepers of Chandrapore go on strike – 'A new spirit seemed abroad, a rearrangement, which no one in the stern little band of whites could explain' (*Passage*, p. 218). In Kipling any direct examination of the relationship between colonizer and colonized is couched in axiomatic terms which presuppose a British monopoly on power – even when the events narrated call this supposition into question. Now there is an urgent need to find out how the Indian is 'disposed', to use Ronny Heaslop's word, towards his ruler. By 1924 the imperial gaze has been turned from the boundaries of its territory – the Russian threat has dissolved into internecine struggle while the Japanese threat is not yet made manifest – inwards upon its own suddenly dissident subjects.

To appreciate the fundamental instability of imperial self-perception in India, and its attendant fears, it is first necessary to understand that the British–Indian relationship is not monological – the British endlessly speaking and issuing orders with no reply – as imperialists and some subsequent critics have believed, but dialogical. Essentially, all Britain's imperial symbolism and pageantry was devoted to impressing the native in order to involve him in a kind of transaction resulting in acquiescence in imperial rule. The Indian is to be impressed both in the sense of being overawed by displays of power, and by being impressed with a kind of mark which makes him recognizable and conveys an exchange value regarding his relationship to the 'overseer'. It means he will behave in certain ways according to standards set by the colonizer and his reactions will be antiphonally related to British actions. One might say that the British utterance institutes a rhetorical dialogism which, to quote Allon White on Bakhtin, 'shapes itself to penetrate as deeply as possible the imagined resistance of its addressee … "every word is directed towards an answer and cannot escape the profound influence of the answering word that it anticipates"'.[2] Imperial discourse must, by necessity, be dialogical in a regime that purports to govern by consent. It constitutes a two-way gaze; the ruler looks at his subjects and encourages them to look back at him and his works with the requisite degree of reverence, with which he can, in turn, construct a view of himself as in total control of a situation characterized by the clearcut binarism of victory and defeat. As will be seen, the relationship here described forms a kind of mirror held up by the colonizer to bolster self-esteem and the sense of imperial mission. The expected and desired answer from the Indian is always already anticipated and dealt with in the originating utterance.

Equally, when the correct response is forthcoming it can be used to confirm British maxims about the Indian character and reinforce the current typologies of the childlike, untrustworthy, lazy native – those Anglo-Indian 'hints' which Forster tells us, in 'Salute to the Orient', 'have usurped the whole of speech' (*Abinger Harvest*, p. 287). Conversely, British identity automatically becomes the opposite of everything the Indian 'admits' to being. Such an antithesis even applies to positions of apparent opposition to British rule, like that held by Mahmoud Ali in *Passage*, whose antagonism to Britain is organized from within structures – party politics (Congress, The Muslim League) and the Law – instituted by Britain in the first instance. For imperialism, India must be seen either to mould itself into a shape favourable to Britain – to curry favour and Westernize, as does Dr Panna Lal in the novel – or to react against the colonizer in recognizable ways: through the attempt to fight Britain on its own terms and using its own legislative and juridical systems, as do Hamidullah and the nationalist lawyer Amritrao. This phenomenon, whereby even oppositional attitudes can be incorporated into an imperially devised framework, has drawn comment from Ashis Nandy:

> Many Indians ... saw their salvation in becoming more like the British in friendship or in enmity ... colonialism tried to supplant the Indian consciousness to erect an Indian self-image which in its opposition to the West, would remain in essence a Western construction.[3]

Under these circumstances, the one thing imperial discourse cannot stand is having its tenets ignored: the mirror which throws back no image at all.

Thus, while what is described is a dialogue, it is clear that it is in no sense a free dialogue with both partners choosing their own position in relation to the other's discourse. The perplexing development for Anglo-India in the 1920s was the appearance of an element which rejected the simplistic replication of imperialism's linguistic polarities – what I would call self-definition through opposition – and instead assembled an idea of Indianness based on a simple life philosophy and a rejection of modernity. This element was led by Mahatma Gandhi.

Yet, I would argue, E. M. Forster also recognized the dialogical nature of the colonial relationship and looks for ways to release the dialogue from predetermined channels in his novel. He finds a congenial option inherent in the novel form itself: in polyphony, the many voices circulating in the novel's dialogic structure. The variety of discourses introduced in the text 'establish[es] a resistance ... to the dominance of any one discourse'.[4] In this way it is also an expression of that sympathetic, but ideologically ambiguous liberal humanism which characterizes the author's own world-view. By the use of many voices, often in the form of parody and pastiche, Forster foregrounds the dialogics of the British–Indian relationship, the readings mutually taken. In one of the novel's earliest scenes Hamidullah, Mahmoud Ali and Aziz discuss 'whether or not it is possible to be friends with an Englishman' (*Passage*, p. 33) illustrating the centrality of the colonizer to their lives and demeanour, and shortly afterwards the visitors Mrs Moore and Adela receive the benefit of the British Club's accumulated wisdom on Indians: 'Natives don't respect one any the more after meeting one, you see' (*Passage*, p. 48). In a memorable spoof of Kipling's transgressive figures, McBryde is described, during the racial panic attack at the Club, as being down in the city 'disguised as a Holy Man' (*Passage*, p. 189), while before the trial Ronny discovers 'an Indian close outside the window ... picking up sounds' (*Passage*, p. 207).

Moreover, Forster seeks to equalize the voices he allows by undercutting them to differing degrees. In this way he can avoid appearing to be in agreement with, or privileging one voice rather than another. This results in the extensive use of burlesque, irony and other alienation techniques in rendering the voices of the Anglo-Indians after the Marabar Caves incident and at the Club in the evening. The narrator-figure describes Mrs Turton's regrets about her previous coldness to Adela and she is depicted, in mock-heroic terms, 'ennobled by an unselfish sorrow' (*Passage*, p. 187), after which the collective voice of the memsahibs takes up the self-flagellating tone:

> Ah, why had they not all been kinder to the stranger, more patient, given her not only hospitality but their hearts? ... If she wasn't one of them, they ought to have made her one, and they never could do that now ... 'Why don't one think more of other people?' sighed pleasure loving Miss Derek. (*Passage*, pp. 187–8)

Yet, characteristically, the narrative voice immediately interjects to set the mock tragic voice in perspective; 'These regrets only lasted in their pure form for a few hours. Before sunset, other considerations adulterated them, and the sense of guilt ... had begun to wear away' (*Passage*, p. 188). Likewise, Mrs Blakiston, the golden haired emblem of pure English womanhood – that other synonym of 'whiteness' who 'symbolised all that is worth fighting and dying for; a more permanent symbol, perhaps than poor Adela', sees her moment of self-dramatization ruined by her baby blowing bubbles down its chin, and the narrative voice further deflates the discourse's propensity for creating heroic symbols when it interrupts to describe Mrs Turton 'towering at her side like Pallas Athene' (*Passage*, p. 188). Parodic voices, and the periodic intrusion of narrative pointers, reveal the extent to which Anglo-India's tones are borrowed for the occasion; Mrs Turton assumes her 'public-safety voice' (*Passage*, p. 189), and the defence-conscious Collector launches into what is described as his 'august colloquy', interspersed with offerings from his internal monologue on 'the old weary business of compromise and moderation' enforced by that 'caucus of cranks and cravens, the British Parliament' (*Passage*, p. 190). The meeting culminates in a verbalization of the pseudo-religion of the White Man's Burden when Ronny arrives, prompting the congregation to reflect 'young Heaslop was a martyr ... he was bearing the sahib's cross', and Major Callendar to beat his breast over giving Aziz leave to take the ladies to the Marabar – 'That is what I did, my sons, that is what I did' (*Passage*, p. 192) – in tones straight from Kipling's less ambitious verse.

That natives also speak in heightened or artificial language when in the presence of their rulers, and recognize the fact, is suggested when Nawab Bahadur reflects on the part he will have to play at the Collector's Bridge Party where the sterility of racial intercourse is thrown into sharpest relief; 'The Lieutenant-Governor may be my very good friend but I give him no trouble – "How do you do, Nawab Bahadur?" "Quite well, thank you, Sir Gilbert; how are you?" – and all is over'. Forster attempts to offset this necessitated affectation by showing Indians in private contemplation and in conversation with other Indians.

However, problems occur in this dialogic technique when, as occasionally, Forster's own position in relation to domineering registers becomes ambiguous. The blending of voices in the novel which promotes polyphony becomes a treacherous blurring as some of the ethnocentric judgements placed in Anglo-Indian mouths have actually originated in Forster's diary entries and letters home, many of which have been published under the collective title *The Hill of Devi*. As Bette London has observed, certain of the commonplace

Anglo-Indian phrases attributed to Ronny in *Passage* originate with Forster himself.[5] When the young City Magistrate comments, 'Whether the native swaggers or cringes there's always something behind every remark he makes, always something, and if nothing else he's trying to increase his izzat – in plain Anglo-Saxon, to score' (*Passage*, p. 54) he echoes, in sentiment and phraseology, Forster's diary entry on the Indian character; 'No line between the insolent and the servile in social intercourse. In every remark and gesture, does not the Indian prince either decrease his own "izzat" or that of his interlocutor' (*Hill*, p. 23). Similarly, the diarist's eagerness to 'give some account of this amazing little state, which can have no parallel, except in a Gilbert and Sullivan opera' (*Hill*, p. 15), finds its counterpart in Miss Derek's quoted idea of 'the entire peninsula as a comic opera' (*Passage*, p. 67). The elision of author and character's ethnographic utterance is the more disconcerting given that an 'expert' orientalist voice is elsewhere proffered in a clearly ironic vernacular – as during the trial when Anglo-India reacts to the commotion by nodding sagely: 'There is no stay in your native. He blazes up over a minor point and has nothing left for the crisis' (*Passage*, p. 229).

Forster's adjacency to orientalist axioms also creates grey areas at points in the narrative where it is not clear to whom an utterance belongs. For example, at the very end of the novel, after Aziz and Fielding have rehearsed heatedly the respective Indian and British positions on the subject of independence, a passage of Aziz's direct speech – 'India shall be a nation!' – is followed by an indirect paragraph:

> India a nation! What an apotheosis! Last comer to the drab nineteenth-century sisterhood! Waddling in at this hour of the world to take her seat! She, whose only peer was the Holy Roman Empire, she shall rank with Guatemala and Belgium perhaps! Fielding mocked again. And Aziz in an awful rage danced this way and that ... (*Passage*, p. 315)

It is not made clear whether these unallocated impressions belong to Fielding, as part of his defence of British rule, or to Forster. Much of the ambiguity revolves around the status of the sentence, 'Fielding mocked again'. Does it refer to the ideas expressed immediately before it – about the devaluation India would undergo if she became a nation – in which case they are Fielding's, or to an un-narrated speech act by Fielding which we do not hear, or to the narrator himself interposing his opinion at a vital point in the argument.

Certainly, indirect speech here gives an added objectivity to the view expressed. One might claim that here is a doubly oriented speech act, or 'hybrid construction', in the best Bakhtin tradition where 'one and the same word figures as the speech of the author and as the speech of another – and at the same time'.[6] However, in a dialogue between the violently opposed polarities of the colonial debate such hybridity – especially when, as here, mediating a position more or less antagonistic to nationalist aspirations – is not a site of innocent narrative capriciousness but a tacit endorsement of a reactionary stance.

The same kind of reading reveals the author-narrator's equally perilous location when he refers to the Mediterranean as 'the human norm'. As Fielding returns to England via Venice he muses on 'the beauty of form', forgotten in India but magnificently brought home to him in the Mediterranean, and rendered with an appropriate smattering of awestruck exclamation marks. His thoughts are given in an indirect mode and in the conditional tense as he assumes that his Indian friends would be able to see, but not fully partake of, the joys of classical form: 'they would see the sumptuousness of Venice, not its shape' (*Passage*, p. 288). But at this point the text launches into a disembodied encomium on the Mediterranean:

> The Mediterranean is the human norm. When men leave that exquisite lake, whether through the Bosphorus or the Pillars of Hercules, they approach the monstrous and the extraordinary; and the southern exit leads to the strangest experience of all. (*Passage*, p. 288)

The change to present tense suggests a step back; the gnomic present is often the tense associated with direct narratorial comment. Also, after the quoted passage, the form immediately changes again, this time to epic preterite to describe Fielding's journey home and the 'tender romantic fancies' that await him there.

The concept of a definitive 'human norm' is dangerous in a novel about the imperial relationship which seeks to embrace diversity, particularly when it refers to an area of the world whose cultural productions have served as the foundation for Western culture. It undermines the relativity Forster embodies in his work, setting up the kinds of exclusions he otherwise attacks. Clearly, we are in the presence of deep-rooted ambivalence of tone and outlook which reflect Forster's position as a 'cultured subject', in both senses of the phrase.[7] Yet here is a novel in which the English liberal would empathize with the native and, in stark contrast to the ideological conservatism noted above, Forster can provide interesting and destabilizing examples of narrative infiltration using the dialogic approach. For instance, the 'Caves' section of *Passage* begins with the voice of the Western guidebook presenting geological and historical information about the area around the Marabar Caves where the book's central incident, the alleged assault on Adela, will take place. The timbre is largely prosaic although tinged with a little local colour – the gods who took their seats on the mountains to contrive the River Ganges, for example. Even when the imagery becomes most florid – as where we are told of the mountains that 'the sun who has watched them for countless aeons may still discern in their outlines forms that were his before our globe was torn from his bosom' (*Passage*, p. 137) – it is still the grandiloquence of the travel writer trying to capture the imagination, the type of language with which viewers of modern travel documentaries would be familiar.

However, in describing the curious non-experience of seeing the caves, the guidebook register becomes less assured, begins to doubt its own adequacy to its task: 'Having seen one such cave, having seen two, having seen three, four, fourteen, twenty-four, the visitor returns to Chandrapore uncertain whether he has had an interesting experience or a dull one or any experience at all' (*Passage*, p. 138). Here is an eventuality for which the voice of the guidebook whose job is exposition, is unprepared. The strain of attempting to describe that which will not yield to description causes a rupture of the measured, and measuring, tone and heavily ironizes the narrative's earlier claim that 'the caves are readily described'. The increasing frenzy of the random mathematical progression, 'three, four, fourteen, twenty-four', is underlined by the discomfiting effects of the visit on the visitor – not at all likely to encourage the casual tourist.[8] And quietly, in the interstices, another voice is born. As it describes the interior of the caves the narrative's register becomes filled with a spirit of poetry. Yet this is not purely English poetry. We learn that when one strikes a match 'another flame rises in the depths of the rock and moves toward the surface *like an imprisoned spirit*'; the two flames are described as lovers divided by the 'delicate stars of pink and grey' that shine in the polished wall, which also contains '*shadings fainter than the tail of a comet* or the mid-day moon'; they are '*smoother than windless water, more voluptuous than love*' (*Passage*, pp. 138–9). What this voice recalls is nothing so much as the Indian poetic register as represented in previous Anglo-Indian literature, with its languorous pathos and taste for similes, conjunctions and quasi-prepositions – when Aziz quotes poetry we learn that pathos for the Indian is the highest quality in art: 'a poem should touch the hearer with a sense of his own weakness, and should institute some *comparison* between mankind and flowers' (*Passage*, p. 118).

Overall, this is a section which speaks against the possibility of English knowledge of archaic, 'Ancient Night', just as Adela's inability to say what happened in the caves frustrates the British power-through-knowledge programme. We are told, 'if man grew curious and excavated', as would the Western archaeologist for example, 'nothing, nothing would be added to the sum of good and evil' (*Passage*, p. 139). The voice of the guidebook, elsewhere manifest in Forster's trusted Baedeker, is subverted by a voice that is more fundamentally 'of the land'. Here is a dynamic and disturbing use of dialogism. As such it runs completely contrary to the examples given earlier of the way Forster is involved in orientalist generalizations. Here Forster utilizes the conventions of the exotic, only to subvert them. How is the reader to reconcile the 'two Forsters' we discover in the one book? Obviously, the author to some extent sanctions the disclosure of his preconceptions by publishing his contemporary letters and diaries. Yet, I feel, it is an insufficient response to say, as does Bette London, that Forster is simply 'a preeminent example of the ways we are all implicated in and by the conditions of our discourse'.[9] Ambivalence exists and an examination of instances where it bubbles to the textual surface is more rewarding than demonstrating the author's predetermined ideological allegiance. I would argue that a full investigation of equivocality in *Passage* requires quite another, contrapuntal, way of reading in order to understand Forster's project in the novel. In what follows I am not suggesting that the technique accredited to the author is a conscious one, but that such a reading as that given is a direct result of ambivalence – that ambivalence makes it possible.

Once more, Mikhail Bakhtin may provide the beginnings of an answer to the problem of Forster's narrative stance in its relation to imperialist orthodoxies, when he suggests:

> The relationship of the author to a language conceived as the common view is not static – it is always found in a state of movement and oscillation that is more or less alive ... the author exaggerates, now strongly, now weakly, one or another aspect of the 'common language', sometimes abruptly exposing its inadequacy to its object and sometimes, on the contrary ... maintaining an almost imperceptible distance, sometimes even forcing it to reverberate with his own 'truth', which occurs when the author completely merges his own voice with the common view.[10]

This idea has certain useful resonances when applied to Forster. The narrative voice's occasional close proximity to the dominant language, the 'common view', it elsewhere satirizes is, I would suggest, a textual reflection of an unsettling ideological position Forster recognizes as his own. His brand of individualist liberalism is important in considering the narrative-power link, as it causes an inevitable degree of contradiction in Forster's attitude both to his project in 'writing India' and to the imperial position in general.

I believe Forster realizes the shortcomings of liberalism in the face of imperialism, and its complicity in that same imperialism's perpetuation. The problem of enlisting a liberal construction of empire is repeated in the work of Paul Scott: for example, in the figure of the benevolent matriarch Mabel Layton. Characters must be provided to articulate a 'best self', to validate a sense of responsibility in a situation of inequality and exploitation. The liberal construction of empire on a national level – incorporating the civilizing mission and the preparation of the child-like native for an accession to 'man's estate' sometime in the conveniently distant future – serves as a counterpoint to the baldness of financial greed and territorial acquisitiveness. On a personal level and as reflected in numerous novels of India, the liberal ethic is expressed as the desire to make the best of an imperfect situation, and to forge links between members of the ruling and ruled races. Edmund Candler, Edward Thompson, Paul Scott, John Masters and Forster all express a desire for personal contact and cultural exchange, a sharing of the best of both worlds. Yet the inescapable and repeated reservation present in their work is that the best is decided on their own terms, that is the terms of Western humanism. 'Human norms' are ineluctably Western norms whether they take the form of the privileged terrain and artistic heritage of the Mediterranean or the cumbersome baggage of European taste.

Forster's is, by and large, the dilemma of both liberal writings and re-writings about empire which would empathize with the colonized but repeatedly find something in the way. One can agree with Benita Parry when she says:

> The text deliberately reveals the crisis of liberal-humanist ideology – its impotence as a code in an embattled situation where moderation and compromise are not possible ... It is because the novel is mediated through this world-view and returns there for repose that the advance into new and profoundly astonishing perceptions is accompanied by retreats to the confines of known sterilities.[11]

Thus Forster can at one moment unironically utter such classic 'orientalisms' as 'Suspicion in the Oriental is a sort of malignant tumour' (*Passage*, p. 276), 'like most Orientals, Aziz over-rated hospitality' (*Passage*, p. 154) and, 'It's so typical of the Oriental who makes a howling mess over one thing and does another with perfect grace' (*Hill*, p. 28) – while at the next reflect upon 'the difference between the real East ... and the faked East ... which exists to be the background of some European adultery' ('Salute to the Orient', in *Abinger*, p. 290). Forster shows a remarkable insight into the faking nature of orientalism's projective, deflective motives. Yet having pierced the cover of writing which is merely interested in the East as a device providing automatic exoticism, Forster cannot take a further step and recognize that his own conceptions of the Orient, for all his personal contact with it, are products of the same ideological soil. He can include startling divide-hopping acts of narrative inclusiveness, yet still retain an ethnographical catch in his voice.

However, this is not to say that he is unaware that there is a problem, that he cannot 'connect'. Moreover, one must say that he recognizes the ineffectual nature of liberal principles and writes this realization into *Passage* in the undercutting of the liberal figures, Fielding and Mrs Moore. Indeed, the sacrifice of these two voices to the experiences they undergo, and in Mrs Moore's case to the 'voice' of the caves, can be read as an abdication of the liberal code's authority to speak for India, since the motives and registers of the two benign English characters – summed up in the phrase 'goodwill plus culture and intelligence' – are closely related to Forster's own.

More radically, I wish to argue, Forster etches this doubt about the efficacy and ethics of an Englishman claiming to speak for India, into the textual strategy. If one accepts such a premise the way is cleared to a more dynamic reading of the novel's project of representation which also provides an answer to the problem of Forster's position in relation to the voices he would caricature. I would propose that *Passage* explicitly dramatizes the impossibility of any English interlocutor claiming to stand aside from his fellows and 'speak for' India. All English voices eventually overlap and meld. So Adela is merely and unavoidably succumbing to an ideological *fait accompli* when she assumes the role of assailed Englishwoman for the book's most momentous event. Likewise, it is equally inevitable that Fielding should eventually 'come into line with the oppressors of India', after his marriage to Heaslop's sister and acceptance of a government inspectorate. As Brenda Silver points out, 'Just as Fielding's defiance after Aziz's arrest was contained by the relations of power that made Ronny and him antagonists who spoke the same language, the form of his resistance corroborates rather than undermines the system'.[12] It does so in that it underwrites the 'true' English values of fair play from which the embattled Anglo-Indians have deviated, but which has, nonetheless, participated in – and provided a legitimizing ethic for – imperial expansion. This is E. M. Forster's position too, and while the voices of Fielding and Forster are not identical or interchangeable, the writer does recognize that the overlap applies to his own voice as well as to the kind of English people he imagines. (One could claim that this is one of the reasons why the narrator's voice is so muted in *Passage* and why the text strives to remain open for all the voices that would speak.)

In fact, Forster can write his difficulties into the structure of the novel in the form of those problematic episodes surrounding the status of voice considered earlier, in a tactic which offers the reader a choice of interpretations. To contextualize, previous attempts at representing India have been inadequate inasmuch as they simplistically partake of, and perpetuate, an overall image, or 'vision', built upon a prescribed list of orientalist 'truths': statements, metaphors, analogies and so forth which the writer is allowed to use in connection with the East and which make his representations 'authentic' and 'valid'. If one accepts that Forster is conscious of this difficulty – and the quotation from 'Salute to the Orient' given above would suggest this to be the case – one can claim that those 'grey areas' where the origin of voice is unclear, in fact, constitute a framing of the perils of an English writer representing India.

Accordingly, even that poetic Indian voice which subverts the orderly tones of the English guidebook at the start of the 'Caves' section can be read, I would suggest, not as a straightforward presentation of an insubordinate Indian voice, but as a marker for the shortfall between Indian art and English artifice in trying to adopt or purloin the tones of that art. The text's Indian inflection here distinctly becomes the voice of India as perceived by the voice of British culture: a spotlighted case of mediating and speaking for India. Anxieties over the loyalty of the Indian voice which, I have been arguing, are a central concern of the British in India in the 1920s, mean that the conscious artist can no longer naively claim to be able to make the Indian speak, in the way that Kipling could. All voices purported to be Indian must now be bracketed in some way, accentuated as not what India says, but as a trace of the very fact that India cannot speak in the British realist novel as it has developed, and that such voices are substitutions to fill the inevitable breach that follows from this. In saying this I do not mean that it is impossible for an English writer to speak about and for Indian characters *per se*, rather that historical anxieties such as those I have briefly outlined make this a highly charged aesthetic and political issue in the years leading to independence. Obliquely the point is made that any English attempt to make Indians speak is literally a case of putting words into their mouths: the words the English auditor wants to hear, the reader wants to see.

Historically, one can view the imperial parade and pageant, the royal progresses of this era, at which dutiful natives were trotted out to proclaim their allegiance to the crown in tones of obeisance – either hushed or joyous, depending on the surroundings – as fulfilling the British need to hear their imperial subjects making reassuring noises. Thus, the Prince of Wales, on his way to India in 1921 was confronted in Aden by rows of 'natives' assembled under a banner boldly requesting him to 'TELL DADDY WE ARE ALL HAPPY UNDER BRITISH RULE'.[13] The palpable inauthenticity of such voices, with their childish, pidgin quality and, at the other extreme, the surrogate 'Babuisms' of the traduced educated Indian, have by the 1920s crawled off the pages of imperial adventure fiction into the public policy and comportment of the empire proper. The uneasy, antiquated, pseudo-biblical phrases – the peppering of 'thees' and 'thous' with their suggestion of prostration – one finds in Kipling may bear little relation to reality but they are just the type of carefully formulaic exchange the harassed imperial administrator wants to hear, and encourages his charges to reproduce. The felt need for such an appropriation of language reveals the British awareness of the potential objection, of the sudden unpredictability of the other voice in the dialogue.[14]

However, the days of appropriation's efficacy for the serious writer wishing to explore the shifting undertones of the imperial relationship, are long over. Forster unmasks the artifice involved in English representations of India, and the rich, purple diction which takes over from geological precision in the first chapter of 'Caves' provides him with an opportunity. Rebecca West was perhaps more perceptive than she realized when she described the writing in this section as 'perfectly beautiful in a strange way that occasionally recalls *Kubla Khan*',[15] that other imagined Orient with its 'caverns measureless to man'. Likewise, the suggestion of the Mediterranean as 'the human norm' can be immediately relativized by such a reading – can become a site of ideological contestation. One might say that the narrator, for once, steps out, clothed in the present tense, to utter a 'truth' and reanimate the cultural values of the West as a benchmark. But he is instantly swept aside by the tide of the polyphonic narrative which straightaway plunges into the cacophonic Gokul Ashtami festival with its ecstatic worshippers, its Sweepers' Band, its excited children and its 'frustration of reason and form' (*Passage*, p. 282). In this way the idea of a 'norm', of the exclusion and hierarchy that have gone before, is boldly challenged. The one-eyed, tunnel vision of empire is never allowed to settle into a complacent general or authorized view. (In this way the section is symptomatic of the whole device, which foregoes resolution.) Moreover, Western values are geopolitically decentred too, through the passage taken by the novel's protagonists. The Mediterranean is always at the edges of the text: seen in passing by the peregrinating characters, Fielding and Adela, and cited in passing by the constantly shifting narrative voice. The Mediterranean, like Suez, is a gateway, a portal to another world through which the traveller passes but in which he or she can never stop. In this way the 'human norm' is parenthesized, becomes wafer-thin, transparent, and is effectively revealed as no norm at all, but a conceit of the Western-centred consciousness and peripheral to the action of the novel.

Many of the contradictions in Forster's fluctuating position regarding dominant sentiments and registers can be explained if one reads them as framed examples of how all attempts to speak about and for India are implicated in the mental imperialism of governing ideologies. Yet, once the writer has recognized this, can he find any more essential way of disrupting power-through-knowledge? In a small way Forster begins to do this in the method he uses to convey Professor Godbole's song at Fielding's gathering. Refusing to ape the easily assumed quasi-Eastern poetic tongue – which, we have seen, is an outmoded and insidious vehicle for British strategies of power – the narrative merely reveals what the song is about: a milkmaiden's invocation to Shri Krishna and that 'he neglects to come' (*Passage*, p. 96). Then, instead of an English transcription, the reader is merely offered an impressionistic description of Godbole's singing using only western musical terminology of the type with which the narrator is familiar:

> His thin voice rose, and gave out one sound after another. At times there seemed rhythm, at times there was the illusion of a Western melody. But the ear, baffled repeatedly, soon lost any clue, and wandered in a maze of noises ... none intelligible ... The sounds continued and ceased after a few moments as casually as they had begun – apparently halfway through a bar, and upon the subdominant. (*Passage*, p. 95)

Here is the suggestion of form rather than the rendition of content. But the question remains, once one has realized, as a writer, the mendacity of inscribing the Indian voice into the English text, how does one bridge the resultant cavity and, more pressingly, how does one provide a space for those Indian voices which are speaking now in a language other than that of the predetermined binarism of controller and controlled? How is it possible, in a text where all voices are not only speaking but spoken for, to create an area for those who remain ideologically 'unimpressed'?

Ostensibly, all imperial roles have been inscribed within the English-dominated dialogue, from the sycophantic Dr Panna Lal to the conventional militant Mahmoud Ali. Yet I wish to claim that Forster leaves 'unimpressed' or 'uninscribed' areas in *Passage*, parts whose reading in terms of the existing dialogue is impossible or at least ambiguous. At the outset it might be helpful to define what I have chosen to call Forster's technique of 'uninscription'. Briefly, one may say that to inscribe a character in a novel awash with, and typified by, many merging and eddying voices, is to bathe the character in one or more of the available discursive registers. In this way the character is 'brought to life': that is, brought into the realm of speech, spoken for. He may speak directly or have his voice rendered in indirect speech, but in either case what he would say and how he would say it are determined by external organizing agencies – the speech-types he quotes and alludes to and, of course, the aegis of the narrative's organizing grammar. Clearly this involves a degree of manipulation on the part of the author-narrator, a straining to make the voice fit the overall scheme. To refuse to do this – to 'uninscribe' – is to acknowledge that one cannot speak for, but only of, India. The contrast is stark and is identifiable at various points in *Passage*.

One can see Forster groping towards a realization of the potential of such a technique by examining Professor Godbole again. As a 'mystical Hindu' in an age of unavoidable social contention, Godbole is both involved in events at the Marabar Caves and, literally, removed from them. His reaction to the catastrophe in a subsequent conversation with Fielding, and his seemingly abstruse philosophizing, reveal the extent to which his outlook differs from Western intellectual systems; '[Fielding] stared again – a most useless operation, for no eye could see what lay at the bottom of the Brahman's mind' (*Passage*, p. 184). Although one could claim that Godbole's other-worldly position is catered for in the typological vision of Anglo-India, which sees Indians debilitated by spirituality, his circumlocution after Aziz's arrest constitutes an example of the disconcerting power of the refusal, first, to respond predictably and, second, to respond at all, especially at a time of crisis for British power-through-knowledge. As Benita Parry points out, the Brahman is 'not indifferent to human needs and mortal concerns. It is his way of interceding which radically departs from expected means'.[16] Similarly, when Ronny's brash rudeness spoils the mood of Fielding's gathering Godbole remains unperturbed, 'with downcast eyes and hands folded as if nothing was noticeable' (*Passage*, p. 94), thereby demonstrating that he is unimpressed by petulant antics as well as by Britain's desire to know everything.

These examples show Godbole as a disturbingly elusive figure – 'he always did possess the knack of slipping off' (*Passage*, p. 198) – who refuses to throw back the images his overlords would see. However, his radical potency is irremediably diluted by the use Forster makes of this enigmatic figure as a harmonizing textual device. For instance, he is described as wearing:

> a turban that looked like pale purple macaroni, coat, waistcoat, dhoti, socks with clocks. The clocks matched the turban and his whole appearance suggested harmony – as if he had reconciled the products of East and West, mental as well as physical, and could never be discomposed. (*Passage*, p. 89)

Indeed, this is the core of the 'other space' as Forster consciously writes it. It is not really a different space at all as it draws on existing East/West reference points. In fact, Godbole is not a symbol of asceticism, not unimpressed at all. He merely exhibits a highly qualified anti-materialism – its limits are revealed by his copious feeding while Fielding's guest. His obscurantist Hinduism is useful to Forster as a way of legitimizing a sympathetic, optimistic world-view against the nihilistic grain of the novel as a whole. An example of this occurs when he 'impels' the vision of Mrs Moore during the Gokul Ashtami festival.

> He was a Brahman, she Christian, but it made no difference ... It was his duty, as it was his desire, to place himself in the position of the God and to love her, and to place himself in her position and to say to the God, 'Come, come, come, come'. (*Passage*, p. 287)

Here he is performing Forster's wishes; in the absence of a corporeal Mrs Moore, Godbole takes on the mantle of inclusive humanist presence. Forster succumbs to the temptation of completing Godbole by reference to Mrs Moore in a transcultural translation of value.

If Godbole cannot be said to be totally successful as an uninscribed character there are figures who stray on to the novelistic canvas and do preserve their independence from the broad brush-strokes of the dialogic technique. Foremost among these is the punkah-wallah at the trial. He represents another space into which the British all-seeing eye cannot penetrate, but one which preserves for itself a greater measure of potential for socially significant action in the new India struggling to be born in the 1920s. The description of him – given in unadorned, unironic yet curiously heightened prose – reveals him, 'Almost naked':

> he seemed to control the proceedings ... Pulling the rope towards him, relaxing it rhythmically, he seemed apart from human destinies, a male Fate, a winnower of souls. Opposite him ... sat the Little Assistant Magistrate, cultivated, self-conscious and conscientious. The punkah-wallah was none of these things, he scarcely knew that he existed and did not understand why the court was fuller than usual, didn't even know he worked a fan, though he thought he pulled a rope. (*Passage*, p. 221)

In other words, he is emptied out – utterly. The punkah-wallah is an ideological blank page, a *tabula rasa* for Mahatma Gandhi, with his appeal to the dispossessed, the outcastes, the untouchables to write upon. He is the ultimate unimpressed subject. Richard Lannoy reminds us:

> The true revolutionary power, at that point in history, lay in Gandhi's harnessing the energies not of the Western-oriented middle classes nor of the urban or industrial proletariat, but of those who had been disinherited, the mute, the powerless.[17]

Moreover, the punkah-wallah is given a position of power here at the heart of the novel. Seated on a raised platform at the back of the court, he occupies the centre of the view from where Adela sits, effectively providing the focal point of proceedings – a situation which radically decentres the icons of imperial power, the Assistant Magistrate and the English who temporarily occupy the dais opposite him and constantly clamour to be the centre of attention. In this state of peculiarly powerful powerlessness he anticipates another uninscribed figure, the servitor who drowns the model village of Gokul at the end of the Mau festivities. He too is an emptied figure in a position of power – 'the Indian body again triumphant' (*Passage*, p. 309) – as, with 'his beautiful dark face expressionless', he performs his hereditary office of closing 'the gates of salvation', as will the dispossessed, under Gandhi's inspiration, to the British. Aesthetically, uninscribed spaces militate against the completion towards which the text aspires. Despite the book's lauded 'shape' there is always an area that is unfinished, a story that is untold. It seems that here, in the innocuous-seeming depiction of those about whom he admittedly knows nothing, Forster has perhaps unwittingly anticipated a new locus of possible resistance in both narrative and politics: 'an island bared by the turning tide, and bound to grow' (*Passage*, p. 61).

It will be seen from this that problems of authority are also problems of speech. The uninscribed subject provides a dynamic which the method of polyphony cannot replicate, owing to its double-edged, acquisitive quality. One might claim that the liberal tradition in English fiction is a master discourse which can simultaneously present and emasculate the irreconcilability of contending voices. To borrow a phrase from Michael Orange, it allows Forster to 'induce belief in his verbal structures while disavowing their efficacy'.[18] He does so by using certain distancing devices: different voices, none of which are wholly endorsed; irony, as in the blatant undercutting of the histrionics at Chandrapore's Anglo-Indian club; direct narratorial comment, like that which deflates power-seeking narratives; and indirect speech which seems to set the controlling narrative at an immediate remove from what is being said under its auspices. In short, the liberal master narrative tolerates. Forster effaces himself as narrator among other voices – like the god Krishna obscured by bric-à-brac in the Gokul Ashtami festival. In a replica of the method of decentring power icons and monumental voices noted earlier, Forster for the most part refuses the centrality and power of omniscient narrator he finds more conducive in the earlier novels where the narrator's voice is more detached and self-confident (though not nearly as much as traditional criticism would have us believe). In *Passage*, voices provide a spectrum of difference which apparently holds any resolution of the polyphonic contest in abeyance. It means that a decision of authority is also deferred. The author-narrator can keep in remission the authoritarianism his own grammar would display if he was a conventional, interventionist, omniscient narrator. Seemingly, there is no decisive vehicle of utterance. A middle ground is sought and the inflection of all voices is blurred.

However, this Pilate-like stance on the part of the author-narrator is, in fact, jeopardized by one of the devices with which he would sustain it. Indirect speech is both a vehicle for the attempt at impartiality and an indicator of its inevitable failure. For a writer the ploy of rendering speech, or thought, in an indirect mimetic mode means that he can hold back from appearing to be in agreement with the sentiments he chronicles. So, for example, when we learn that 'Ronny had not disliked his day, for it proved that the British were necessary to India; there would certainly have been bloodshed without them' (*Passage*, p. 110), or that, as Fielding muses on the Marabar incident, 'Great is information and she shall prevail' (*Passage*, p. 197), such ideas are immediately qualified by other voices and, as we discover, ultimately invalidated by subsequent events. Another instance of distancing occurs in the repeated use of the word 'perhaps' noted by Barbara Rosecrance[19]; the theological debate over divine inclusiveness involving the missionaries old Mr Graysford and young Mr Sorley, thus begins 'All invitations must proceed from heaven perhaps' (*Passage*, p. 58), while even the narrating voice itself, in one of its implosive moments, questions the meaning of the festival and whether a 'silver doll', a 'mud village' or a 'pious resolution' has been born: 'Perhaps all these things! Perhaps none! Perhaps all birth is an allegory!' (*Passage*, p. 287). Thus liberalism, in its crudest sense of 'seeing both sides', would appear to be written into the form of the narrative. Such a strategy relativizes all voices, including the narrator's own, and is therefore outwardly opposed to, and working against, monolithic utterances such as that of imperialism which claims centrality for itself.

Yet another, countervailing, tendency of *oratio obliqua* (indirect speech) is that it blunts differences between heterogeneous speech acts. As Barthes reminds us, spoken language is full of hesitations, errors, amendments and so forth:

> a word cannot be *retracted*, except precisely by saying that one retracts it … if I want to erase what I have just said, I cannot do it without showing the eraser itself (I must say, 'or rather …' 'I expressed myself badly …') … All that one can do in the case of a spoken utterance is to tack on another utterance.[20]

In written language these confusions and hiatuses are often disguised by forms of finishing and revision – nowhere more so than in reported speech. This applies equally to thoughts and feelings; the meandering, undisciplined avenues of the mind are tidied up in the realist novel. Divergent forms of speech are markers of cultural difference. The transformation that takes place when spoken language becomes reported speech is composed of elisions and artistic alterations – a directly instituted narrative control. In the same way the moment or heat of utterance is also a mark of linguistic diversity, a mark which indirect speech takes no account of as it steamrolls, or rather skims, its way towards the homogenization of language. (In this connection it is useful to remember that the alternative designation of indirect speech is 'reported speech', with all that name implies about mediation and power.) One can say that in a narrative technique utilizing totally direct speech the narrator would appear as a foregrounded 'presenter', showing the action to the reader and having the last word: 'he said', 'she said', and so forth. With indirect mimetic speech there may be no orchestrating presenter but there is an overall grammar – in Forster's case that of urbane liberal humanism. For a prime example of what happens to speech diversity in the face of the overriding grammar one need look no further than Aziz. As several critics have observed his directly quoted speech is allowed subtle individualization and turns of phrase which make it recognizable and give it *an air* of authenticity. Even when the content of his speech remains romantically stoical, his register retains its own distinctive quality:

> 'We can't build up India except on what we feel. What is the use of all these reforms, and Conciliation Committees for Mohurram, and shall we cut the tazia short or shall we carry it another route, and Councils of Notables and official parties where the English sneer at our skins?' (*Passage*, p. 128)

However, as soon as the narrative claims to be faithfully recording his thoughts an uncharacteristic but tell-tale measure and order infect the previously undisciplined sentences, and bring him closer to those narrative values espoused by his author, creating a hybrid or mixed voice:

> He vowed to see more of Indians who were not Mohammedans, and never to look backward. It is the only healthy course. Of what help, in this latitude and hour, are the glories of Cordova and Samarcand? They have gone and while we lament them the English occupy Delhi and exclude us from East Africa. Islam itself, though true, throws cross-lights over the path to freedom. The song of the future must transcend creed. (*Passage*, p. 265)

Here again the controlling voice is supposed to change from that of the narrator, in the first sentence, to that of Aziz but, I feel, without the accompanying change of register. The give-away references to 'we' and 'us' are not enough to prevent the speech remaining resolutely alien. Concomitantly illuminated and denied, a conflict exists between the many unruly grammars of characters' speech and the centripetal unitary language.

The single voice seeks to orchestrate all other voices in indirect speech and thereby emasculates the difference it claims to preserve. This is important for a novel dealing with empire and racial difference since it replicates an imperialism within the text. It might be claimed that what is set up is a kind of heteroglot contest, a dialogue of the many voices against the one concerting voice. Then what comes into existence on the plane of narrative technique is essentially the same battle for the right to speak, and 'speak for', as Forster dramatizes in the text's own polyphony – his refusal to speak authoritatively – and in the political situation, with its anxieties over the expected response, his story presents. Thus battle is joined on several levels, at the deepest of which E. M. Forster, the writer, finds himself ensnared in the power drives of his national discourse and its cultural form, the novel. Speech acts always return to the writer-grammarian, they are seen through his filter. So, while *oratio obliqua* appears to allow a disavowal and renunciation of power through speech, it is also actually implicated in such a programme at the same time. The radical part of Forster's technique, then, is not tossing all available voices into the novel's melting pot and in this way claiming to disavow the intention of speaking for India – we should here recall Barthes' point about repressive discourse's links with equilibrium:

> Hence the taste shown by such discourse for motives of balance, verbal opposites, antitheses formulated and evaded, being *neither* for this *nor* for that (if however, you do the double addition of the neithers and the nors, it will be seen that our *impartial, objective, human* speaker is *for* this, *against* that). Repressive discourse is the discourse of good conscience, liberal discourse.[21]

Rather, it is precisely the presence of those who are not given a voice – and it is given or bestowed by the English writer – those I have described as unimpressed or uninscribed, that represents the fundamental challenge. Perhaps paradoxically, Indian figures in the novel can approach freedom only when the narrator takes direct responsibility for them – as he does with the punkah-wallah – and does not inscribe them in the sense of inducting them mimetically into the text's indirect, polyphonic approach nor presume to give them 'their own' voice. Just as Professor Godbole is ultimately not subversive precisely because he is given a voice, and that voice is used for the author-narrator's own purposes, the punkah-wallah, despite falling under the jurisdiction of the over-ruling grammar, is a site of resistance because Forster has not called him into speech and claimed to talk for him.[22]

It takes a post-1947 perspective to be able to read the interruption in the text occasioned by the punkah-wallah in this way. One might say that a new interpretative possibility has been brought to the dialogue between text and reader. He, the servitor and the rest of 'humanity grading and drifting beyond the educated vision' (*Passage*, p. 58), become subjects with voices as part of the independence struggle. In view of this, Forster's true achievement in *Passage* is not to give them a 'voice' at all – which would of course be controlled by him like all the others. Forster, as controlling English author(ity), cannot introduce the *truly* free dialogue.

To summarize, Anglo-India must control all meanings, written, spoken and symbolic. *Passage* intervenes at a time when this control is being called into question and reflects and participates in this process. Colonial discourse in all its forms should confirm Anglo-India's sense of difference and superiority by drawing an appropriate response from the colonized – either meek abasement or recognizable opposition. In either case the colonized, like a mirror, throws back an image of the colonizer which affirms him in what Said describes as 'positional superiority'.[23] The Englishman calls all the shots. A rejection of this relationship, a refusal to return the required image, a refusal to be impressed, is a tactic which allows escape from colonially determined reactive and subjugated positions. I have argued that Forster effectively imprints a space for such a tactic in his novel, within the parameters of what is otherwise an anguished liberal humanist tract – and that his incorporation in this discourse in part prevents him from realizing the potential of such a ploy. Instead, Forster offers another, more characteristic resolution in the novel.

As one can see from essays included in *Abinger Harvest*, and from *The Hill of Devi* and *Passage*, the princely or native state, with its emphasis on pre-capitalist social relations and ruled over by the often highly individual personality of the Rajah, offers the liberal individualist Forster an alternative to engagement with imperialism. This is summed up by the way in which Forster repeatedly invokes 'the Oriental', as individual, against 'the European nation', especially in the essays in *Abinger Harvest*. It is almost as if he sees in this resilient, unreconstructed East the ideal manifestation of his beloved individuality, against the soulless, clanking efficiency of the European nation state. (It is worth recalling Forster's regret, expressed in the preface to *The Hill of Devi*, that the newly independent nation created in 1947 chose to call itself India – a reservation related, I think, to the ambiguous mockery of the notion of India as a nation noted at the end of *Passage*.)

All this is reflected in Aziz's own tenacious individualism, made manifest in poetry instead of politics, dreaming instead of action. His own passage is to a watery political commitment, abstract and theoretical. He will still compose idealistic verse and 'express what is deepest in his heart' and, one feels, his creator will respect him the more for it. He retires to the native state of Mau and for Forster this is not so much an act of resistance against imperialism, as a token gesture against centralizing tendencies, which include both imperialism and Indian nationalism. One can deduce, from the tone of the essay 'The Mind of the Indian Native State' (*Abinger*, pp. 368–79), that, while recognizing their idiosyncrasies and anachronisms, Forster values princely fiefdoms as rural models presided over by distinguishable and sometimes odd personalities, to set against centralized rule, either British or Indian. (It is revealing, in this essay, that he indiscriminately refers to nationalists as 'extremists'.) They are not, strictly speaking, British India (the empire) nor Nationalist India (the 'anti-empire') but a third kind of space Forster seeks, above grubby politics.

He comments in this essay:

> So long as his subjects are uneducated peasants, a Prince is in a strong position from every point of view. They revere him with the old Indian loyalty, and a glimpse of his half-divine figure brings poetry into their lives. And he understands them even when he is indifferent or unjust, because like them he is rooted in the soil. ('The Mind of the Indian Native State', *Abinger*, p. 378)

It is tempting to rest one's case, so well does this extract reveal Forster's faith in individuals and 'the personal touch'. However, it is worth examining this quotation in detail and taking note of the ideological 'slippage' that takes place both in language and thought. Unwittingly, Forster uses exactly the same rhetoric and phrases as the British in India to describe a political ideal. He emphasizes 'the old Indian loyalty' as if it was involuntary and genetic, as does Kipling: 'uneducated peasants', and the Raj prefers these too as they are less trouble and more impressionable, and obviously prefers native rulers to have them for the same reason; and the 'half-divine figure' of the Prince himself, who has an interchangeable relationship with the 'heaven-born' sahib – the process of domination through impressive display and personal veneration being a well-chronicled imperial tactic, of course. Likewise, the final sentence, proclaiming empathy between ruler and ruled through mutual rootedness is at once a panegyric on 'natural law' and a possible mechanism for despotic power. And it does not seem to matter that it is despotic. Forster's libertarian principles are immediately suspended when the Grail of individual contact, of personal relations, is in sight. Indeed, there is a distinct impression that such feudal societies, because they are pre-capitalist, have a particular appeal for Forster. Perhaps they act to salve the conscience of the nineteenth-century liberal who recognizes, in the essay 'The Challenge of our Time' (*Two Cheers for Democracy*, p. 67), that his privileges have been built on the profits of capitalism's imperial adventurism. In this context it is worth comparing the appeal of such pastoral fantasias as the pre-industrial 'pleasant land' of England in works like the 'Abinger Pageant'. Forster says of the native princes, 'they do not in their heart of hearts regard anything but Royalty as permanent, or the movements against it more than domestic mutinies. They cannot understand, because they cannot experience, the modern world' ('Mind of Native State', *Abinger*, p. 370). Although presumably the fruit of Forster's stay in the state of Dewas Senior, this sounds like, and is, orientalism at work: Forster claiming to understand the 'heart of hearts' of the Indian Prince. It is instructive here to recall the point made concisely in *Aspects of the Novel* (pp. 63–70), that fiction differs from life precisely because in life one cannot know the hearts and minds of people. Here, I think, we reach the core of Forster's nostalgic vision. The native state has become an idealized and *fictionalized* locale; Forster can speak for it, control it and it need never change. Essentially, the native state joins Abinger, Italy, Howards End and the mythical Greenwood as Forster's sanctuary from the harsh realities of modernity.

The contradictions of Forster's liberalism are most clearly disclosed in the essays, letters and diary entries, where they are stripped of the novelistic context in which they can be read as framed or ironic utterances. The desire to transgress, to transcend cultural barriers, expressed in Forster's work is always thwarted by the conditions and history of the very tongue which expresses it. So, Forster's notion of the authentic India in the native state is conservative when set against other possible identities and authenticities – that created by Gandhi, for example. Indeed, it is interchangeable with old Anglo-Indian aphorisms about the representative quality of the princes and 'the countryside' – 'the real

India' – as opposed to the less reliable civic population. It sits uneasily in the political climate of 1924 proclaiming its ideological innocence when, as Said says, 'The battle between native and white man had to be visibly joined'.[24] The view is essentially a product of Forster's romantic idealism. He would kill all nationalisms, including English and Indian, with individual kindness if he could – 'kindness, more kindness, and even after that more kindness', says Aziz, 'I assure you it is the only hope' (*Passage*, p. 128).

Ultimately, *A Passage to India* might be described as the limit-text of liberalism's critique of empire. Forster presents difference and 'unknowability', but in order to convey it he must make it known. If one admits that a power-through-knowledge programme is inevitably blind in certain areas, one is then faced with the question of how to set up one's own narrative and claim to 'know better'. Forster addresses this problem in the recurrent mystifications and ambiguities he leaves intact, both in event – we never discover what did happen in the caves – and by problematizing the reader's interpretative interaction with the text. That is, he adopts a posture of disavowal. And that area he knows least about – the 'undiscovered India' – provides the truly radical narrative dynamic. This is the text beyond *Passage*, the text of arrival, the text Forster could never, himself, have written. Yet in setting up spaces which anticipate a power beyond the already known, he both marks the existence of another voice and concedes the inability of his own discourse to speak for it. Henceforth, liberalism can never be seen as an adequate response to imperialism. Perhaps more importantly it can no longer see itself as an adequate response either. The chimes of Forster's midnight for liberalism, intoned in *Passage*, echo as resonantly for British writers on India who antedate 15 August 1947 as does the date itself for post-colonial writers like Salman Rushdie. The legacy is at once paralysing and invigorating.

Notes

1. James Morris, *Farewell the Trumpets*, p. 303.
2. Allon White, 'Bakhtin, Sociolinguistics and Deconstruction', in Frank Gloversmith (ed.), *The Theory of Reading*, p. 128.
3. Ashis Nandy, *The Intimate Enemy: Loss and Recovery of Self Under Colonialism*, pp. 7, 72. See also Partha Chatterjee, *Nationalist Thought and the Colonial World: A Derivative Discourse?*
4. David Lodge, *After Bakhtin: Essays on Fiction and Criticism*, p. 22.
5. Bette London, *The Appropriated Voice: Narrative Authority in Conrad,*

Forster and Woolf, pp. 91–2.

6. Mikhail Bakhtin, *The Dialogic Imagination*, p. 307.
7. Bette London reads *A Passage to India* against the background of the Indian letters, journals and essays 'to suggest the complexities of his position as a cultured subject bound up with historically available discourses on race, class and nationality', London, *The Appropriated Voice*, p. 8.
8. Sara Suleri says of the instability of register in the description of the caves at this point, 'Such a geography denies both connection and chronology, in that it forces cultural description into a recognition of its own vacuity. The touristic experience of colonialism is deglamorized into mathematical computations of how literally banal the exotic may be', Sara Suleri, *The Rhetoric of English India*, p. 145.
9. London, *Appropriated Voice*, p. 89.
10. Bakhtin, *Dialogic Imagination*, p. 302.
11. Benita Parry, '"A Passage to India": Epitaph or Manifesto?', pp. 130–1.
12. Brenda R. Silver, 'Periphrasis, Power and Rape in A Passage to India', p. 99.
13. *His Majesty the King 1910–1935: Twenty Five Years of a Glorious Reign told in Pictures* (with an introduction by H. W. Wilson), not paginated.
14. Steps were constantly being taken to counteract this other voice. Bernard S. Cohn, in 'Representing Authority in Victorian India', gives a history of the Durbar and its appropriation by the British as part of a 'cultural-symbolic constitution'. He comments, 'It is significant that the major present [given by the Viceroy to the native princes during the Assemblage or Durbar of 1877] was a representation of the British version of the Indian rulers' pasts as represented in their coats of arms', p. 204.

    Edward Thompson, in his classic *The Other Side of the Medal*, quotes an interesting example of Indian resistance to the plundering of their past, and refusal to sanction the British version of the dialogue:

    > A missionary told the present writer that in his earlier and less experienced days he instructed his class of catechists to write an essay on the Mutiny. Every youth sent in a sheet of blank paper! It was a silent, unanimous and unapologetic refusal to perform the task. (W. M. Fitchett, *The Tale of the Great Mutiny* (6th impression) pp. 440–1, quoted in Edward Thompson, *The Other Side of the Medal*, p. 120)
15. Rebecca West, 'Interpreters of Their Age', p. 254.
16. Parry, *Delusions and Discoveries*, p. 311.
17. Richard Lannoy, *The Speaking Tree: A Study of Indian Culture and Society*, p. 384. Gayatri Spivak has described the punkah-wallah as an 'ex-orbitant tribal': 'that other that can be neither excluded or recuperated', 'Draupadi' by Mahasveta Devi, p. 381. The extent to which Gandhi did in fact 'speak for' untouchables like the punkah-

wallah has been contested in recent Indian historiography, with the Subaltern Studies group of historians attempting to reinvest such figures with power as speaking subjects who could, and did, speak and act for themselves in the struggle against colonialism.

18. Michael Orange, 'Language and Silence in A Passage to India', p. 144.
19. Barbara Rosecrance, *Forster's Narrative Vision*.
20. Roland Barthes, *Image, Music, Text*, p. 190.
21. Ibid., p. 209.
22. In *Whose India?* Teresa Hubel also works through to a positive conclusion about the 'powerful silences' of both the punkah-wallah and the servitor, albeit via an examination of gender and sexual complications in the novel and their relationship to power. She remarks:

    The figures of the punkah-wallah and the temple servitor ... are both products of Orientalism, for both are imagined as somehow existing outside time, in that eternal and changeless India that the West cannot and should not touch. As such they are exempt from the narrator's sceptical analysis, which usually examines the objects, people and beliefs of India in order to absorb them into a western narrative ... Instead of seeing these images as turning us back to an imperialist arena, we can allow them to point us to a perspective that the text obliquely endorses but is completely unable to articulate given the limits of its vision. This is the perspective of the peasant or subaltern. (Teresa Hubel, *Whose India? The Independence Struggle in British and Indian Fiction and History*, p. 107)

    For a completely different reading of these figures see Jenny Sharpe, *Allegories of Empire: The Figure of Woman in the Colonial Text*.
23. Said, *Orientalism*, p. 7.
24. Said, *Culture and Imperialism*, p. 249.

III John Masters: Writing as Staying On

> 'I don't know what's right for India – I thought I did once. I don't know who should decide – there are too many voices.' (John Masters, *Nightrunners of Bengal*)
>
> 'It is not your country. It is mine. I made it, from a hundred countries, I and my great-great-grandfather, and my great grandfather and so on.' (John Masters, *To the Coral Strand*)

John Masters was of the fifth generation of his family to have served in India. His background is essential to the series of novels he wrote during the 1950s and 1960s, chronicling the adventures of an Anglo-Indian dynasty, the Savages.[1] The novels depict the British–Indian relationship at various crisis points in its development. Masters' heroes are involved in the violence surrounding the Mutiny, fight the system of religious robbery and murder known as Thuggee, take part in The Great Game with Russia, and so on. Events are always mediated from the point of view of the Anglo-Indian protagonist, whose internal monologue forms the main thread of narrative, abutted on, and added to, by occasional forays from an omniscient narrator. One might claim that the use of an omniscient narrator here acts as a way of controlling India as an imaginative resource as well as the narrative: an India which has, in reality, become uncontrollable and independent by 1951 when the novel cycle begins. Indeed by concentrating on the English ruler facing various challenges, Masters can be said to resuscitate and participate in the myth of the White Man's Burden; nor is this his only connection with Kipling. Masters' writing allows a confirmation of imperial aims after they have been discredited in actuality. By writing the sort of adventure fiction which has so often hymned the imperial project – one thinks of Henty, Brereton and A. E. W. Mason – he can re-collect a number of figurings of the colonized: children who need a father, deviants requiring correction, or treacherous orientals to be vanquished. In this way history can be rewritten to show that British imperialism was a good venture at some level. In addition, Masters expresses a concern for objectivity and a desire to 'tell it like it is'.[2] He has no sense of himself as peddling, and being implicated in, a ruling ideology, in the way that Forster shows an awareness of this. Nevertheless, the end of empire also means the end of the era when the imperial adventure story could claim to be politically innocent. The post-independence heroic narrative of empire confronts its own *telos* and the ideological complicity of imperial romance fiction, often in the 'writing back' of India's own novelists. The result is an uncertainty over how to tell the old story and a challenge to find new ways of representing the imperial encounter.[3] Masters' particular interest for a post-colonial reader is in the way he expresses this uncertainty, yet is ultimately unable to struggle free of the shackles of an imperial mindset.

As has been suggested, Masters has several thematic and technical affinities with Rudyard Kipling, a writer he much admired. His best-known use of a Kiplingesque genre is in the motif which might be called cultural cross-dressing. In Masters, as in Kipling, the walnut-stained and suitably attired Englishman frequently passes among the natives, incognito, on some errand which will result in the preservation of truth, justice and the British Raj. Such structures characterize *The Deceivers*, *Coromandel!*, *The Lotus and the Wind* and *Nightrunners of Bengal*.[4] In fact, one may observe a number of generic features at work in *Nightrunners of Bengal*, whose lineage can be traced to Kipling. There is the same sense of vocation displayed by the hero, Rodney Savage: the idea of being part of a great imperial family which carries the weight of responsibility for its immature native charges. Not only does Rodney remind the reader of Kipling's Anglo-Indian stalwart John Chinn from the story 'The Tomb of his Ancestors' (*The Day's Work*), in the close relationship, borne of heredity, he enjoys with India and Indians – 'he found it a strange thing to hate his exile, and yet love the country which was its place' (*Nightrunners of Bengal*, p. 20) – like Chinn he also waits restlessly for 'some great thing to turn up for him to do'. Equally, Rodney's dedication to the regiment, its traditions and paraphernalia, recall Kipling's paean to the White Hussars in 'The Man Who Was' (*Life's Handicap*). Rodney testifies to the reassurance derived from membership of the Thirteenth Rifles and the sacramental quality of its traditions; 'the officers partook of the continuing body of the regiment and of the blood spilled in its battles' (*Nightrunners of Bengal*, p. 119). Masters himself displays the same adulatory zeal in his autobiography, *Bugles and a Tiger*:

> It was for this spirit that we drilled together, got drunk together, hunted, danced, played, killed and saved life together. It was from this spirit that no man was alone, neither on the field of battle ... nor in the chasm of death, nor in the dark places of life. (*Bugles and a Tiger*, p. 106)

The tone of this memoir, recalling an austere life on the North West Frontier in the 1930s, and other aspects of Masters' retrospective, make him the incarnation of Leonard Woolf's celebrated comment that he was uncertain whether Kipling had modelled his characters on Anglo-Indians or vice versa.

However, there are undoubted differences between the two writers' attitudes, and these mainly arise from their respective proximity to the metropolitan 'centre'. Kipling's stay in India was comparatively brief and after the publication of *Plain Tales from the Hills* he had at least one eye on the tastes and preferences of an English readership. Therefore, his relation to the peripheral society which formed his subject matter became increasingly tenuous. This is a complex phenomenon and may best be grasped by remembering that while in India Kipling tasted the wrath of the Anglo-Indian community over his newspaper's stance on the Ilbert Bill, had to take care to avoid offending the grass-widows he often satirized, and was generally viewed with some suspicion. However, on his return to England and acceptance into the literary pantheon, he came to be fêted in India as the voice of the English in residence, and was felt to speak on their behalf. Masters, in contrast, is always eager to identify himself with Anglo-India, to speak for those who know the natives and have first-hand experience of land and man management in India. One feels there is a dependence complex at work in Masters, which is subtly different from Kipling's famous need to 'belong'. In Masters there is a psychological overlap involving the identities of the sahib, the regiment (for Masters, personally, the Gurkhas), and the tribal peoples of India. All these groups are felt to be on the periphery of a monolithic, functioning 'system' – Britain, the British Army, the empire in India – to which they are only loosely affiliated. Each group has a sense of its members as individuals yet interdependent, gaining identity in the group and losing it outside (this loss is the theme of *To the Coral Strand*). Masters' heroes are always champions of these peoples on the periphery, and can call back to the centre to remind it of its duties and draw attention to its oversights. In a sense this was the justification of the liberal wing of Anglo-Indian society throughout its existence.

Given the faith in regimental bonds and trust evinced by Rodney, their betrayal in the Mutiny comes as a life-shattering shock. Yet his subject matter presents the author himself with the problem of registering infidelity in a relationship based on faith and an ideal to which he too subscribes. His answer is largely to ignore the political and cultural complexities leading to the revolt and to regress to a thin, Kipling-like grasp on the social polemics of empire. There is an air of involuntariness about the mutineers, even at the height of the rebellion: 'their faces shone in the irregular glare, and were *dark and frightened*. They had become strangers, Hottentots, and there was no way of making contact with them' (*Nightrunners of Bengal*, p. 191). In this version of the Mutiny, the many are led like cattle by the few. The masses have no affinity with the aims of the rebellion, orchestrated by a few malevolent rajahs and their ministers,[5] but just follow blindly and somewhat stupidly, succumbing in the process to what is presented as a potential for reversion to inhuman acts. Also, in the midst of the carnage, the obligatory faithful natives appear to verbalize the (ir)rationale of the Mutiny in terms of madness which recall Kipling.

One figure who partly escapes this orientalizing tendency and comes near to being a fully rounded character is the Rani of Kishanpur. While, perhaps predictably, the other speaks through an overblown sexuality during the rapes and excesses perpetrated by the sepoys, Rani Sumitra enjoys a more complex association with orientalist precepts. She dupes Rodney and gains useful information for the rebels by playing on the Englishman's preconception about licentious Eastern women. Her combination of resilience, resourcefulness and psychological complexity raises her above the other rebels. Yet even her strength and independence is undermined by the attraction she is made to feel for the dashing Captain Savage:

> She went soft, and even in his anger he knew that this was not that other clinging softness. This was a helpless, moving softness, shivering and moaning under him. This was a composite of all women east and west, and of all female need. (*Nightrunners of Bengal*, p. 84)

Sumitra's yielding to Rodney is simultaneously that of her gender and of her race. Just as Caroline Langford, the companion of his escape, is only completed when she realizes her need for Rodney, the proto-feminist Rani of the novel's first pages is diluted in this way. Yet critics who complain about the inaccuracy and chauvinism in Masters' portrayal of Rodney and Sumitra's relationship perhaps overlook the symbolic undertones of its presentation. The point is that Rodney, and the imperial family he represents, hereby *embraces* (literally and metaphorically) *all India*, including the rebellious element. This is related to the love and forgiveness he is to personify by the close. It might be described as an imperialist attempt to smother recalcitrant India with affection.

What Masters really finds difficult in *Nightrunners of Bengal* is reconciling the two antagonistic perspectives he must juggle. As the novel's language is the taut, tense argot of the mid-twentieth-century adventure story relating a nineteenth-century event, so a shift in viewpoint must necessarily occur if only to take account of decolonization. Masters is a writer who comes after and therefore literally 'knows more' about the empire than Kipling. He can use aspects of Kipling's technique but must accommodate subsequent events. He attempts this through a technique of 'typicality'. John Clay explains the strategy:

> Each member of the Savage family would, in every succeeding generation, act as a kind of measuring rod to the major historical events happening around him, and the way he witnessed and reacted to these events would be in a manner typical of the British in India at that time.[6]

In *Nightrunners of Bengal*, Rodney is made to reflect British positions in respect of the Indian and how they change after the Mutiny. We are supposed to see Anglo-India's position in microcosm: benevolent paternalism giving way to righteous retribution and steely suspicion. However, Rodney is idealistically taken a stage further through the therapeutic experience symbolized by the fight against cholera in the village of Chalisgon. Masters' heroes are supposed to be typical of the British response to any of a number of given imperial situations. But they are not. They are really indicative of an ideal response that is Masters' own retrospective code.

The Chalisgon episode as a whole discloses more about Masters' tactics and bias than anything else in the novel. It is another example of the white 'Anglo-Indian family' man making himself at home in India. Having stumbled upon the village during his flight, and still raging against Indians for what he has seen, Rodney murders a young villager who has come to help him hunt for food. Caroline tells him that everyone in the village knows he has killed the man, yet no one confronts him about this, nor even threatens to hand him over to the importunate mutineers. Chalisgon is the white man's fantasy island in a sea of troubles: a place where Rodney's faith in humanity, and particularly Indians, can be restored. When the cholera arrives it provides an opportunity for an imagined working out of England's potential for service in India. Caroline exhorts him: 'if we're to be accepted in India it will be because of things like this – not victories or dams or telegraphs or doctors' (*Nightrunners of Bengal*, p. 257) and Rodney himself comes to see that:

> to men of English blood had been given an opportunity such as God grants but once in a thousand years. After the blind selfishness of two centuries, the hour had come. From here they could ruin themselves with power, or step forward as giants of understanding, forerunners of a new world of service. (*Nightrunners of Bengal*, p. 265)

Humanitarian action is here recommended above a purely national and imperial interest. Yet the one is usurped by the other in Masters' imperial discourse, as Caroline's presupposition about being accepted in India makes clear. There is no conception that service ceases to be service when it is unwanted, that it then becomes occupation and oppression. It is implied that India will welcome such service if it is conducted in a spirit of love and, therefore, that the Mutiny leaders have betrayed India because their actions are not motivated by love: Rodney muses, 'he and every Englishman need not be foreigners anywhere. The task was plain – to love, as a father his son, as a son his father' (*Nightrunners of Bengal*, p. 264). The most important by-product of all this is that it invalidates the mutineers' aims and claims: just as the Rani sobs in Rodney's arms, 'None of you English are quite foreigners, or ever will be. I wish I did not think so' (*Nightrunners of Bengal*, p. 59).[7]

Some even heavier narrative artillery is rolled out to confront the Silver Guru, one of the few coherent nationalist voices in the book; although significantly he represents not Indian but Irish Nationalism since we discover that he is a deserter of long-standing from Donegal. Rodney accosts his militant adversary with the butt-end of the civilizing mission:

> The Company is *not* going to lose India ... And if it did, do you think Indians are fit to rule themselves, or protect themselves yet? There'd be a year of anarchy, civil wars between rajahs mad for power ... And who would suffer in all this but the ordinary people of India? And afterwards – Russia! (*Nightrunners of Bengal*, p. 281)

To which the Guru's suitably chastened, almost embarrassed reply is, 'Perhaps. But when a country has learned how to throw off one lot of foreigners, it can do it again. *Let us not talk about it anymore*'. The faltering, unconvincing reply, the unwillingness to take the argument further attributed to the rebel, suggest fatal flaws in his logic without ever having to explore them. Masters operates a rhetorical system constructed around discursive limits and boundaries. Refusing to accept that by 1951 the revolutionary balloon has not only gone up, but is comfortably airborne, Masters attempts a narrative choking like the actual choking of the Silver Guru by the faithful native, Piroo. The rebel script is turned back on itself and forced to re-examine its motives in the highly refracted light of a vague humanist notion of love, masquerading as apolitical but in fact conscripted for Britain, and find them transfigured into jealousy and hate and thus, wanting. Rationally, there is only one possible outcome. The Silver Guru must die because he has been completely compromised as a repository for the power of the other, and his cause discredited.

What Masters cannot allow in *Nightrunners of Bengal* is any voice which would draw the reader's attention away from the narrative of the white man learning to love his fractious wards again after their miscreant behaviour, and resolving to serve them all his days. In the teeth of the evidence, he believes that a new world of service was indeed created, and the heroes of his subsequent novels set about proving it. One can say that while Masters' project in this novel may not be to monumentalize the Mutiny in the way that the church builders and mourning angel designers did in India itself after the most bitter and protracted campaign of reprisals in imperial history, it *is* to commemorate the ethic of service he believes to be the root and flower of British intentions and which he dates from the event. Perhaps inadvertently, he does monumentalize the Mutiny as the watershed in British–Indian relations, both in what the novel chooses to say and in what it refuses to sanction. (This tendency is manifest in British writing about the Mutiny from Flora Annie Steel's *On the Face of the Waters* to M. M. Kaye's *Shadow of the Moon*.)

Masters' post-independence perspective is more attenuated and self-serving in that it hinges on the better knowledge of the Anglo-Indian patriarch and his ability to forgive his 'children' a multitude of sins. So, Rodney Savage rediscovers an unconvincing affection for Indians by the end of the novel, despite the fact that his wife and all his colleagues have been butchered before his eyes. David Rubin has described this kind of reaction, which typifies Masters and Kaye, as 'the gushing of a willed emotion ... a mid-twentieth century liberal anachronism'.[8] In the same way, in *Far, Far the Mountain Peak*, Peter Savage and Adam Khan are representatives of a cross-racial liberal consensus, co-opted for the forces of 'progress'. By making them appear to be enablers of independence at some stage in the future, a role is reserved for the English in India's achievements: that is, *in the time-honoured sense of preparing the native for man's* estate. Peter's wife Emily reports the reaction to her husband's return to his ICS (Indian Civil Service) duties; 'everyone is keyed up to do great things, now that Peter is back. The Congress people know they won't be able to get away with vague slogans anymore, but will have to be precise and bold' (*Far, Far, the Mountain Peak*, p. 289). Independence agitation is presented as a kind of game the old Cambridge undergraduates, Peter and Adam, are involved in: tactically approaching autonomy in a series of set-piece moves. The English-educated Indian leader of the Nehru variety is clearly indicated in the character of Adam, who also goes to prison for his beliefs, and the foundation of his Committee for Good Government is emblematic of the loyalist beginnings of the Congress Party. Moreover, 'extremists' like Harnarayan, the obstructive local politico, are marginalized by a framework of consensual political progress in which the British, through a kind of dialectic, can be seen as active agents for change. A post-1947 authorial consciousness can be seen at work here in that Masters knows independence is coming for his imagined India although the action takes place between 1900 and 1920. In order to justify the activities of his English hero he must incorporate him into the enterprise of preparing India for self-government, hence the ICS background. His use of the post-independence perspective enshrines the white man as champion for both sides. His heroes and heroines are always representatives of an enlightened British-Indian aristocracy benevolently overseeing the process of change, always, one might say, on the side of the liberal-imperialist angels.

However, the real point about the way Masters inscribes a post-independence perspective has nothing to do with either authenticity or anachronism. Rather it is that his novels' avowal of a libertarian tolerance is actually inconsistent with their narrative strategies of power. One can see this most clearly in what is, paradoxically, his most ambitious work, *Bhowani Junction*. The adventure narrative of empire came into being to tell the story of paternalism's self-denial. However, this is a tale which no longer finds a ready audience in the later colonial scenario where such myths come under scrutiny. By the time of independence, portrayed in *Bhowani Junction*, the project is concerned with damage limitation: the attempt to maintain the image of the happy imperial family even if some of its members are showing signs of more than delinquency. The novel confronts and dramatizes that which works with an earlier setting can comfortably defer: the possibility of the Indian who no longer wants the old familial relationships. (Masters used to court and enjoy comparisons with his hero Kipling, but it is in their adamant refusal to admit that any Indians worthy of the name can be unhappy with British rule that the two authors are most similar.) By 1954, the novel of empire comes up against the brute fact of that empire's demise; as Avtar Singh Bhullar puts it, 'reality overtakes a myth'.[9] Hence, for Masters, with his vested interest in the integrity and happiness of the imperial family, the challenge is now to relativize narrative power, to accede to historical fact and admit that other voices exist and are not just easily assumed Indianized derivatives of the English master-voice, but to do so in such a way that the original ethic is somehow vindicated. His answer is to allow three first-person narratives to guide *Bhowani Junction*, providing different voices and viewpoints on events during the months before independence.

The plot involves three characters – two Eurasians, Patrick Taylor and Victoria Jones, and an Englishman, Colonel Rodney Savage – in attempts to track down a Communist agitator, K. P. Roy, who is bent on derailing the process of peaceful change to Indian rule. The action takes place in the railway district of Bhowani over a few weeks in 1946. The narrating characters are carefully delineated through their use of English and their motivation and concerns about independence. The decisions they will have to make concerning identity and belonging are teased out in the course of a linear plot-line during which the baton of narrative is passed from one speaker to another. Thus we meet the wrong-headed, boorish District Traffic Superintendent, Patrick, who is proud of the status, albeit orbital, his half-English background confers: who calls all Indians 'wogs' and fears that they are driving his fellow Eurasians off the railways; and who is in love with his childhood sweetheart, Victoria. For her part, Victoria has just returned from a spell in the Women's Army Corps which has given her a new, more cosmopolitan outlook. She condemns Patrick for his racism and self-deluding insularity and is a model displaced person, commenting, 'Why must we torture ourselves with ideas that we are better than some people and worse than others? Why don't we put on dhotis or saris if we want to, and marry Indians?' (*Bhowani Junction*, p. 27). In fact, this is just the process Victoria does undergo in the course of the novel, and which provides the main focus of interest. She swings from a total acceptance of her Indian side, which drives her to the point of marrying the Sikh union leader and Congress supporter, Ranjit, to a brief affair with Colonel Savage to placate the drives of her English 'blood', before settling for her original Eurasian identity and deciding to accept Patrick's proposal of marriage.

In a break with mechanical novels detailing Anglo-Indian feats of derring-do, Masters explores the sense of uncertainty and displacement, shared by Eurasian and Anglo-Indian alike, caused by the rapid course of events carrying them towards independence. Variation, colour and interest are derived from the first-person narrative technique, not least in characterization, where the protagonists are no longer cardboard adventure heroes. However, the linear, unselfconscious quality of three people happily giving their sequential instalments of the unfolding drama – no section actually concludes, 'and now over to you Victoria/Rodney/Patrick', but this is the spirit in which the first-person narrators operate – contributes to the narrative's curious overall quality of being both rounded and flat at the same time. To explain: Patrick's narrative is given in straightforward, unironic prose and without making use of hindsight, although he relates his first portion of the story long after the events described, in the past tense, and the subsequent narrators refer back to it. It is worth considering whether this reluctance to show hindsight does not counteract the bold characterization a first-person narrative lends itself to. After all, if Patrick is as ego-centric and self-satisfied as some of his utterances show him to be, and as the other 'tellers' say he is, surely his narrative, written after the fact, would register *some* tremor revealing the way in which his faults are going to be exposed: either by admitting his foolishness or by attempting to exonerate himself in some way. The fact that Patrick never attempts this, suggests that we can trust his narrative as an accurate, if prejudiced, retelling of events. Yet what I think this uncovers is the beginning of the text's affiliation to a more subtle strategy of power, something I will attempt to trace in many of its manifestations in this novel. Here, it might be helpful to return to the example of Kipling's 'The Phantom Rickshaw', discussed in Chapter 1. If one is going to use a multi-narrative technique – either explicit, as here, or implied, as in 'The Phantom Rickshaw' – one can make interpretation more problematic if versions of events are not the same. But here the narrators are undercut in how they speak, not in what they say; Patrick is racist, Rodney is initially a macho man. Similarly, while Victoria's tone is assured and she is evidently more at home with the language than Patrick, this makes no difference to the facts she relates; she is neither more nor less reliable. The narration never emanates from a source which is in opposition to them or the imperially defined positions they embody.

In fact, one can see disclosed, in a series of narrative anomalies, of slippages in tone, the presence of an overall metanarrative which carefully controls the first-person voices and what they are allowed to say. Take, for example, a sentence from the first paragraph of Colonel Savage's narration where he describes Victoria, to whom he has just made love; 'She looked as beautiful as – a naked woman kneeling by a naked man's head' (*Bhowani Junction*, p. 263). Here is the distinctive voice of the unimaginative army officer with no pretension to being a writer, giving up the search for a suitably literary simile. The reader accepts this as a carefully drawn and distinctive piece of characterization. What, then, is one to make of the Colonel's language when describing Victoria's abduction by the fugitive K. P. Roy on the railway; 'She heard the shimmer of sound in the rails as soon as he did. Straining her ears, she could hear the slow beat of the engine's exhaust' (*Bhowani Junction*, p. 310). Is this still Savage's voice? The non-storytelling army officer has here been miraculously transfigured into something which resembles in tone an omniscient narrator. Indeed, Masters finds it hard to resist his interventionist instincts despite the autonomy his first-person technique claims. Just occasionally this lapse of register intrudes and suggests the existence of a secret, omnipotent, 'colonizing' narrator standing above his characters and pulling their strings.

Part of the difficulty stems from Masters' persistent use of a segregated narrative technique in his novels. In the other texts, an omniscient narrator is used in tandem with one of the central characters and, through a mixture of direct and indirect speech and narratorial interjection a single view is forged. The problem occurs because, as Masters uses it, the technique is not flexible enough to admit more than one character as mediating consciousness in a single chapter or section. It is only at the end of a chapter or, as here, a 'book' that Masters allows another voice to take over. This unwieldy 'alternate consciousness' approach means that, to present a full picture, as the characters always strive to do, they must literally take up mind-reading. Thus Savage says of Victoria's father, Mr Jones, 'I could read her father's mind as easily as I could read hers'; and, later, of Victoria, 'I could almost hear her saying to herself, Men are extraordinary' (*Bhowani Junction*, pp. 324 and 325). Besides showing how clever the Anglo-Indian hero is, these examples of Savage claiming to know the thoughts of other characters and narrating them as fact is a sign of the way having space to tell a story gives power. What might be called a coercion of interpretation takes place, stamping out any possibility of these other characters Savage narrates behaving, speaking or thinking in any way not governed and allowed for by his over-mastering narrative. In short, a coercion of interpretation takes place when the reader's full interpretative interaction with the text – for instance, in Kipling through the questionable narrator and in Forster through cultural ambivalence – is foreclosed or hindered in some way. In *Bhowani Junction* this occurs in that nominal relativization of the first-person narrative which really leaves a totalizing system of narrative hegemony intact: the voice which says 'I am Eurasian and am here speaking freely', while remaining under the control of an intrusive omniscient power. Coercion of interpretation may be compared and contrasted with Kipling's technique of 'colonizing' narratives in 'The Phantom Rickshaw', to show how Masters' device is actually more oppressive. 'The Phantom Rickshaw' shows its own workings and how the suppression of other narratives is achieved, thereby preserving the reader's uncertainty about the events reported and his or her interpretative engagement with the text. A coercion of interpretation is designed to disguise the operation of interpellative ideology through what one could term, borrowing from Gerard Genette, a sham internal-focalization.[10] The narrative is supposed to be focalized through the eyes of characters whose points of view orientate the text's perspective, but their vision is deliberately impaired by an overview which is at once more 'objective' and yet reveals the underlying ideology informing the work. The English writer/narrator supposedly lets others speak, but in fact lulls his reader into a perhaps unwitting complicity with conservative narrative strategies. Irony can find a place in this project, in that Savage's arrogant assumptions about the future course of his relationship with Victoria are shown to be flawed. Yet this is an allowance the English text can afford, can even encourage, as it *is actually about self-effacement*. As Masters' own power to direct interpretation as omniscient narrator is deliberately relativized in a way that leaves the Englishman blame-free and able to demonstrate his affinity with the true, as opposed to the false, thrusting, India, so Savage's own sexual presumptuousness is undercut, but he is still shown as being a 'power in the land'. (Above all, it is through his intervention that the inept Patrick achieves full manly status by killing Roy, and becomes worthy of Victoria.)

The text may, in one way, stand as evidence that the English no longer have the right to be the only voices heard, but its constitutionalist bias – the law-giving English and the natives and Eurasians who co-operate with them are 'goodies'; Roy, the Sirdarni and the extremists are 'baddies' – means that while *Bhowani Junction* may articulate a rueful farewell to British India, the validated liberal discourse inculcated by Britain will remain dominant. The Eurasians are shown throughout trying to be more English than the English, while Govindaswami and Ranjit help smooth the transfer of power on the understanding that the British-bequeathed system will be better than an unspecified alternative represented only by homicidal maniacs and Communist ideologues. While the English text does not say 'believe in me' directly, we are invited to judge the imperial legacy in such a way that other possible systems are discredited. The Indian oppositional voice does not get a chance to tell its tale, not because Masters, à la Forster, realizes the problems of speaking for Indians – after all, he has no qualms about inscribing a 'chee-chee' voice, nor about speaking for Krishna Ram in *The Ravi Lancers* and Mohan Singh in *The Venus of Konpara* – but because in its version the Anglo-Indian would no longer be the hero. One could say that the Indian's own discourse is pushed from the train of imperial narrative as it passes through *Bhowani Junction*.

I use the word 'version' to describe the various narratives circulating in this text in order to convey a sense of the way in which views of, and responses to, events are made deliberately contentious. Propaganda and disinformation are at the heart of the plot as British and nationalist discourses vie for the minds of the populace. The Congress leader Surabhai tries to make an official raid on the Sirdarni's house into a publicity coup for his side by photographing the party breaking down the door (*Bhowani Junction*, p. 234). Victoria herself, during her brief dalliance with the extremists, hears their theories about British torture during the Naval Mutiny, but in Savage's presence is forced to admit her uncertainty (*Bhowani Junction*, p. 142). Even the Collector himself suggests the contingent nature of right and wrong in modern Indian affairs when he expresses the hope that a shared religion will unite Victoria and Ranjit under:

> 'things in India that are older and better than this.' He waved his hand, perhaps at the sound of motor engines in the distance, perhaps at the atmosphere of squabbling and mistrust hanging about in the room, perhaps at the portrait of Queen Victoria over his desk. (*Bhowani Junction*, p. 226)

All this may help to foster the impression that nothing can be proved to be entirely true, but it does not alter the text's assertion that some things *are* entirely false. The Communist plotters display caricatural properties; the Sirdarni laments the conciliatory attitudes of Nehru and Gandhi, without whom 'this street would be running in blood ...', and uses words like 'lickspittle' (*Bhowani Junction*, p. 203). No really effective counterbalancing figures are offered. They are always seen through the eyes of characters fundamentally unsympathetic to them. A further sample of the novel's weighting occurs when it falls to the pro-British Collector to explain the opposition's motives:

> 'Some Congress men genuinely believe a social revolution is the way to get rid of the British. But some people in Congress want revolution for quite another reason – to make it impossible for the Congress itself to rule after the British go ... Their masters, and their minds, are in Moscow. The thing they must prevent is an orderly hand-over to Congress ... Everything must fail so that the people have only one hope, only one friend they can turn to. (*Bhowani Junction*, pp. 31–2)

If other Masters novels schematically enact an imaginative recolonization of the now independent India, *Bhowani Junction*, with its individualized narrators, appears to enjoy a more complex relationship with England's claim to be 'author' of the East. Yet what must always be remembered is the manipulation of the so-called 'other' versions we are presented with.

The most blatant example occurs during an exchange between Colonel Savage and the Sirdarni at a meeting with Govindaswami. Savage remarks:

> 'This is the lady who was urging the Congress men to charge my fellows in the Street of Suttees. The one who wanted to cause another Jallianwalla Bagh.'
>
> ... 'I was at the Jallianwalla Bagh,' the Sirdarni said unexpectedly in English.
>
> 'Were you responsible for that, too, Beji?' Savage asked in Hindustani.
>
> The Sirdarni shot him a hard look, said, 'I don't understand English,' and pressed her lips together. (*Bhowani Junction*, p. 224)

As we have witnessed the rabble-rousing antics of the Sirdarni at first hand in the novel, when she incites the mob to attack the Army and later the Kutcherry building, Savage's interjection is evidently designed both to goad the Sirdarni and maintain the possibility that it really was Indian malevolence that caused the Amritsar massacre. It foregrounds the idea, reiterated in this novel, that the 'truth' of the Indian troubles is always subject to different interpretations. Yet the choice of this incident as an illustration is significant as it reveals the English version's manipulative tendency. It is in the interest of the liberal imperial narrative which is at the book's core, to keep motivation vague, to keep all versions alive and so avoid responsibility. It is in this atmosphere of suspended culpability that what Masters calls, in the novel's dedication, 'an obstinate ideal of service' can continue to breathe. The writer can slip in this sort of whitewash because the technique of multiple first-person narrative supposedly operates on the principle that all voices are equal. Nevertheless, the Indians get the blame in Savage's version and there is no speaker to oppose his construction. The different versions Victoria must juggle and choose from here – she comments uncertainly, 'Some people said General Dyer's soldiers meant to kill all the civilians; others said the massacre happened because there was a panic' (*Bhowani Junction*, p. 224) – are comparable with the different cultural positions with which she experiments. But her choice, in both cases, is predetermined.

The Anglo-Indian family Masters and his Savage heroes belong to has roots deeper than the Raj itself. Because of this Masters feels free to stand outside and criticize the Raj as an institution. In fact, versions are only relativized in so far as they exonerate the Anglo-Indian hero-figure. For example, although two Eurasian figures are allowed to sit in the narrative driving seat, the historical fact that the Eurasian community was created by England and subsequently left to its fate at independence, becomes a side-issue.[11] Power, in the novel, is quite accurately shown as some vague, unearthly force which operates on the Eurasian community but to which it has no access. Yet the same is claimed of Colonel Savage, the military man who is just obeying orders and who speaks on behalf of those who implement imperial power, not those who devise it. That quality of peripherality in the Savage family and its India, referred to earlier, supports their claims to a better knowledge of India and its needs. Beneath the text which sees the independence agitation and cries, 'what a mess, but we're all in it together', lies a subtext which disclaims on behalf of the Anglo-Indian family, 'it's not *our* fault, you know'.

In tandem with a narrative based on responsibility disclaimed, there exists one based on responsibility displaced. One can see the latter swinging into action when Victoria, accompanying Savage to the Bhowani European Club, is forced to confront the subtle racism she will encounter if she 'turns West' and marries him. Her enthusiasm for the pictures on the wall is accounted an example of her bad taste and the habitual Anglo-Indian conversation about 'Home' leaves her out in the cold. Colonel Savage explains the unintentional nature of much of this treatment and how others attempt to use Victoria as a way to get at him personally. However, none of this is presented as vicious or racial. In fact Molly Dickson's intervention is supposedly for Victoria's own good, as the latter reflects:

> she was really trying to warn me that everything isn't wonderful for Anglo-Indians [Eurasians] in England, not in the upper classes. Then she was reminding me that if we had children one might be as white as you and the other very dark, darker than Mater. (*Bhowani Junction*, p. 293)

Racism is thus displaced from British India, regardless of that society's increasing division along racial lines in the pre-Independence period, on to an ignorant, narrow-minded metropolis. Where are the sly bigots of Scott's Pankot sisterhood?

No, the Savages' India is a land of milk and honey into which a few villainous pinkos have thoughtlessly strayed. Colonel Savage, like his creator, is happiest in an India for which he feels he can still speak. What he says when he is there provides the final evidence of the text's ideological loading. Shortly before the novel's climax, Savage takes Victoria on a weekend leopard hunt in the jungle to discover whether they are truly compatible. Here they will be far away from cultural, political and racial taboos. Savage wants to:

> *delete every frame of reference*, both hers and mine, so that we could examine each other by nothing but what was in us. This valley was to be our Eden. In the jungle there is neither white or brown, black nor khaki. In the jungle the history of men doesn't count; the quality of one man does. (*Bhowani Junction*, p. 331)

Here, in a sense, lies the heart of the novel's project of relativization, 'deleting every frame of reference'. The jungle is to feature as a desocialized, dehistoricized space where some essentialist core of human nature is to be reached. But the purity of this project is very quickly shown as false, when Savage joins the villagers' celebrations after he has, with their assistance, caught the leopard. He enthuses:

> This was my India, not because of the capering or the drunkenness but because these people had no desire to be like me, nor I like them. There had been a place for me round such fires as this

> for three hundred years. The Ranjits and the Surabhais, who were trying to change themselves, didn't light bonfires and dance round them. They read Paine and Burke and spoke in English because the ideas they were trying to express did not exist in their own language. If I and my sort had an idea it was to make Indian wood into better wood, not change it into bakelite. In general, I thought, our great virtue was *not* having an idea. (*Bhowani Junction*, p. 341)

Here the 'frame of reference' Savage claims to be seeking to delete is reimposed, in fact, by the man himself. What he praises is not a vacuous, prelapsarian jungle but a carefully defined, dependence-based set of relationships; the two-way father and son bond he enjoys with his regimental sergeant-major and rifleman underscores the fact and its relation to power. *His* India, that of the hereditary sahib, is here imbued with a primal authenticity to set against the book-learning of Westernized nationalists who are supposedly trying to express ideas that do not exist in their own language and are, by extension, inappropriate to India.

Hence, the white author is empowered to say what is really Indian and what is not. Inevitably, he and his kind end up being more Indian than the nationalists by this set of criteria. What I think one can see here is an example of the tendency towards miscegenation which stamps Masters' work. Just as the Savage men enjoy the favours of Indian women with no consequences, and extract themselves in time to marry the pure white girl at the end,[12] a situation is created in *Bhowani Junction* in which the Englishman as 'father' reserves the right to define and limit relationships within his imperial family: reserves the right always to define the true nature of the Other while simultaneously insulating himself from it *and* claiming to be part of it. At work in *Bhowani Junction* is a desperate, back-pedalling preservation of the English storyteller's linguistic hegemony, which is akin to that intrusion of a 'wide-angle' narrator-controlled perspective into the first-person testimonies, and which exposes the hollow tactic of relativization the novel espouses. Masters makes a feint of giving other voices the chance to speak, whereas in reality he keeps a firm grip on their enunciative possibilities, and on his reader's reaction to them. Despite this, a symptomatic reading of narrative anomalies can reveal the imperious bearing of his rhetorical strategies.

One of the issues arising from the reading of British representations of India I have been offering in this study could be framed as the question, what does the true voice of India sound like in the British book? It is tempting to reply that one does not know, although it seems obvious that it does not sound like the syrupy accents of fawning self-abasement, as some writers would have us believe. Yet the question is worthy of more serious attention since it is germinal for a consideration of how post-colonial writers have broken free of old imperial positions and stereotypes and how they may continue to do so in the future. One could start by looking backwards since my point is not that it is impossible for an English writer to create Indian characters and have them speak, but that they must recognize that the tradition of India as a fictional resource has been compliant, in a highly refined yet traceable way, with imperial power. They must then rewrite accordingly.

As I have tried to indicate, this problem was at its most pressing for anti-imperial writers in the first half of the century – what Allen J. Greenberger calls the 'Era of Doubt' about the imperial project[13] – so that, for Forster, experimentation with the problematics of speaking for India is an inevitable corollary of a radical critique of that still-existent empire's forms of depiction, enunciation and control. However, the issue is still alive for post-independence writers like John Masters because the degree to which they are prepared to asterisk or jettison old tropes, types and forms – from the greasy Babu to the childlike peasant; from the quaint descriptive story to the didactic realist tome – appears to be commensurate with their degree of seriousness about enacting a liberation of India in the text. To take an example, every writer has his or her own way of describing Indians. The problem arises when compressive, synecdochic techniques are repeated with sufficient frequency for certain words and phrases to solidify into axioms of 'easternness'. Not only does this absolve the writer of the responsibility for original thought and descriptions of different Indian characters in different situations, it also adds, directly or indirectly, to the image-store of orientalism since the features chosen for accentuation are nearly always of the traditional kind sufficient to conjure up an Indian from a few strokes of the pen on a blank page. Masters is particularly guilty of this. Seemingly every other Indian we meet in his fiction is described as 'wheat-coloured' and has the curiously ill-defined and essentialist habit of 'spreading his/her hands'. In *To the Coral Strand*, Rodney Savage says of his native employer that he 'stretched out his hands, turning them palm upward in a very Indian gesture, which I was pleased and reassured to see' (*To the Coral Strand*, p. 146) and a cursory re-reading has revealed seven other instances of these instant passwords to Indianness.[14] I am not suggesting that some Indians are not similar to wheat in colouration, nor that they may not occasionally 'spread their hands'. I am saying that the repetition of these descriptions is indicative of a compartmentalizing tendency in which a few words come to signifiy ethnicity *and* moral worth.

One note towards the definition of non-acquisitive, non-essentialist writing may be provided by Hélène Cixous when she suggests, 'The most difficult thing to do is to arrive at the most extreme proximity while guarding against the trap of projection, of identification. The other must remain in all its extreme strangeness within the greatest possible proximity'.[15] It is this spirit which moves in E. M. Forster's drawing of the punkah wallah. Masters' fiction, and that of his Anglo-Indian contemporary M. M. Kaye, is, in contrast, a homogenizing discourse which has as its end the creation of a corporate national identity. Krishna Ram in *The Ravi Lancers* is made to realize that England is a foreign land, which 'had forced its tongue on him' (*Ravi Lancers*, p. 257), and yet this is exactly what Masters' work does when it speaks for Indians, forcing them to conform to an image of India which includes the liberal-minded sahib as an integral component. Masters' consensus, the 'real India' which includes the Anglo-Indian family and those natives who play by its rules, reinforces the experience of domination for the newly unseated white man, despite Masters' assertion that domination was 'almost immaterial' in the colonial relationship (*Road Past Mandalay*, p. 312).

However, Masters' particular version of the Anglo-Indian inheritance does not so much dehumanize Indians as superhumanize the hereditary sahib; in terms of endurance, determination and dedication, Rodney, Peter, Jason and the other early Savages and Savage-types have powers beyond the human and form a breed of imperial supermen. When set against them Indian characters inevitably pale into a subsidiary significance. Native 'sidekicks' are there to show that it is only through love and co-operation that the Raj, and the true India, can survive. Yet we are never allowed to forget that the white man is the real hero; see, for example the end of *The Lotus and the Wind*, when Robin Savage's Gurkha orderly Jagbir, who has shared his adventures, kneels to wipe the dust off his master's boots before they are presented with their medals (*The Lotus and the Wind*, p. 280).[16] Indeed, India is a theatre in which white men, particularly English, but also Portuguese, Dutch and even Russian, can act out the imperial fantasy. They do so by defeating Thuggee, taking part in espionage and counter-espionage, and, in an overworked metaphor for getting to the top, climbing mountains.

All this marks a tendency towards the depopulation of the colonial territory. What is absolutely essential for an understanding of Masters is to realize the coextensive relationship between colonizing and writing. Both depend on dreams of a world emptied of human beings and bonds into which can be projected images from the unconscious, creatures of the imagination, who will obey the directives of their 'author'. Hence the attraction in the beginnings of the colonial encounter to which Masters responds by writing *Coromandel!* set in 1627; 'no maps, no tourist reports, only the smallest commerce and that passing through a score of intermediaries. A time of wonder, when anything could be believed, and was, about the mysterious East' (*Pilgrim Son*, pp. 248–9). I think one can see the results of this in the lurid, 'Gorgeous East' descriptions which dot the novel, particularly the fantastic account of the Tsaparang Monastery where Jason makes sojourn near the end of his quest.

Coromandel itself is an example of the alluring colonial open space: a clean page for the restless Jason Savage to write upon. The thrill produced by the map of the Coromandel coast which Old Voy sells to Jason reminds one of the effect of the blank space on Marlow's map in *Heart of Darkness*, and Stevenson's recollection that *Treasure Island* began with the drawing of a map:[17]

> Jason gazed breathlessly at the map. He could not read, but this map hardly needed reading. There were pictures. There were the blue waves of the sea, and a row of thin trees with feathery tops. There was a big dark-red stain in one corner, and writing everywhere. (*Coromandel!*, p. 22)

The textual introduction to the colonizable space is reinforced in the artifacts he discovers at the Shrewford Pennel manor; two big globes – meant to symbolize Britain's post-Tudor expansionist outlook – and a travel book which is like 'a key to heaven' (*Coromandel!*, pp. 50–1). India, for the humble Jason as for Masters, is a screen for the projection of the Englishman's colonial fantasy, Cixous' strictures notwithstanding. It becomes in Ashis Nandy's terms:

> a projective test; it invites one not only to project onto it one's deepest fantasies, but also to reveal, through such self-projection, the interpreter rather than the interpreted. All interpretations of India are ultimately autobiographical.[18]

Of course, Jason finds his India not quite as blank a space as Crusoe's island – the Dutch and Portuguese are already there – and indeed part of the novel is about Jason's acquisition of a sense of social responsibility. Yet the Savage novels as a sequence stress that this social responsibility is what enables and justifies the eventual role of Jason's descendants. Jason is an archetype in that he is shown as having the twin qualities of imagination and determination, dreaming and action, which allow exploration and conquest. The novel is quite coy about the relation of these qualities to imperial ideology, as can be seen from the fairytale quality of the ending, but a post-colonial reader need not be taken in by the apparent innocence of Jason's abstraction:

> I know that the magic mountain is always the one beyond the one you have climbed, the coast of Coromandel is always over the horizon. If it were not so, magic would be at an end and a man could only dream, or only do, but never both. (*Coromandel!*, p. 298)

Three hundred and fifty years of colonial experience have made us more sceptical.[19]

Coromandel! does share with its central character certain archetypical qualities. It fuses common colonialist motifs such as the *foreign field as a promised land for those thwarted by social custom* in England; a tradition which included, and pandered to, the dreams of the younger sons, those who, because of primogeniture, would not inherit ancestral lands and who felt the need for a surrogate hereditary space. Although Jason does not fall into this category it is made clear that he feels his potential is being frustrated by England's rigid social hierarchy and the example of his considerable and undirected energies marks the novel's intersection with another colonial theme, that of the colony as repository for social misfits and criminals. Jason has killed the local squire's son – though not through any revolutionary propensity but because he was interrupted while making love to the squire's daughter – and finds India an arena where this action has no consequences. He is beyond mundane law and can find other outlets for his transgressive energies.

Yet *Coromandel!* has a curious, elliptical relation to what should be one of its central concerns. In invoking the age of the merchant adventurer, and the early operations of the East India Company, the text encounters commerce, a prime ingredient of imperialism and one which leaves a more bitter taste than Masters' usual exculpatory fricassee of self-fulfilment, duty and service. In *Dreams of Adventure, Deeds of Empire*, Martin Green defines the two main strains of imperial adventure fiction, and defines them in terms of two castes and groups of antecedents: the merchant caste from Defoe, and the aristo-military caste from Sir Walter Scott.[20] Clearly John Masters belongs to the aristo-military branch of this tradition. His fiction is designed to laud the exploits of Anglo-India's military and civil services and need not, elsewhere, dirty its hands with the more squalid motives of commercialism. However, because his theme is the first contact between the Savages and their future 'subjects', and this meeting would historically have to take place in a commercial setting, Masters dutifully sends Jason to Coromandel on an East India Company trading ship. Yet throughout the novel military adventure paradigms, centring on an anachronistic idea of service, wrestle with, and eventually strangle, mercantile patterns.[21] Mark the unaccustomed altruism in Jason's concern for the creation of a (better) functioning economy. He is amazed at the poverty of the local pearl fishers, learns that it is caused by fishing restrictions and poor remuneration imposed by the king, and determines to go and confront him. His altruism is later overtaken by personal ambition when he dreams of riches and a post as the king's chief minister (*Coromandel!*, pp. 127, 130, 154), but after that the text focuses firmly on the hero's voyage of self-discovery, from which he finally emerges a chastened and better man and one with suitable qualities to found a ruling dynasty. Somewhere along the narrative – one can possibly date it from the departure of the English traders – the story of the bartering white men with their calico and rum has been subsumed under that of the heroic empire builder in the making. Masters' treatment of Jason is at odds with historical veracity, but is necessary in order to incorporate the hero into the service ethic which motivates the other Savages. Without wishing to be prescriptive, a story around the beginnings of imperial commercialism would need to engage with displacement and exploitation, but *Coromandel!* evades this and recasts the moment of inception for mercantile adventurism in India. Although he must learn other things about himself Jason knows in his bones that he must be good to Indians. There is never any suggestion that he will begin organizing them into coolie gangs and sending the profits from their labour home to England.

Writing here is not only a reinvention of the first colonial encounter, but also an extended act of imaginative recolonization, or of staying on, since Masters writes after independence. (In the same way, Colonel Rodney Savage attempts to stay on in *To the Coral Strand*.) As such it involves a mythologizing of the imperial enterprise. It has no interest, *per se*, in attempting any kind of cultural relativism. Indeed, any view which decentres British authority is alien to this programme. To enlist Nandy's assistance once again, Masters and his characters have no conception of the British in India 'as a subculture meaningful in itself, and important though not all important, in the Indian context'.[22] This is because what might be termed the Kiplingesque view, which Masters shares, unashamedly luxuriates in its relation to power. It sees the British in India as a defining presence without which India the nation would not exist. It is Masters' avowed belief that the British created modern India out of a collection of disparate and hostile states and gave them unity and stability. In *Road Past Mandalay* he comments on the Indian troops passing into recaptured Mandalay:

> Twenty races, a dozen religions, a score of languages passed in those trucks and tanks. When my great-great-grandfather first went to India there had been as many nations; now there was one – India; and he and I and a few thousand others, over two and a half centuries, sometimes with intent, sometimes unwittingly, sometimes in miraculous sympathy, sometimes in brutal folly, had made it. (*Road Past Mandalay*, p. 312)

Writing as staying on works both to make and preserve the English sahib as India's hero, and simultaneously to ensure that his political and moral legacy is seen to live on in the new India. This is how England becomes a defining presence in India. Understanding this helps to explain the contradictory aspect of this type of Anglo-Indian discourse: one can cover all eventualities by saying that the old, rural India is the real India, while in the same breath saying that it was England which created the modern Indian nation.

As has been demonstrated the true India and the true Indian are decided in terms of their sympathy towards Britain. Although Masters disclaims the importance of domination, it is beyond the scope of his social imagination to accept the British in India as only a blip on the continuum of Indian life. Even when he comes closest to doing so the urge to mythologize becomes overpowering. For example, there are explicit and repeated comparisons between the British empire and the legacy of Alexander the Great in *The Lotus and the Wind*, as Robin Savage chases the Russian agents through central Asia:

> Here Alexander had stood and made his final decision – to go on or to go back. Bombastic petty conquerors, passing this way, had carved their fame in the rocks and were forgotten. He had written nothing, and had retreated, but was remembered. (*The Lotus and the Wind*, p. 179)

There is an elegiac quality in Masters' writing here. It seems apparent that part of his post-independence perspective in this novel consists of the idea that just as Alexander's empire passed away so too will the British and Russian models – the novel was published in 1953 – but that what is important is having once been here and shaped the land and its people, having created one's own legend.[23] Given such a reading, even the spymaster Hayling's insight into Robin's misanthropic nature and its uses in the Great Game has hidden ideological assumptions sewn in. He says:

> You have a feeling, an affinity, for emptiness ... The part of Asia where the solution to our problem lies consists of emptiness. Therefore I feel that the intrusion of *the world* there, however carefully concealed, will be more apparent to you than to others. Any Russian plan will involve the intrusion of the world. The desert and the mountains will look different, feel different – to you, not to me. (*The Lotus and the Wind*, p. 152)

Robin is the man who knows the colonial space, as the other Savages know its people. He has an eye for space *as* space and will know if it has been intruded upon by 'the world' – a euphemism for Russia. But, of course, he is already there himself. The false naivety one sees here bears comparison with the desocialized jungle idyll of *Bhowani Junction*. Neither is ideologically possible. The energizing myth of the colonial blank space is sheer wishful thinking in a world undergoing what Fenner Brockway called the 'Colonial Revolution', conducted by the very people who are not supposed to populate blank spaces such as this.[24] Thus, *The Lotus and the Wind* uses its post-independence perspective to immortalize the British in India in spite of the empire's demise. A functioning Anglo-Indian mythology is clearly evident in the bizarre yet seriously intended descriptions of Gurkhas' eyes glowing red in battle and their ability to sprint at full speed down vertical slopes (*The Lotus and the Wind*, pp. 44 and 252).

Indeed, what Masters is concerned to create in *Coromandel!*, *The Lotus and the Wind* and his other Indian novels, is mythopoeic rather than historical fiction which will operate to resolve ideological contradictions at work in society – such as the mercantile/aristo-military traditions which contend for the soul of British imperialism – in the way suggested by Lévi-Strauss' reading of myth.[25] So much of Masters' first memoir, *Bugles and a Tiger*, is involved in mythologizing imperial relationships and encounters. A concern for posterity and that stories, legends and myths should be seen to grow around the Anglo-Indian sahib is, in fact, directly articulated in *To the Coral Strand* when Rodney joins the villagers in an orgy at a Pattan temple; '*It was said afterwards* that the whole village of Pattan joined in the orgy on the old temple platform. This is not true ...' (*To the Coral Strand*, p. 117). The phrase I have italicized shows how the Englishman desires that folklore should preserve his image and confirm him not just as one of them, but as a defining presence and, as elsewhere in this novel, a Solomon figure, a Gora Raja (Pale Face King).

Such mythologizing preserves a sense of what Paul Scott describes as 'unfinished business' about the British in India. Yet whereas Scott uses the phrase to indicate Britain's hurried and regretful departure, Masters' refusal to end the imperial encounter means that somewhere, in the imagination and on the page, the British are still paternally lording it over their Indian vassals.

Make no mistake, John Masters writes adventure stories of tremendous pace and energy which carry the reader along to an invariably thunderous climax. However, his perspective and preoccupations lead him towards an unquestioning replication of imperial narrative forms in a post-imperial world. Angus Wilson has commented that Masters' style is 'tender, cynical or sensual, seldom sensitive, ironic or passionate'.[26] I would agree and add that irony is not an option for Masters since it would undermine the service ethic on which his writing and family history are predicated. If he introduced an undercutting irony he would be at the very least devaluing his family legacy and history as received. For the same reason he presents action shorn of its relation to hegemony; indeed by incorporating his Britons into a progressive consensus each time, the nature of that hegemony is deliberately obscured. The exposure of such hegemony, its constituent narrative conventions and ideological assumptions, is the explicit project of J. G. Farrell's contrasting Mutiny novel, *The Siege of Krishnapur*, in which the deployment of irony is instrumental in the radical disruption of self-serving and complacent imperial mindsets. In a dynamic way J. G. Farrell and Paul Scott represent the possibilities of a British narrative of India which, while using existing genres, situations and types, so transforms and qualifies them that the end result is an undermining of would-be dominant discourses.

Notes

1. There are nine novels with an Indian setting, discussing Indian themes: *Nightrunners of Bengal* (1951); *The Deceivers* (1952); *The Lotus and the Wind* (1953); *Bhowani Junction* (1954); *Coromandel!* (1955); *Far, Far the Mountain Peak* (1957); *The Venus of Konpara* (1960); *To the Coral Strand* (1962) and *The Ravi Lancers* (1972). In addition Masters wrote three autobiographical volumes, *Bugles and a Tiger* (1956), *The Road Past Mandalay* (1961) and *Pilgrim Son* (1971) which detail Indian experiences and reflections.
2. Avtar Singh Bhullar remarks that Masters 'was desperately concerned with transmitting the reality' of India, Avtar Singh Bhullar, *India: Myth and Reality*, p. 110.
3. This uncertainty is characteristic of several British representations of the imperial past in the immediate post-independence era. Another example occurs in the medium of film, in Marcel Hellman's *North West Frontier* (Rank Film Distributors, 1959). In this picture Kenneth More's traditional English hero, the army officer keeping order between quarrelsome natives, is placed on a train with a Muslim nationalist reporter, played by Herbert Lom, during intercommunal disturbances in 1905. Lom's character presents a coherent and well-argued case against the British presence in India, to which More can only reply by keeping a stiff upper lip, showing a jolly countenance and quoting Kipling. The film can only resolve the ideological contradiction embodied in these two strong characters by eventually reducing the nationalist to a sweating, treacherous oriental stereotype – he tries to murder More's young Hindu charge and turns a Gatling gun on his fellow passengers – before having him shot from the roof of the train during a struggle with the hero. As I will try to show, the technique of pushing the nationalist voice off the imperial train is a particular favourite of Masters too.
4. Masters seems to have something of an obsession with this fantasy, but does not always use it judiciously. For example, one can compare Robin's disguise as an Afghan horse trader in *The Lotus and the Wind* with Kipling's Mahbub Ali in that other Great Game novel, *Kim*. An act of much deeper penetration into the unsupervised East is allowed by the English protagonist *actually being* the Afghan horse trader, rather than just dealing with him. Robin is *engagé* in a way that Kim is not. Conversely, the whole dimension of cultural ambivalence offered by Kim's attachment to the Lama is absent here. Alongside it, Robin's misanthropic wanderlust is a poor substitute. While Kim is pulled in the conflicting directions of different loyalties, Robin will do his bit for the empire, get the DSO (Distinguished Service Order) and *only then* disappear on his personal quest.

5. The Dewan of Kishanpur is described as exuding an air 'alternatively cringing and bullying, and both attitudes façades for something deeper' (*Nightrunners of Bengal*, p. 44). He is a caricatured oriental villain – he even loses an eye and has to wear an eye patch – who exclaims, 'I want the killing to begin. My fingers itch' (*Nightrunners of Bengal*, p. 137).
6. John Clay, *John Masters: A Regimented Life*, p. 166.
7. Masters has also contracted from Kipling the habit of unconcernedly transferring his thoughts, opinions and even his words into the mouths of his Indian characters. Thus, in *Bugles and a Tiger*, he rejoices, 'We were none of us quite strangers, nor ever would be', in India. So much for Sumitra's independence!
8. David Rubin, *After the Raj: British Novels of India since 1947*, p. 32.
9. Bhullar, *India: Myth and Reality*, p. 133.
10. Gerard Genette, *Narrative Discourse*, p. 186.
11. See Frank Anthony, *Britain's Betrayal in India: The Story of the Anglo-Indian Community*, p. ii.
12. See the denouements of *Nightrunners of Bengal*, *The Deceivers*, *Coromandel!* and *To the Coral Strand* for prime examples. See also; Rubin, *After the Raj*, pp. 49–50.
13. Allen J. Greenberger, *The British Image of India: A Study in the Literature of Imperialism 1880–1960*. Greenberger shows a good understanding of the relationship between literature, preconception and policy in imperial affairs. However, his definition of the three periods – Era of Confidence 1880–1910; Era of Doubt 1910–1935; Era of Melancholy 1935–1960 – is over-schematic and does not take into account those cracks in the wall of imperial narrative which, I have tried to show, were a feature of the first period and that suggest something other than 'the image of a confident and secure empire' (p. 5).
14. Adam Khan, Krishna Ram, Mohan Singh and Sumitra are all described as wheat-coloured (*Far, Far the Mountain Peak*, p. 11; *The Ravi Lancers*, p. 16; *The Venus of Konpara*, p. 14; and *To the Coral Strand*, p. 36), while Krishna, Rukmini and Victoria all display the habit of spreading their hands (*The Ravi Lancers*, p. 34; *The Venus of Konpara*, p. 52; *Bhowani Junction*, p. 133). There are other examples but these will surely suffice.
15. Hélène Cixous, 'Extreme Fidelity', in Susan Sellers (ed.), *Writing Differences: Readings from the Seminar of Hélène Cixous*, p. 29. Although this volume is concerned chiefly with gender differences, many of its prognoses have a fruitful application to problems of cultural difference too.
16. Edward Thompson offers an amusing vignette of this phenomenon when he describes how Indians have been treated as:

   the 'trusty servants' of countless thrilling boys' stories. When all

> their compatriots have turned into 'swarthy devils' these splendid fellows have stopped bullets and knife-thrusts meant for their masters and have died murmuring, 'It all right, sahib. I happy – dying for master.' And the sahibs, pausing ere they pass on to renewed slaughter of the treacherous villains in front of them, wipe away a manly tear and say, 'Poor Gopal! He was a good fellow, though he did worship false gods.' (Thompson, *Other Side of the Medal*, pp. 17–18)

And this is almost exactly what does happen in *The Deceivers* when Hussein, who has assisted William Savage in his pursuit of the Thugs, saves the Englishman by setting the Deceivers' lair on fire. The helpful native is expendable, dying in the flames with the chuprassi's (doorkeeper's) cry to his master on his lips, 'Ane walla hun' – I am coming!). The last word on him comes in an almost parodic exchange between William and his wife, Mary. On learning of Hussein's fate, Mary remarks to her husband:

> 'Oh, darling! I think he died happy though ... You must tell me more about him later ...'
>
> 'He wanted to be a chuprassi and was faithful.
>
> 'That's it. William, have you got anything we can eat? My insides are rumbling.' (*The Deceivers*, p. 232)

17. Green, *Dreams of Adventure, Deeds of Empire*, p. 228. Green also observes; 'geography became a sort of heraldry of imperialism – every mountain and river evokes the excitement of conquest and possession' (p. 270).
18. Nandy, *The Intimate Enemy*, p. 79.
19. See, for example, Julian Evans' review of *The Oxford Book of Exploration*, edited by Robin Hanbury-Tenison, in *The Guardian*, 2 November 1993. Evans points out the allure of exploration which can trap even the most aware of editors into ideologically naive compilations.
20. Green, *Dreams of Adventure, Deeds of Empire*, p. 15ff.
21. Brian Gardner comments of Sir Thomas Roe, a successful East India Company Ambassador to the Count of Jahangir at Agra in the early seventeenth century:

> unlike those who came much later, his interests were solely to serve the East India Company and, through it, his country; in that he was typical of the coming regime of the East India Company; the notion of service to India and Indians was to come much later. (Brian Gardner, *The East India Company*, pp. 37–8)

22. Nandy, *The Intimate Enemy*, p. 75.
23. Speaking of Fourier's *Description de l'Egypte*, Edward Said reveals the cumulative effect of narrative tactics like this:

> The resonances of the great names ... [Pompey, Caesar, Mark Antony and Augustus] the normalizing of foreign conquest within the cultural orbit of European existence – all this transmutes conquest

> from an event into a process that is much longer, slower and more acceptable to the European sensibility enfolded within its own cultural super-structure. (Edward W. Said, 'Intellectuals in the Post-Colonial World', pp. 44–64)

24. Fenner Brockway, *The Colonial Revolution*.
25. Claude Lévi-Strauss, 'The Structural Study of Myth', *Structural Anthropology*.

    George Woodcock comments:

    > Once an era is past one can treat it as myth or as history. Late English writers about the Raj do both. Except for *Bhowani Junction*, Masters embellishes the myth, while Scott's *Raj Quartet*, demonstrating the irrational working of human feelings within a rigid social framework, comes as near to history as fiction can approach. (Woodcock, 'The Sometime Sahibs: Two Post-Independence British Novelists of India', pp. 48–9)

26. Angus Wilson, Review of *Bhowani Junction*, in *The Observer*, 23 May 1954.

IV The Burden of Representation: Counter-Discourse through Cultural Texts in J. G. Farrell's *The Siege of Krishnapur*

> The history of the novel is the history of forms rejected and modified, by parody, manifesto, neglect, as absurd. Nowhere else, perhaps, are we so conscious of the dissidence between inherited forms and our own reality. (Frank Kermode, *The Sense of an Ending*)

> 'You have a name for everything ... but a name does not give knowledge. Beyond thinking and imagination, there are subtle bodies which remain forever outside mortal sense. Our Vedas said that, before your microscope and telescopes. No one will ever see the world as it really is, even the greatest *guru*.' (Francis Yeats-Brown, *Bengal Lancer*)

After the Indian Mutiny of 1857, Alfred, Lord Tennyson joined the line of literary and artistic luminaries queuing to commemorate the heroic deeds of the British. He did so in a poem called 'The Defence of Lucknow' which contained the following encomium:

> Banner of England, not for a season, O banner of Britain, has thou
> Floated in conquering battle or flapt to the battle-cry!
> Never with mightier glory than when we had reared thee on high
> Flying at top of the roofs in the ghastly siege of Lucknow –
> Shot through the staff or the halyard, but ever we raised thee anew,
> And ever upon the topmost roof our banner of England flew.
> ...
> Handful of men as we were, we were English in heart and in limb,
> Strong with the strength of the race to command, to obey, to endure,
> Each of us fought as if hope for the garrison hung but on him;
> Still – could we watch at all points? we were every day fewer and fewer.

> There was a whisper among us, but only a whisper that past:
> 'Children and wives – if the tigers leap into the fold unawares –
> Every man die at his post – and the foe may outlive us at last –
> Better to fall by the hands that they love, than to fall into theirs!'
> ...
> And ever upon the topmost roof our banner of England blew.[1]

J. G. Farrell's fifth novel, *The Siege of Krishnapur* (1973) offers a wry, twentieth-century take on this spirit of melodrama doused with sentiment, and on Victorian confidence and faith in progress more generally. In doing so it explores notions of civilization and history in a specifically post-colonial context. What distinguishes Farrell's work from that of elegists of empire such as John Masters and M. M. Kaye is, in part, that he recognizes the basis of imperial modes of self-perception in cultural forms and that access to, and rethinking of, a past which still bears on the present can best be achieved through an ironic reworking of such cultural forms. In his novel he attempts not only cultural retrieval by using the popular nineteenth-century genre of imperial adventure fiction, but also its subversion through a technique of ironic distancing, pastiche and the mock-heroic. Farrell foregrounds issues of representation and those fantasies of power through surveillance seen in the work of writers such as Rudyard Kipling and John Masters, by inverting the gaze and making the colonizer suddenly the object of the 'othering' view of the natives who come to watch the progress of the siege from a nearby hillside. In fact, I wish to argue, the text is structured around set-piece scenes illustrating the slippery nature of the power of the gaze and of representation. From the Englishman, Fleury, in the Indian prince's photographer's chair and the relieving General's fantasy of immortality through painting, to the Collector's feverish supervision of the residency defences through his telescope, the text offers a sustained critique of those validated national archives, the exhibition, the painting, the photograph and the novel. Completing its analysis of the ideology of modes of representation, *Siege* adopts a twentieth-century, filmic structure to explore the blind-spots, the limitations on perspective imposed by colonial discourse's framing, editing and point-of-view. In this book, Farrell invokes an ironic distance in time between a contemporary implied reader and the society of the nineteenth century. The technique of generic bricolage produces an effect of defamiliarization through the juxtaposition of comedy and pathos. In doing so it draws attention to the text *as* text, and to the textual apprehension of 'history' in a way that is clearly postmodern.

Thomas Richards has described the mid-nineteenth century as the era of spectacle in which, 'a rhetorical mode of amplification and excess ... came to pervade and structure public and private life ...'.[2] The 1851 Great Exhibition was a nodal event in this process. Its exhibits formed part of the mid-Victorian faith in power-through-knowledge, as did wider strategies of representation and domestication such as travel writing, painting and imperial adventure fiction. Yet only six years later the Indian Mutiny, or First Sepoy War, catastrophically exposed the complacency at the heart of British power in India. It is the contradiction between confidence in Western progress, materialism and surveillance, and the shattering privations of a siege during the Mutiny which is played out in Farrell's text. In his character, Mr Hopkins the Collector, Farrell embodies the values of confidence in European notions of superiority expressed by the Exhibition.

The cultural confidence which built both the Crystal Palace and the British empire was in a large measure based on a faith in the ability of educated men to know, frame, shape and represent the world they perceived about them. Indeed, it is not too much to claim that this confidence found its literary manifestation in realism. One can see the realist novel, with its post-Newtonian ideology of linear time and its dutiful observation of the Aristotelian conventions of beginning, middle and end – ideally suited to express doctrines of homogeneity – as having characteristics reflective of the modes of perception of the imperial age. Bernard Bergonzi perhaps unwittingly uses a significant metaphor for our purposes in describing the development of the realist novel 'as the successive opening up of tracts of unexplored territory'.[3] When writing a novel set in the age of empire, Farrell utilized part of this convention: the relaxed, orderly tones of the Victorian omniscient narrator. (Indeed, the subtlety of his use of this voice has seduced several critics into missing the corrosive irony with which it is laced.) The text subverts and manipulates realistic conventions in order to depict, in a striking and original way, the interaction of individuals and the larger forces of history. For Farrell history is the logic of practices *and* the lived experience of individuals. Moreover, the formal disruption of the text reflects the fragmentation and disruption of the imperial outlook of certain of the central characters.

At the outset it may be worthwhile contextualizing Farrell's narrative strategies by charting briefly the already well-known literary climate of the time of writing. The 1960s saw a backlash against the resurgent use of unproblematic realism, which had been a feature of British novels during the 1950s and which has been described in Rubin Rabinowitz's tellingly entitled book, *The Reaction against Experiment in the English Novel: 1950–1960*. 'Pure' realism was discarded by many writers in Europe and America as well as Britain, and alternatives ranged from the *'nouveau roman'* of Alain Robbe-Grillet – with its rejection of traditional concepts of plot, character and subjectivity – to the less belligerent options of multiple voices and blank parody favoured by previously realist-orientated writers such as Angus Wilson. Other possibilities included: the non-fiction novel championed by Truman Capote and Norman Mailer; B. S. Johnson's varied and innovative experiments aimed at disrupting the illusion of reality; and powerfully imaginative writing of the kind practised by Thomas Pynchon, John Barth and Gunther Grass. Indeed, just the names and devices which have since been gathered into the pantheon of postmodernism.[4] Furthermore, the decline of realism leads to an inevitable problematization of the age-old relationship between realism and history. Indeed, it had been for many years axiomatic that the successful literary depiction of history depended on the scrupulous use of realism. This was an assumption which J. G. Farrell, along with John Fowles, David Caute, John Berger and others, challenged in the 1960s and 1970s. The common assumptions which realism reflects – and that, to a large degree, it creates – are explored by Farrell and Fowles in their 'historical novels', works which at the same time attempt something more dynamic than straightforward realism allows.

Yet Farrell's alternative to ordinary realism is radically different from those of his contemporaries. Using a basis in realism for his three novels of British imperial crisis (*Troubles* (1970), *The Siege of Krishnapur* (1973) and *The Singapore Grip* (1978)), he then subverts the realist mode inserting other literary genres and styles of writing including fairytale, Gothicism, romance, farce and parodies of the tones of writers from the literary canon such as Austen, Dickens, Matthew Arnold and Stendhal.[5] Farrell innovates by cramming numerous styles into a single novel to produce an atmosphere of 'larger-than-life' surrealism and fantasticality caused by their rapid and subtle interchange, often in the form of free indirect speech. Farrell deals with the burden of preconstructed imperialism and characters can only come to terms with the apocalyptic events that engulf them by shedding the received opinions of empire. What runs through the three books is the sense of an imperial narrative, fostered and sustained by the kinds of fiction Farrell uses and parodies, told so often that no one can tell any longer if it is true. Certainly, the characters do not recognize it breaking down before events fully overtake them.

In rethinking the possibilities of the novel of history, Farrell follows in the footsteps of Forster and Conrad – whose distinctive styles proved so attractive to his magpie instincts – and anticipates the efforts of writers such as Graham Swift, Peter Ackroyd and Salman Rushdie to transcend realism when dealing with historical subjects, in a manner which has become known as 'historiographical metafiction'. However, one is unlikely to find Farrell mentioned in any of the current lists of postmodern practitioners: this despite the fact that his texts conform to Patricia Waugh's definition of metafiction as, 'fictional writing which self-consciously and systematically draws attention to its status as an artefact in order to pose questions about the relationship between fiction and reality', and which 'offers both innovation *and* familiarity through the individual reworking and undermining of familiar conventions'.[6] Such definitions clearly and accurately describe the tendency of much fiction in the second half of the twentieth century – including Farrell's – to challenge assumptions about the relationship between art, reality and notions of truth. Yet, in some respects, the very nature of the topic seems to have led to a proscriptive narrowing of focus which excludes a writer who works in what some would see as a parochial tradition, to undermine realism from within. Instead, critical treatises often privilege Continental European or American writing of the 1960s and 1970s over its British counterpart as containing purer or more 'radical' examples of metafiction – examples which have a particularly overt and demonstrable relationship to philosophical developments after structuralism which posit a closed system of merely self-referential signification. Indeed, on surveying much of the available critical literature on metafiction, an uncharitable reader might conclude that subtlety has never figured highly in the list of postmodernist beatitudes: the result being the canonisation of authors who – their theoretically declared 'deaths' notwithstanding – leap in and out of their own texts with alacrity, button-holing their readers along the way with reflections on everything from their visits to the laundry to the contingent status of ontological knowledge and the difficulties of writing the novel itself. And innovation is least likely to appear in the cobwebbed corner occupied by colonial fiction, with its tradition of empiricism and its often pragmatic concern with politics of a particularly intractable variety.[7] This is unfortunate since *The Siege of Krishnapur* could be offered as a pre-eminent example of the kind of fiction which foregrounds the process of framing in the construction of an image of reality, and perfectly illustrates Waugh's dictum that, 'Parody of an earlier literary norm or mode unavoidably lays bare the relations of that norm to its original historical context, through its defamiliarizing contextualization within an historical present whose literary and social norms have shifted'.[8]

It is worth dwelling on such ideas because in their interstices they carry the question of politics. To claim that history is only accessible in textual form is one thing, what is more important is to examine the relation of such strategies as those employed in *Siege* to the ideologies underpinning the parodied form at its original moment. In short, how do such forms inscribe and carry the dominant discourse, and how does Farrell's intervention change this? To examine this issue I propose to draw on the notion of counter-discourse as proposed by Richard Terdiman in his book *Discourse/Counter-Discourse*, and, in the remainder of the chapter, to show how Farrell litters *Siege* with moments of counter-discursive implosion.

If we define discourse as a set of socially situated speech acts it will be seen that Farrell is writing counter-discursively about liberal views of empire at the level of content, exposing contradictions and undermining the ideological assumptions of characters, but also as a strategy from within the very vehicles of that discourse: realism, omniscience, the long view etc. Terdiman's study of counter-discursive resistance in nineteenth-century French bourgeois writing begins from a Bakhtinian understanding of linguistic functions in which language presupposes difference and no statement is ever a monologue, free from the gravitational pull of contradictory utterances. Just as Bakhtin reveals the inherently dialogic quality of the sign at a micro-linguistic level, so for Terdiman, competing discourses reproduce at the macro-level – the level of socio-political practice – the competitive stress inherent in the sign.[9] Within a Gramscian framework the nineteenth century witnessed a shift from an authoritarian social system which directly suppressed dissidence, to a more recognizably modern mode of civil society which could countenance contestatory social fragments as part of a capitalist discourse internalizing notions of competition and 'the market': a shift from 'rule' to 'hegemony'.[10] Thus, a space opened up for multivalent strategies of dissent. Dominant discourses in modern society are all-pervasive and 'taken as read', as common sense. Counter-discourses operate by exposing the weaknesses and internal contradictions of dominant discourses, such as bourgeois liberalism. In Terdiman's model they:

> sought to disturb the easy reproduction and reception of dominant discourse. They wanted to breach its self-evidence, to

> make it appear curious, puzzling ... for the dominant discourse within a liberal formation functions smoothly only as long as its means of functioning go unnoticed.

And the most characteristic strategy of counter-discourse is irony. Irony is the repository of difference which functions to insinuate an alternative view and thereby subvert the apparently seamless quality of the view of the dominant power.[11]

The Siege of Krishnapur is a text which also draws attention to the ideological loading of the structures and ways of representing history which it parodies. Another literary mode introduced into the text, and which provides a particularly persistent strand as battles rage, is the mock-heroic. If mock-realism is the distinctive characteristic of the trilogy as a whole, the parody of the heroic is particularly strong in *Siege*. From the sometimes farcical description of battles between mutinous sepoys and desperate, yet often ludicrously posturing, defenders of the residency, to the reflections of the British upon how they will look in commemorative art, the heroic is ironized and conventional ideas of heroism called into question.[12] For example, the young romantic hero Fleury exchanges his threadbare garments for a green suit cut from the baize of a billiard table, which makes him resemble that archetypical English hero Robin Hood, but which also has the unfortunate consequence of rendering him a highly visible and popular target for sepoy snipers; at one of the many funerals Fleury struggles to convince himself that the heroic stature of the dead defender George Cutter is not 'a tiny bit reduced' by his unfortunate middle name, Foxlett; and, at the height of a sepoy attack, the fundamentalist Padre – convinced that the siege is a judgement from God – relentlessly pursues the deist free-thinker Fleury with anti-evolutionary arguments for supreme design. The climax is reached in an uproarious scene in Chapter 30, where Fleury fights a huge and seemingly indestructible sepoy:

> In desperation Fleury leapt for the chandelier, with the intention of swinging on it and kicking the sepoy in the face. But the chandelier declined to bear his weight and instead of swinging, he merely sat down heavily on the floor in a hail of diamonds and plaster. But as the sepoy lunged forward to put an end to the struggle he stumbled, blinded by the dust and plaster from the ceiling, and fetched up choking on the floor beside Fleury ... His opponent was clumsily getting to his feet as Fleury snatched a violin from a rack of worm-eaten instruments ... snapped it over

> his knee and leapt on to the sepoy's back, at the same time whipping the violin strings tightly round the sepoy's neck and dragging on them like reins. (*Siege*, p. 293)

There is certainly an element of 'The Boy's Own Paper' in all this; here is another form of the adventure story for Farrell to travesty. However, rather than the purpose of reinforcing idealized forms of heroic behaviour and encouraging feats of emulation, Farrell imbues his narrative with quite other meanings, implied through the modern, ironic authorial voice and the overblown nature of such encounters. He is writing 'after' imperial adventure novelists such as G. A. Henty in both the sequential and imitative meanings of that preposition.

This is all part of the text's deconstruction of notions of cultural superiority often articulated in these cultural forms. Judged in its own terms, those of colonial discourse, civilization should be 'a beneficial disease'. However, in its haughty imperial incarnation it comes to be described as a contagion isolated by fire: the description referring to the residency and its British inhabitants and the fires that blaze all around them. European civilization is personified by the giant marble busts of Plato and Socrates that gaze implacably over the hostile plain, and which provide cover for Harry Dunstaple's cannon on the ramparts. Their final appearance, 'terribly pocked by round shot and musket-fire' (*Siege*, p. 308), reveals the inability of Western systems of thought to contain and 'speak for' the East. With rationalism and positivism tangibly undermined their only remaining value is military, just as the Collector comes to judge the utility of the great men of letters, electro-metal effigies of whom dot the residency, less by their ideas than by the ballistic properties of their heads.

With his collection of artefacts from the Great Exhibition, the Collector begins the novel as the embodiment of that part of Victorianism which sought to exploit the potential offered by cultural and technological innovation to bring Western civilization to the 'uncivilized' East. The wealth engendered by capitalism (and colonialism of course) should also be used to this end. He says, 'It's not simply to acquire wealth, but to acquire through wealth, that superior way of life which we loosely term civilization and which includes so many things ... both spiritual and practical' (*Siege*, p. 50). And later, 'The foundations on which the new men will build their lives are Faith, Science, Respectability, Geology, Mechanical Invention, Ventilation and Rotation of Crops' (*Siege*, p. 80). His confidence in the possibilities for 'advancement' echoes that of the

Prince Consort who likewise found evidence in the Great Exhibition of, 'a period of most wonderful transition, which tends rapidly to accomplish that great end to which indeed all history points – the realisation of the unity of mankind'. One might add that this 'unity of mankind' might very well come to mean unity under the yoke of the British empire; as Walter Houghton remarks, pride in man's achievements rapidly came to be replaced by pride in *English*-man's achievements.[13] Moreover, the unity of mankind is in any case directly antithetical to the legitimizing ethos of colonialism which depends on what is ultimately a Manichean intellectual framework positing the irredeemable 'otherness' of the colonized. Add to this the onset of Darwinian ideas about natural selection, rehearsed in embryonic form by Fleury and the Padre, and we have the ingredients for the opium agent, Mr Rayne's dehumanization of his servants in the text, whom he christens Ant, Ram and Monkey.

Inversion of generic norms and expectations is a key part of Farrell's counter-discursive strategy. As the siege takes its toll the previously clearcut racial divide is increasingly problematized. As personal hygiene becomes difficult to maintain Louise Dunstaple finds that a spot has appeared on her forehead, recalling of course the Hindu caste mark. Later she makes a poultice for the boils that have appeared on her head which, at first sight, resembles a turban. Still later both the Collector and the previously voluptuous but now sadly deflated Lucy Hughes squat or sit cross-legged in the native fashion. The text's counter-discursive tactic operates through the simultaneous invocation and inversion of racist stereotypes about contamination and decorum. The horrified General who arrives to relieve the siege reflects that the heroes of Krishnapur are 'a pretty rum lot': 'he had never seen Englishmen get themselves into such a state before; they looked like untouchables' (*Siege*, p. 309).

As the siege wears on the British become exhibits in a Great Exhibition not of their own devising when they notice that their frantic defence has attracted a crowd of native on-lookers who observe proceedings from a slope above the melon beds using telescopes, opera glasses and carrying their own picnic hampers. The British find themselves in the presence of a complex alternative culture ironically now utilising paraphernalia previously the preserve of Western civilization to effect an inversion of normal power relations. That Indians should always be under the supervisory, disciplinary gaze of the British is something of a prerequisite to successful imperial governance. The colonial subject is observed as part of the British will-to-know which facilitates rule. Here that observation is reversed. (Indeed, there is a complex network of two-way gazes at work in the text: between British and Indian; between the Collector, who has to maintain an appearance of confidence both for the natives and for the community which looks to him to lead and 'oversee' and that community; and between the Collector as Victorian father, casting a paternal eye over his dutiful daughters, and those daughters themselves who watch their father's peripatetic supervision of the defences through the telescope in his bedroom.)

Another counter-discursively performative theme is that of the unreliability of vision, of perspectival illusion. There are many references to the importance of perspective and the potential for misrecognition, beginning with the faintly Forsterian opening, where the inexperienced modern-day visitor to Krishnapur, on seeing 'what appears to be a town in the heat distorted distance', 'is likely to think he has reached the end of his journey a few miles sooner than he expected' (*Siege*, p. 9). On meeting the Maharajah's son Hari, Fleury and Harry Dunstaple are disconcerted by the prince's mimed advance, designed as a compromise between his welcoming nature and the dignity required by royal protocol which has the effect of utterly destroying perspective (*Siege*, p. 71). Even the reader is suddenly disorientated when, after a detailed description of this royal visit at the beginning of Chapter 7, the narrator – pulling up and away to an almost satellitic range – invites us to, 'Picture a map of India as big as a tennis court with two or three hedgehogs crawling over it ...' (*Siege*, p. 91) as an aid to visualizing the summer dust storms.

Collections such as that assembled in 1851 also form part of the colonial will-to-power/knowledge. One might say that, in true imperial style, the Victorians were keen to collect as many things as possible in order to extend their domain of knowledge. These collections were not only scientific and artistic but, in terms of colonized peoples, anthropological too, contributing to what Thomas Richards has called 'the imperial archive'.[14] Indices of nigrescence, cephalic measurements and facial angles are aspects of a colonial strategy of power-through-knowledge which, in Edward Said's words, 'made it possible to create not only an orderly discipline of study but a set of institutions, a latent vocabulary ... a subject matter and subject races'.[15] This 'latent vocabulary' was institutionalized in the mid-nineteenth century when evolutionary theory appeared to reinforce existing Linnean racial classifications and hierarchies, with the Caucasian at the top and the Negro at the bottom of a biologically determined great chain.

The will-to-know was also manifest in the use of photography in the nineteenth century to supplement disciplinary regimes by producing visual reproductions to augment written documentation. John Tagg has chronicled the development of such uses of photography in *The Burden of Representation*. He acknowledges the application of photography to colonial policy when describing how it functions in an economy of power:

> In the nineteenth century ... we are dealing with the instrumental deployment of photography in privileged administrative practices and the professionalised discourses of new social sciences ... In terms of such discourses ... colonized people ... were constituted as the passive ... objects of knowledge. Subjected to a scrutinizing gaze, forced to emit signs, yet cut off from command of meaning, such groups were represented as, and wishfully rendered, incapable of speaking, acting or organizing for themselves.[16]

Anthropology in India allowed the Victorians to indulge their highly developed taxonomical predilections. A number of methods of data collection were favoured before the spread of photography. For instance, osteological material and skulls were used in an attempt to construct a 'history' of the development of distinct human races. The significance of such ventures for our purposes is that they clearly show the desire to discover representative types, which could then be classified: an urge that feeds deeply on established beliefs about character and physiognomy, and affects cultural narratives in profound and immanent ways. As one can tell from character-drawing in nineteenth-century literature, for the Victorians character was directly deducible from physiognomy: an idea which can be traced back to Johann Casper Lavater, father of the science of physiognomy and author of *Physiognomische Fragmente* (1774–78).[17] However, what distinguishes the application of this notion in the colonial sphere is precisely that the observer is no longer seeking confirmation of individual qualities, but evidence of presumed racial or tribal propensities which carry with them other, evaluative implications. As Christopher Pinney puts it:

> This dichotomy between, on the one hand, a complex Europe bearing the marks of an intricate history, giving rise to an individuality of countenance, and on the other, a non-Western sphere of uniformity, resulting from a lack of history, can also be understood in the context of an emerging Orientalist paradigm in which Europe alone was endowed with agency and historicity.[18]

(In *Siege*, Farrell parodies this impulse in the Magistrate's interest in phrenology, a 'science' of Western individualism, since it seeks to distinguish *individual* character through cranial measurement, whereas skulls in anthropology formed evidence of the *collective* qualities of other cultures.) What emerges from the ideological uses of new technologies, such as photography, is that peculiarly piquant creature the stereotype. Characteristics of physique or even social custom are made to stand for the generality of an entire culture. One can see the ready application of photography to this mode of apprehending and producing the world, in a number of projects: from Watson and Kaye's eight volume compendium, *The People of India (1868–1875)*, with its 'typical' subjects posed with representative artefacts, and its concern to render tribes and castes in terms of the challenges they posed to administration; to J. H. Lamprey's anthropometric system of sitters arranged in front of a background frame hung with two inch square threads of silk to facilitate measurement; and T. H. Huxley's advocacy of full and half-length photographs of subjects, from various angles accompanied by a clearly marked measuring rod – a sinister antecedent of the modern mug-shot.[19] Clearly, the development of photography in the mid-nineteenth century was a major tool in the epistemic shift from power based on displays of might to power based on discipline through documentation and the enforced visibility of the subject. Unremitting surveillance produced a new and more detailed kind of knowledge of the colonial subject, which, in turn, led to new effects of power. Tagg shows how these photographs were staged to provide information leading to categorization: 'The format hardly varies at all. There are bodies and spaces. The bodies are taken one by one; isolated in a shallow contained space; turned full face and subjected to an unreturnable gaze; illuminated, focussed, measured, numbered and named'.[20]

However, Talal Asad cautions against viewing anthropology in the colonial era simply as a reflection of colonial ideology, since, 'bourgeois consciousness, of which social anthropology is merely one fragment, has always contained within itself profound contradictions and ambiguities',[21] and hence must be open to counter-discursive strategies. I would argue that *Siege* engages with issues arising from a fundamental change in the function of representation, in the recurring motifs of painting and photography. In the feudal age painting was one of the few forms of self-perpetuation and thus available only to the rich and powerful. As Foucault says, 'the more one possesses power or privilege, the more one is marked as an individual, by rituals, written accounts or visual reproductions'.[22]

Selective monuments of various kinds are the procedures of an 'ascending individualisation'. As has been suggested, the onset of photography extended the process of representation to those who were objects of control. Anyone could be documented, framed, controlled and widespread representation became an aspect of a 'descending individualisation', characteristic of the disciplinary regime or 'carceral network'.

The Siege of Krishnapur plays upon the idea that representation through painting in the imperial age is generally heroizing, while the new daguerreotype is essentially documentary and therefore more ambiguous in its potential application. This idea is introduced when the Maharajah's Anglophile son Hari resolves to photograph his visitor Fleury using his new camera box. The description of the process of clamping, framing and containment Fleury undergoes is immediately reminiscent of the taxonomical pictures of nineteenth-century anthropology:

> Fleury was steered towards the chair and made to sit down; it had a rod at the back surrounded by an iron crescent for keeping the sitter's head still. Fleury's head was forced firmly back into it and some adjustments were made behind him, tightening two thin metal clamps which nestled in his hair above each ear. (*Siege*, p. 81)

Here the Englishman Fleury is forced to experience a process of control and representation normally suffered by the colonial subject, now represented in the photographer Hari. It is another inversion of the colonial power relations set up by Victorian anthropology: here the Indian frames and represents the Englishman. Irony is added by the fact that during this scene Fleury dismisses the Great Exhibition as a collection of rubbish 'utterly without significance', yet chooses as his example an Observatory Hive. He says, 'ah, the tedious comparisons that were made between mankind and the hive's "quietly employed inhabitants, those living emblems of industry and order"' (*Siege*, p. 83). Of course, it is just such techniques of observation and control – one of which he is now experiencing himself – which have augmented the power of the British in India, through the East India Company, and assisted the march of that 'civilization' which he is in India to record. Regulation and observation of many by a few is no longer merely a dream of Bentham's projected Panopticon; it is the realized strategy of power on which the empire rests, and which is threatened by the Mutiny.

Writing functions in exactly the same way. It is significant that the Cutcherry building, full of documentary information on India is blown up, causing a 'snowstorm' of paper – a decidedly British meteorological phenomenon here – which thwarts a sepoy advance. Also, the ironic narrator reminds us that a young gentleman like Fleury on his first visit to India might be tempted to record his impressions in a journal subsequently to appear under a title such as 'Highways and Byways of Hindustan'; in other words he might perform the duty of even the most casual orientalist and attempt to define, depict and control the colonial space too. Additionally, during one of the most furious engagements of the siege, Fleury imagines how he would look in a 'historical' representation in the *Illustrated London News*: newspapers and journals being important repositories for ideas about the heroic in Victorian society. Despite the desperate nature of the situation Fleury dreamily appends an inappropriate and laconic caption; 'This was the Banqueting Hall Redoubt in the Battle of Krishnapur. On the left, Mr Fleury, the poet, who conducted himself so gallantly throughout; on the right, Lieutenant Dunstaple, who commanded the Battery, and a faithful native, Ram' (*Siege*, p. 139). By adding this caption the scene is recontextualized and the meaning of the image decisively altered. As part of a counter-discursive strategy it can be claimed that the discrepancy between the text and the image opens up a space allowing a view of the workings of ideology in representation and particularly heroization.[23]

The difference between the disciplinary gaze of the camera and the celebratory gaze of the artist is further highlighted in the figure of the General who appears to relieve the siege at the end. He muses on how he will be portrayed in a commemorative painting:

> he would have to pose for hours, holding a sword and perched on a trestle or wooden horse while some artist-wallah depicted 'The Relief of Krishnapur'! He must remember to insist on being in the foreground, however; then it would not be so bad. With luck this wretched selection of 'heroes' would be given the soft pedal ... an indistinct crowd of corpses and a few grateful faces, cannons and prancing horses would be best. (*Siege*, p. 311)

The General's intervention here shows a concern not only for his personal prestige and the claims of posterity, but for the urgent need to reinscribe the myth of imperial invincibility, decorum and sang-froid: in other words, the foundation of the enabling self-image of imperialism.

Indeed, artistic depictions of the British empire in general, as of events connected with the Mutiny, displayed preoccupations which were very different from the forensic tendencies of imperial anthropological photography: the composition privileging the heroic British figure or figures in a celebrated line of Victorian imperial paintings from Sir David Wilkie's depiction of General Baird's discovery of the body of Tipu Sultan at Seringapatam, to G. W. Joy's painting of the death of General Gordon at Khartoum, where the hero is presented showing typical British pluck, standing bravely on some steps attempting to outface his 'fanatical Mahomedan assailants'. One may contextualize such representations by reference to the increasing proximity of painting to an invigorated sense of a national culture. There is also, of course, a growing fascination, after Carlyle, with the idea of the hero and the flotation of the kind of 'great men' view of history which Farrell's text is in the business of bursting. As far as the Mutiny is concerned, perhaps the best-known representation is T. J. Barker's *The Relief of Lucknow*, showing the meeting of three of the most celebrated figures of the campaign, Campbell, Havelock and Outram. J. W. M. Hichberger relates that:

> Outram and Havelock had become trapped in Lucknow after attempting to lift the siege, and it was Sir Colin Campbell's force of Highlanders who finally rescued them and the British garrison. The meeting between the three had been absorbed into the national mythology ... Campbell, having force-marched hundreds of miles in gruelling conditions, against 'overwhelming odds', walked forward to greet them [in a manner worthy of Farrell himself], raising his cap and holding out his hand: 'How do you do, Sir James?'[24]

This was how the British liked to see themselves. It was their corporate image. Indeed, a reviewer in the *Art Journal* was so taken with Barker's picture that he commented that it was, 'a work which looks as if it must have been painted *photograph fashion*, on the spot ...' (my emphasis).[25] This is ironic for the reasons I have outlined above: because of the divergent concerns of photography and painting at this period. What divides these forms of representation is their content and the staging, selection and emphases chosen. What unites them is, quite simply, *their frames*: the quality in both kinds of representation which makes them partial, selective and, in the case of photographs of the colonized, decontextualized. In each case the British eye whether beneath the hood of a camera box, or hazed with the clouds of imagination in the artist's studio, only really sees what it wants to see when it looks at the colonial situation in India. In both instances text and context are split asunder and reconfigured to produce the requisite ideological message. In photography, the 'type' is redefined and classified through decontextualization and, importantly *denarrativization*, producing in Susan Sontag's words, 'fragmented continuities' and 'possibilities of control'.[26] However, both forms attempt to remove the trace of the frame and efface its effects to make the image and its meaning appear natural. *The Siege of Krishnapur* contains many examples of the use of framing devices which subtly draw our attention to the inevitably circumscribed perspectives displayed by characters. When we first meet the Collector he is pausing, framed in an open doorway, considering whether to plunge into the combative atmosphere of the Krishnapur Poetry Society, and later, at a ball, viewers in the galleries appear framed by 'ferns and red plush screens, in a good position to survey the floor below' (*Siege*, p. 40). Perhaps even more significant is the introduction of framing devices in the very structure of the text itself, which lead the reader to register the distance between twentieth-century narration and nineteenth-century event. Serious events are narrated in tones of barely suppressed relish at the counter-discursive potential of incongruity; for example, the *sowars'* attempts to carry the dying General Jackson into the residency without spilling his blood on the 'rather expensive carpet' is compared to the way in which, 'someone eating toast and honey might try, by vigilance and dexterity, to prevent it dripping' (*Siege*, p. 89).[27]

In the twentieth century the task of heroization has largely been usurped by the Hollywood motion picture. It is more than a coincidence that the British empire has provided so many plots and backgrounds for action and adventure films. In his writing Farrell shows a marked taste for cinematic images: one which runs more towards the self-conscious and sometimes surrealist productions of European art cinema than Hollywood romps. Most importantly for us there is no doubt that he recognized the cultural currency of the moving image in the twentieth century as a vehicle for ideas about the present and the past. (This seems borne out particularly clearly in his last completed novel *The Singapore Grip*, with its profusion of cinematic techniques and references which create an image of wartime Malaya through the filter of popular culture.)[28] Indeed, at a strategic point in the text the issue of moving pictures and their potential is raised explicitly. At a tea party organized during a lull in the fighting, Lucy Hughes is besieged by flying bugs which attach themselves to her body in such numbers that, even though she attempts to escape by tearing off all her clothes, she eventually stands 'as black and glistening as an African slave-girl' (*Siege*, p. 230). As the weight of the cockchafers becomes too great for them to cling on successfully, cakes of them fall away only to be rapidly replaced by others:

> But hardly had a white part been exposed before blackness covered it again. This coming and going of black and white was just fast enough to give a faint flickering image of Lucy's delightful nakedness and all of a sudden gave Fleury an idea. Could one have a series of daguerreotypes which would give the impression of movement? 'I must invent the "moving daguerreotype" later on when I have a moment to spare', he told himself, but an instant later this important idea had gone out of his mind, for this was an emergency. (*Siege*, p. 231)

Three significant points are raised by this farcical incident. First, it is another example of the problematization of race that characterizes this text, with perhaps a suggestion here that the all-important categories and ways of understanding race may be arbitrary, or at least that race-consciousness is a notional construct, a habit of mind that is donned and may be discarded. Second, the nature of the incident and the manner in which it is described – Fleury and Harry are bewildered by the unexpected revelation that Lucy has pubic hair – gestures towards the salacious, voyeuristic potential of cinema: an extension of the female objectification and commodification of 'high art', the only point of reference about the naked female body Fleury and Harry have. Finally, and most significantly for the counter-discursive potential of Farrell's use of cinema, *movement signals narrative signals change*. As such it can work against the classificatory stasis of the imperial gaze. As Susan Sontag suggests, photographs display, they do not narrate. And in order to understand process *in time* we need narrative.[29]

However, a serious problem confronts the text in its negotiation between the demands of image and those of narrative. Specifically, it is that the development of mainstream cinema in the twentieth century has been in the direction of a replication of a perceived reality constructed from within the same nineteenth-century aesthetic system as literary realism – the very form *Siege* seeks to disestablish. Moreover, colonial narrative's relation to the central tendency of realism to record events-in-time becomes even more fraught when one considers that:

> since the colonialist wants to maintain his privileges by preserving the status quo, his representation of the world contains neither a sense of historical becoming nor a concrete vision of a future different from the present ... In short, it does not contain any syncretic cultural possibility, which alone would open up the historical process once more.[30]

Almost by definition, cinema carries within it a possibility of challenging the stasis imposed by the colonial preoccupation with posed, framed and contained moments out of time. In fact, I wish to suggest that Farrell constructs *Siege* in a visual, filmic mode to be viewed as much as read. Writing retrospectively, he sets his story at a time when photography was in its infancy, and film not yet conceived. Instead, he uses a telescope as substitute for the seeing eye of the camera lens, which, although it does not produce a material film nevertheless functions as a nineteenth-century equivalent of the movie camera. In Chapter 19, the Collector becomes the conduit for interrogating the colonial gaze under stress as it attempts to construct and project its image of desire, in Lacanian terms, on to a screen at the intersection of the imaginary and symbolic realms: a screen which functions to mark the 'real' of the colonized, but which a twentieth-century reader/viewer is invited to recognize *as* a screen. It will be remembered that for Lacan the subject accedes to the symbolic order of social intersubjectivity and language, from the imaginary or pre-verbal realm, in a process which alienates the subject's desire for the perceived, previously manifest in identification *and* aggression towards the specular image. However, this dynamic of identification and aggression from the imaginary phase remains, although sublimated and modified, in the symbolic order.[31] In a colonial scenario, it can be argued that the gaze of the colonizer upon the colonized transmits the desire of the spectating subject to recapture what is lacking or absent. Abdul JanMohamed argues that this desire to project oneself on to, and be recognized by the other finds an ideal setting under colonialism where the European seeks to compel the native to recognize him as speaking subject.

However, in the process, the colonizer's own identity becomes dependent on his position of mastery as the native, in turn, is not recognized as a subject but as an object on to which the European projects his own negative self-image. In time the colonizer, alienated from his unconscious desire, becomes trapped in his own projected image, he is forced to live out the 'superior' role he has created for himself; one can see this process at work in several of the most celebrated colonial texts, from Forster's Britons in *A Passage to India* to the colonial policeman in Orwell's 'Shooting an Elephant' and, more ambivalently, Kurtz in *Heart of Darkness*. JanMohammed suggests that although, 'the native is negated by the projection of the inverted image, his presence is an absence that can never be cancelled'.[32]

We can relate this to film, and hence to *Siege*, by adopting Stephen Heath's suggestion in *Questions of Cinema*, that suture in film – the cutting, editing, movement and framing that form its grammar, create its meaning, and thus carry its ideology – continually poses an absence. (In short, we are aware that in film characters continue to exist 'outside the frame' of a particular shot.) At the same time suture ceaselessly recaptures what is lacking, in a process which binds 'the spectator as subject in the relation of the film's space'.[33] The camera is the culminating realization of the quattrocento perspective system, essential to realist literature too, in which space is arranged as spectacle for the eye of the beholder. And with the potential for steady observation, for vision and knowledge, comes the potential for mastery of the visible space. The camera projects a utopian vision where characters are centred, perspective is sharp and the image is in every sense clearly directed. Frame space becomes narrative space. The idea is that of 'the spectator at a window ... that gives a view on the world – framed, centred, harmonious ...'.[34]

This is just where Farrell places his subject, the Collector, in Chapter 19: in a fixed position watching an attack by the rebellious sepoys through a telescope which is itself positioned in a frame formed by a window. The 'dazzling circle of crystal' of the Collector's telescope is repeated in the 'screen space' circumscribed by the perimeter of the besieged garrison. Initially, the Collector's own 'empire' – his area of jurisdiction – ran as far in every direction as his colonial eye could see, but during the siege the possible field for projecting his colonial image shrinks back, contracting his (and the empire's) narrative space. Heath reminds us of the ideological ambiguity inherent in cinema's narrative-through-suture; 'mobility is exactly what is *possible* in film, complicit – the possibility of holding film within a certain vision, thereby 'perfected' – and radical – the possibility of film disturbing that vision ...'.[35]

For Farrell, cinema reintroduces movement, process and *change* (history), as against imperial photography and painting with their investment in conservative stasis. Yet more particularly in *Siege* he demonstrates that classic, realistic film perspective and points-of-view such as the colonial, attempt to contain and elide signs of suture to create their illusion of seamlessness and hence naturalness, whereas a self-conscious or postmodern grasp of the potentialities of film offers alternative, counter-discursive kinds of perspective by foregrounding the process of production and interpellation – thus exposing the arbitrary dominance of the quattrocento perspective system. Hence vision is impaired and perspective is out of kilter in Chapter 19. Now, as the attacking Indians reduce the scope of colonial narrative space, the Collector, who is suffering from erysipelas – one of the symptoms of which is an inflamed eye – feels faint and is soon feverish and ill. In this semi-delirious state his telescope, no longer the means of offering the long, authoritative view, appears to magnify the size of a Sikh helping the British to blow up the Cutcherry. We are told that a similar operation is taking place 'out of the field of his lens' (*Siege*, p. 213): something out of frame. Movement across the space of the frame and movement in and out of frame, carry the potential to challenge the construction of space which has positioned the spectator as unified and unifying subject of vision.[36] It is the violent intrusion of another 'view', that of the sepoys invading the frame, that disturbs the Collector's previously harmonious view. Shaken by the challenge to his vision and narrative space, the Collector reframes the scene by resting his telescope on the windowsill to stabilize his point of view, but even this support is shattered and the telescope trembles 'uncomprehendingly'. By panning his telescope he can see that the sepoys are on the offensive and dominating the British. (Perhaps it is what the Collector is observing through his telescope that is searing his eye and making his face throb: the destruction of his carefully constructed, projected image of colonial appropriation.) As the Collector watches the sepoy advance his telescope starts to wander as if it has taken on a life of its own, subverting his control. The explosion in the Cutcherry which produces 'a flash that burnt itself so deeply into the Collector's brain that he reeled, as if struck in the eye with a musketball' (*Siege*, p. 215), dislodges a picture from the wall behind him – perhaps it is the revered portrait of the young Queen Victoria with her bulging eyes, that can no longer guarantee a coherent colonial image. At a cheer from the Indian audience above the melon beds he drops his telescope and his authoritative masterview has gone. Perhaps the Collector is being forced to confront a similarly heretical notion to that which persuaded Galileo, when he observed the heavens and endorsed the Copernican view that the earth did not occupy a fixed position at the centre of the universe. Perhaps he too has to accommodate a nineteenth-century heresy: that there are other viewpoints, and that the point of view of the colonized may in time come to encompass the available space. Although he has now lost his telescope, the Collector can see 'perfectly well without it'. His mind clears momentarily and he recognizes for the first time the true reality of the scene before him. The sepoys are moving across the open ground and occupying the available space, the screen as place. In so doing they are beginning to look back and question the site of the colonial spectator's gaze, implicating it in 'a failure of a binding fiction that would assume and make sense of the images given'.[37] For the first time the Collector is forced to acknowledge these looks which threaten to turn the colonizer into the object. The native's look has at last become significant. The movement of the Indians in revolt, both within the frame and moving into the frame from without, serves to recentre the view on the screen of the Collector's imagination, so giving the faintest glimmer of another point of view. As modern, distanced spectators we are able to recognize the *signs of representation* in this scene and in the colonial world view, the lines of suture of the symbolic and imaginary. We are no longer close enough for its discursive ordering to unify us within its projected image. At the end of the scene the sepoys have been temporarily repulsed. However:

> The Collector had been unable to see the latter part of this action, which had taken place in thick yellow dust and smoke (the snow having mysteriously ceased). But even if there had been no dust, smoke or snow, he would still have been unable to see it, because he was lying on the floor beside the window, having fallen off his chair. Pain had come to stretch out beside him. Unseen by either Pain or the Collector, the fat pariah dog in the shade of the tamarind was whining and jumping up and down with excitement at the prospect of a square meal or two, when all the fuss was over. (*Siege*, pp. 216–17)

After the relief of Krishnapur, the Collector is taken by carriage to the railhead across the vast dusty plain. The 'widening perspective' causes him to muse on the relative insignificance of the siege he has just endured. The effect here is equivalent to the conventional mode of cinematic closure where the camera is slowly pulled back so that the subject is swallowed up by his or her surroundings. This signifies the withdrawal of our attention but also, importantly, it can heighten a sense of ambiguity of emotional response.[38] Our distance from the complacencies and prejudices on display may be temporal and ideological, but it is never cosy or safe. Without the strong sense of a society still structured on, and influenced by, the residue of preconceptions fostered in the age of empire, we risk misreading Farrell's novel and its implications for our own time. Ultimately, the point of Farrell's analysis of imperial modes of self-perception is that they, and their offspring are still with us in the only partly attenuated form of racism, xenophobia and continuing notions of British cultural superiority, illustrated in any number of contemporary events. As Nicholas Shrimpton has noted, 'Farrell's remarkable trilogy ... suggests that we too, the British, will not properly understand how we live now until we make sense of our neglected national memories'.[39]

Notes

1. Alfred, Lord Tennyson, 'The Defence of Lucknow', in Elleke Boehmer (ed.), *Empire Writing: An Anthology of Colonial Literature 1870–1918*, pp. 59–63. Christina Rossetti also contributed five maudlin but inspirational stanzas in a poem entitled 'In the Round Tower at Jhansi, June 8, 1857', R. W. Crump (ed.), *The Complete Poems of Christina Rossetti*. As 'conductor' of *Household Words*, Dickens published one or two particularly intemperate diatribes: see especially 'A Sermon for Sepoys', *Household Words*, No. 414, Saturday 27 February 1858; and 'Blown Away', *Household Words*, No. 418, Saturday 27 March 1858. An interesting selection of literary responses to the Mutiny is offered in Michael Edwardes, *Red Year: The Indian Rebellion of 1857*, pp. 174–82. Another accessible account of the events of 1857 appears in Christopher Hibbert, *Great Mutiny: India 1857*.
2. Thomas Richards, *The Commodity Culture of Victorian England: Advertising and Spectacle 1851–1914*, p. 54.
3. Bernard Bergonzi, *The Situation of the Novel*, 2nd edn, p. 16. For an extended discussion of this relationship see Said, *Culture and Imperialism*, 'Chapter Two: Consolidated Vision'.
4. See Bernard Bergonzi, 'Fictions of History', in Malcolm Bradbury and David Palmer (eds), *The Contemporary English Novel*; David Lodge, 'The Novelist at the Crossroads'; Stuart Laing, 'Novels and the Novel', in Alan Sinfield (ed.), *Society and Literature 1945–1970*. See also Alain Robbe-Grillet, *For a New Novel: Essays on Fiction*.
5. See Ronald Binns, *J. G. Farrell*, p. 18. Ralph Crane and Jennifer Livett point out that Farrell's use of other writers' styles is more in the spirit of postmodern intertextuality than mere allusion or a Bloomian concern for 'influence' in Ralph Crane and Jennifer Livett, *Troubled Pleasures: The Fiction of J.G. Farrell*, pp. 20–1.
6. Patricia Waugh, *Metafiction: The Theory and Practice of Self-Conscious Fiction*, pp. 2, 12. For more specific ideas on 'historiographic meta-

fiction' see Linda Hutcheon, *A Poetics of Postmodernism: History, Theory, Fiction*, pp. 105–23. See also, Robert Alter, *Partial Magic: The Novel as Self-Conscious Genre*; Mark Currie (ed.), *Metafiction*; Linda Hutcheon, *Narcissistic Narrative: The Metafictional Paradox*; Brian McHale, *Postmodernist Fiction*; Wenche Ommundsen, *Metafictions? Reflexivity in Contemporary Texts*.

7. An honourable exception to the proscriptive caricaturists of metafiction, Wenche Ommundsen acknowledges the act of reading and the 'context of reception', together with a 'metafictional competence' which produce metafictional meaning. Critical of those who narrow metafiction to a sub-genre, or a phenomenon entirely divorced from any mimetic tendency, Ommundsen says, 'Separating metafiction from "mainstream" novelistic practice seems destined to impoverish both', Wenche Ommundsen, *Metafictions?*, p. 21. Other perspicacious critics have located a strong postmodern dimension in Farrell's work. See John McLeod, 'Exhibiting Empire in J. G. Farrell's *The Siege of Krishnapur*', p. 120; also Crane and Livett, *Troubled Pleasures*, p. 18; Michael Prusse, *'Tomorrow is Another Day': The Fictions of James Gordon Farrell*, pp. 76–8.
8. Waugh, *Metafiction*, p. 66.
9. Richard Terdiman, *Discourse/Counter-Discourse: The Theory and Practice of Symbolic Resistance in Nineteenth-Century France*, pp. 15, 43.
10. Ibid., pp. 52–3.
11. Ibid., pp. 75, 76–7.
12. For more on Farrell's ironizing of the heroic, see McLeod, 'Exhibiting Empire', pp. 122–3; and Crane and Livett, *Troubled Pleasures*, pp. 53–5, 88–91.
13. Walter Houghton, *The Victorian Frame of Mind, 1830–1870*, p. 43.
14. Thomas Richards, *The Imperial Archive: Knowledge and the Fantasy of Empire*.
15. Said, *The World, the Text and the Critic*, p. 222.
16. John Tagg, *The Burden of Representation: Essays on Photographies and Histories*, p. 11.
17. Christopher Pinney, *Camera Indica: The Social Life of Indian Photographs*, p. 51. See also Michael Shortland, 'Skin Deep: Barthes, Lavater and the Legible Body', p. 284.
18. Pinney, *Camera Indica*, pp. 52–3.
19. Christopher Pinney, 'Classification and Fantasy in the Photographic Construction of Caste and Tribe', in Joanna Cohan Scherer (ed.), *Picturing Cultures: Historical Photographs in Anthropological Enquiry*, pp. 259–88; also Elizabeth Edwards, 'Photographic "Types": The Pursuit of Method', in Scherer (ed.), *Picturing Cultures*, pp. 235–58.
20. Tagg, *Burden*, p. 64.
21. Talal Asad (ed.), *Anthropology and the Colonial Encounter*, p. 18.
22. Foucault, *Discipline and Punish*, p. 193.

23. John McLeod comments, 'Farrell ironizes the value of heroic behaviour by highlighting a disparity between the discourse of heroism and the experience of battle', McLeod, 'Exhibiting Empire', p. 123.
24. J. W. M. Hichberger, *Images of the Army: The Military in British Art, 1815–1914*, p. 61.
25. Ibid., p. 61. For a consideration of the ideology of British imperial painting at a slightly earlier stage in the colonial encounter in India, see Kate Teltscher, *India Inscribed: European and British Writing on India 1600–1800*.
26. Susan Sontag, *On Photography*, p. 156.
27. Margaret Drabble and Crane and Livett are among the critics who have remarked upon Farrell's use of distancing through incongruity. John Berger says, 'The meaning of an image is changed according to what one sees immediately beside it or what comes immediately after it'. The same is certainly true of Farrell's technique and its effects: see John Berger, *Ways of Seeing*, p. 29; also Margaret Drabble, 'Things Fall Apart', in J. G. Farrell, *The Hill Station*, p. 178; and Crane and Livett, *Troubled Pleasures*, pp. 23, 92.
28. Crane and Livett, *Troubled Pleasures*, pp. 115–16. In her recent biography Lavinia Greacen notes Farrell's passion for cinema and narrates how, during his Harkness Fellowship in the United States, he was a keen student on a course at Yale entitled 'Writing for the Camera'. It seems clear that Farrell internalized aspects of screen-writing technique and applied them strategically to his fiction, see Lavinia Greacen, *J.G. Farrell: The Making of a Writer*, pp. 209–12.
29. Sontag, *On Photography*, p. 23. For high art and the male gaze see Berger, *Ways of Seeing*, pp. 45–64. The classic statement on the male gaze in cinema remains Laura Mulvey, 'Visual Pleasure and Narrative Cinema'.
30. Abdul JanMohamed, 'The Economy of Manichean Allegory: The Function of Racial Difference in Colonialist Literature', in H. L. Gates, Jr (ed.), *'Race', Writing and Difference*, p. 88. For more thoughts on the relation between film narrative and literary realism, see Graeme Turner, *Film as Social Practice* (2nd edn), p. 12.
31. JanMohamed, '*Race*', p. 105.
32. Ibid., pp. 85–6. For a similar treatment of David Lean's film adaptation of *A Passage to India* see Laura Donaldson, *Decolonizing Feminisms: Race, Gender and Empire Building*, p. 95. As John Berger says, 'According to the convention of perspective there is no visual reciprocity. There is no need for God to situate himself in relation to others: he is himself the situation', Berger, *Ways of Seeing*, p. 16.
33. Stephen Heath, *Questions of Cinema*, p. 52.
34. Ibid., pp. 36, 28.
35. Ibid., p. 32.
36. Ibid., p. 38.

37. Ibid., p. 99.
38. Turner, *Film*, p. 53. Chris Ferns comments on the almost 'blank screen' at the end of the novel, Chris Ferns, '"First as Tragedy, Then as Farce": J. G. Farrell's Retelling of History', p. 284.
39. Nicholas Shrimpton, 'Talent for Thought', p. 18. Margaret Drabble likewise comments, 'All the distancing is directed towards one end – the revelation of the absurdity and injustice of things as they are, and the need for radical change', Drabble, *Hill Station*, p. 191.

V The God that Left the Temple: Unravelling the Imperial Narrative in Paul Scott's *Raj Quartet*

> In the books I write about the last days of British India ... I am conscious of the present, the one I am living in, leaning its weight on the vanished world I attempt to illustrate ... so that it is sometimes difficult for me to determine what was then, what is now, and what is yet to be. (Paul Scott, *My Appointment with the Muse*)

> The Raj Quartet appears not as another instalment of a bankrupt attempt to retrieve the imperatives of Englishness ... but as precisely the reverse: an early, uneven and contradictory bid to think through historically the enormity of these epochal changes. There is a case for viewing Scott as white England's first novelist of decolonization. (Bill Schwartz, 'An Englishman Abroad ... and at Home', *New Formations*)

One of the most fruitful branches of inquiry in current post-colonial criticism concerns the relationship between narrative and nation and centres on the 'discursive temporality' of nationhood. Works such as Benedict Anderson's *Imagined Communities* and, more recently, the tightly argued essays of Homi Bhabha, have investigated how institutions and cultural forms produce the idea of a homogeneous communal identity, and work on behalf of cultural and national cohesion. For Anderson, one of the most efficient tools in the creation of such a sense is the novel. He comments, 'The idea of a sociological organism moving calendrically through homogeneous, empty time is a precise analogue of the idea of the nation which is also conceived as a solid community moving steadily down (or up) history'.[1] It is the discursive temporality of a mythology of British India, articulated through generic convention, and Paul Scott's interrogation and deconstruction of this mythology which I wish to address in this chapter. However, it must be borne in mind that in Anglo-Indian literature we are not dealing with a national literature as such, but specifically a *literature of exile*, with all the pathos, self-dramatization, lamentation and hyperbole that that entails. The historian Robin Moore has defined the foundations of the Anglo-Indian sense of community as based on 'companionship in exile', expressed in insularity in the face of a threatening dark tide; 'pride in experience' and shared membership of an exclusive club (both literal and metaphorical); and the possession of rights and obligations these were felt to confer.[2] While metropolitan communities may have expressed and found confirmation of their sense of unity through cultural productions, Anglo-Indians did not need confirmation of their unity; exile made them acutely aware of it and their formation into a racial elite underlines the fact. What they needed was confirmation and reassurance about the worth of their presence and their perceived sacrifices. Traditionally, this engendered a two-fold response in literature. The first is epitomized by all those stories, sedulously fostered in the Victorian and Edwardian eras – most memorably by Kipling himself – in which melancholic subalterns and wan imperial servants wilt in the hot weather and walk a narrow path between the temptations of blissful oblivion through suicide, on the one hand, and the soul-destroying ingratitude of parliament, Travelling Gentlemen and their native charges on the other. The second reply comes in the shape of a calming, clear-voiced, prearranged dialogue with the Indian subject which, in form and content, will articulate the unchanging nature of the imperial relationship. The Indian in British fiction is not only seen *by* the British but, in almost all cases, seen only in relation to the British. In this construction the selected knowable community in conventional British fictions of India is also a selected set of relations between English and Indian deployed and replayed over and over again. The form these fictions take is always linear, their tendency towards unity.

It was because the fictional debate about the empire in India was conducted in these terms for so long – 'are we doing good in India? Do they still want/need us?' – that literary representations frequently give the impression of endlessly ploughing the same stony furrow, both in theme and formal preferences. Thus, George Woodcock is right to observe of the 'literature of the sahibs':

> It tended to be descriptive and didactic rather than formally experimental and displayed little more daring in the latter sense than the use of colloquial forms of speech and realistic settings, in which Orwell in the 1930s did not go far beyond Kipling almost half a century before. The intent of the sahib writer was to reassure or criticize; he could not risk obscurity by innovation.[3]

Paul Scott's *Raj Quartet* – comprising *The Jewel in the Crown, The Day of the Scorpion, The Towers of Silence* and *A Division of the Spoils* – represents an important disruption of this comfortable script. It charts the demise of the British in India by examining representative figures and communities in the crucial years between Gandhi's Quit India movement in 1942 and partition in 1947. Taking as its starting point two heavily symbolic incidents, the rape of a young Englishwoman, Daphne Manners, in the Bibighar Gardens of Mayapore, and the attack on an English missionary and her Indian companion elsewhere in the district, the *Quartet* charts the irreversible decline in Indo-British relations and the accompanying sense of fragmentation and loss experienced by the British community, steeped in the military and patriarchal traditions and outlook of the Raj. Scott's own professed position retains a residual admiration for the work ethic and sense of dedication behind the empire. He recognizes them as the fabric of an assiduously embroidered myth, but wishes to illustrate Anglo-Indians in the defining context of their work, since it is by their sense of vocation they may best be understood.[4] His main point of interest for a contemporary reader lies in the way the relativizing technical innovations he brings to British fictions of India enact a distinctly post-colonial deconstruction of the generic conventions of imperial romance, and indeed the myth itself, and offer a potential reading that coincides with the preoccupations of current post-colonial debate.

Scott's concern in *The Raj Quartet* was to find a form appropriate to the moment of imperial dissolution. The texts are formally fragmented in a number of ways: most obviously in the division of the first novel, *The Jewel in the Crown,* into parts corresponding to the sources and stages of an investigation carried out by the historian figure who is looking into events surrounding the rape, and whose occasional musings bind the disparate narratives into a coherent whole. Each 'Part' of the novel, 'Miss Crane', 'The MacGregor House', 'Sister Ludmila' and so on, introduces a different perspective on events and characters given by witnesses with varying degrees of involvement or knowledge. The fractionary narrative structure calls on newspaper articles, depositions, reminiscences and memoirs, letters, verbal and written transcripts of interviews, and lengthy 'reconstructions' in which the historian-writer persona imagines characters' feelings and motivations. Indeed, it is here, immediately, that one finds an example of Scott's frustration of generic expectation and the beginning of his unravelling of the imperial narrative, since the medium is poised between the dynamic, story-led impulses of the novel and the meticulous collation of the history book. Likewise, the narrating voice remains at the midpoint between historiographical disengagement and omniscient novelese, occasionally forsaking its lofty perch to plunge into the 'minds' of characters like Miss Crane who, anticipating trouble after Gandhi's arrest, asks her Indian colleague Mr Chaudhuri whether he thinks the situation dangerous: 'They always know, she thought, and then: This is how it happens too, to call them "they" as though they are different' (*Jewel*, p. 66). What is instituted is a tension between a putative master-narrative – the history book, the novel – and other modes of discourse, which mirrors the irruption of a determined nay-saying Indian narrative in the political sphere. (In this way Scott can conflate and deflate the pretensions of two forms of authoritative Western narrative.)

Modern historiography, like the novel, was made possible in a cosmology sanctioned by the Enlightenment's greatest thinker, Newton. As David Goldknopf comments, 'The principal Newtonian signals were the emboldening of empiricism, faith in formula, and a heightened time sense. Newton had shown that the natural laws were *there*, awaiting only systematic observation and experiment to be discovered'.[5] But the same tide of empiricism brought with it notions about ideal forms of government which had a distinctly ambivalent application in what was also the age of empire. At an ideological level, the requirements of Enlightenment thought were pressed into service as a legitimizing adjunct to imperialist practice and eventually made manifest as the civilizing mission. Along with political control, a cornucopia of flowering theories and pseudo-sciences such as ethnography came to be validated by Enlightenment ideas, but used for distinctly unenlightened purposes. As they developed, official imperial histories worked to blur the contradiction that dogged the co-existence of 'enlightened' thought and imperialism, a contradiction ably summarized by Partha Chatterjee: 'For Enlightenment itself, to assert its sovereignty as the universal ideal, needs its Other; if it could ever actualize itself in the real world as truly universal, it would in fact destroy itself'.[6] That other is simultaneously admitted and emasculated in histories of the British presence in India and the fiction it generated.

By contrast, Scott's history confronts the idea of the adequacy of a single authoritative voice. This is a book about writing histories. The mode of articulation is documentary and forensic, calling many witnesses and examining evidence. (Even the interrogation of the accused, Hari Kumar, by the sadistic District Superintendent Merrick becomes the kind of writing which, in itself, interrogates the processes and expediencies of imperial governance.) The patchwork of contending versions created in *Jewel* provides an opportunity to pastiche the stock voices of Anglo-Indian narrative. Thus we are furnished with 'Edited Extracts from the unpublished memoirs of Brigadier A.V. Reid, D.S.O., M.C.: "A Simple Life"' (*Jewel*, pp. 337–97): a brilliant parody of Anglo-Indian forms of memorializing and their unctuous titles. Reid's world is populated by red-faced stereotypes with fatuous public-school nicknames, like General 'Tubby' Carter, and national archetypes such as 'Johnny Jawan' and 'Tommy Atkins' who display appropriate propensities in times of peril – like the civil unrest Reid is charged with quelling (in attitude, action and anagram he is a surrogate General Dyer). Against him is set 'An edited transcript of written and spoken comments by Robin White, C.I.E. (ex-I.C.S)' (*Jewel*, pp. 398–428), a representative of the civil authorities who recognizes factual inaccuracies in Reid's account but that, 'he had somehow managed to make everything that happened look logical in his own terms' (*Jewel*, p. 402). The clipped, limited voice of the army officer is set against that of the self-conscious liberal in a technique of true dialogism. The historian narrator stands back to allow this hall-of-mirrors method to provide different perspectives on events and thus highlight the difficulty of arriving at a definitive truth. It serves to remind us that a truth may be seen from many sides – including Daphne's journal which purports to contain the facts about the rape – and refuses the kind of foreclosure archival records crave. Indeed, there is a delight in the play of different versions throughout *Jewel*. Each race has its own variants on the legends surrounding the MacGregor House and Bibighar Gardens, and conflicting accounts circulate about the troubles of August 1942; 'Everyone in Mayapore at that time would have a different story to tell' (*Jewel*, p. 81). Versions are wound up and allowed to run, especially in this first volume, without any of the irritable reaching after equilibrium or fairness one occasionally detects in Forster.

Versions and their juxtaposition militate against the seamless imperial narrative and foreground the problematics of constructing an authoritative retelling. The obligations of historical narration – order, explication, resolution – which it shares with realist, linear fictions of empire, are imploded and what we are given instead are the raw materials of a history, personal testimony, *not the whole picture at once*. We never get to read the historian's finished book and he asks despairingly, 'Where does one draw the line under the story of Hari Kumar?' (*Jewel*, p. 302). In such a fashion the idea of adequate historical narratives is questioned. Voices are not corralled into a preconceived, homomorphic pattern. In fact, the orchestrating voice is decentred and dispossessed of the power to force through an interpretation. His meta-text, the physical unit of the text itself, provides a playground for versions. It governs the articulation of differences, not those differences themselves. The vestigial narrator,[7] a thing of threads and patches, is forced on to the margins in place of traditionally subordinate but now riotous speakers (it is significant that three of them, Lili Chatterjee, Srinivasan and Vidyasagar, are Indian).

Scott uses multiple focalization punctuated by 'reconstruction' in *Jewel* to enact on a formal level the first of many displacements that come to corrupt the would-be pukka narrative. They take the form of a displacement, or rather here a persistent redeployment of the locus of narration among the characters and between characters and 'narrator'. Subsequent books are more overtly novelistic in their integration of these elements but, I wish to argue, this constitutes a refinement of, rather than a retreat from, these positions. An important component in this is free indirect speech. We have seen in our study of Forster how free indirect speech preserves ambivalence through 'hybrid constructions'. Yet, whereas Forster's use tends towards the isolation, but not rejection of, ethnocentric postures, Scott's undermines dominant discourses by what one might describe as subversive articulation through unaccountable voices. Mention has been made of the infection and inflection of the omniscient tone by characters' voices, and on numerous occasions in the *Quartet* Scott verbalizes the collective consciousness of Anglo-India. Events are viewed from the perspectives, and using the voices, of the entrenched and reactionary wives at the military hill station of Pankot. An example of an unproblematic use of this approach occurs when the community reflects on the 'inevitable' failure of Cripps' mission of reconciliation to Indian leaders. We are told:

> it was entirely to placate Roosevelt that Churchill (who knew a thing or two ...) had sent out that Fabian old maid, Stafford Cripps, to do what Churchill knew couldn't be done: put pepper into Indian civilians and politicians by offering them what they'd been offered before, but which a pinko-red like Cripps, unused to office, would see as new, generous, advantageous, a Left-Wing invention ... Its total and inevitable failure had been a smack in the eye to Cripps who went home eating crow as well as his bloody vegetables. (*Towers*, p. 57)

Yet there are moments when the locus of free indirect narration hovers disturbingly between narrator and collective consciousness and begins to articulate discomfort and fears in striking imagery which remains tantalisingly beyond the range of expression of Anglo-Indian society. For instance, the narrating voice swoops to indulge in the memsahibs' aggregate reflections on Mildred Layton's increased drinking, seeing it as symptomatic of imperial dissolution (*Towers*, p. 51), and her unstable daughter Susan is escorted from a roomful of mems by her psychiatrist who, 'bore himself like a man taking someone out of an area of contagion' (*Towers*, p. 419). Although the ladies would register disquiet on both these counts, it seems unlikely that they would express their unease in this way, by extrapolating from the private to the public worlds. They certainly would not equate themselves with an area of contagion. However, the most striking use of subversive articulation through an unaccountable voice occurs after the death of Mabel Layton, a figure emblematic of a lost golden age of the Raj, whose increasing withdrawal from Anglo-Indian rituals has been taken as eccentricity rather than disapproval. But now:

> dead, she emerged as a monument which, falling suddenly, had caused a tremor which continued to reverberate, echo, in the wake of [her best friend] Miss Batchelor who, bowling down Club Road in the back of a tonga, now guarded the fibre suitcase as if it were crammed with numbered pieces of the fallen tower that had been her friend, and as if it were her intention to re-erect it in the garden of the rectory bungalow or even in a more public position, in the churchyard perhaps or at the intersection of Church and Club Roads where – imperfectly assembled – it might lean a little and dominate the whole area with a peculiar and critical intensity, make it impossible to go past the spot without having one's confidence further impaired and one's doubts increased by this post-mortem reversal of roles. (*Towers*, p. 301)

This extraordinary sentence, with its curious metaphysical conceit, reveals the ironic tone of an ambiguous narrating presence. Whose voice is speaking? The startling and elaborately worked image suggests the historian-narrator, but the concluding sentiments about the debilitating effects on 'one's' confidence appear to anchor the sentence to the Pankot sisterhood. Yet it is certainly another of those things they would be unable to verbalize in this way. The long, multi-clausal sentences, pitted by the 'modalizing locutions',[8] 'as if', 'perhaps' and 'might', work to create the sense of processes of assimilation and interpretation at work, without stipulating in whom. A kind of modernist rhythm of accretion, reminiscent of the opening of Faulkner's *Absalom, Absalom!*, or Virginia Woolf's mature style, sets adrift the locus of the subject of the sentence; the more it builds the harder it becomes to attribute.[9] Scott's transgressive mode crosses conventional boundaries and breaches epistemological dividing lines. It is this sort of free indirect speech that is potentially subversive as it undermines those certainties of voice which characterize colonial discourse. By articulating a collective consciousness in crisis, and giving voice to anxieties that must remain suppressed for the sake of the patrimonial narrative, he can hasten, and participate in, the collapse of Anglo-India's enunciative possibilities. In the same way, the garrulous former missionary Barbie Batchelor figures as the voice that goes on and on after discursive limits have been reached. The Pankot women try to avoid Barbie and her chatter. She is interested in saturating her consciousness with words, the means of interrogation and communication. For the rest of them reticence prevails and words are confined to platitudes, intolerant rhetoric and imperialist cliché. Their words seek to bolster the crumbling edifice, hers seek to explore it.

As the technique of multiple focalizations and redeployment of the locus of narration might indicate, these are books about ways of seeing. They are also about ways of memorializing and the operation of memory, since the historian-narrator is carrying out his research in the late 1960s and early 1970s. Accordingly, the assumptions of linear narrative – the basic design of British fictions of India – are challenged as the story shuttles between its twin contexts, and orbits the Bibighar incident which the historian senses is the key to understanding wider events. Indeed, there is a pronounced cyclical quality in the narrative structure which Patrick Swinden has described as a 'curve around from the future into the past and back into the present again – which is always Bibighar, the assault, the arrest, the arrival of Daphne Manners ... and the search for Hari Kumar by Ronald Merrick'.[10] Realistic linear chronology is further violated by the mediation of time within the 'Books', 'Parts' and subsections into which each volume is divided. At its simplest this may consist of one subsection being dominated by the ideas, outlook and current circumstances of the central mediating consciousness, while the next may take the form of a 'flashback' or recollection of the same consciousness, or may be mediated by an entirely different consciousness picking up the story at another point altogether. Scott calls on devices familiar from Genette's study of *A la Recherche du Temps Perdu*.[11] Narrative loops – and loops within loops – frustrate the linear, successional imperatives of the realist imperial storyline. Thus, from the incident of Ahmed Kasim and Sarah Layton's ride on the waste ground near the Mirat Palace in *The Day of the Scorpion* (pp. 140–9), the reader is propelled back in time, via a discussion of Susan Layton's impending marriage to Captain Teddie Bingham, to the drive which has led the party to Mirat where the wedding will take place. In turn, on page 180 we loop – forward in 'real' time/backward in narrative time – to rejoin Sarah and Ahmed on their ride. The books display that zig-zagging movement, 'a highly complex and deliberate transgression of chronological order',[12] Genette finds characteristic of Proust. Such overt time loops are only the most obvious illustration of many such 'anachronisms'. Analepsis (retrospection) occurs in the descriptions of Teddie and Susan's ill-starred wedding in *Day* and Merrick's death in *A Division of the Spoils*, rendered at a later point in the overall flow of events; while the anticipation of Ahmed's death on page 140 of *Division* – in a projection by the historian back in 'real' time from the 1970s/forward in narrative time to August 1947 – is a complex interweaving of analepsis and prolepsis.[13] Sister Ludmila's comment to the historian at the start of his research sums up Scott's own methodology:

> there is ... in you an understanding that a specific historical event has no definite beginning, no satisfactory end? It is as if ... time were telescoped and space dovetailed? As if Bibighar almost had not happened yet, and yet has happened, so that at once past, present and future are contained in your cupped palm. (*Jewel*, pp. 156–7)

The *Raj Quartet* has no discernible beginning and, as the urgency of the historian's investigations and concern to ground them in the 1960s and 1970s demonstrate, no satisfactory conclusion. This anti-teleological thrust is appropriate for a work dealing with an empire of 'unfinished business' and suggests the novels are also an attempt to come to terms with an imperial past which is, somehow, not yet over.

In *The Historical Novel*, Lukács defines an authentic historical novel as one which would rouse the present and which contemporaries would recognize as their own prehistory. *The Raj Quartet* makes this connection explicitly at various points by referring to its *grounding* – the ultimate perspective, the temporal setting of the historical narrative as it emerges. Grounding the *Quartet* in the moment of writing 1964–75 aligns it with the period of Indo-Pakistani conflict and those post-colonial incidents conjured simply by the names Bangladesh, Rhodesia, Angola. Most pertinently for Scott his novels become associated with the time of immigration to Britain from the former colonies and of the white backlash personified by Enoch Powell.[14] This, along with the 'written of' era 1942–47 provides a double frame with which any critic must contend. The narrative reflects this duality in both thematics and form. Hence, in the section of *Jewel* entitled 'An Evening at the Club', the historian witnesses at first-hand lingering racism in Mr Srinivasan's treatment at the hands of a new generation of British in the Mayapore Club seventeen years after independence. (The historical perspective shows that little has changed. The text does not exist in an atemporal liberal Anglo-Indian vacuum where everyone is fundamentally nice to each other.) In terms of form, spatial and temporal oscillation destabilizes a lengthy and apparently solid narrative, just as it will dislocate the characters who populate it. The full impact of this can be gauged from a close analysis of the opening page of the novel cycle. Note the shifting temporal loci which I have emphasized – 1942, several years earlier, the 'uneasy present', a few hours before the moment of narration, back to 1942, and so on – reflected in the ever-changing tense, which never allows the reader to settle:

> Imagine, then, a flat landscape, dark for the moment, but even so conveying to a girl running in the still deeper shadow cast by the wall of the Bibighar Gardens an idea of immensity, of distance [/] such as years before Miss Crane had been conscious of, standing where a lane ended and cultivation began ... [/] ...
>
> This is the story of a rape, of the events that led up to it and followed it and of the place in which it happened.[/]
>
> In the Bibighar Gardens case there were several arrests and an investigation. There was no kind of trial in the judicial sense. [/] Since then people have said [/] there was a trial of sorts going on. [/] In fact, such people say [/] the affair that began on the evening of 9th August 1942 in Mayapore [/] ended with the spectacle of two nations in violent opposition, not for the first time nor as yet for the last because they were then locked in an imperial embrace of such long standing and subtlety it was no longer possible for them to know whether they hated or loved one another, or what it was that held them together and seemed to have confused the image of their separate destinies. (*Jewel*, pp. 9–10)

The final sentence states explicitly what the structure implies. The reader's attention is drawn not only to the different times and places described, but also to the time and place in which these strands are being interwoven, the time of writing – and, in the invocation to 'imagine then', to the time and place of reading, whenever and wherever that may be.

Time is telescoped, space dovetailed. The replication of character relationships and incident is complemented by a Forsterian 'repetition-plus-variation' in the multiplicity of multi-functional symbols used. The love-triangle of the MacGregor legend is replayed in the Merrick-Daphne-Hari situation; Daphne and Hari's love is reflected in attenuated form in Sarah and Ahmed's friendship; and Edwina, Barbie and Mabel undergo a conflation of identities in the minds of other characters. Similarly, roses, towers, silver, possessions and costumes, imprisonment, service, rainstorms, colours, and dreams are among the countless images which take on shifting symbolic meanings. Martin Green has described Scott's technique as 'synthetic' in that it imposes Kiplingesque subjects on a Forsterian rape plot.[15] One might claim to be witnessing less the flouting of generic conventions in *The Raj Quartet* than a complete re-working of the grand archetypes of British fiction of India. This is accomplished most clearly in the critique of character and society.

Scott takes the commonplaces of Anglo-Indian literature, the motifs and the myths, and reveals their inadequacy for a writer after decolonization: particularly a writer whose concern is to dramatize the actual moment of decolonization. Central to this is an exposure of the mechanics of the imperial script, an unpicking of the stitches holding together imperial modes of (self-)perception. Most importantly it jolts the reader out of any complicity with the generic traditions bred by previous fictions. Thus, *The Day of the Scorpion* opens with a modern-day view of the British administrative centre, Ranpur. An example of the wholesale transplanting of English values and characteristics typical of imperial settlement occurs not only in the complex, hierarchical system of administration set up, but also in the reported description of Ranpur as 'Aldershot with trees planted', each road and building having, 'an air of being turned inwards on itself to withstand a siege' (*Day*, p. 11). However, such transplanting is reported to be less striking than the hurried vacation of such towns by the colonials after the Second World War. Civic buildings such as Government House are less impressive than the sense that in places like Ranpur, 'the British came to an end of themselves as they were', and the 'humpy graves' in the cemetery of St Luke's record the early demise of many colonial settlers, 'with all that this suggests in the way of unfinished business' (*Day*, p. 12).

Nevertheless, Anglo-Indian communities such as the one at the army-dominated hill station of Pankot do their best to ignore the portents which come thick and fast during the war years. The

Layton family, who come to personify the life and sense of mission in Pankot, continue to maintain their status in the strict, regimental hierarchy which characterizes the life of the womenfolk too. While her husband is a prisoner of the Japanese Mildred Layton upholds the increasingly hollow convention of matriarchal visits to the wives of her husband's native troops, dispensing sympathy and thinly disguised condescension in the name of Man-bap, the tradition of paternal care and imperial solidarity. Yet, in a rapidly changing world – exemplified by the civil unrest of 1942 and the inexorable Japanese advance – such traditions are barely more than charades designed to reassure the Anglo-Indian community and preserve some sense of security. In this atmosphere, Scott constantly refers to such gestures as 'performance', a sense of going through certain preordained, yet nonetheless meaningless motions. The irony is that the Anglo-Indians are aware that such motions are meaningless: from the detached Mabel, whom people visit to ensure that she, like them, is still 'representing it'; to Mildred's daughter Susan who dons the garb of the perfect memsahib and behaves like 'a brick' until her breakdown; to Mildred herself whose drinking and loveless affair with the adjutant is an effort to obliterate the sense of deficiency and loss of mission of a people abandoned by history. The Laytons hold the imperial fort, but are as much imprisoned by it as the real internees Mohammed Ali Kasim and Hari Kumar.

Scott forces his characters to compare the prison where they live unto the world of imagined former glories and legendary feats of bravery and sacrifice. And because that world was populous – fixed in the illusion of permanence and in the myth of Indian gratitude and acquiescence – and here is not a creature but themselves, they cannot do it. His technique can be described as tending towards the deflation and diminution of the grandiose claims of Anglo-India and its cultural productions. This is reflected in the repeated use of certain words to describe the Pankot women at their meeting after the first disturbances. Mildred becomes associated with the word, and thus the appearance of, 'langour'; Clara Fosdick is constantly described as 'maternal'; Lucy Smalley stands for 'dullness' and dependability; Maisie Trehearne is all 'composure'; and the senior among them, Isobel Rankin, exudes 'concentrated energy' (*Towers*, p. 66ff.). The memsahibs are all mistresses of the smaller virtues. Through the words repeatedly used to define them they become representative of types of Englishness. Such a method here becomes a radical, disruptive tactic, running contrary to the source of power or, perhaps, reflecting the breakdown of that power – just as both the Metropolis-Colony and Colonizer-Colonized gazes no longer function effectively.

Despite early attempts to conform, the elder Layton girl, Sarah, is unable to settle for an identity incorporated within the waning imperial fantasy. While at school she writes an essay on 'The Effect of Climate and Topography upon the Human Character', in which she regurgitates the accepted view that the temperate English climate:

> react(s) upon the inhabitants to make them strong, active, energetic and self-sufficient. It is these qualities which they take abroad with them into their tropical and subtropical colonies, lands whose native populations are inclined because of heat and humidity to be less strong, less active, less energetic and more willing to be led. (*Day*, p. 143)

However, on analyzing this imperialist orthodoxy she finds that it fails to reflect her own experience. Eventually Sarah overcomes such stereotypical views and scripting – including the imperial gender scripting which demands marriage and procreation in order to propagate empire – causing Lucy Smalley to question her commitment to the imperial project by suggesting that, 'she doesn't really take it seriously ... sometimes she looked at me as if I were, well, not a real person' (*Day*, pp. 156–7). Lucy and the other Anglo-Indians belong to a derivative discourse whose roles are passed unthinkingly from one generation to the next. In that sense she is indeed 'not a real person' but an epic type and Sarah, reflecting upon the empire and its unchanging rituals realises that, 'A dead hand lay upon the whole enterprise' (*Day*, p. 164). Sarah is perhaps the only character vouchsafed the ability to recognize and deconstruct herself and others as epic types in the imperial pageant – as at the end of the cycle when she consciously adopts her 'brave little memsahib act' for the victims of the train massacre.

The same existential anxiety causes Susan Layton to break down both as an individual, owing to the trauma of her husband's death and her post-natal depression, and as the image of the young imperial matriarch poised to follow in the wake of the recessional older generation. Her attempt to burn her baby son in a circle of fire on the lawn of Rose Cottage is linked to the legend of the scorpion which is supposed to commit suicide when surrounded by fire, and which stands as a symbol of the British at bay; to Edwina Crane's despairing death in the manner of the suttee who immolates herself on her husband's funeral pyre; and to her husband Teddie's heroic yet now ambiguous death by fire while attempting to reclaim deserters. It is also an emphatic gesture and an attack upon the sacrosanct idea of genealogies. Perhaps her breakdown is less a loss of identity than a recognition that she has never had one beyond the collective illusion of the imperial memsahib. She says to her sister, 'Whatever you do and wherever you go you'll always be yourself. But what am I? Why there's nothing to me at all. Nothing. Nothing at all' (*Day*, p. 398). While Sarah has managed to cling to her identity as an individual through a determined refusal to succumb to the collective illusion, Susan, for whom the illusion has been her life, only has recourse to breakdown, introversion and silence.

Before her collapse Susan feels, 'Like a drawing that anyone who wanted to could come along and rub out' (*Day*, p. 410). One character-type who undergoes exactly this process is her first husband Teddie Bingham, Captain in the Muzzafirabad Guides. As a representative of hopelessly outdated systems of belief like Man-bap, Teddie is introduced ironically by the historian-narrator as a man already doomed by the passage of events. We learn that between his departure from Burma and his arrival at Pankot a year later, 'there is a gap, but it is one of many and it plays a perfectly proper schematic part in an account of him because to Teddie himself his whole *history* seems to have been a series of gaps linked by a few notable events' (*Towers*, p. 115). The description of Teddie's life as a 'history' identifies him with the wider 'history' of the British in India, the one that presents itself as unified and natural. Teddie is a man made entirely of, and by, such histories, 'a set of trained and drained responses', and thus Susan's natural counterpart as an identity entirely incorporated within the missionary myth of the Raj. Yet the ominous gaps that appear in his story are a sign of the times in which he is set and of his creator's determination to have no truck with a defunct character-type who would, earlier in the genre, have been hero material. Like Rosa Diamond in *The Satanic Verses,* Teddie imagines himself part of a seamless British imperial narrative, but his real status as a 'creature of gaps and absences'[16] is forced into view by a coy narrative voice which disclaims the kind of knowledge it would need were it to assert omniscience for itself and solidity for its creation. For example, when Teddie's initial courtship of Sarah is terminated the historian-narrator speculates that he '*surely* never felt that she didn't take him seriously as a person ...' (*Towers*, p. 119); and when he is posted to Mirat and fears for the future of his engagement to Susan '*one may fancy*' that 'he could not rid himself of the idea that he might be turning out to be the kind of man around whom things collapsed, not noisily but with a sort of slithering, inexorable, folding-in and -over movement' (*Towers*, p. 130). He too experiences narrative diminution, like the memsahibs, in the double negatives, with their suggestion of a cancelling out, in Sarah's retrospective description of him as 'not unamusing, not unpleasant ... up to a point which was soon reached' (*Towers*, p. 122).

The chink in Teddie's impeccable British identity becomes a gaping hole when Merrick tells him about the Indian troops who, on capture by the Japanese, have defected to the Axis powers and, with assistance and supervision, formed an Indian National Army with the intention of fighting alongside the Japanese and forcing the British from Indian soil. On hearing of such treachery by soldiers of the King Teddie feels distinctly light-headed. Such action is quite contrary to any code of decent behaviour he would have thought possible. It is, for him, 'utterly unspeakable'. The 'tropical disorder' which accompanies Teddie's painful education marks the beginning of his erasure, as his ideology, which *is* his identity, is eroded by the existence of the INA and he has 'a sensation of not being quite himself' (*Towers*, p. 181).[17] The process reaches its inevitable conclusion as Teddie is 'rubbed out' literally when ambushed in pursuit of some of the deserters to whom he would extend the offer of forgiveness inherent in the now delusive principle of Man-bap. He is thus deprived of a success which would have confirmed the imagined consonance of the British–Indian relationship and would have resulted in his elevation into a regimental legend of the sustaining variety. His intended rescuer Merrick observes, 'But of course it didn't come off and nobody will tell the tale like that. And anyway *that kind of tale has had its day*' (*Day*, pp. 471–2). In a time of war Teddie's sacrifice is seen simply as a waste of both lives and equipment. Along with other lamentable developments:

> It drew attention to a situation it was painful to acknowledge: that the god had left the temple, no one knew when, or how, or why. What one was left with were the rites which had once been propitiated, once been obligatory, but were now meaningless because the god was no longer there to receive them. (*Towers*, p. 306)

The erasure of Teddie and Susan is one part of Scott's deconstruction of imperial romance archetypes. Another is the rejection of the essentialist categories 'villain' and 'hero' that find their way into simplistic, schematizing colonial fictions. Scott is always a most sophisticated examiner of character and motivation; *Staying On* is perhaps the most mature British fiction ever written about India, with its eschewal of the exoticism, posturing and mystical philosophizing which typify many other ventures. Accordingly, the basically unsympathetic Merrick is not merely shown abusing his prisoner Hari Kumar, but bravely attempting to rescue Teddie from his blazing vehicle. I wish to return to this point and suggest another way of reading his function, but for now one must also remember that the same ambiguity extends to the rendition of Guy Perron. Despite the efforts of numerous critics to portray the young soldier-historian as the author's champion of the piece, his role is much more complex and questions, in semi-parodic style, the continued efficacy of such character-types. His overblown, heraldic full name, Guy Lancelot Percival Perron sets the tone of this pasquinade. The handsome, amiable Sergeant Perron is a hero in a situation where heroes are no longer required. The first suggestion of this is given when his colleague Purvis refers to the fact that, 'in this country only a man born and bred in the officer class can decline a commission [as Perron had done] without running the risk of having his integrity and future usefulness doubted' (*A Division of the Spoils*, p. 37), and eventually Perron uses an influential relative to secure a transfer out of the clutches of his detested Merrick. (Scott's sense of social reality always prevents him from being seduced into hero worship.) Likewise, Perron saves the depressed Purvis from suicide in the Layton's Bombay apartment only to discover that a subsequent attempt has been successful. Also, this Fabian socialist shares a strong racial consciousness and orientalist assumptions which are not always explicable in terms of his sense of satire. Like Orwell, Perron sees the iniquities of the British empire, yet still retains the kind of impulses most unnervingly encapsulated in Orwell's professed desire, in 'Shooting an Elephant', to stick a bayonet through a Buddhist priest's guts. For despite his education, or perhaps because of it, Perron views Merrick's personal servant, Suleiman, a.k.a. The Red Shadow, as the embodiment of oriental licentiousness when Suleiman offers to show him a sample of the sexual delights of Pankot. This animosity culminates in an attack on the 'thieving Oriental' – Perron has caught him taking ten rupees from his pocket – which P. M. S. Dawson rightly points out, is described in terms akin to those used to present Merrick's assault on Hari.[18] Most damning of all for the heroic mode, Perron experiences a decidedly unheroic paralysis on the last train journey at the moment when Ahmed sacrifices himself:

> A feeling of terrible relief swept over Perron. At the time it was just relief. It was terrible subsequently; when it sank in that it

> had been the relief a man feels when his self-protective instinct tells him he has personally survived a passing danger. (*Division*, p. 700)

One can imagine a John Masters hero, either then or later, taking some decisive action. For Perron and the character-type he represents, here at the dead end of British imperialism in India, there is no longer any such option. Earlier, Perron has described Merrick as 'the man who comes too late and invents himself to make up for it' (*Division*, p. 254). Yet, if there is a single character, among all the lost souls in the *Raj Quartet*, to whom this truly applies it is Perron himself.

Thus far analysis has centred on British characters, and necessarily so since Scott is primarily concerned with articulating the dislocation felt by a ruling elite being dispossessed and driven out. Yet critics who have objected to Scott's focus on the Anglo-Indians as misrepresenting independence, the result of a potent mass movement, as a gentlemen's agreement, fire as wide of the mark as do those who complain about the inauthenticity of those Indians who do exist. For my part, I wish to suggest another way of approaching the depiction and role of Scott's Indian characters. In the perception of Suleiman, and the treatment meted out to him, one sees an example of the stock fodder of British fictions of India; what one might call an epic character-type seen from the perspective of another epic character-type, Perron. However, in the depiction of the Muslim Congress leader Mohammed Ali Kasim, Scott extends the knowable community of Indians – previously restricted to authorial spokesmen or caricatures – by showing an Indian in a position of responsibility discharging his duties honestly and efficiently; we are told that the lights often burned all night at the Secretariat during his pre-war ministry (*Day*, p. 21). Similarly, when interned, M. A. K., as he is known, retains his dignity, neither losing definition as a character, mouthing absurdities, nor collapsing in a heap. The character of M. A. K. throws light into a particularly neglected corner of British India and is one of the book's minor triumphs.

Yet it is symptomatic of Scott's own variety of liberal individualism – a trait which has certainly contributed to the critical tendency he found so irksome to compare his work to Forster's *A Passage to India* – that the two Indian protagonists who most engage our attention and sympathy are the apolitical figures Hari Kumar and Ahmed Kasim. They, in contrast to M. A. K., appear part of a well-known community in British fictions of India in which character resolves itself into epic types based loosely on racial determinism: in this case, the boy who tries to be like us and the faithful native sacrificing himself for the common bond and the old masters. Hari's and Ahmed's heroic actions – keeping mum over the rape and stepping off the train to save the other travellers – are justified in the internal context offered by the novel sequence which valorizes the attempt to cross boundaries and dividing lines. Yet, in the wider framework provided by the historic British project of representing India they conform to an ideal of the British–Indian relationship as it has always been imagined by the colonizer: that in the final instance 'our' type of Indian will do the honourable thing and protect the British. For a post-colonial reader the question arises as to whether this particular figuring of the colonized is necessary or desirable in a fiction which explicitly situates itself in the 1960s and 1970s. How far can one read textual strategies such as the hybrid, apolitical hero and the primary integrity attributed to personal relationships as a further example of ironic generic rewriting? Or are they ideological baggage weighing down the author and his work? While using literary forefathers doesn't Scott end up ensnared by them and their legacies? More damagingly, don't such strategies encourage the dangerous Golden Age nostalgia that feeds neo-imperialistic 'raj revisionism'?

Reservations of this nature have been voiced by critics such as Salman Rushdie and Benita Parry.[19] In an influential essay, Rushdie complains of Scott's 'instinct for the cliché' and strategy of 'borrowing' from Forster, suggesting that the rape motif is the quickest and easiest way 'to conjure up white society's fear of the darkie'.[20] However, Rushdie's critique suffers from an indiscriminate homogenizing programme of its own. He misrepresents Scott's work in order to fit it into a broader cultural phenomenon he calls 'raj revisionism'. His argument is entirely valid in political terms but is not helped by the generalizations through which he lumps Scott together with writers like M. M. Kaye who bears a closer relationship to John Masters in terms of strategy and technique. The *Raj Quartet* is psychologically more complex, historically better defined and has greater depth of character and motivation than anything comparable in Kaye. More serious is Benita Parry's concern over Hari's 'undignified' 'de-racination'. For her, Scott evinces a deeply ambiguous attitude to the Raj, an uneasy mix of swingeing criticism and admiration for an ideal and potential of service that was never realized. Part of the problem is located in Scott's narrative technique of 'disengagement'. She says: 'there are areas where such apparent disengagement can be unsatisfactory and disturbing, for when political conflict and moral choices are opened to *too many possible constructions*, the definition of an author's own controlling intelligence is obscured' (my emphasis).[21]

Engaging with this line of criticism is crucial, not just for our consideration of the *Raj Quartet*, but because it also goes to the very heart of how we read as post-colonial subjects. For my point in this chapter, and to a certain extent throughout this study, is precisely that British fictions have been read in a complicit way which allows *too few* possible constructions. I have called these possible constructions interpretative possibilities. As suggested earlier Anglo-Indian discourse sought to stake out for itself a rigidly demarcated territory embracing words and behaviour ('playing the white man') and dictating the form, content and reception of cultural productions that would engage with it. Far from revealing the dangers of fetishizing plurality of meaning in British fictions of India, the proliferation of perspectives, those possible constructions, is part of the unravelling and withdrawal of the imperial narrative seen particularly clearly in Paul Scott. Read in this way the charge that the author's 'controlling intelligence is obscured' becomes a mark of the text's success in avoiding narrative-ideological complicity. It is then the responsibility of the reader to reconstruct meaning from the multiplicity of fragments the imperial narrative has become. As Wolfgang Iser reminds us, the intention of the text is located in the reader's imagination.[22]

Only when this proliferation is accepted can our readings diversify not just to address the remnants of the imperial narrative itself, but also to begin to recognize the elements which have infiltrated the convention and brought about its disruption, elements which will be immediately familiar to aficionados of post-colonial criticism. For Scott's concern in these novels is with hybrids, margins and places 'between' – like the 'dangerous area of fallibility between a policy and its pursuit' which characterizes Britain's political dealings with the sub-continent for Srinivasan (*Jewel*, p. 236) – and his strategy is to introduce the ambivalent, the metonymic and the dialogic into monolithic, monologically understood situations and relationships. The respective roles of Ahmed and Hari offer a very different interpretative possibility in this construction. Shortly before the disastrous last journey to Ranpur, Perron and Sarah drive out to watch Ahmed hawking on the Nawab of Mirat's land. Both appreciate the grace and beauty of the activity, but the reader is made aware of something anachronistic in the scenario, something that recalls those tableaux which frequently punctuate the *Quartet*. This sense is summed up in Sarah's recognition of the scene as 'something of the old India' (*Division*, p. 620). Ahmed and his lifestyle only take on their full ironic meaning at the end when he freely steps off the hijacked train and into the murderous crowd of Hindu and Sikh fanatics. In this context his death suggests that the world he represents is passing away in an India about to be changed forever by partition. His actions are less those of a faithful native than an indicator of the closure of the old romantic construction of the hawking, hunting India of the princes.[23] Whether Sarah and the rest of the Layton family believe in this old India as the 'real India' is beside the point. Ahmed dies not merely because he is acting according to type but because, in making his gesture, he is revealing his inability to break out of the behaviour patterns demanded by what Sarah calls 'a received life'. The hawking Ahmed stands for the historical-mythical past and his death cordons off one facet of the Anglo-Indian discursive staple, underlining its unsuitability for the post-colonial writer. In so doing, the Ahmed character-type is used in a metonymic rather than a metaphoric way; he comes to stand for a larger body of characters distributed throughout British fictions of India, much in the way the historian-narrator consciously arranges his characters for exploration in *Jewel*, 'like toys sent out by kneeling children intent on pursuing their grim but necessary games' (*Jewel*, p. 145).

If Ahmed can be read as representing the past then, in the same way, Hari represents the future, or at least one possible formulation of it. As much is indicated early in the *Quartet* when he muses on his sense of being exiled from two cultures, in a letter to his fair-weather friend Colin Lindsey; 'At the moment there seems to be no one country that I owe an undivided duty to. Perhaps this is the pattern of the future. I don't know whether that encourages me or alarms me' (*Jewel*, p. 328). Kumar's hybridity, a fusion of English attitudes and learning and Indian colouring and background, leaves him ill at ease, and at home neither in the Anglo-Indian community nor among his fellow Indians. As the embodiment of both English and Indian characteristics he can be read as a paragon of Scott's insistent valorization of duality and, perhaps, indicative of the classic liberal position of the author. However, another potential interpretation of Hari discloses quite different results. In fact, Kumar's cultural hybridity could be seen as a telling intervention which splits the homogeneously imagined community of the English in India. The most obvious occurrence is in his courtship of Daphne. The idea of a black man/white woman combination works against the mores of Anglo-India which, as so often, receive articulation in disconcertingly forthright fashion from Merrick to whom the man in any interracial liaison – if such *must* be undertaken – should be white because there is about whiteness the connotation of 'something more finely, more delicately adjusted. Well – superior. Capable of leading' (*Day*, p. 263). Certainly this configuration contravenes generic traditions as well as Anglo-Indian discourse, since previous writers mainly fought shy of it, preferring the gender and racial reassurance of the white man/black woman alliance. Daphne's actual *choice* of Hari over Merrick would have been unthinkable in the genre previously.[24] For the imagined community of Anglo-India the issue is one of survival, as Count Bronowsky realizes: 'You English all felt that she didn't want you ... and of course among exiles that is a serious breach of faith. It amounts to treachery really ...' (*Day*, p. 235).

This is only one in a number of ways Hari slips the clutches of the taxonomical discourse and its narrative conventions. Daphne recognizes that there is no possibility of him speaking within the parameters of the exclusive, binarist British narrative as it has developed when she admits that, 'for Hari, no story worked' (*Jewel*, p. 542). Just as Hari refuses to concoct an alibi for the night of the rape, as Daphne desperately hopes he will, so we are never given his version of the Bibighar incident. His reticence under interrogation – and later at the second interview with Rowan – is of a different quality from the tight-lipped paranoia of the English community. It is a tactical silence and preserves him as the 'left-over', 'loose-end' of the British-Indian encounter, evading incorporation into a narrative which would offer no space for him to speak. At the end of *A Division of the Spoils* Perron traces Hari to an address in the backstreets of Ranpur. He takes a taxi part of the way but on arrival at the street's entrance the driver refuses to take him any further: 'Taxis, he said, did not go into such places' (*Division*, p. 717). There is a sense in which Perron has stumbled on Anglo-India's own Heart of Darkness, a 'black' hole into which British power-knowledge imperatives cannot venture. Subsequently, it comes as no surprise to discover that when Perron locates Hari's door his knock receives no reply. In a further Conradian touch the occupant is out. Hari and his narrative are, and remain, in Eagleton's phrase, the 'absent centre' of the novel sequence.[25]

The only other character for whom a similar claim can be made is Hari's adversary Merrick; at no point in the *Quartet* is the reader furnished with his direct unmediated voice. In an important sense both characters are the definitive creations of the Raj: more, even, than the Laytons with their affective investment in the paternalist myth. Hari and Merrick reveal how character is created, and human relationships warped, in a society based so clearly on domination and subjection. Merrick, the oddball, the outsider who would be an insider, the victimized lower middle-class schoolboy venting his frustrations in the colony, is a striking example of a particular subject position within class and national ideologies. His repressed homosexuality spills over into a sado-masochism which comes to express the real animus of the British–Indian relationship behind the sense of vocation and mission. Sarah Layton reluctantly acknowledges this when she admits of him, 'You are ... our dark side, the arcane side' (*Day*, p. 476).[26]

More than this, Merrick's frequent and embarrassing interventions on behalf of an ideal of racial superiority he believes the British have lost sight of, begin to produce another series of ruptures in the imagined community of Anglo-India and what it is in India to do. The maverick Merrick prises apart the narrative of beneficent supervision on which the Raj's self-image is based. Ironically, as he does so he leaves space for Hari Kumar, Macaulay's 'brown-skinned Englishman' incarnate, the 'loose end' the British–Indian connection has created but would deny and silence. He enters through the fissures created both by Scott's deconstruction of narrative and character, and by Merrick's sacred dividing lines between colonizer and colonized, which are really cracks in a narrative that, since Kipling, has sought to depict the relationship as one based on sweetness, light and (carefully ordered) union. It is here that Hari finds a locale, and a voice which enunciates a central 'message' of the *Quartet*. While Hari's hybridity is not a valid position in the imperial narrative – he cannot live the life of Anglicized privilege he originally longed for and must eke out a living as a journalist – he can partake of that culture in the persona of 'Philoctetes', the resonant *nom de plume* he adopts to write the article 'Alma Mater', about his lost youth in England, which Perron discovers in a copy of the Ranpur Gazette. He can remake himself in narrative on his own terms and find, in the discrepancy between its tone of nostalgia and the reality of his present circumstances, and between the classical name and form he chooses and his own disempowered cultural position, an appropriate vehicle for his experiences. Moreover, the spiritually battered Hari is empowered precisely in that he comes to articulate and personify all the losses suffered in a novel sequence which depicts individuals and communities in a state of transition, transmigration and depletion. Borders are crossed: literally, for the Hindu travellers to what will become free India, and Muslims journeying to Pakistan, in the fateful exodus in the months before partition. Indians prepare to 'enter' and embark on the government of their own country, while the English make ready to exit from a site of power and prestige and re-embark for home. *The Raj Quartet* is filled with 'comings and goings'. There are frequent 'Journeys into Uneasy Distances' by train; movements in and out of Rose Cottage; Sarah travels to Calcutta and the 'other side' of the dividing line with the parvenu public-school rebel Clark; Barbie urges the removal of Mabel's body to Ranpur; Teddie ventures into the jungle for a rendezvous with death; and, of course, there is the tragic last train to Ranpur – all in a sense prefigured in the initial image of Daphne running from her assailants. In the given scenario displacement, the borders, the margins and their coterminous identities, the outsider, the exile, the hybrid, become the centre of a shifting focus which serves only to underscore the transience of human tenure and the vanity of imperial wishes. As the ever-perceptive Bronowsky remarks, 'now we are all émigrés' (*Division*, p. 666).

The character of Hari Kumar constitutes a powerful irruption on the previously gentle, rolling landscape of British fictions of India. As a position not catered for in Anglo-Indian discourse and ignored or marginalized in the fictional tradition it spawned, hybridity works with Scott's technique of undercutting character-types and narrative expectation to forge a new kind of fiction about India, responsive to the changed perception of subjectivity and national identity in the post-colonial world. The recognition of the necessary historicization of imagined communities and cultural productions need not solely be seen as an issue for the post-colonial writer engaged in the articulation of a colonized, or formerly colonized, identity. To insist on the transference of the fluidity of 'history' and 'culture' to the realm of the colonizer, is to subvert the very identity politics that grounds the claim to authority. By revealing this authority, not as 'natural' or 'given', but as a construct – the uncertain and transitory product of discourses of power – we may begin to shift the power relations which enclose the colonial subject in that space of fantastic otherness. We must insist that the instability of identity is not an attribute of the post-colonial subject, but the necessary position of all identity claims. In the *Raj Quartet* Merrick's split personality and repressions, Hari Kumar's hybridity, and Sarah's and Susan's existential angst in the face of the break-up of 'inherited identity' are only the most prominent examples of such instability.

In one sense, Salman Rushdie is a post-colonial reader *par excellence*. Yet if this section on British fictions of India has taught anything, it should have alerted us to the fact that every reading is above all an indicator of its own historical moment. What his criticisms of the *Raj Quartet* show is not so much shortcomings in the novels themselves as the continuation, in the public sphere, of certain attitudes and prejudices diagnosed in the novels' treatment of race and nation. The unravelling of imperial constructions and perspectives Scott undertakes in his texts has not been realized in actuality. On the contrary, they seemed to have re-emerged at the time Rushdie penned his essay in the euphoria surrounding that curious imperial postscript, the Falklands campaign.[27] It is hard to imagine that Paul Scott would have viewed with anything other than dismay the appropriation, by the resurgent forces of nationalism and apologist 'raj revisionism', of a critique which suggestively links insularity and imperial race consciousness to continued racial tension at the moment of writing. In Rushdie's case, utterances which categorize Scott's work as elegiac, liberal cliche are, of course, signs of the investment the speaker has in the historical events of independence and partition, and the ongoing business of seeking new ways of mediating such experiences. Certainly, Scott can be placed in a tradition of writing which might variously be called 'the novel of empire' or 'the liberal rewriting of the imperial encounter', but, as this reading has sought to propose, Scott participates in the tradition only to dismantle it, to expose its constituents one by one, to unravel the imperial narrative. In its active exposure of the historicity of a tenacious communal fiction, and more particularly in the disjunctive rendering of historical process and subjectivity, *The Raj Quartet* can, in certain respects, be seen as the last stop in the literary line before Rushdie's own epic of partition and its legacy, *Midnight's Children*.[28]

Notes

1. Benedict Anderson, *Imagined Communities: Reflections on the Origins and Spread of Nationalism*, p. 26. See also Homi Bhabha (ed.), *Nation and Narration* and *The Location of Culture*.
2. Robin Moore, *Paul Scott's Raj*, pp. 91–2.
3. George Woodcock, 'The Sometime Sahibs', p. 39.
4. Scott comments on his sense of never having met anyone like Forster's Turtons and Burtons because they were depicted as representatives of an ideology rather than as working individuals; 'To see them occupied is not necessary but without the aura of occupation they lack what was their chief justification', Paul Scott, 'India: A Post-Forsterian View', p. 118.
5. David Goldknopf, *The Life of the Novel*, p. 14. See also, Ian Watt, *The Rise of the Novel: Studies in Defoe, Richardson and Fielding*, pp. 21–5.

6. Partha Chatterjee, from *Nationalist Thought and the Colonial World: A Derivative Discourse*, quoted in Homi K. Bhabha, 'DissemiNation: Time, Narrative, and the Margins of the Modern Nation', in Bhabha (ed.), *Nation and Narration*, p. 293.
7. I am indebted to Robin Moore, *Paul Scott's Raj*, p. 63, for the phrase 'vestigial narrator'.
8. Genette, *Narrative Discourse*, p. 203.
9. Scott was always fond of the elegant, multi-clausal sentence. Two of his literary heroes were the great nineteenth-century exponents of this style, Dickens and Thackeray. This relaxed, luxurious tone – along, no doubt, with the sheer weight of the *Raj Quartet* as a body of work – has misled several critics into viewing the cycle as an example of unproblematic 'nineteenth-century' realism; see Francine Weinbaum, *Paul Scott: A Critical Study*, p. 179; while K. Bhaskara Rao in *Paul Scott* proclaims, 'We have no difficulty in placing the *Quartet*. It is written in the grand tradition of nineteenth-century fiction' (p. 146). In fact, far from being simply linear and realist, Scott's technique is shifting, elusive and allusive. The densely packed apparent 'realism' is pocked by outbursts of dreams, hallucinations and spiritual revelations, mainly associated with Barbie Batchelor in *The Towers of Silence*.

   Ultimately, it may be unhelpful to speak of a realist/modernist schism in relation to Scott. The writer has gurus in either camp – to Dickens and Thackeray add T. S. Eliot – and believes that 'modernist' innovations such as the stream of consciousness have been absorbed into fiction in general, 'not ... as a technique which changed the *form* of novels but as a material – as a new aspect of those human realities which are available to us to see, understand and try to convey', Paul Scott, *My Appointment with the Muse*, p. 88.
10. Patrick Swinden, *Paul Scott: Images of India*, p. 98.
11. Genette, *Narrative Discourse*.
12. Gerard Genette, 'Time and Narrative in *A la Recherche de Temps Perdu*', in Hillis Miller (ed.), *Aspects of Narrative*, p. 96.
13. Genette, *Narrative Discourse*, pp. 48ff. and 67ff.
14. See Bill Schwartz, 'An Englishman Abroad ... and at Home: The Case of Paul Scott', pp. 95–105, which brilliantly sets Scott in historical and ideological context. Also, Moore, *Paul Scott's Raj*, pp. 134–52; Hilary Spurling, *Paul Scott: A Life*, p. 303; Tom Nairn, *The Break-Up of Britain: Crisis and Neo-Nationalism*, pp. 256–88, on Enoch Powell. Tariq Ali makes the connection between the psychologies and upbringing of Powell and Ronald Merrick and adds:

    > I have always thought it a bit of a cop-out to kill Merrick off at the end. Surely he returned to Britain after Independence, joined the Conservative Party, became a Cabinet Minister and then began to be haunted by the sight of odd Asian faces in *his* sweet and pleasant land. (Tariq Ali quoted in Moore, *Paul Scott's Raj*, p. 139)

That Scott recognized it too is implied in the title and content of his speech on race consciousness and cultural shock, 'Enoch Sahib: A Slight Case of Cultural Shock', in *My Appointment with the Muse*, pp. 90–104.

15. Green, *Dreams of Adventure, Deeds of Empire*, pp. 336–7.
16. Salman Rushdie, *The Satanic Verses*, p. 130.
17. In the same way Barbie's breakdown and death at the conclusion of *The Towers of Silence* mark the end of the efficacy of Christianity – like empire itself one of Kermode's 'apocalyptic types' – as an explanatory meta-narrative in the colonial situation.
18. P. M. S. Dawson, 'Race, Sex and Class in Paul Scott's *Raj Quartet*', in Moore-Gilbert (ed.), *Literature and Imperialism*, p. 177.
19. Salman Rushdie, 'Outside the Whale', in *Imaginary Homelands*, pp. 87–101; and Benita Parry, 'Paul Scott's Raj', pp. 359–69.
20. Rushdie, *Imaginary Homelands*, p. 88. As has been suggested the 'borrowing' from Forster and use of 'cliché' characters and situations is part of the strategy of pushing Anglo-Indian generic convention to its limits. Rushdie is right, however, in suspecting that: 'it is useless ... to suggest that if rape must be used as the metaphor of the Indo-British connection, then surely ... it should be the rape of an Indian woman by one or more Englishmen of whatever class' (p. 88). It is useless because it becomes clear as the novels proceed that the real assault is by Ronald Merrick on Hari Kumar. Taking a synoptic view it might be possible to claim that the motif of heterosexual rape is redundant because self-explanatory, stale and obvious. When this schematic, however 'accurate', has been imposed it is hard to imagine an original way it could be developed. It would take an artist of very exceptional talent indeed to blow any life into this particular cadaver, whereas Scott's metaphor constantly demands the explanation and exploration he undertakes.
21. Parry, 'Paul Scott's Raj', pp. 359–60.
22. Wolfgang Iser, 'Indeterminacy and the Reader's Response in Prose Fiction', in Hillis Miller, *Aspects of Narrative*, p. 43. Scott reaches the same conclusion by empirical means in the essay 'The Architecture of the Arts', in *Muse*, pp. 75–89. He says that the novelist's work, 'does not begin to exist until someone picks it up and reads it, and that then it will not exist as the writer wrote it but as the reader reads it' (p. 79).
23. The same view is suggested by the demise of the native state of Mirat which is to accede to India. In *The Raj Quartet*, as in *The Birds of Paradise* (1962), Scott does not romanticize the princely states in the way Forster and Masters are wont to do. They are used instead as an illustration of Britain's duplicity and contentment with the divisions it created in Indian society and which eventually bedevilled independence.
24. D. C. R. A. Goonetilleke, *Images of the Raj*, p. 143. Another post-

independence novel which deals with the same transgressive romance motif is Ruth Prawer Jhabvala's *Heat and Dust*. The unspeakable can now be spoken. In his analysis of Paul Scott's *Raj Quartet* in *After Empire*, Michael Gorra offers a more extended consideration than is found in these pages of Hari's hybridity, its roots and wider significance for racially exclusive imaginings of Britishness, and of his symbiotic relationship to that other outsider, Merrick. Gorra agrees that 'the *Quartet* itself mounts a critique of its own Orientalism', and concludes, like Bill Schwartz, that Scott's novels stand 'as the first anti-essentialist account of national identity in modern British literature', see Michael Gorra, *After Empire: Scott, Naipaul, Rushdie*, pp. 24, 45.

25. Terry Eagleton, *Criticism and Ideology: A Study in Marxist Literary Theory*, p. 138.
26. There is also a sense in which he represents the subversion and termination of the generic convention of cultural cross-dressing, when he dons Pathan costume to cruise in search of young Indian boys. And, of course, he is killed wearing it: the end of that particular fantasy!
27. Rushdie sees that 'raj revisionism' he identifies in his essay, as 'the artistic counterpart of the rise of conservative ideologies in modern Britain', *Imaginary Homelands*, p. 92.
28. Tariq Ali, 'Midnight's Children', p. 88, quoted in Schwartz, 'An Englishman Abroad ... and at Home, p. 97.

VI Post-Colonial DestiNations: Spacial Re(con)figurings in Khushwant Singh's *Train to Pakistan* and Rohinton Mistry's *A Fine Balance*

> The idea of India ... is based on ... multiplicity ... plurality and tolerance ... There can be no one way – religious, cultural or linguistic – of being an Indian; let difference reign. (Salman Rushdie, 'The Assassination of Indira Gandhi', in *Imaginary Homelands*)

> 'Part of the importance of the "fragmentary" point of view lies in this, that it resists the drive for a shallow homogenisation and struggles for other, potentially richer definitions of the "nation", and the future political community.' (Gyanendra Pandey quoted in Partha Chatterjee, *The Nation and Its Fragments*)

In an essay which has become a seminal text in post-colonial literary and cultural studies, Fredric Jameson analyses what he describes as 'Third World Literature in the Era of Multinational Capitalism'. This piece is probably well enough known to require only a cursory synopsis here. Briefly then, Jameson contends that in 'third world' writing, 'the story of the private individual destiny is always an allegory of the embattled situation of the public third world culture and society'. He argues that the split between the private and public domains, characteristic of the industrialized, individualistic bourgeois West, does not exist to such an extent in the community-oriented 'third world', with the result that in third-world literary productions the fate of the individual is always inextricably linked to the fate of his or her collectivity, understood within late colonialism in terms of the nation. This concern for typicality and representativeness recalls, for Jameson, earlier modes of Western literature, superseded by the atomized, psychologically preoccupied modernist subject. The typicality of the individual or, in literary terms, the character, results in third-world literary texts taking the form of allegory. Furthermore, 'in distinction to the unconscious allegories of our own [*sic*] cultural texts, third world national allegories are conscious and overt'.[1] Now, there are a number of tendentious generalizations in Jameson's essay, and its Euro-Americanist objectifying shortcomings have been noted by critics such as Aijaz Ahmad and Rosemary Marangoly George.[2] However, it has proved influential for several subsequent considerations of the relation of the nation and the literary work in post-colonial criticism. For my part, I wish to take issue with two elements of Jameson's thesis, one explicit and the other implicit. The first is that national allegories need to be 'conscious and overt'. The second is the apparent argument that each literary text is an allegory, discrete and complete unto itself. Certainly there are several South Asian writers whose texts, as multifarious but self-contained accounts of Indian history, lend themselves to interpretation is such terms: one thinks of the encyclopaedic quality in texts such as Manohar Malgonkar's *A Bend in the Ganges* (1964), Salman Rushdie's *Midnight's Children* (1981), Shashi Tharoor's *The Great Indian Novel* (1989) or Mukul Kesavan's *Looking Through Glass* (1995). However, in this chapter I will argue that the recurring thematic and tropological deployment of space and the body in post-independence Indian literature may indeed be seen as elements of a national allegory, but one which, rather than being offered complete in each individual text, is instead accretional, cumulative and continually being created and worked out as the body of English language Indian fiction grows. In this way an ever-expanding literary space is created for the multiplicity of communal, ethnic, caste and class voices that comprise India. These tropes, repeated and reworked, then constitute part of an attempt to think through partition and subsequent Indian history – including Indira Gandhi's State of Emergency 1975–77 – and reclaim colonized space and its bodies from external and internal forces of oppression. Specifically, in relation to our central concern with narrative and power, colonial power gives way to the homogenizing power moves of the nation-state, and the issue once again becomes one of narrative as resistance. Although Indian fiction in English, and in other tongues, offers numerous examples, in pursuing my argument I shall compare *Train to Pakistan* (1956) by the Sikh writer Khushwant Singh and the Canadian-based Parsi novelist Rohinton Mistry's *A Fine Balance* (1996).

Of course, it might immediately be objected that all literary fiction is concerned with spaces and bodies, as characters in locations. However, as previous chapters have demonstrated, under colonialism, and especially within the patterns of colonial and post-colonial literature, these seemingly innocent juxtapositions are linked indissolubly with the issue of power. Colonialism operates both *spatially* – in the acquisition and adaptation of the land – and on the *body* of the colonized, both through physical coercion where necessary, and through the enforcement of and limitations on *movements of the body in space*. Hence the somewhat embroidered quality of my chapter title. I use the term re(con)figurings as a correlation of the palimpsest-like layers of significance I seek to indicate: first, 'configuration' as a mode of arrangement or relative positions (of spaces, bodies or things); second, the verb 'to figure', in the sense of being a symbol, representing typically or imagining; and finally, 'figure' in its nounal form, indicating external shape and, more specifically, the body. It goes without saying that, after the demise of colonial power 'on the ground', the drive to control the body in space becomes an issue of establishing and defending national borders, a project often requiring the kind of direct physical intervention previously associated with the former ruler. Such construction, along with attempts at interrogation and deconstruction, have a profile in both politics and literature which it is interesting to trace.

So, while this paper is prepared to read along with Jameson's somewhat totalizing definitions of national allegory to a certain extent, an immediate distinction needs to be made between the conditions for its manifestation in India and those in other 'third-world' countries to which Jameson might be referring. In particular, the history of Indian nationalism offers a highly visible example of the necessary elisions and forcible yokings of a national project with regard to the different communities occupying the space of the projected nation. This is clearest in the years approaching independence in 1947. Significantly, although Indian nationalism remained the main focus for Muslims until the 1920s, the conditions for a belief in a national entity which could call forth attitudes of unquestioning loyalty from both Hindus and Muslims, inasmuch as they existed, did so only sporadically and often locally: for example in the Lucknow Pact of 1916, brokered by Tilak and Jinnah, and in the subsequent Anti-Rowlatt Act agitation (1919) and the Khilafat and Non-Cooperation Movements (1919–22); and even here, in the latter case, nationalist aims required articulation in terms of the specifically religious rhetoric of 'Islam under attack'. The reasons for the tenuous nature of the Hindu-Muslim rapprochement are too involved to bear more than a superficial examination in an essay of this nature. However, primary among them is the British role in fostering communalism, including the establishment of separate electorates under the Morley-Minto Reforms of 1908 which encouraged Indians to think and vote communally, and the compounding of this policy in the 1932 Communal Award, and the Government of

India Act (1935). Such moments can be seen as the most visible markers of longer-term British support for the Muslim League as a bulwark against the recalcitrant and predominantly Hindu, Congress. As Bipan Chandra points out, there were also a number of deep-seated factors within traditional society itself militating against totally successful union: such as the older pre-colonial identifications which survived primarily in rural areas, and rushed in to fill the vacuum during lulls in nationalist activity; demographic complications, as in areas where landlords were predominantly Hindu and their tenants mainly Muslim; the Hindu nature of much early nationalist rhetoric, idiom and symbol which alienated Muslims; and, finally, a distorted and compartmentalized view of Indian history – fostered by British historiographical paradigms – as an era of Hindu artistic and cultural achievement followed by decline, defeat and eclipse by a Muslim 'golden age', after which the British appeared as saviours of the Hindu in the eighteenth century.[3]

Communal antipathy between Hindu and Muslim, along with caste antagonism, posed particular problems for any attempt to portray a national future free from the colonizer in holistic terms. So too did programmes with a marked suspicion toward modern nationalism such as Gandhi's vision of India less as a nation-state than as a vast affiliation of 'self-sufficient village republics' operating along pre-industrial lines.[4] Moreover, the imperative of reclaiming a pre-colonial culture whose very existence had been denied by the colonizing power did not arise in the same way as for, say, subsequent African nationalisms. The work of English orientalists and the process of Anglicized education for selected Indians initiated by Macaulay, meant that expressions of nationalist sentiment in Indian fiction often took hybrid forms, marrying the conventions of the English nineteenth-century novel with the storytelling traditions of the Hindu epics. This remained the case for Indian writers in the twentieth century, such as Raja Rao whose *Kanthapura* (1938) utilizes oral patterns within a novelistic form. However, for *Kanthapura*, as for another key text which examines the state of pre-independence India through representative figures and scenario – Mulk Raj Anand's *Untouchable* (1935) – attempts to imagine the nation as a unit are constantly hindered by the intrusion of India as she is, stratified and segregated by caste and community, rather than as the nationalist project would wish her to be. As national allegories in Jamesonian terms, Mulk Raj Anand's and Raja Rao's texts make certain strategically necessary elisions. The myth of national unity is confronted by India's polymorphous, polyglot reality. In suggesting this it is not my intention to repeat the hoary imperialist shibboleth that India has always been hopelessly divided along sectarian lines and therefore cannot be a nation; fifty years of history firmly refute such an argument. My point is, rather, on the level of representation. It is that India offers a particularly striking instance of the representational process by which nations unify across differences. Playing a central role in this, literary images of the nation are always already predicated on the simultaneous exposure and emasculation of religious, cultural and ethnic differences. The distinction between pre-independence and post-independence writers is in part related to their investment in the nation as a supra-representational given; the former seek to delimit while the latter celebrate the many narratives within the textual borders.[5]

For example, *Untouchable* with its Joycean day-in-the-life technique and use of almost Brechtian stereotypes, a legacy of its author's sojourn in modernist Europe, conceives of the move from colonial subjecthood to independent national citizenship in terms of a bridging of existing rifts in the contemporary body politic. Specifically, having illustrated the problem – the horrific treatment meted out to the untouchable protagonist Bakha by orthodox Hindu society – and rehearsed the putative remedies, such as Christianity and Gandhism, it is seen to be the absence of the technological modern spirit which Marxism can rectify which will liberate the untouchables and create an atmosphere in which true nationhood can breathe. Rao's *Kanthapura* inscribes difference in the myth, legend and song that create the text's multiple perspectives. The technique of situating the story of the independence movement in a single village with a representative Gandhi figure and, unlike Anand, a rapprochement between the untouchables and other castes, reveals the text to be as much an idealized account of what the early nationalist leaders had called a 'nation-in-the-making'[6] as a commentary on actual contemporary developments. The book charts the rise of a national consciousness among the peasant classes, while also encapsulating the 1930s move from the direct action of the civil disobedience era (1930–31) to the constitutionalism of the later years of the decade and, for a certain generation, the move from Gandhism to the kind of socialist materialist critique offered by Nehru. Although this move is symbolically undertaken at the end by the hero Moorthy, overall the text can be read as an illustration of what Partha Chatterjee has described as Gandhi's 'critique of civil society' and also the larger tactics and phases of the nationalist struggle.[7] With its use of tradition and legend to articulate the dynamics of struggle, *Kanthapura* is very consciously a text about nation building. This is evident not merely in the metaphorical correspondence of

Kanthapura to India and Moorthy to Gandhi, but also in the features of *satyagraha* – the fasts, the boycotts and so on – described, and in the formation of the socially representative Kanthapura Congress Committee which includes those previously disfranchised such as women and untouchables. But the text also shows how nationalism met opposition from conservative elements even within Hindu society, backed and supported by the British. The villagers struggle bravely to a bitter-sweet victory, but one is all the while aware that this embryonic nation is constantly being formed across and against difference. For example, after a meeting in which their leader Moorthy has told the villagers about Gandhi's imminent Salt March, we learn that, 'Seenu rang the gong, and eyes shut themselves in silence, and the brahmin heart and the weaver heart and pariah heart seemed to beat the one beat of Siva dancing' (*Kanthapura*, p. 124). Similarly, when the nationalist lawyer Sankar begins Hindi classes another faultline is exposed:

> He said Hindi would be the national language of India, and though Kannada is good enough for our province, Hindi must become the national tongue, and whenever he met a man in the street, he did not say 'How are you?' in Kannada, but took to the northern manner and said 'Ram-Ram'. But what was shameful was the way he began to talk Hindi to his mother, who understood not a word of it, but he said she would learn it one day. (*Kanthapura*, p. 103)

In this way *Kanthapura* stands both as a tribute to the idealism involved in anti-colonial nationalism and as a marker of its internal contradictions.

Later, 'allegorical' views of India often call attention to the fragmentary nature of the society they describe. The tropes and devices they use to connect the fate of character and country correspondingly become more partial and contingent: dates and events which significantly yoke the fates of character and nation – most famously *Midnight's Children* of course, but also Nayantara Sahgal's *A Time to be Happy* (1958); accidents of genealogy – Rushdie again but also K. A. Abbas' *Inquilab* (1955); tentative intercommunal relationships – *Train to Pakistan* and Chaman Nahal's *Azadi* (1975); and most insistently the movement of bodies on the railways during partition, as in countless novels including the texts to which I will return, *Train to Pakistan* and *A Fine Balance*.[8] So, just as the nation was felt to be 'in-the-making' during the independence struggle, but has since had its internal self-definition challenged from various quarters, so too Indian novels in English have developed from participation in the project of articulating the idea of an Indian nation, to questioning the monolithic coherence of this imagined community. Since the death of Nehru in 1964 and the rise of, among other things, a rather less visionary and altruistic form of politics interested more in the immediate electoral gains to be derived from fostering special interest groups, rather than seeking to support and serve the secular ideal – the novel in India has had, according to Kavila Matthai:

> to confront an authoritarian state-sponsored version of national identity and the erosion of the idealism that had accompanied nationalism ... In a situation where the official version is the only one, purporting to be the authentic version as well, the role of literature becomes crucial in releasing alternative versions.[9]

In an arena in which certain class, cultural and indeed gender identities are taken to be representative of some essential Indianness, and made to stand for the whole nation, those outside such a definition risk marginalization and, in extreme cases, victimization. Thus, like all nations India is an experiment in selective inclusions and exclusions but one that uses particularly volatile ingredients. In recent years, revived communalism has arisen in the ugly mask of Hindu nationalism and trampled in atavistic frenzy over the ruins of the Babri Mosque at Ayodhya, destroyed by Hindu militants who claim the site as sacred to Hindusim, and which also marked another attack on anti-colonial nationalism's enshrined secularism by the monological – and curiously colonial – forces of religious identification.[10] Effacing signs of non-Hinduness is something which can only be achieved by a revisionist view of history and culture, and the attempted imposition of a single set of acceptable narratives of Indianness. This, in turn, can only succeed by turning a deaf ear to the multitudinous stories reverberating around the cavernous echo-chamber of the nation, stories which often diverge from the state-sanctioned version. As Arun Mukherjee notes:

> in India, the newspaper version is not the end of a story. It is recast and embroidered around roadside tea shops and family compounds every day. One person begins it and others interject in between speculating about the several possible ways the event could be narrativised. The event continuously calls for re-narrativisations and remains forever inconclusive.[11]

It is this diversity that emboldens me to suggest a different way of understanding 'national allegory'. Instead of reading individual literary texts as free-standing attempts to 'tell the story of India', it might be more rewarding – and more libertarian – to think of these texts as fragments in an ongoing superallegory more faithfully reflecting the multiplicitous make-up of India. Recent writers such as Rushdie, Amitav Ghosh and Bapsi Sidhwa have incorporated an acknowledgement of the diversity of the culture they seek to describe in narrative techniques emphasizing the nation as split, fragmented and always 'in process'. In addition, writers like Boman Desai and Allan Sealy have taken it upon themselves to articulate, in allegorized form, epic narratives of their respective marginal communities, the Parsis and the Eurasians or Anglo-Indians.[12] To think of these stories as cohering into part of an all-embracing allegory, we then need to think about those recurring tropes, images and thematic concerns which they may share. It is for this reason that I wish to argue for space and the body as elements of a larger transtextual national allegory brought into being through the variety of figurings of nation, subjects and events in Indian writing. In fact, in important ways, both Khushwant Singh and Rohinton Mistry are in the business of interrogating loopholes in the national project – the ongoing task of promoting national identifications and affiliations – and the various tribulations involved when the rhetoric fails: indeed, which are always immanent in such rhetoric. The differences in their approach are (in part) related to the periods in which they write: for Khushwant Singh the 1950s and for Mistry the 1990s. Khushwant Singh records events but also – in the guardedly utopian village of Mano Majra at the start of *Train to Pakistan* – seems to be positing, retrospectively, an alternative, if history had not 'switched points' so to speak. Consequently, images of connecting, of bridges and bridging come to play a central role in the novel. For Rohinton Mistry, writing forty years later and interested in the vast pattern of interconnections between individuals and communities – and between times, in the form of memory, and spatial location – the image of a quilt, representing the interlinked stories of his central characters, acquires almost talismanic significance. The image of the quilt with its squares of different materials, shades and patterns sitting side by side, might serve us too as a metaphor for all those stories that go to make up India.

Edward Said has commented that what 'radically distinguishes the imagination of anti-imperialism ... is the primacy of the geographical in it', based on the need to imaginatively regain the land lost to the colonizer.[13] There is a discernible preoccupation with images of the land in post-colonial fiction and particularly with modes of movement across, through and between aspects of the physical terrain which sometimes owe their origins to colonial technological as well as discursive practices; one thinks of the prevalence of the road as a channel for colonialism, neo-colonialism and resistance in the work of many African writers. In India the struggle most frequently coheres around the image of the railway journey and the vast spaces it traverses and hence brings into proximity. Space is both that which is being contested and the site of that contest. In India, the great imperial cities Bombay, Calcutta and New Delhi became, in Sunil Khilnani's words, 'a stage where the regalia of British sovereignty was displayed, where the Indian was ruled, where space was most explicitly governed'.[14] In his view it was the achievement of Gandhi, with his 'vaunted idea of the village as a counter to the colonial city', who, in his long marches across the countryside, 'constructed a new topography of India defined not by the railway tracks that linked cities but by routes that connected villages ... Most importantly, he invented ways in which Indians could occupy and act in the public spaces of the Raj ...'.[15]

Beneath the surface one detects an ambivalence at the heart of certain Indian nationalist attitudes to the railways – 'British-made', yet built by Indian labour of course. On the one hand, railways were a visible symbol of intrusive imperial power: scars inflicted on the body of India by the invader and anathema to Gandhi's anti-technological vision. On the other hand, they were soon co-opted by the nationalists and used to spread the anti-British message far and wide. Initially unwelcome, the foreign mode of transport was quickly internalized and adapted to suit indigenous needs. And, as in life, so in art: the railway in imperial adventure fiction, such as Kipling's tales or Masters' novels, becomes a dehistoricized space with a double function; it is a potential thread for sedition, used by malcontents and sabotaged by communists and, conversely, it becomes a space for the Englishman to perform heroic deeds of saving India from impending chaos. In imperial romance the railway signifies Britain's technological and unifying legacy, it works centripetally. As well as a practical way of policing the empire it is also a conduit for what Benita Parry calls the 'capitalist specific' discursive practices of empire expressing the 'reterritorialization of space and the commitment to compulsory modernisation'.[16]

In *Train to Pakistan*, ironically, it is the railway, a result of capitalism and industrialization, that at first confirms the 'unquestioned ritualistic time of village life'[17] in Mano Majra. Prayers, work, food and sleep are all initially regulated by the passage of trains through the small station. The early morning mail train blows its whistle and wakes the mullah providing the cue for the Muslim call to prayer, which in turns wakes Meet Singh, the Sikh priest. In this way the train comes to stand for interdependence rather than communal rivalry and suggests Mano Majra as enjoying an idealized, trans-historical existence in its position on the frontier of the new nation in the soon to be divided Punjab of 1947. So too does its symbolic topography wherein the three brick buildings enclosing a common at the hub of the village are the Hindu moneylender's house, the mosque and the Sikh temple. But the imminent collision of the old harmonious and violent new worlds is suggested early on, not least in the tense shifts of the novel's opening. The first two paragraphs, placing the story that is to follow in the wider context of a maddeningly hot summer and late monsoon, and the communal riots heralding partition, are related in a quasi-oral storytelling tone reminiscent of Rao's *Kanthapura* and, significantly, in *the past tense.* They serve to historicize what follows, setting the story and the community it depicts at a specific moment in the past. Then, when we are told, 'Mano Majra is a tiny place' (*Train to Pakistan,* p. 10), the shift to present tense at once conjures a sense of immediacy and 'the now', and suggests a quality of timelessness which gives the subsequent description of the village an air of unreality. Thereafter, we are brought back to the fateful summer of 1947, and the text resumes its more conventional perfect tense narration, focusing in on the main protagonists of the story that is to follow. The zig-zagging temporal narrative here invoked continues in the early sections, producing an effect of simultaneity as characters' actions and whereabouts at the time of the murder of the Hindu money-lender Ram Lal are plotted.

The painstaking opening, setting the reader down gently in the apparently unchanging world of Mano Majra, with its time-honoured ritual and observances, has the effect of lulling the reader into a sense of familiarity and comfort. There is little direct speech by characters in the establishing present tense section, instead the evening goods train seems to say 'goodnight' for them. The train, and the nearby bridge, are used by the community to regulate life. A British innovation has been internalized and woven into the native social fabric. Likewise, mankind seems to be in harmony with nature. We learn that:

> By the time the 10.30 morning passenger train from Delhi comes in, life in Mano Majra has settled down to its dull daily routine. Men are in the fields. Women are busy with their daily chores.

> Children are out grazing cattle by the river. Persian wheels squeak and groan as bullocks go round and round ... Sparrows fly about the roofs, trailing straw in their beaks. Pye-dogs seek the shade of the long mud walls. Bats settle their arguments, fold their wings, and suspend themselves in sleep. (*Train to Pakistan*, p. 13)

We seem here to be witnessing what one might almost call an Indian pastoral scene. However, what subverts the idyll is the fact that the daily routine is described as 'dull' and, more tellingly, the image of bats 'settling their arguments'. It gestures towards bigger arguments that cannot be so easily settled and the end in store for this well-ordered society, as the madness of partition's communal butchery seeps into the village.

In fact, the whole of the opening is, with hindsight, highly ambiguous. There is a sense in which this society carries within in it the seeds of its own destruction. For example, the village is, despite appearances, carefully stratified; 'The Sikhs own all the land around the village; the Muslims are tenants'. Similarly, the train whistle, which punctuates the secretive trysts of the Sikh *budmash* Juggut Singh and his lover, Nooran the Muslim weaver's daughter, also provides the signal for the *dacoit* attack which culminates in the murder of Ram Lal. Later, the train brings the bodies of those killed fleeing the ethnic conflict to Mano Majra, and along with them, the seeds of communal strife itself. In contrast to the static idyll so beloved of imperial romance writers like John Masters, the Mano Majra 'idyll' is revealed as flawed, vulnerable and ripe for destruction. Indeed the text incorporates romance structures – heroic adventure and love story conventions – but places them at the service of a keenly observed and culturally specific narrative of a people caught in the tide of history. Once again, this is partly symbolized by the way in which communal time, previously regulated by the trains, starts to break down. We are told that:

> Early in September the time schedule in Mano Majra started to go wrong. Trains became less punctual than before ... Some days it seemed as though the alarm clock had been set for the wrong hour. On others, it was as if no one had remembered to wind it. Imam Baksh waited for Meet Singh to make the first start. Meet Singh waited for the mullah's call to prayer before getting up. People stayed in bed late without realising that times had changed and the mail train might not run through at all. Children did not know when to be hungry and clamoured for food all the time. (*Train to Pakistan*, pp. 92–3)

The railway brings the riven outside world into the measured rhythmic life of Mano Majra in the trainloads of bodies the villagers view with trepidation. It breaks up that life. As such it works centrifugally. By the end of the novel, with the Muslims effectively expelled and sent on their way across the new border to Pakistan, the railway becomes a space for Juggut Singh's heroic self-sacrifice on the line to save a trainload of his erstwhile Muslim neighbours, including Nooran. The heroic act is reclaimed for the Indian body; even if it culminates in that body's death and fails to arrest the demise of the old community.

Khushwant Singh's use of such images suggests the pre-eminence of the body within his symbolic arsenal. I would argue that the political connotations of the deployment of images of the body change between the colonial and post-colonial era. As David Arnold has pointed out in connection with medical discourse, colonialism in India was essentially a 'colonization of the body', concerned with the collection and classification of data about its subject's corporality; but that opposing readings meant that 'the body formed a site of contestation and not simply of colonial appropriation'.[18] The body also takes on a heightened significance at the time of partition, in that it bears the signs of ethnic allegiance, marking subjects as belonging on one or other side of a now unbridgeable divide. As *Train to Pakistan* demonstrates the resultant carnage often took place on trains carrying huge numbers of passengers to either national site of perceived safety, India or Pakistan; 'In India Sikhs and Hindus prowled the cars of ambushed trains, slaughtering every male they found who was circumcised. In Pakistan, Muslims raced along the trains murdering every man who was not'.[19] The bloody circumstances of partition give the lie to the cosy idea that nationhood was a benediction generously bestowed by the departing Raj. By the time of the late monsoon of 1947 almost a million people were dead and ten million had lost land and homes. Indeed, partition can be said to be the contest around the body in space that brings the nation into being. For Khushwant Singh, contending physical spaces and communal interest groups are constantly clashing and colliding. The text plays out the competing demands of the village community of Mano Majra, the affiliations of religion – here Sikhism and Islam – and finally the unitarian moves of the nation.

This is a novel that teems with bodies: from the spare, lean prose of the descriptions of the trainloads of corpses (*Train to Pakistan*, pp. 100–2) and the burning of those bodies; the dead floating in the river Sutlej after a massacre upstream (*Train to Pakistan*, pp. 164–5);

the extreme physical violence of the attack on Ram Lal; to the intense physicality in the description of Juggut and Nooran's love-making. It is there too in the bulky frame of Hukum Chand, Magistrate and Deputy District Commissioner with his seemingly emblematic corpulence and decay – he is 'the Government' personified, and is addressed as such by the old woman who brings the young singer Haseena whose services Hukum is keen to procure. (Hukum Chand is a complex character. Venal, corrupt and with an eye for the politically expedient, he is nevertheless revealed to be vulnerable – he seeks solace and affection from the girl rather than physical gratification – and humane – his pragmatic plan to release the incarcerated Jugga saves many Muslim lives, including Haseena's.) And finally there is the imposing form of the giant Juggut Singh. Detained by the local police on the false suspicion of being involved in Ram Lal's murder, abuse of the body by those in power comes as no surprise to Jugga, a veteran of police torture:

> He had been through it once. Hands and feet pinned under legs of charpoys with half a dozen policemen sitting on them. Testicles twisted and squeezed till one became senseless with pain. Powdered red chillies thrust up the rectum by rough hands, and the sense of having the tail on fire for several days. All this, and no food and water, or hot spicy food with a bowl of shimmering cool water put outside the cell just beyond one's reach. (*Train to Pakistan*, pp. 91–2)

Among all the communal madness, Jugga becomes an agent of that connection across difference vaunted by the novel in using his body as both bridge and sacrifice, ensuring the Muslims' survival by hanging on to and severing the rope designed to sweep as many as possible from the roof of the train. Indeed, this is a text that builds and valorizes bridges of various kinds, most clearly in the intercommunal relationships of Jugga/Nooran and Hukum Chand/Haseena. In addition, *Train to Pakistan* raises the issue of those transgressive spaces and identities which defy the reductive classifications of bigotry. For instance, in Mano Majra:

> There are a few families of sweepers whose religion is uncertain. The Muslims claim them as their own, yet when American missionaries visit Mano Majra the sweepers wear khaki sola topees and join their womenfolk in singing hymns to the accompaniment of a harmonium. Sometimes they visit the Sikh temple, too. (*Train to Pakistan*, p. 10)

Haseena claims exemption on the grounds of her art, remarking, 'Singers are neither Hindu nor Muslim in that way. All communities come to hear me', and tells the story of how a group of *hijras* (hermaphrodites) in Chundunugger defied a bloodthirsty Hindu and Sikh mob by displaying their lack of any bodily communal marks: 'You can call them Muslim, Hindu or Sikh or anything, male or female' (*Train to Pakistan*, p. 122). The arbitrary, almost farcical nature of physically inscribed communal hatred is figured by the *hijras* here; how is it possible to read their bodies in a situation where the body is the ultimate signifier both of gender and communal affiliation? As the disillusioned communist agitator Iqbal muses, 'Where on earth except in India would a man's life depend on whether or not his foreskin had been removed? It would be laughable if it were not tragic' (*Train to Pakistan*, p. 188).

Indeed, it is in the character of Iqbal that this issue of unattributable cultural identity is most memorably manifested. Unable to discern from the name Iqbal the ethnic allegiance of the young activist who has recently appeared in Mano Majra – he could be Iqbal Mohammed, Iqbal Singh or Iqbal Chand – the sub-inspector orders a strip search to try to fix a cultural identity. Although it ultimately transpires that he is a Sikh, Iqbal is circumcized and has fashionable modern short hair. The cross-communal quality of the name remains a fluid and potent counterpoint to the senselessness of entrenched sectarianism. The authorities 'read' Iqbal as a Muslim when attempting to implicate him in Ram Lal's murder, in order to encourage a Muslim exodus before the real storm of communal violence breaks. Later, when manipulating his release in an attempt to prevent the planned rail sabotage, Hukum Chand conveniently reinterprets Iqbal as a Sikh. The name Iqbal is therefore a transgressive signifier. Indeed, the word 'transgressive' itself is a key one in this novel. To transgress – literally to go beyond set boundaries – is what Jugga and Nooran, Hukum and Haseena, the sweepers, and the *hijras* do. It is also, of course, what borders exist to prevent. Transgression is what Khushwant Singh appears to valorize, against rampant communal nationalism. As an image of this, the text's bridges, real and symbolic, are perhaps the most readily available metaphor in the 1950s when the wounds of partition were still raw.

Writing in the 1990s, Rohinton Mistry is also interested in interlinked individual and collective subjectivities, but the images he uses to metaphorize them stress the multiple kaleidoscopic interconnections of experience, time, the body and space. In *A Fine Balance*, published in 1996 but portraying the lives of four characters thrown together during the State of Emergency twenty-one years earlier, the significatory potential of railways and the body is deployed in a strikingly different way, as the Prologue immediately reveals. The student Maneck and the tailors Ishvar and Omprakash are travelling to a rendezvous with Maneck's 'Aunt' Dina in the city by the sea:

> The morning express bloated with passengers slowed to a crawl, then lurched forward suddenly, as though to resume full speed. The train's brief deception jolted its riders. The bulge of humans hanging out of the doorway distended perilously like a soap bubble at its limit ... The men who had wandered outside came back with the news that another body had been found by the tracks, near the level-crossing.

One of the passengers grumbles:

> 'Why does everybody have to choose the railway tracks only for dying. No consideration for people like us. Murder, suicide, Naxalite terrorist killing, police custody death – everything ends up delaying the trains. What is wrong with poison or tall buildings or knives?' (*A Fine Balance*, pp. 3, 5–6)

The equation of the railway with a preferred form of death is an instantly striking metaphor for a nation that runs over people while, itself, going 'off the rails'. Indeed, this is only part of the symbolic freight the railway is made to carry in this novel. Metaphorically and literally the railway provides a link between the domains of the novel made explicit in several of the chapter headings: the 'City by the Sea', where Dina lives and to which the other characters gravitate; the 'Village by a River', from where the tailors originally hail; and the 'Mountains' which are home to Maneck and to which he often returns in memory. It joins the rural and the urban and is a vehicle for the theme of connection/disconnection – between country and city, self and others, past and present – which runs through the text, and is symbolized in Dina's lovingly created patchwork quilt. On their arrival in the big city, Ishvar and Omprakash are amazed by the number of people expectantly thronging the station platform in wait for their train; 'Passengers poured out into the sea of waiting friends and families. There were shrieks of recognition, tears of happiness. The platform became a roiling swirl of humanity' (*A Fine Balance*, p. 153). As times goes by, and particularly after the tailors have found a temporary domicile on just such a busy station platform during one of their temporary separations from Dina, they come to appreciate the mixing, melding and merging such places offer, in particular contrast to the strictly enforced caste segregation of their home village. As Maneck reflects, remembering his first exciting train journey as a child, trains take one away from the familiar; in a sense they carry the notion of movement and change in their very function. This should in turn, provide one with the opportunity for a rewarding engagement with difference: different people, different places, a different way of life. However, as was prefigured by the sinister delay to the train in the Prologue, under the Emergency – as elsewhere in history – although more trains run on time, the railway system becomes a channel for some of the regime's worst excesses; for instance, the railway provides the location and the putative reason for the death of the troublesome student leader Avinash. Ultimately, it will also be the site of Maneck's despairing plunge to death.

A railway journey is also the setting for Maneck's meeting with the allergic proofreader, Vasantrao Valmik BA LLB, with his penchant for quoting Yeats. In Mistry's text the proofreader seems to 'read' the nation. Abandoning a law career – synchronous with the birth of the nation but, perhaps allegorically, stifled almost at once – Valmik took up his post working for the *Times of India*. He says, 'For twenty four years the triumphs and tragedies of our country quickened my breath, making my pulse sing with joy or quiver with sorrow' (*A Fine Balance*, p. 230). Valmik reads 'stories of misery, caste violence, government callousness, official arrogance, police brutality' (*A Fine Balance*, p. 229), in other words what Homi Bhabha calls the 'scraps, patches and rags of daily life [which] must be *repeatedly* turned into the signs of a national culture'.[20] But his little 'kingdom' of print, like all 'cities and thrones and powers' cannot last forever. In his list of ailments – suddenly developing an allergy to printing ink when reading an editorial about governmental corruption, and damaging his throat in a subsequent career producing rally slogans for different political parties – Valmik seems literally to embody the malaise of an India weighed down by cynicism and opportunism. Continuing in Swiftian vein, Valmik replies to Maneck's observation that if everyone in the country roused themselves in anger against current injustice things might change:

> 'In theory, yes, I agree with you. But in practice, it might lead to the onset of more major disasters. Just try to imagine six hundred million raging, howling, sobbing humans. Everyone in the country – including airline pilots, engine drivers, bus and train

conductors – all losing control of themselves. What a catastrophe. Aeroplanes falling from the skies, trains going off the tracks, boats sinking, buses and lorries crashing. Chaos. Complete chaos.' (*A Fine Balance*, p. 229)

Valmik is the pre-eminent storyteller in a text which, like Mistry's other works, *Tales from Firozsha Baag* (1987), and *Such a Long Journey* (1991), advocates the spinning and sharing of stories. He comments that telling stories is 'extremely important because it helps to remind yourself of who you are. Then you can go forward, without fear of losing yourself in this ever-changing world. Ah, yes, to share the story redeems everything' (*A Fine Balance*, p. 604). Stories act as a defence against the randomness of life. The city is variously described as a 'story factory' and a 'story spinning mill' and characters establish connection with others by sharing their stories.[21] At the heart of this process are the occupants of Dina Dalal's cramped and crumbling flat – it is described as bearing 'wounds' – which is home to Dina and Maneck, and workplace for Ishvar and Om. As their relationship grows and trust develops they relate their memories and the respective journeys which have brought them to this point: Dina's tragically curtailed marriage and burdensome indebtedness to her overbearing brother; Ishvar and Om's family background and the caste atrocity which has driven them to the city; and Maneck's idyllic childhood in the mountains ended by increasing disagreement with his father and the need for education. Yet it is not only the past which they share. Day by day their experiences are symbolically stitched into a quilt Dina is making from the diverse, brightly coloured scraps left over from the tailors' labour. Just as tailoring involved the sewing together of different pieces of material according to some larger pattern, so the quilt comes to represent the many memories and stories which serve to forge identity. Narratives, including of course the one we are reading, create order out of the flux and chaos of heterogeneous experiences. The quilt takes on the redemptive qualities of a work of art. Its squares allow the tailors to see their life as a whole, the small connections symbolizing the larger ones they have made in the wider world. Maneck allows himself to imagine that 'God is a giant quilt maker', but that the universal quilt has grown so large that it is impossible to trace the pattern anymore (*A Fine Balance*, p. 340).

Indeed, Maneck's own failure to sustain the connections becomes the book's final tragedy, and undermines any simple redemptive, modernistic vision of wholeness through art. Maneck's memories, and reaction to time and loss, finally reveal him as incapable of coming to terms with mutability – one of the key themes here, vigorously played out in the tumult of the Emergency. This is revealed most tangibly in his reaction to the spaces in which he finds himself. Unable to endure the squalid conditions in his college's hall of residence, Maneck moves into Dina's flat. Significantly, it is the sight of worms – symbols of parasitism and death – crawling out of the drain in Dina's bathroom that is the cue for an extended reverie about his home in the mountains. In the text, Maneck becomes the fulcrum for an exploration of what Gaston Bachelard, in *The Poetics of Space*, has called 'topophilia': the investigation of 'the human value of the sorts of space that may be grasped, that may be defended against adverse forces, the space we love'.[22] Despite finding a habitation in Dina's flat with his aunt and the tailors, Maneck continues to dream of home: in Bachelard's words to 'travel to the land of Motionless Childhood, motionless the way all immemorial things are. We live fixations, fixations of happiness. We comfort ourselves by reliving our memories of protection'.[23] However, such obsessive retrospective musings are unhealthy in this text as they foster fantasies of stasis which prevent one from confronting time and change. Maneck and other characters, such as Dina's bereaved mother, who attempt to cling too desperately to the past, are ultimately lost. Symbols of the past, like Dina's husband's bicycle, return but only to remind us of the inevitability of decay. Against this Maneck's furious attempts to pedal backwards in time to an era of primal safety bear out Bachelard's observation:

> At times we think we know ourselves in time, when all we know is a sequence of fixations in the spaces of the being's stability – a being who does not want to melt away, and who, even in the past, when he sets out in search of things past, wants time to 'suspend' its flight. In its countless alveoli space contains compressed time. That is what space is for.[24]

Maneck's father, Mr Kohlah, has an even more intense identification with much-loved spaces. His relationship with the landscape around his mountain home is evidenced by his habit of patting favourite rocks and trees when taking his regular walks. His body is also related to the body of the land in direct symbolic ways reminiscent of Rushdie's Saleem Sinai. (After partition a neighbour wonders if the sundered parts of the country will some day be sewn together again, at which Mr Kohlah fingers the eye-patch covering his own mutilation; he has suffered the loss of an eye to an exploding bottle of his home-made carbonated drink.) However, the biggest blow comes with the intrusion of developers. Mr Kohlah's anthropomorphic outlook is echoed in the narrative tone:

> the day soon came when the mountains began to leave them. It started with roads. Engineers in sola topis arrived with their sinister instruments and charted their designs on reams of paper. These were to be modern roads, they promised, roads that would hum with the swift passage of modern traffic. Roads wide and heavy-duty, to replace scenic mountain paths too narrow for the broad vision of nation-builders and World Bank officials. (*A Fine Balance*, p. 215)

The road inches up the hills leaving them 'gashed and scarred', and Mr Kohlah thinks of it as 'a malevolent growth' – appropriately prefiguring the corporeal one which will kill him near the end of the book. Maneck's father's beloved mountain community is torn apart by the influx of capital, so-called 'improved' communications and, eventually, a multinational cola company which spells the end for his own home-brewed variety. However, thinking back to these events through the haze of nostalgia, Maneck fails to make the necessary connections between the personal and the political. As Edward Soja reminds us, space – even the apparently virginal space of 'pure' nature – is always socially produced. Soja contrasts idealizing 'cognitive or mental space' with an analysis of the development of the material landscape 'as a process of the mode of production'. He says, 'To seek to interpret spatiality from the purview of socially independent processes of semiotic representation is consequently ... inappropriate and misleading, for it tends to bury social origins and potential social transformation under a distorting screen of idealism'.[25] Maneck's tragedy is that he fails to recognize and contest the capitalist social forces behind the transformation of his, and his father's space – just as he fails to confront the abuses of space and of the body taking place before him during the Emergency. In fact, in a direct symbolic contravention of the text's insistence on the destructiveness of artificially preserving pristine sites of permanence and holism, he leaves to chase the petro-dollar in Dubai working in, of all things, refrigeration.

In 'Transfiguring: Colonial Body into Postcolonial Narrative', Elleke Boehmer notes that:

> Class and gender exclusions dictate that not all colonised bodies get the chance to represent themselves. Nationalist discourses

> impose their own definitions, certain dominant recuperative selves stand in place of others. There are those among the once-colonised for whom the silences of history have not ended.[26]

This also seems to be the message of *A Fine Balance* where degrees of disempowerment are played out through bodies, their natural functions and their fragility. This occurs most vividly in the figure of the legless beggar Shankar (a.k.a. 'Worm') who sits on a wheeled platform outside the Vishram Vegetarian Hotel, but also in the tailors Ishvar and Om whose personal tragedy reflects that of the nation, and who in the end come to replace Shankar as crippled beggars in one of the novel's many cyclical repetitions. Having fled caste oppression in their village, Ishvar and Om come to the city in search of work only to be caught up in the darkly absurd events of the Emergency, visited most spectacularly upon the homes and bodies of the poor. Boehmer says, 'when national histories are revealed as stochastic, divided, painful, the body, too, is exposed as fissured, reduced'.[27] This is certainly the case in Mistry's treatment of the State of Emergency declared by Indira Gandhi's beleaguered and deeply unpopular government on 27 June 1975, which resulted in the mass arrest of opposition leaders, the cancellation of elections, a ban on strikes and the suspension of press freedom. It culminated in the infamous policies of indiscriminate slum clearance and enforced sterilization: the latter claiming almost as many victims as partition itself. Ishvar and Om undergo these experiences in grim and inexorable sequence. All Mistry's characters are physically or emotionally scarred in some way, often because of the very barriers they erect to protect themselves from the outside world (as disastrous for characters here as it was in his earlier novel, *Such a Long Journey*).[28] But in the tailors' case mistakes and malice reduce them to broken but still living embodiments of folly on a national scale.

Moreover, Mistry is of that generation of writers who recognize that it is not the case that some pre-existing national reality creates self-serving symbols, but that symbols themselves generate an imagined nationhood. As such, national politics as symbolic display, exemplified by the contemporary slogan 'Indira is India' and the much devalued image of Mother India promoted by Indira's followers, must be fought on the symbolic level. In *A Fine Balance* this is memorably demonstrated in the scene where the gargantuan body of Mrs Gandhi, in cardboard and plywood form, topples on to the crowd at a political rally. A circling helicopter, dropping leaflets into the crowd, causes the effigy to wobble perilously:

> the Prime Minister's eighty foot cutout began to sway in the tempest of the helicopter's blades. The crowd shouted in alarm. The figure with outstretched arms groaned, and the ropes strained at their moorings. Security men waved frantically at the helicopter while struggling to hold on to the ropes and braces. But the whirlwind was much too strong to withstand. The cutout started to topple slowly, face forward. Those in the vicinity of the cardboard-and-plywood giant ran for their lives.
>
> 'Nobody wants to be caught in the Prime Minister's embrace,' said Rajaram.
>
> 'But she tries to get on top of everyone,' said Om. (*A Fine Balance*, p. 267)

Soon ambulances arrive 'to collect the casualties of the eighty-foot Prime Minister's collapse'.[29] This is only one of the more overtly 'allegorical' moments in the text: other examples include the satirical patter of a village potency-potion salesman who compares the physical effect produced by his products to the hardness of the government's heart; and the splurge of disorganized colour in the market square – symbolic of the nation's descent into chaos – following a raid by the sterilization police: 'In seconds the square was littered with tomatoes, onions, earthen pots, flour, spinach, coriander, chillies – patches of orange and white and green [the colours of the Indian flag] dissolving in chaos out of their neat rows' (*A Fine Balance*, p. 529).

Finally, there are bodies of people living together, in families – just as Dina, Maneck, Ishvar and Om form a temporary supportive family unit in the flat – and communities. As in *Train to Pakistan*, communities, whether they are urban or rural, middle class or the community of the dispossessed who congregate on the station platform, are easily torn apart. Unlike the imperial romance, Mistry's novel recognizes the role of capitalism and neo-colonialism in dividing people and making it difficult to keep body and soul together. Indeed all characters and relationships are affected by the machinations of the capitalist economy: from the piece-working tailors and their well-intentioned employer Dina, who is nonetheless implicated as an exploiter of cheap non-unionized labour; the poisonous Mrs Gupta, whose mania for control finds expression in persistent visits to the hairdresser to tame her unruly hair, and who sells the garments the tailors produce to an overseas buyer; to the beggars whose place in the warped economy of beggary is determined by the severity of their mutilation; and to the sinister Beggarmaster who, as he points out, at least ensures that the street people make a living of sorts. That he also becomes Dina's protector, after a tortuous series of twists of fate, emphasizes the text's interest in moral culpability and the impossibility of total insulation against the taint of money in a society where anything or anyone can be bought and sold. This is not to say that Mistry is nostalgic for some idealized, pre-capitalist rural society. He recognizes that the roots of India's problems lie also in the concept of caste, and portrays rural society as often brutal and superstitious. Significantly, it is when urban and rural modes of exploitation, caste and class, ancient and modern, come together – and their arch-enemy and murderer of their family Thakur Dharamsi becomes a Congress Party official – that Ishvar and Om's fate is sealed and their tragedy enacted.

The poor we may always have with us, but Mistry is not content with this as an explanation of social injustice. *A Fine Balance* is a book about why they are poor, whose interests are secured by keeping them poor and, most chillingly, what happens to the poor when they become an eyesore. In this case the enforced sterilizations and slum clearances are the most damning indictment of a body politic, which attempts to perfect the larger body of India by getting rid of its anonymous imperfect bodies and preventing their proliferation. Under the direction of Sanjay Gandhi a terrible beautification is born. Once more Mistry's apparent spokesman, Vasantrao Valmik, articulates the central absurdity when talking with Dina:

> 'Who knows why, madam? Why is there disease and starvation and suffering? We can only answer the how and the where and the when of it. The Prime Minister cheats in an election, and the relevant law is promptly modified. Ergo, she is not guilty. We poor mortals have to accept that bygone events are beyond our clutch, while the Prime Minister performs juggling acts with time past.' (*A Fine Balance*, p. 563)

A nation which does not learn from the oppressions of the colonial past seems doomed to repeat them. This is one reading of the State of Emergency in this text. Valmik concludes, a little forlornly, 'There is always hope – hope enough to balance our despair. Or we would be lost' (*A Fine Balance*, p. 563). The clarity of vision his experience vouchsafes him, expressed in his determination to 'maintain a fine balance between hope and despair' (*A Fine Balance*, p. 231) is lost on Maneck whose own disconnection eventually leads him to throw himself under another train, repeating the fate of those earlier victims in the only act of identification left open to him (thereby effectively inverting Juggut Singh's heroic self-sacrifice at the denouement of *Train to Pakistan*). Putting one's life 'on the line' is now less an appropriation of colonial space than a signifier of psycho-social isolation in an age of dislocation and Kafkaesque midnight knocks.

Mistry's technique blends satire and pathos, tragedy and broad farce. The shifts between prolepsis and analepsis, which weave an intricate pattern of temporal connections, provide a means of understanding motivation and character, as well as examining historical and political causality. In this way they are a formal corollary of the thematic concern for pattern, exemplified by Dina's quilt. Indeed, the text performs a subtle synthesis of the available modes of novelistic writing in the post-colonial world, in its mixture of the mimetic qualities of realism (the social detail, the concern for historical verisimilitude) and the deliberate artifice and excess associated with much post-colonial Indian writing – often homogenized, somewhat misleadingly, under the heading 'magic realism'. Nilufer Bharucha says of Mistry, 'As a Parsi he is on the periphery even in India so his discourse also challenges and resists the totalization of the dominant [Hindu] culture within India itself'.[30] As a result of this marginality Mistry's writing is able to stand as an oblique commentary on the processes of identity formation the Indian nation has undergone pre- and post-1947, based, of course, on selective inclusions and exclusions. Stylistically, this, and the traditional Parsi proximity to colonial culture, accounts for the generically hybrid nature of the novel's tone. It is why the collapsing Mrs Gandhi cut-out scene, the Vasantrao Valmik character and so on, appear susceptible to being read *either* as an example of the fantastical, larger-than-life allegorical mode bursting through, and exposing, the facade of social realism, *or* as idiosyncratic, quasi-Dickensian irony and exaggeration within a broad, empathetic liberal realist novel. Mistry's writing radically disturbs such aesthetic categories with its self-conscious reference to canonical European writers – Yeats, Eliot, Balzac – awareness of the role of the storyteller in a predominantly oral society, and nods in the direction of his great Bengali forerunner Rabindranath Tagore. I would argue that the universal identifications available to many different readers, along with the specific social, political and cultural detail of India under the Emergency, have allowed several critics to misrecognize Mistry as merely perpetuating the traditions of the nineteenth-century European realist novel. Rather than being an example of 'documentary realism', as Hilary Mantel suggests, *A Fine Balance* is about imposed patterns, and the double-edged search for order in flux on both individual and national levels. It uses patterns of recurrence and cyclicality and metafictional elements. It can only be read as 'over-determined', as Mantel complains, if one accepts the dubious assertion that this is simply and solely a text in the business of holding that infamous mirror up to nature. Everything about the text's search for pattern indicates that this is not the case, and that it is fundamentally about fiction-making: an example of what one might describe as post-colonial metarealism.[31]

A Fine Balance represents an expansion from the previous tight focus on Parsi communities in Mistry's work and gives space for other social perspectives. What Nila Shah describes as 'a proliferation of "alternative histories of the excluded" produces a pluralist anarchy on the one hand and recreates the nation it belongs to on the other'.[32] This inclusiveness is the quality which makes *A Fine Balance* a prime example of a national allegory in the collectivist sense I have been advocating. In an era in which post-colonial study has increasingly come to record and celebrate the uprooted, the displaced and the exiled, Mistry's writing manages both to carry the hallmarks of a diasporic consciousness and concern for the mutability of people and places, and also to display a quality of rootedness and a celebration of those shelters, albeit temporary, which become homes. That he does so in a manner which manages to avoid – indeed often to expose – the oppressive and stultifying definitions of homes as places of exclusion, is testimony to the way his locations are open to occupation by all manner of Indian identities regardless of religion, class, caste or gender. Just as Mistry has moved outward from the ghettoized locations of Firozsha Baag and the Khodadad Building, so too in *Train to Pakistan,* Khushwant Singh transcends the specifically Sikh concerns which characterize a novel such as *I Shall Not Hear the Nightingale* (1959); although several main protagonists are Sikh there is a strong sense of tragedy and rupture for the whole village community in *Train to Pakistan*. Paradoxically, however, the strength of each text, its ability to articulate marginality, seems to grow from the very specificity, and hence partiality, of its cultural site of production: the Sikh perspective and the Parsi and diasporic sensibility. This alone should alert us to the implausibility of elevating either writer to the giddy heights of 'national spokesperson'.[33] Instead, in the manner recommended by Salman Rushdie in the quotation at the head of this chapter, they are attentive to the multiplicity and plurality characteristic of Indian society,[34] and recreate it in their fiction.

I would suggest that such inclusiveness could profitably be extended to our ways of reading fictions of India and thinking about national allegories. If we consider the 'Indian national allegory' less as the *story* of the nation in a finite, self-contained textual space than as the proliferation of *stories* that go to make up India, we enrich our understanding of cultural diversity beyond the bounds of that often negative social unit privileged above all others since the rise of capitalism. Writing of the shortcomings of the predominant modes of Indian historiography, Partha Chatterjee laments, 'Until such time that we accept that it is the very singularity of the idea of a national history of India which divides Indians from one another, we will not create the conditions for writing ... alternative histories'.[35] If we turn then to Indian fiction in English we will see that such strictures are unduly pessimistic. I have tried in the spirit of Jameson's critique to suggest how two novels may be read as containing motifs – space and the body – whose repetition and modification has an allegorical relationship to an ongoing narrative of India. In these texts the fate of India is played out on the bodies of their central characters in a landscape ribbed by a railway which conveys those bound for their own undiscovered countries. 'The body complex', says Elleke Boehmer:

> as a palimpsest of different symbolic layers – land, mother, scored flesh – is disclosed opened out and ultimately divided up into multiple constituent narratives of bodily/national investment. Symbol is expanded into plot, or plots, history in the epic sense of the tale of a nation becomes biography, autobiography, anecdote, tales of growing up ... in other words, becomes individual or communal narrative, less lofty than national epic, certainly not as coherent, not as authoritative.[36]

It seems to me that this is how the liberation of symbolic resources, the metaphorical decolonization (the decolonization *of* metaphor) often takes place in post-colonial Indian writing in English. Such a strategy more than answers the claim to speak for India asserted by centralizing, monological discourses of power from colonialism onwards. It also enables us to read *Train to Pakistan* and *A Fine Balance* as parts of a grand national narrative still in the making.

Notes

1. Fredric Jameson, 'Third World Literature in the Era of Multinational Capitalism', pp. 69, 79–80.
2. See Aijaz Ahmad, 'Jameson's Rhetoric of Otherness and the National Allegory', in *In Theory: Classes, Nations, Literatures*, pp. 95–122, and

Rosemary Marangoly George, 'Nostalgic Theorising: At Home in "Third World" Fictions', in *The Politics of Home: Postcolonial Relocations and Twentieth Century Fiction*. George questions how we read texts from locations other than our own. For Jameson third-world texts are necessarily national allegories because he reads the societies they come from, recently emerged from anti-colonial struggle, as based on a collectivism lost to the individualistic West. In fact, in the Western academy and publishing houses nationalism has become *the* issue in reading non-Western cultural texts. Every non-Western text is read as some kind of national allegory and third-world writers are pressured to produce easily categorizable material, to the extent that writing which cannot be read in this way risks not being published. As a corrective, George foregrounds the location of reception. Nationalism provides a topic which makes this literature easier to teach for a cultural outsider. George then propounds two readings of R. K. Narayan's *The Dark Room*: the first as national allegory, the second, more rewardingly, through Hinduism and ideologies of domesticity. National allegorical readings emerge as the last refuge of those who cannot read the 'alien dynamic' (p. 121) of the text. Western academics (including this one) beware!

3. See Bipan Chandra (ed.), *India's Struggle for Independence, 1857–1947*, especially 'Chapter 31: The Rise and Growth of Communalism', pp. 398–413; 'Chapter 32: Communalism – The Liberal Phase', pp. 414–27; and 'Chapter 33: Jinnah, Golwalkar and Extreme Communalism', pp. 428–42. See also R. J. Moore, *The Crisis of Indian Unity, 1917–1940*.
4. Partha Chatterjee, *Nationalist Thought in the Colonial World: A Derivative Discourse?*, p. 121. Sunil Khilnani has described Gandhi's social vision as 'anarcho-communitarianism', in Sunil Khilnani, *The Idea of India*.
5. Elleke Boehmer says that in the early phase of anticolonial national literature, 'Narrative had the capacity to project communal wholeness, to enact nationalist wish-fulfilment in text, and to provide role models', *Colonial and Postcolonial Literature*, p. 197.
6. Chandra, *India's Struggle*, p. 23.
7. Chatterjee, 'The Moment of Manoeuvre: Gandhi and the Critique of Civil Society', in *Nationalist Thought*, pp. 85–130.
8. Khushwant Singh, *Train to Pakistan* (1956, 1988) and Rohinton Mistry, *A Fine Balance* (1996, 1997). For more on the strategies and texts mentioned here see Menakshee Mukherjee, *The Twice Born Fiction: Themes and Techniques of the Indian Novel in English*.
9. Kavila Matthai, 'National Identity in Recent Indian Novels in English', in Wolfgang Zach and Ken L. Goodwin (eds), *Nationalism vs. Internationalism: (Inter)National Dimensions of Literatures in English*, p. 436.
10. See Khilnani, *Idea of India*, pp. 141–9.

11. Arun Mukherjee, 'Narrating India', p. 82.
12. See Boman Desai, *The Memory of Elephants* (1988); Amitav Ghosh, *The Shadow Lines* (1988); Salman Rushdie, *Midnight's Children* (1981); I. Allan Sealy, *The Trotter Nama* (1988); Bapsi Sidhwa, *Ice-Candy-Man* (1988).
13. Said, *Culture and Imperialism*, p. 271. Of course, as Viney Kirpal reminds us, it would be misleading to suggest that the power of description over land was in the sole possession of the colonizer during the Raj. One might with justification read the tradition of the *sthala-purana*, the legendary history of a place – also referred to by Raja Rao in the Foreword to *Kanthapura* – as an ongoing technique of geographical and metaphorical anti-colonial resistance. Kirpal says, 'The Indian novel has many a *sthala-purana*, its purpose being to provide linkages between the living ancient past (that is, the pantheon of gods, goddesses and saints) and the contemporaneous present', Viney Kirpal, 'Has the Indian Novel been Understood?', in Anna Rutherford (ed.), *From Commonwealth to Post-Colonial*, p. 310. See also Raja Rao, *Kanthapura* (2nd edn).
14. Khilnani, *Idea of India*, p. 118. On imperial cartography in India see Matthew H. Edney, *Mapping an Empire: The Geographical Construction of British India, 1765–1843*.
15. Khilnani, *Idea of India*, pp. 125–6.
16. Benita Parry, 'A Critique Mishandled', pp. 132–3. Partha Chatterjee has noted how the arrival of the British communications infrastructure, including the railway, represents, 'the advance of the modern regime of power, a regime in which power is meant not to prohibit but to produce', Partha Chatterjee, *The Nation and Its Fragments: Colonial and Postcolonial Histories*, p. 15. For specific discussions on the history of the railway in India see Bill Aitken, *Exploring Indian Railways*; Ian J. Kerr, *Building the Railways of the Raj, 1850–1900*; and G. S. Khosla, *A History of Indian Railways*. An interesting general Marxist interpretation of the social impact of railways in the nineteenth century is offered in Wolfgang Schivelbusch, *The Railway Journey: The Industrialization of Time and Space in the Nineteenth Century*.
17. Jameson quoted in Ahmad, *In Theory*, p. 108.
18. David Arnold, *Colonizing the Body: State Medicine and Epidemic Disease in Nineteenth Century India*, pp. 8 and 10. V. A. Shahane has noted that, 'The artist's preoccupation with the body and blood is one of the most significant aspects of Punjabi literature', V. A. Shahane, *Khushwant Singh*, p. 29. Once again it was Gandhi who managed to combine symbolically the nation and the body in his carefully targeted tactic of fasting.
19. Larry Collins and Dominique Lapierre, *Freedom at Midnight: The Epic Drama of India's Struggle for Independence*, p. 378. A flavour of this

atmosphere of fear and mistrust in a tale of bodies in transit across a riven landscape, can be gained from Bhisham Sahni's story 'We have Arrived in Amritsar', in Stephen Alter and Wimal Dissanayake (eds), *The Penguin Book of Modern Indian Short Stories.*

20. Homi Bhabha, *The Location of Culture*, p. 145.
21. In an interview with Robert McLay, Rohinton Mistry comments; 'In the city everything can become everything else; homes, hostels, workplaces, prisons, doorways, streets, whatever. In this sense the city helps to inhibit line drawing', Robert McLay, 'Rohinton Mistry talks to Robert McLay', p. 17.
22. Gaston Bachelard, *The Poetics of Space*, p. xxxv.
23. Ibid., p. 6.
24. Ibid., p. 8.
25. Edward W. Soja, *Postmodern Geographies: The Reassertion of Space in Critical Social Theory*, pp. 121, 122.
26. Elleke Boehmer, 'Transfiguring: Colonial Body into Postcolonial Narrative', p. 272.
27. Ibid., p. 274. John Ball notes a similarity between Mistry and Salman Rushdie in their 'unflinching attention to the bodily inscriptions of history' and remarks on Mistry's use of 'motifs of mutilation and severance (of limbs, of hair) as both literal effects and grotesque symbols of Partition and Emergency', John Ball, 'Taking the Measure of India's Emergency', p. 86. Parsi writers seem to have a particularly keen apprehension of the metaphorical possibilities of the body and its vulnerability, see, for example, Bapsi Sidhwa, *Ice-Candy-Man* and Firdaus Kanga, *Trying to Grow.*
28. McLay, 'Mistry talks to McLay', pp. 16–18.
29. For interesting synopses and analysis of the Emergency see Tariq Ali, *The Nehrus and the Gandhis: An Indian Dynasty*; Nayantara Sahgal, *Indira Gandhi: Her Road to Power*. A 'popular' history which is rather more sympathetic to Indira Gandhi than either of the above is, Jad Adams and Phillip Whitehead, *The Dynasty: The Nehru-Gandhi Story.*
30. Nilufer E. Bharucha, '"When Old Tracks are Lost": Rohinton Mistry's Fiction and Diasporic Discourse', p. 59.
31. Hilary Mantel, 'States of Emergency', pp. 4 and 6. That metafictional insights form part of Mistry's armoury can be seen from a reading of 'Swimming Lessons', the last story in *Tales from Firozsha Baag*, where we discover that the narrator's parents have been reading the text along with us and now finally enter it as characters. For the role of oral techniques in Mistry see Amin Malak, 'The Shaharazadic Tradition: Rohinton Mistry's *Such a Long Journey* and the Art of Storytelling', pp. 108–18.
32. Nila Shah, 'Novel as History: A Study of *Such a Long Journey* and *A Fine Balance*', in Jaydipsinh Dodiya (ed.), *The Fiction of Rohinton*

Mistry: Critical Studies, p. 100.

33. An additional obstacle to any reading of Khushwant Singh as a national spokesperson must be his support for Indira and Sanjay Gandhi during the Emergency while editor of *The Illustrated Weekly of India*. For a more specific examination of Rohinton Mistry as a Parsi writer see Nilufer E. Bharucha, 'The Parsi Voice in Recent Indian English Fiction: An Assertion of Ethnic Identity', in N. Bharucha and V. Sarang (eds), *Indian-English Fiction 1980–1990: An Assessment*.
34. An example of the mixing of the multiple traditions of India occurs in the realm of cuisine. Arjun Appadurai has shown that the 'construction of a national cuisine' is a syncretic process, and how foods from different regional and communal centres often transcend the social barriers humans are unable to traverse. He says:

    > The idea of an 'Indian' cuisine has emerged because of ... the increasing articulation of regional and ethnic cuisines. As in other modalities of identity and ideology in emergent nations, cosmopolitanism and parochial expressions enrich and sharpen each other by dialectical interaction. (Arjun Appadurai, 'How to Make a National Cuisine: Cookbooks in Contemporary India', pp. 21–2)

    Bill Aitken also comments on the diversity of food to be found at railway stalls:

    > It is now common to find on railway stalls in the south *rumali rotis*, just as *dosas* and *idlis* have become trendy items in the north. The language promoters might take a lesson in how to encourage Hindi from the spontaneous interchange of subcontinental diets. (Bill Aitken, *Exploring Indian Railways*, p. 251)

35. Chatterjee, *Nation and Its Fragments*, p. 115.
36. Boehmer, 'Transfiguring', p. 275.

Bibliography

The bibliography lists all works mentioned in this study, and others which, though not cited directly, were of value in preparing the book.

Adam, Ian and Tiffin, Helen (eds) (1991) *Past the Last Post: Theorizing Post-Colonialism and Post-Modernism*, Harvester Wheatsheaf.

Adams, Jad and Whitehead, Phillip (1997) *The Dynasty: The Nehru-Gandhi Story*, Penguin/BBC Books.

Adorno, T. W. (1974) *Minima Moralia: Reflections from a Damaged Life*, New Left Books.

Adorno, T. W., Adorno, G. and Tiedemann, R. (1984) *Aesthetic Theory*, Routledge and Kegan Paul.

Ahmad, Aijaz (1992) *In Theory: Classes, Nations, Literatures*, Verso.

Aitken, Bill (1994) *Exploring Indian Railways*, Oxford University Press.

Ali, Tariq (1982) 'Midnight's Children', *New Left Review* 136, Nov–Dec, pp. 87–95.

——(1985) *The Nehrus and the Gandhis: An Indian Dynasty*, Picador.

Allen, Glenn O. (1955) 'Structure, Symbol and Theme in E. M. Forster's *A Passage to India*', *P.M.L.A.* LXX, December, pp. 934–54.

Alter, Robert (1975) *Partial Magic: The Novel as Self-Conscious Genre*, University of California Press.

Anand, Mulk Raj (1935) *Untouchable*, Penguin, 1940.

——(1972) *Coolie*, Bodley Head.

Anderson, Benedict (1991) *Imagined Communities: Reflections on the Origins and Spread of Nationalism*, rev. edn, Verso.

Annan, Noel (1964) 'Kipling's Place in the History of Ideas', in Andrew Rutherford (ed.), *Kipling's Mind and Art*, Oliver, pp. 99–124.

Anon. (1966) 'Review of *The Jewel in the Crown* by Paul Scott', *The Times* 21 July, p. 16.

——(1951) 'Review of *Nightrunners of Bengal* by John Masters', *Times Literary Supplement* 22 June, p. 385.

Anstey, F. E. (1897) *Baboo Jabberjee, B.A.*, J. M. Dent and Sons Ltd.

Anthony, Frank (1969) *Britain's Betrayal in India: The Story of the Anglo-Indian Community*, Allied Publishers.

Appadurai, Arjun (1988) 'How to Make a National Cuisine: Cookbooks in Contemporary India', *Comparative Studies in History and Society* 38.

Appiah, Kwame Anthony (1991) 'Is the Post- in Postmodernism the Post- in Postcolonial?', *Critical Inquiry* 17, Winter, p. 353.

Apter, T. E. (1982) *Fantasy Literature: An Approach to Reality*, Macmillan.

Arendt, Hannah (1968) *The Origins of Totalitarianism: Part Two: Imperialism*, Harcourt Brace Jovanovic.

Arnold, David (1993) *Colonizing the Body: State Medicine and Epidemic Disease in Nineteenth Century India*, University of California Press.

Arnold, Matthew (1894) *Culture and Anarchy*, Smith.

Arnold, William Delafield (1973) *Oakfield, or Fellowship in the East*, Leicester University Press.

Asad, Talal (1973) *Anthropology and the Colonial Encounter*, Ithaca Press.

Ashcroft, B., Griffiths, G. and Tiffin, H. (1989) *The Empire Writes Back: Theory and Practice in Post-colonial Literatures*, Routledge.

Ashe, Geoffrey (1968) *Gandhi*, Stein and Day.

Bachelard, Gaston (1994) *The Poetics of Space*, trans. Maria Jolas, Beacon Press.

Bakhtin, Mikhail (1981) *The Dialogic Imagination*, Michael Holquist (ed.), trans. Caryl Emerson and Michael Holquist, University of Texas Press.

——(1984) *Problems of Dostoevsky's Poetics*, Manchester University Press.

Balibar, Etienne and Wallerstein, Immanuel (1981) *Race, Nation, Class: Ambiguous Identities*, Verso.

Ball, John (1996) 'Taking the Measure of India's Emergency', *Toronto Review of Contemporary Writing Abroad* 14, 2, pp. 83–7.

Ballhatchet, Kenneth (1980) *Race, Sex and Class Under the Raj*, Weidenfeld and Nicholson.

Bardolph, J. (ed.) (1989) 'Short Fiction in the New Literatures in English: Proceedings of the Nice Conference of the European Association for Commonwealth Literature and Language Studies', Faculté des Lettres et Sciences Humaines, Nice.

Barthes, Roland (1967) *Writing Degree Zero*, trans. Annette Lavers and Colin Smith, Jonathan Cape.

——(1976) *The Pleasure of the Text*, trans. Richard Miller, Jonathan Cape.

——(1977) *Image, Music, Text*, ed. and trans. Stephen Heath, Fontana Press.

Beer, John (1985) *A Passage to India: Essays in Interpretation*, Macmillan.

Belliappa, K. C. (1980) 'The Elusive Classic: Khushwant Singh's *Train to Pakistan* and Chaman Nahal's *Azadi*', *The Literary Criterion* (Bangalore) 15, 2, pp. 62–73.

Beloff, Max (1976) 'The End of the Raj: Paul Scott's Novels as History', *Encounter* May, pp. 65–70.

Benjamin, Walter (1970) *Illuminations*, Hannah Arendt (ed.), Fontana/Collins.

Berger, John (1972) *Ways of Seeing*, BBC/Harmondsworth.

Bergonzi, Bernard (1979) *The Situation of the Novel*, 2nd edn, Macmillan.

Bhabha, Homi K. (1983) 'The Other Question: The Stereotype and Colonial Discourse', *Screen* 24, Nov–Dec, pp. 18–36.

——(1984) 'Of Mimicry and Men: The Ambivalence of Colonial Discourse', *October* 28, pp. 125–33.

——(1984) 'Representation and the Colonial Text: A Critical Exploration of Some Forms of Mimeticism', in Frank Gloversmith (ed.), *The Theory of Reading*, Harvester Press, pp. 93–122.

——(1985) 'Signs Taken for Wonders: Questions of Ambivalence and Authority under a Tree Outside Delhi, May 1817', *Critical Inquiry* 12, Autumn, pp. 155–8.

——(1990) *Nation and Narration*, Routledge.

——(1994) *The Location of Culture*, Routledge.

Bharucha, Nilufer E. (1995) 'Reflections in Broken Mirrors: Diverse Diasporas in Recent Parsi Fiction', *Wasafiri* 21, Spring, pp. 32–5.

——(1995) '"When Old Tracks are Lost": Rohinton Mistry's Fiction as Diasporic Discourse', *Journal of Commonwealth Literature* XXX, 2.

Bharucha, Nilufer E. and Sarang, Vilas (eds) (1994) *Indian-English Fiction 1980–1990: An Assessment*, BR Publishing Corporation.

Bhullar, Avtar Singh (1985) *India: Myth and Reality*, Ajanta Books.

Bindella, M.-T. and Davis, G. V. (eds) (1993) *Imagination and the Creative Impulse in the New Literatures in English*, Rodopi.

Binns, Ronald (1979) 'The Novelist as Historian', *Critical Quarterly* 21, 2, Summer.

——(1986) *J .G. Farrell*, Methuen.

Boehmer, Elleke (1992) 'Transfiguring: Colonial Body into Postcolonial Narrative', *Novel* 26, 3, pp. 286–98.

——(1995) *Colonial and Postcolonial Literature: Migrant Metaphors*, Oxford University Press.

——(ed.) (1998) *Empire Writing: An Anthology of Colonial Literature 1870–1918*, Oxford University Press.

Bolt, Christine (1984) 'Race and the Victorians', in C. C. Eldridge (ed.), *British Imperialism in the Nineteenth Century*, Macmillan, pp. 129–47.

Bondurant, Joan (1958) *Conquest of Violence: The Gandhian Philosophy of Conflict*, University of California Press.

Booth, Wayne C. (1961) *The Rhetoric of Fiction*, University of Chicago Press.

Bose, Sujit (1990) *Attitudes to Imperialism: Kipling, Forster and Scott*, Amar Prakashan.

Boyer, Allen (1985) 'Love, Sex and History in The Raj Quartet', *Modern Language Quarterly* 46, pp. 64–80.

Bradbury, Malcolm (ed.) (1970) *E.M. Forster: A Passage to India – A Casebook*, Macmillan.

Bradbury, Malcolm and Palmer, David (eds) (1979) *The Contemporary English Novel*, Edward Arnold.

Brailsford, H. N. (1931) *Rebel India*, Leonard Stein and Victor Gollancz Ltd.

——(1943) *Subject India*, Victor Gollancz Ltd.

Brander, L. (1968) *E.M. Forster: A Critical Study*, Rupert Hart-Davis.

Brantlinger, Patrick (1988) *Rule of Darkness: British Literature and Imperialism, 1830–1914*, Cornell University Press.

Brewer, Anthony (1980) *Marxist Theories of Imperialism: A Critical Study,* Routledge and Kegan Paul.

Briggs, Julia (1977) *Night Visitors: The Rise and Fall of the English Ghost Story,* Faber and Faber.

Bristow, Joseph (1991) *Empire Boys: Adventures in a Man's World,* Harper Collins.

Brock, M. (1988) 'Outside his Art: Rudyard Kipling in Politics', *Essays by Divers Hands* XXXVI, pp. 103–26.

Brockway, Fenner (1973) *The Colonial Revolution,* Hart-Davis, MacGibbon.

Bronowski, J. and Mazlish, Bruce (1960) *The Western Intellectual Tradition,* Penguin.

Brookes, Lyn (1977) 'A Study of John Masters', unpublished MA thesis, University of Birmingham.

Brown E. K. (1950) *Rhythm in the Novel,* University of Toronto Press.

Burra, Peter (1985) 'Introduction to the Everyman Edition', in E. M. Forster, *A Passage to India,* Penguin, pp. 317–33.

Butcher, Maggie (ed.) (1983) *The Eye of the Beholder: Indian Writing in English,* Commonwealth Institute.

Cairns, David and Richards, Shaun (1988) *Writing Ireland: Colonialism, Nationalism and Culture,* Manchester University Press.

Candler, Edmund (1922) *Abdication,* Constable and Co.

——(1924) *Youth and the East: An Unconventional Autobiography,* Blackwood.

Carrington, C. E. (1965) *Rudyard Kipling: His Life and Work,* Macmillan.

Césaire, Aimé (1972) *Discourse on Colonialism,* trans. Joan Pinkham, Monthly Review Press.

Chakrabarty, Dipesh (1992) 'Postcoloniality and the Artifice of History: Who Speaks for "Indian" Pasts?', *Representations* 37, Winter.

Chandra, Bipan (ed.) (1989) *India's Struggle for Independence, 1857–1947,* Penguin Books India.

Chandra, Vikram (1995) *Red Earth and Pouring Rain,* Faber and Faber.

Chatman, Seymour (1978) *Story and Discourse: Narrative Structure in Fiction and Film,* Ithaca Press.

Chatterjee, Lola (ed.) (1986) *Woman, Image, Text: Feminist Readings of Literary Texts,* Trianka.

Chatterjee, Partha (1986) *Nationalist Thought and the Colonial World: A Derivative Discourse?,* Zed Book.

——(1993) *The Nation and Its Fragments: Colonial and Postcolonial Histories,* Princeton University Press.

Chaudhuri, Nirad C. (1954) 'Passage To and From India', *Encounter* II, June, pp. 19–24.

——(1979) 'India in English Literature', *Essays by Divers Hands* XL, pp. 15–34.

Childs, Peter and Williams, Patrick (eds) (1997) *An Introduction to Post-Colonial Theory,* Harveseter Wheatsheaf.

Clay, John (1992) *John Masters: A Regimented Life,* Michael Joseph.

Cocks, Joan (1989) *The Oppositional Imagination: Feminism, Critique and Political Theory*, Routledge.

Cohn, Bernard S. (1983) 'Representing Authority in Victorian India', in Eric Hobsbawm and Terence Ranger (eds.), *The Invention of Tradition*, Cambridge University Press, pp. 165–210.

Collini, Stefan (1988) *Arnold*, Oxford University Press.

Collins, Larry and Lapierre, Dominique (1997) *Freedom at Midnight: The Epic Drama of India's Struggle for Independence*, Harper Collins.

Colls, Robert and Dodd, Philip (eds) (1986) *Englishness: Politics and Culture 1880–1920*, Croom Helm.

Colmer, John (1967) *E.M. Forster: A Passage to India – Studies in English Literature*, Edward Arnold.

——(1975) *E. M. Forster: The Personal Voice*, Routledge and Kegan Paul.

Conan Doyle, Arthur (1898) *The Adventures of Sherlock Holmes*, George Newnes.

Conrad, Joseph (1973) *Heart of Darkness*, Penguin.

Cornell, L. L. (1966) *Kipling in India*, Macmillan.

Couto, Maria (1983) 'The Search for Identity', in Maggie Butcher (ed.), *The Eye of the Beholder: Indian Writing in English*, Commonwealth Institute.

Cowasjee, Saros (ed.) (1983) *Stories from the Raj: From Kipling to Independence*, Granada.

Cox, C. B. (1963) *The Free Spirit: A Study of Liberal Humanism in the Novels of George Eliot, Henry James, E.M. Forster, Virginia Woolf, Angus Wilson*, Oxford University Press.

Crane, Ralph J. (1992) *Inventing India: A History of India in English Language Fiction*, Macmillan.

Crane, Ralph J. and Livett, Jennifer (1997) *Troubled Pleasures: The Fiction of J.G. Farrell*, Four Courts Press.

Crews, Frederick C. (1962) *E.M. Forster: The Perils of Humanism*, Princeton University Press.

Cronin, Richard (1989) *Imagining India*, Macmillan.

Culler, Jonathan (1893) *On Deconstruction: Theory and Criticism after Structuralism*, Routledge and Kegan Paul.

——(1981) *The Pursuit of Signs*, Cornell University Press.

Currie, Mark (ed.) (1995) *Metafiction*, Longman.

Dabydeen, David (ed.) (1985) *The Black Presence in English Literature*, Manchester University Press.

Das, G. K. and Beer, John (eds) (1979) *E.M. Forster: A Human Exploration*, Macmillan.

Dawson, P. M. S. (1983) 'Race, Sex and Class in Paul Scott's *Raj Quartet*', in B. J. Moore-Gilbert (ed.), *Literature and Imperialism*, English Department of the Roehampton Institute of Higher Education, pp. 170–80.

Dempsey, David (1953) 'File on Masters', in 'In and Out of Books', *New York Times Book Review* 11 January, p. 8.

Dickens, Charles (1858) *Household Words* 414, Saturday 27 February; and 418, Saturday 17 March.

Dirlik, Arif (1994) 'The Postcolonial Aura: Third World Criticism in the Age of Global Capitalism', *Critical Inquiry* 20, Winter, pp. 328–56.

Dobrée, Bonamy (1951) *Rudyard Kipling*, Longmans, Green and Co.

Dodiya, Jaydipsinh (ed.) (1998) *The Fiction of Rohinton Mistry: Critical Studies*, Sangam Books.

Donaldson, Laura (1992) *Decolonizing Feminisms: Race, Gender and Empire Building*, Routledge.

Duncan, Sara Jeanette (1909) *The Simple Adventures of a Memsahib*, Thomas Nelson and Sons.

Eagleton, Terry (1978) *Criticism and Ideology: A Study in Marxist Literary Theory*, Verso.

——(1986) *Against the Grain: Essays 1975–85*, New Left Books.

Edney, Matthew H. (1997) *Mapping an Empire: The Geographical Construction of British India 1765–1843*, University of Chicago Press.

Edwardes, Michael (1963) *The Last Years of British India*, Cassell and Co. Ltd.

——(1975) *Red Year: The Indian Rebellion of 1857*, Sphere Books.

——(1988) *The Sahibs and the Lotus: The British in India*, Constable.

Edwards, Owen Dudley (1988) 'Kipling and the Irish', *London Review of Books* 4 February, pp. 22–3.

Eldridge, C. C. (ed.) (1984) *British Imperialism in the Nineteenth Century*, Macmillan.

Eliot, T. S. (1951) *Selected Essays*, Faber and Faber.

Evans, Julian (1993) Review of Robin Hanbury-Tenison (ed.), *The Oxford Book of Exploration, The Guardian* 2 November, p. 9.

Fanon, Frantz (1965) *The Wretched of the Earth*, MacGibbon, 1967.

——(1967) *Black Skins, White Masks*, Grove Press.

Farrell J. G. (1970) *Troubles*, Fontana Paperbacks, 1984.

——(1973) *The Siege of Krishnapur*, Fontana Paperbacks, 1985.

——(1978) *The Singapore Grip*, Fontana Paperbacks, 1984.

——(1982) *The Hill Station*, Fontana Paperbacks.

Faulkner, Peter (ed.) (1986) *A Modernist Reader: Modernism in England 1910–1930*, Batsford.

Ferns, Chris (1987) '"First as Tragedy, Then as Farce": J.G. Farrell's Retelling of History', *The Dalhousie Review* 67, 213.

——(1994) 'Regions of the Empire: Scott, Raddall, Farrell and the Voices of the Colonized', *The Swansea Review*, pp. 208–20.

Forster, E. M. (1936) *Abinger Harvest*, Edward Arnold.

——(1947) *Collected Short Stories*, Sidgwick and Jackson Limited.

——(1951) *Two Cheers for Democracy*, Edward Arnold.

——(1962) 'Indian Entries', *Encounter* XVIII, January, pp. 20–7.

——(1972) *The Life to Come and Other Stories*, Edward Arnold.

——(1976) *Where Angels Fear to Tread*, Penguin.

——(1983) *The Hill of Devi, and Other Indian Writings*, Edward Arnold.

——(1985) *A Passage to India*, Penguin.

——(1985) *Maurice*, Penguin.

——(1986) *A Room with a View*, Penguin.

——(1989) *Howards End*, Penguin.

——(1989) *The Longest Journey*, Penguin.

——(1990) *Aspects of the Novel*, Penguin.

Foucault, Michel (1970) *The Order of Things: An Archaeology of the Human Sciences*, Tavistock Publications.

——(1979) *Discipline and Punish: The Birth of the Prison*, Penguin, 1991.

——(1980) *Power/Knowledge: Selected Interviews and Other Writings 1972–1977*, ed. Colin Gordon, Harvester Wheatsheaf.

——(1986) 'Of Other Spaces', *Diacritics: A Review of Contemporary Criticism* 16, 1, Spring, pp. 22–7.

French, Sean (1985) 'Look Back in Angst', *The Sunday Times* 21 April, p. 39.

Furbank, P. N. (1977 and 1978) *E.M. Forster: A Life*, 2 vols, Secker and Warburg.

Gandhi, Mohandas K. (1940) *An Autobiography: Or, The Story of My Experiments with Truth*, Navajivan, Ahmedabad.

Gardner, Brian (1971) *The East India Company*, Rupert Hart-Davis.

Gardner, Phillip (1973) *E.M. Forster: The Critical Heritage*, Routledge and Kegan Paul.

Gates, Jr, H. L. (ed.) (1986) *'Race', Writing and Difference*, University of Chicago Press.

Genette, Gerard (1971) 'Time and Narrative in *A la Recherche du Temps Perdu*', in J. Hillis Miller (ed.), *Aspects of Narrative: Selected Papers from the English Institute*, Columbia University Press, pp. 93–118.

——(1980) *Narrative Discourse*, trans. Jane E. Lewin, Basil Blackwell.

George, Rosemary Marangoly (1996) *The Politics of Home: Postcolonial Relocations and Twentieth-century Fiction*, Cambridge University Press.

Gloversmith, Frank (ed.) (1984) *The Theory of Reading*, Harvester Press.

Goldknopf, David (1972) *The Life of the Novel*, University of Chicago Press.

Goonetilleke, D. C. R. A. (1988) *Images of the Raj*, Macmillan.

Gorra, Michael (1997) *After Empire: Scott, Naipaul, Rushdie*, University of Chicago Press.

Gramsci, Antonio (1971) *Selections from the Prison Notebooks of Antonio Gramsci*, ed. and trans. by Quintin Hoare and Geoffrey Nowell Smith, Lawrence and Wishart.

Greacen, Lavinia (1999) *J.G. Farrell: The Making of a Writer*, Bloomsbury.

Green, Martin (1980) *Dreams of Adventure, Deeds of Empire*, Routledge and Kegan Paul.

——(1984) *The English Novel in the Twentieth Century: The Doom of Empire*, Routledge and Kegan Paul.

Greenberger, Allen J. (1969) *The British Image of India: A Study in the Literature of Imperialism 1880–1960*, Oxford University Press.

Hall, Stuart (1991) 'Old and New Identities, Old and New Ethnicities', in Anthony D. King (ed.), *Culture, Globalization and the World-system*, Macmillan, pp. 41–68.

Hanson, Clare (1985) *Short Stories and Short Fictions 1880–1980*, Macmillan.

——(1989) 'Limits and Renewals: The Meaning of Form in the Stories of Rudyard Kipling', in P. Mallett (ed.), *Kipling Considered*, Macmillan, pp. 85–96.

——(1989) *Re-reading the Short Story*, Macmillan.

Heath, Stephen (1981) *Questions of Cinema*, Macmillan.

Heble, Ajay (1993) '"A Foreign Presence in the Stall": Towards a Poetics of Cultural Hybridity in Rohinton Mistry's Migration Stories', *Canadian Literature* 137, Summer, pp. 51–61.

Henty, G. A. (1884) *With Clive in India*, Blackie and Son Ltd.

Herz, Judith S. and Martin, Robert K. (eds) (1982) *E.M. Forster: Centenary Revaluations*, Macmillan.

Hibbert, Christopher (1978) *Great Mutiny: India 1857*, Penguin.

Hichberger, J. W. M. (1988) *Images of the Army: The Military in British Art, 1815–1914*, Manchester University Press.

His Majesty the King, 1910–1935: Twenty Five Years of a Glorious Reign Told in Pictures (1935) intro. H. W. Wilson, Associated Newspapers.

Hitchens, Christopher (1989) *Prepared for the Worst: Selected Essays and Minority Reports*, Chatto and Windus.

Hobsbawm, Eric and Ranger, Terence (1983) *The Invention of Tradition*, Cambridge University Press.

Houghton, Walter (1957) *The Victorian Frame of Mind 1830–1870*, Yale University Press.

Howe, Suzanne (1969) *Novels of Empire*, Columbia University Press.

Hubel, Teresa (1996) *Whose India? The Independence Struggle in British and Indian Fiction and History*, Leicester University Press.

Hutcheon, Linda (1984) *Narcissistic Narrative: The Metafictional Paradox*, Methuen.

——(1988) *A Poetics of Postmodernmism: History, Theory, Fiction*, Routledge.

Hutchins, Francis G. (1967) *The Illusion of Permanence: British Imperialism in India*, Princeton University Press.

Isaacs, Harold R. (1972) *Images of Asia: American Views of China and India*, Harper and Rowe.

Iser, Wolfgang (1971) 'Indeterminacy and the Reader's Response in Prose Fiction', in J. Hillis Miller (ed.), *Aspects of Narrative: Selected Papers from the English Institute*, Columbia University Press, pp. 1–45.

——(1978) *The Act of Reading: A Theory of Aesthetic Response*, Routledge and Kegan Paul.

Islam, Shamsul (1979) *Chronicles of the Raj*, Macmillan.

Jackson, Rosemary (1988) *Fantasy: The Literature of Subversion*, Routledge.

James, Henry (1969) *The Turn of the Screw and Other Stories*, Penguin.

James, Richard Rhodes (1979) 'In the Steps of Paul Scott', *The Listener* 8 March, pp. 359–61.

Jameson, Fredric (1981) *The Political Unconscious: Narrative as a Socially Symbolic Act*, Methuen.

——(1986) 'Third World Literature in the Era of Multinational Capitalism', *Social Text* 15, Fall, pp. 65–88.

——(1988) *Nationalism, Colonialism and Literature: Modernism and Imperialism*, Field Day.

JanMohammed, Abdul (1985) 'The Economy of Manichaean Allegory: The Function of Racial Difference in Colonialist Literature', *Critical Inquiry* 12, Autumn, pp. 58–87.

Jhabvala, Ruth Prawer (1975) *Heat and Dust*, Futura Publications.

Kabbani, Rana (1986) *Europe's Myths of Orient: Devise and Rule*, Macmillan.

Kanga, Firdaus (1990) *Trying to Grow*, Ravi Dayal.

Kaplan, Caren (1990) 'Reconfigurations of Geography and Historical Narrative: A Review Essay', *Public Culture* 3, 1, Fall, pp. 25–32.

Karlin, Danny (1989) 'Plain Tales?', in P. Mallett (ed.), *Kipling Considered*, Macmillan, pp. 2–18.

Katrak, K. (1992) 'Indian Nationalism, Gandhian "Satyagraha" and Representations of Female Sexuality', in Andrew Parker, Mary Russo, Doris Sommer and Patricia Yaeger (eds), *Nationalisms and Sexualities*, Routledge, pp. 395–406.

Kaye, M. M. (1979) *The Far Pavilions*, Penguin.

——(1979) *Shadow of the Moon*, Penguin.

Kemp, Sandra (1988) *Kipling's Hidden Narratives*, Basil Blackwell.

Kermode, Frank (1967) *The Sense of an Ending: Studies in the Theory of Fiction*, Oxford University Press.

Kerr, Ian J. (1995) *Building the Railways of the Raj 1850–1900*, Oxford University Press.

Kesavan, Mukul (1995) *Looking Through Glass*, Chatto and Windus.

Khattak, Zahir Jang (1987) *British Novelists Writing About India – Pakistan's Independence: Christine Weston, John Masters, Ruth Prawer Jhabvala and Paul Scott*, University Microfilms International.

Khilnani, Sunil (1998) *The Idea of India*, Penguin.

Khosla, G. S. (1988) *A History of Indian Railways*, Government of India.

Kiernan, V. G. (1969) *The Lords of Human Kind: European Attitudes Towards the Outside World in the Imperial Age*, Weidenfeld and Nicholson.

Kipling, Rudyard (1895) *Soldiers Three*, Macmillan.

——(1899) *Stalky and Co.*, Macmillan.

——(1904) *Traffics and Discoveries*, Macmillan.

——(1909) *Actions and Reactions*, Macmillan.

——(1910) *Rewards and Fairies*, Macmillan.

——(1917) *A Diversity of Creatures*, Macmillan.

——(1926) *Debits and Credits*, Macmillan.

——(1927) *A Book of Words*, Macmillan.

——(1932) *Limits and Renewals*, Macmillan.

——(1965) *Puck of Pook's Hill*, Macmillan.

——(1982) *Life's Handicap*, Macmillan.

——(1982) *Many Inventions*, Macmillan.

——(1982) *Wee Willie Winkie*, Macmillan.

——(1987) *The Day's Work*, Oxford University Press.

——(1987) *The Jungle Books*, Penguin.

——(1987) *Kim*, Penguin.
——(1987) *Plain Tales from the Hills*, Penguin.
——(1987) *Something of Myself: For My Friends Known and Unknown*, Penguin.
Kipling, Rudyard and Balestier, Wolcott (1901) *The Naulahka*, Macmillan.
Kohli, Indira (1987) *Paul Scott: His Art and Ideas*, Vimal Prakashan, Ghazibad.
Kovel, Joel (1970) *White Racism: A Psychohistory*, Penguin.
Krishna Rao, A. V. (1988) 'History and the Art of Fiction: J.G. Farrell's Example: *The Siege of Krishnapur*', *The Literary Criterion* 23, 3, pp. 38–48.
Lane, Christopher (1995) *The Ruling Passion: British Colonial Allegory and the Paradox of Homosexual Desire*, Duke University Press.
Lannoy, Richard (1971) *The Speaking Tree: A Study of Indian Culture and Society*, Oxford University Press.
Lévi-Strauss, Claude (1972) *Structural Anthropology*, Penguin.
Levine, J. P. (1971) *Creation and Criticism: A Passage to India*, Chatto and Windus.
Lewis, Robin Jared (1990) 'The Literature of the Raj', in Robin W. Winks and James R. Rush (eds), *Asia in Western Fiction*, Manchester University Press, pp. 53–70.
Lodge, David (1969) 'The Novelist at the Crossroads', *Critical Quarterly* 11, 2.
——(1989) 'Mrs Bathurst: Indeterminacy in Modern Narrative', in P. Mallett (ed.), *Kipling Considered*, Macmillan, pp. 71–84.
——(1990) *After Bakhtin: Essays on Fiction and Criticism*, Routledge.
London, Bette (1990) *The Appropriated Voice: Narrative Authority in Conrad, Forster and Woolf*, University of Michigan Press.
Low, Gail Ching-Liang (1996) *White Skins/Black Masks: Representation and Colonialism*, Routledge.
MacDonald, G. (1980) *Held Fast for England*, Hamish Hamilton.
Macherey, Pierre (1978) *A Theory of Literary Production*, trans. Geoffrey Wall, Routledge and Kegan Paul.
MacKenzie, John M. (1984) *Propaganda and Empire: The Manipulation of Public Opinion 1880–1960*, Manchester University Press.
Mahood, M. M. (1983) 'Paul Scott's Guardians', *The Yearbook of English Studies* 13, pp. 244–58.
Malak, Amin (1993) 'The Shaharazadic Tradition: Rohinton Mistry's *Such a Long Journey* and the Art of Storytelling', *The Journal of Commonwealth Literature* XXVIII, 2, pp. 108–18.
Mallett, P. (ed.) (1989) *Kipling Considered*, Macmillan.
Mannoni, O. (1956) *Prospero and Caliban: The Psychology of Colonization*, Frederick A. Praeger.
Mannsaker, Frances M. (1985) 'The Dog that Didn't Bark: The Subject Races in Imperial Fiction at the Turn of the Century', in David Dabydeen (ed.), *The Black Presence in English Literature*, Manchester University Press, pp. 112–34.

Mantel, Hilary (1996) 'States of Emergency', *The New York Review of Books* 43, 8, 20 June, pp. 4 and 6.

Mason, Philip (1962) *Prospero's Magic: Some Thoughts on Class and Race*, Oxford University Press.

——(1979) *The Wild Sweet Witch*, Penguin.

Masselos, Jim (1993) *Indian Nationalism: An History*, Sterling Publishers.

Massey, Irving (1976) *The Gaping Pig: Literature and Metamorphosis*, University of California Press.

Masters, John (1948) 'Through the Films Darkly', *Atlantic Monthly* September, pp. 91–2.

——(1951) *Nightrunners of Bengal*, Sphere Books, 1977.

——(1952) *The Deceivers*, Penguin, 1955.

——(1953) *The Lotus and the Wind*, Sphere Books, 1984.

——(1954) *Bhowani Junction*, Penguin, 1960.

——(1955) *Coromandel!*, Penguin, 1958.

——(1956) *Bugles and a Tiger*, New English Library, 1962.

——(1957) *Far, Far, the Mountain Peak*, Penguin, 1961.

——(1960) *The Venus of Konpara*, Michael Joseph, 1980.

——(1961) *The Road Past Mandalay*, Michael Joseph.

——(1962) *To the Coral Strand*, New English Library, 1965.

——(1971) *Pilgrim Son*, Michael Joseph.

——(1972) *The Ravi Lancers*, Sphere Books, 1985.

Masters, John and MacQuitty, William (1982) *The Glory of India*, Collins.

McClure, J. A. (1981) *Kipling and Conrad: The Colonial Fiction*, Harvard University Press.

——(1985) 'Problematic Presence: The Colonial Other in Kipling and Conrad', in David Dabydeen (ed.), *The Black Presence in English Literature*, Manchester University Press, pp. 154–67.

McConkey, J. (1957) *The Novels of E.M. Forster*, Cornell University Press.

McDowell, Frederick P. W. (1969) *E.M. Forster*, Twayne.

McEwan, Neil (1987) *Perspective in British Historical Fiction Today*, Macmillan.

McHale, Brian (1987) *Postmodernist Fiction*, Methuen.

McLay, Robert (1996) 'Rohinton Mistry talks to Robert McLay', *Wasafiri* 23, Spring, pp. 16–18.

McLeod, John (1994) 'Exhibiting Empire in J.G. Farrell's *The Siege of Krishnapur*', *Journal of Commonwealth Literature* XXIX, 2.

McLeod, W. H. (1996) *The Evolution of the Sikh Community: Five Essays*, Oxford University Press.

McLuhan, Herbert Marshall (1944) 'Kipling and Forster', *Sewanee Review* LII, Summer, pp. 332–42.

Mehta, Gita (1989) *Raj*, Jonathan Cape.

Mellors, John (1974) 'Noble Savages: The Novels of John Masters', *London Magazine* 14, 4, Oct/Nov, pp. 57–64.

Meyers, Jeffrey (1973) *Fiction and the Colonial Experience*, The Boydell Press.

Miller, J. Hillis (ed.) (1971) *Aspects of Narrative: Selected Papers from the English Institute*, Columbia University Press.

Mistry, Rohinton (1987) *Tales from Firozsha Baag*, Faber and Faber, 1992.

——(1991) *Such a Long Journey*, Faber and Faber, 1992.

——(1996) *A Fine Balance*, Faber and Faber, 1997.

Mo, Timothy (1978) 'Magpie Man', *New Statesman* 15 September.

Mohan, Ramesh (ed.) (1978) *Indian Writing in English: Papers Read at the Seminar on Indian English held at the Central Institute of English and Foreign Languages, Hyderabad, July 1972*, Orient Longman, Bombay.

Moore, R. J. (1974) *The Crisis of Indian Unity, 1917–1940*, Clarendon Press.

Moore, Robin (1990) *Paul Scott's Raj*, Heinemann.

Moore-Gilbert, B. J. (ed.) (1983) *Literature and Imperialism*, English Department of the Roehampton Institute of Higher Education.

——(1986) *Kipling and 'Orientalism'*, Croom Helm.

Moorehead, Caroline (1975) 'Getting Engrossed in the Death-throes of the Raj', *The Times* 20 October, p. 7.

——(1978) 'Writing in the Dark and not a Detail Missed', *The Times* 9 September.

Moorhouse, Geoffrey (1983) *India Britannica*, Harvill Press.

Moraes, Frank and Howe, Edward (eds) (1974) *John Kenneth Galbraith Introduces India*, Andre Deutsch.

Morris, James (1973) *Heaven's Command: An Imperial Progress*, Faber and Faber.

——(1978) *Farewell the Trumpets: An Imperial Retreat*, Faber and Faber.

——(1978) *Pax Britannica: The Climax of an Empire*, Faber and Faber.

Morse, Ruth (1988) 'Impossible Dreams: Miscegenation and Building Nations', *Southerly: A Review of Australian Literature* 48, 1, pp. 80–96.

Mukherjee, Arun (1992) 'Narrating India', *Toronto South Asian Review* 10, 2, pp. 82–91.

Mukherjee, Meenakshi (1971) *The Twice Born Fiction: Themes and Techniques of the Indian Novel in English*, Heinemann.

Mulvey, Laura (1975) 'Visual Pleasure and Narrative Cinema', *Screen* 16, 3.

Nairn, Tom (1981) *The Break-Up of Britain: Crisis and Neo-Nationalism*, 2nd edn, Verso.

Nandy, Ashis (1983) *The Intimate Enemy: Loss and Recovery of Self Under Colonialism*, Oxford University Press.

Nehru, Jawaharlal (1947) *The Discovery of India*, Meridian Books Limited.

Ommundsen, Wenche (1993) *Metafictions? Reflexivity in Contemporary Texts*, Melbourne University Press.

Orange, Michael (1979) 'Language and Silence in *A Passage to India*', in G. K. Das and John Beer (eds), *E.M. Forster: A Human Exploration*, Macmillan, pp. 142–60.

Orel, H. (1982) *Kipling: Interviews and Recollections*, Barnes and Noble.

Orwell, George (1944) *Burmese Days*, Penguin.

——(1957) *Inside the Whale and Other Essays*, Penguin.

——(1965) *The Decline of the English Murder and Other Essays*, Penguin.

——(1968) 'Reflections on Gandhi', in Sonia Orwell and Ian Angus (eds), *Collected Essays, Journalism and Letters of George Orwell, Vol. IV, 'In Front of Your Nose' 1945–1950*, Secker and Warburg, pp. 463–70.

Owen, R. and Sutcliffe, R. (eds) (1972) *Studies in the Theory of Imperialism*, Longman.

Oxford Literary Review (1987) Vol. 9, Colonialism and Other Essays.

Palliser, Charles (1979) 'J.G. Farrell and the Wisdom of Comedy', *The Literary Review* 1, p. 14.

Pannikar, K. M. (1959) *Asia and Western Dominance*, Allen and Unwin.

Parkinson Zamora, Lois and Farris, Wendy B. (eds) (1995) *Magical Realism: Theory, History, Community*, Duke University Press.

Parry, Benita (1972) *Delusions and Discoveries: Studies on India in the British Imagination 1880–1930*, Penguin.

——(1975) 'Paul Scott's Raj', *South Asian Review* 8, 4, July/October, pp. 359–69.

——(1979) '"A Passage to India": Epitaph or Manifesto?', in G. K. Das and John Beer (eds), *E.M. Forster: A Human Exploration*, Macmillan, pp. 129–41.

——(1987) 'Problems in Current Theories of Colonial Discourse', *Oxford Literary Review* 9, Colonialism and Other Essays, pp. 27–58.

——(1993) 'A Critique Mishandled', *Social Text* 35, pp. 121–33.

Pascal, Roy (1977) *The Dual Voice*, Manchester University Press.

Pinney, Christopher (1997) *Camera Indica: The Social Life of Indian Photographs*, Reaktion Books.

Pinney, T. (1985) *Kipling's India: Uncollected Sketches 1884–1888*, Schocken Books.

Poe, Edgar Allan (1949) *Tales of Mystery*, Pan Books.

Pradhan, N. S. (ed.) (1985) *Major Indian Novels: An Evaluation*, Arnold-Heinemann.

——(1989) 'John Masters's India', *The Commonwealth Review* 1, l, pp. 97–110.

Prusse, Michael C. (1997) *'Tomorrow is Another Day': The Fictions of James Gordon Farrell*, Franke Verlag.

Rai, Vijay Shankar (1990) *The Last Phase of the Transfer of Power in India*, Arnold.

Rao, K. Bhaskara (1980) *Paul Scott*, Twayne.

Rao, Raja (1989) *Kanthapura*, 2nd edn, Oxford University Press.

Raphael, Frederic (1975) *Bookmarks*, Jonathan Cape.

Richards, Glyn (1991) *The Philosophy of Gandhi: A Study of His Basic Ideas*, Curzon Press.

Richards, Thomas (1990) *The Commodity Culture of Victorian England: Advertising and Spectacle 1851–1914*, Stanford University Press.

——(1993) *The Imperial Archive: Knowledge and the Fantasy of Empire*, Verso.

Ridley, Hugh (1983) *Images of Imperial Rule*, Croom Helm.

Robbe-Grillet, Alain (1965) *For a New Novel: Essays on Fiction*, trans. Richard Howard, Grove Press.

Rosecrance, Barbara (1982) *Forster's Narrative Vision*, Cornell University Press.

Rosenthal, M. (1986) *The Character Factory: Baden Powell's Boy Scouts and the Imperatives of Empire*, Collins.

Ross, Angus (ed.) (1987) *Kipling 86: Papers Read at the University of Sussex in May 1986 as Part of the Commemoration of the Fiftieth Anniversary of Rudyard Kipling's Death*, University of Sussex Library.

Rossetti, Christina (1979) *The Complete Poems of Christine Rossetti*, Vol. 1, ed. R. W. Crump, Louisiana State University Press.

Rubin, David (1986) *After the Raj: British Novels of India since 1947*, University of New England Press.

Rushdie, Salman (1981) *Midnight's Children*, Picador, Pan Books.

——(1988) *The Satanic Verses*, Viking Press.

——(1991) *Imaginary Homelands: Essays and Criticism 1981–1991*, Granta.

Rutherford, Andrew (1964) *Kipling's Mind and Art*, Oliver.

Rutherford, Anna (ed.) (1992) *From Commonwealth to Post-Colonial*, Danganoo Press.

Sahgal, Nayantara (1983) *Indira Gandhi: Her Road to Power*, Macdonald and Co.

Sahni, Bhisham (1989) 'We Have Arrived in Amritsar', in Stephen Alter and Wimal Dissanayake (eds), *The Penguin Book of Modern Indian Short Stories*, Penguin.

Said, Edward W. (1978) *Orientalism: Western Conceptions of the Orient*, Penguin, 1991.

——(1984) *The World, the Text and the Critic*, Faber and Faber.

——(1985) 'Orientalism Reconsidered', *Cultural Critique* 1, Fall, pp. 89–107.

——(1986) 'Intellectuals in the Post-Colonial World', *Salmagundi* 70–1, Spring/Summer, pp. 44–64.

——(1993) *Culture and Imperialism*, Chatto and Windus.

Samuel, Raphael (ed.) (1989) *Patriotism: The Making and Unmaking of British National Identity, Volume III, National Fictions*, Routledge.

Sarma, G. V. L. N. (ed.) (1977) *Essays and Studies: Festschrift in Honour of Prof. K. Viswanathan*, Triveni Publishers.

Scarry, Elaine (1985) *The Body in Pain: The Making and Unmaking of the World*, Oxford University Press.

Scherer, Joanna Cohan (1990) *Picturing Cultures: Historical Photographs in Anthropological Enquiry*, Harwood Academic Publishers.

Schivelbusch, Wolfgang (1986) *The Railway Journey: The Industrialization of Time and Space in the Nineteenth-Century*, University of California Press.

Schwartz, Bill (1986) 'Conservatism, Nationalism and Imperialism', in James Donald and Stuart Hall (eds), *Politics and Ideology*, Open University Press, pp. 154–86.

——(1992) 'An Englishman Abroad ... and at Home: The Case of Paul Scott', *New Formations* 17, Summer, pp. 95–105.

Scott, Paul (1952) *Johnnie Sahib*, Heinemann.

——(1953) *The Alien Sky*, Heinemann.
——(1956) *A Male Child*, Heinemann.
——(1962) *The Birds of Paradise*, Penguin.
——(1963) *The Bender*, Heinemann.
——(1966) 'How Well Have They Worn? No. 1: *A Passage to India*', *The Times* 6 January, p. 15.
——(1967) *The Mark of the Warrior*, Heinemann.
——(1969) 'The End of the Raj', *Times Literary Supplement* 30 October.
——(1970), 'India: A Post-Forsterian View', in *Essays by Divers Hands* XXXVI, pp. 113–32.
——(1974) '*The Raj*', in Frank Moraes and Edward Howe (eds), *John Kenneth Galbraith Introduces India*, Andre Deutsch, pp. 70–87.
——(1977) *Staying On*, Granada Publishing.
——(1986) *My Appointment with the Muse: Essays 1961–75*, ed. Shelley C. Reece, Heinemann.
——(1988) *The Day of the Scorpion*, Pan Books.
——(1988) *A Division of the Spoils*, Pan Books.
——(1988) *The Jewel in the Crown*, Pan Books.
——(1988) *The Towers of Silence*, Pan Books.

Sealy, I. Allan (1988) *The Trotter Nama*, Alfred Knopf Inc.

Sellers, Susan (ed.) (1988) *Writing Differences: Readings from the Seminar of Hélène Cixous*, Open University Press.

Shahane, V. A. (1968) *Perspectives on E.M. Forster's A Passage to India*, Barnes and Noble.
——(1972) *Khushwant Singh*, Twayne Publishers.

Sharpe, Jenny (1993) *Allegories of Empire: The Figure of Woman in the Colonial Text*, University of Minnesota Press.

Shohat, Ella (1993) 'Notes on the "Post-Colonial"', *Social Text* 31–2, p. 103.

Shonfield, Andrew (1968) 'The Politics of Forster's India', *Encounter* XXX, January, pp. 62–9.

Shortland, Michael (1985) 'Skin Deep: Barthes, Lavater and the Legible Body', *Economy and Society* XIV, 3.

Shrimpton, Nicholas (1981) 'Talent for Thought', *New Statesman* 24 April.

Shusterman, David (1961) 'The Curious Case of Professor Godbole: A Passage to India Re-examined', *P.M.L.A.* LXXVI, September, pp. 426–35.

Sidhwa, Bapsi (1988) *Ice-Candy-Man*, Heinemann.

Silver, Brenda R. (1988) 'Periphrasis, Power and Rape in A Passage to India', *Novel* 22, Fall, pp. 86–105.

Sinfield, Alan (ed.) (1983) *Society and Literature 1945–1970*, Methuen and Co.

Singh, Khushwant (1956) *Train to Pakistan*, Ravi Dayal, 1988.
——(1959) *I Shall Not Hear the Nightingale*, Ravi Dayal, 1997.
——(1972) 'Problems of the Indian Writer in English', *Punjab University Research Bulletin (Arts)* 3, 1, pp. 177–82.
——(1989) *The Collected Short Stories of Khushwant Singh*, Ravi Dayal.

Singh, Rahul (1969) *Khushwant Singh's India: A Mirror for its Monsters and Monstrosities*, IBH Publishing.

Singh, Shailendra Dhari (1973) *Novels on the Indian Mutiny*, Arnold Heinemann.

Soja, Edward W. (1989) *Postmodern Geographies: The Reassertion of Space in Critical Social Theory*, Verso.

Sontag, Susan (1979) *On Photography*, Penguin.

Spivak, Gayatri Chakravorty (1981) '"Draupadi" by Mahasveta Devi', *Critical Inquiry* 8, pp. 381–402.

Sprinker, Michael (1993) 'The National Question: Said, Ahmad, Jameson', *Public Culture* 6, 1, Fall, pp. 3–30.

Spurling, Hilary (1991) *Paul Scott: A Life*, Pimlico.

Srinath, C. N. (1990) 'The Writer as Historical Witness: Khushwant Singh's *Train to Pakistan* and Chaman Nahal's *Azadi*', *The Literary Criterion* (Bangalore) 25, 2, pp. 58–66.

Steel, Flora Annie (1897) *On the Face of the Waters*, Heinemann.

Stevenson, Randall (1986) *The British Novel since the Thirties: An Introduction*, Batsford Limited.

Stevenson, Robert Louis (1987) *The Strange Case of Dr Jekyll and Mr Hyde, and Weir of Hermiston*, Oxford University Press.

Stocking Jr, George W. (1991) *Colonial Situations: Essays on the Contextualization of Ethnographic Knowledge*, University of Wisconsin Press.

Stone, Wilfred (1966) *The Cave and the Mountain: A Study of E.M. Forster*, Oxford University Press.

Street, Brian (1985) 'Reading the Novels of Empire: Race and Ideology in the Classic "Tale of Adventure"', in David Dabydeen (ed.), *The Black Presence in English Literature*, Manchester University Press, pp. 95–111.

Sturrock, John (ed.) (1979) *Structuralism and Since*, Oxford University Press.

Suleri, Sara (1992) *The Rhetoric of English India*, University of Chicago Press.

Sullivan, Zoreh T. (1984) 'Kipling the Nightwalker', *Modern Fiction Studies* 30, 2, Summer, pp. 217–35.

Sunwani, V. K. (1997) 'Rohinton Mistry's *A Fine Balance:* A Critique', *Journal of Indian Writing in English* 25, 1–2, pp. 107–12.

Swinden, Patrick (1980) *Paul Scott: Images of India*, Macmillan.

Sykes, J. B. (ed.) (1982) *Concise Oxford Dictionary*, 7th edn, Clarendon Press.

Tagg, John (1988) *The Burden of Representation: Essays on Photographies and Histories*, Macmillan.

Tambling, Jeremy (1991) *Narrative and Ideology*, Open University Press.

Tedesco, Janis and Popham, Janet (1985) *Introduction to the Raj Quartet*, University Press of America.

Teltscher, Kate (1995) *India Inscribed: European and British Writing on India 1600–1800*, Oxford University Press.

Tennyson, Alfred (1899) *Poetical Works of Alfred Lord Tennyson, Poet Laureate*, Macmillan.

Terdiman, Richard (1985) *Discourse/Counter-Discourse: The Theory and Practice of Symbolic Resistance in Nineteenth-Century France*, Cornell University Press.

Tharoor, Shashi (1989) *The Great Indian Novel*, Viking.

Thompson, Edward (1925) *The Other Side of the Medal*, Hogarth Press.

——(1927) *An Indian Day*, Alfred A. Knopf.

——(1931) *A Farewell to India*, Ernest Benn Ltd.

——(1938) *An End of the Hours*, Macmillan and Co.

Thorburn, S. S. (1987) *His Majesty's Greatest Subject*, Appleton.

Thorpe, Michael (1997) 'A Fine Balance', *World Literature Today* 71, 1, Winter, pp. 224–5.

Tinsley, Molly B. (1982) 'Muddle Et Cetera: Syntax in *A Passage to India*', in Judith Scherer Herz and Robert K. Martin (eds), *E.M. Forster: Centenary Revaluations*, Macmillan, pp. 257–66.

Todorov, Tzvetan (1970) 'The Fantastic in Fiction', *Twentieth Century Studies* May, pp. 76–92.

——*(1984) Mikhail Bakhtin: The Dialogical Principle*, Manchester University Press.

Tompkins, J. M. S. (1959) *The Art of Rudyard Kipling*, Methuen.

Trilling, Lionel (1944) *E.M. Forster*, Hogarth Press.

Turner, Graeme (1993) *Film as Social Practice*, 2nd edn, Routledge.

Vinson, James (ed.) (1976) *Contemporary Novelists*, 2nd edn, St James Press.

Walsh, William (1990) *Indian Literature in English*, Longman.

Watt, Ian (1963) *The Rise of the Novel: Studies in Defoe, Richardson and Fielding*, Chatto and Windus.

Waugh, Patricia (1984) *Metafiction: The Theory and Practice of Self-Conscious Fiction*, Routledge.

Weinbaum, F. S. (1978) 'Paul Scott's India: The Raj Quartet', *Critique* 20, 1, pp. 100–10.

——(1992) *Paul Scott: A Critical Study*, University of Texas Press.

Wellek, René (1941) *The Rise of English Literary History*, University of North Carolina Press.

Wells, H. G. (1963) *Three Novels: The Time Machine, The War of the World, The Island of Doctor Moreau*, Companion Book Club.

West, Rebecca (1973) 'Interpreters of Their Age', in Philip Gardner (ed.), *E.M. Forster: The Critical Heritage*, Routledge and Kegan Paul.

Weston, Christine (1930) *The World is a Bridge*, Charles Scribner's Sons.

White, Allon (1984) 'Bakhtin, Sociolinguistics and Deconstruction', in Frank Gloversmith (ed.), *The Theory of Reading*, Harvester Press, pp. 123–46.

Wilde, A. (1964) *Art and Order: A Study of E.M. Forster*, New York University Press.

Williams, David (1996) 'Cyberwriting and the Borders of Identity: "What's in a Name" in Kroetsch's *The Puppeteer* and Mistry's *Such a Long Journey*', *Canadian Literature* 149, Summer, p. 55–71.

Williams, Patrick (1989) 'Kim and Orientalism', in P. Mallett (ed.), *Kipling Considered*, Macmillan, pp. 33–54.

Williams, Patrick and Chrisman, Laura (eds) (1993) *Colonial Discourse and Post-Colonial Theory: A Reader*, Harvester/Wheatsheaf.

Williams, Raymond (1961) *The Long Revolution*, Penguin.

——(1973) *The Country and the City*, Chatto and Windus.

——(1980) *Problems in Materialism and Culture*, N.L.B..

Wills, Clair (1991) 'Language Politics, Narrative, Political Violence', *Oxford Literary Review* 13, Neocolonialism, pp. 20–60.

Wilson, Angus (1954) Review of *Bhowani Junction*, *The Observer* 23 May.

——(1957) 'A Conversation with E.M. Forster', *Encounter* 9, 5, November, pp. 52–7.

——(1977) *The Strange Ride of Rudyard Kipling*, Secker and Warburg.

Wilson, Edmund (1961) *The Wound and the Bow*, Methuen.

——(1964) 'The Kipling that Nobody Read', in Andrew Rutherford (ed.), *Kipling's Mind and Art*, Oliver, pp. 17–69.

Winks, Robin W. and Rush, James R. (eds) (1990) *Asia in Western Fiction*, Manchester University Press.

Woodcock, George (1979) 'The Sometime Sahibs: Two Post-Independence British Novelists of India', *Queen's Quarterly* 86, pp. 39–49.

Woolf, Leonard (1928) *Imperialism and Civilization*, Hogarth Press.

——(1961) *Growing: An Autobiography of the Years 1904–1911*, Hogarth Press.

Wurgraft, Lewis D. (1983) *The Imperial Imagination: Magic and Myth in Kipling's India*, Wesleyan University Press.

Yeats-Brown, Francis (1930) *Bengal Lancer*, Victor Gollancz Ltd.

Young, Robert (1990) *White Mythologies: Writing History and the West*, Routledge.

Zach, Wolfgang, and Goodwin, Ken L. (eds) (1996) *Nationalism vs Internationalism: (Inter)National Dimensions of Literatures in English*, Stauffenburg Verlag, Tübingen.

Zorn, Jean G. (1977) 'Talk with Paul Scott', *New York Times Book Review* 21 August, p. 37.

Index